FRAUGHT WITH DIFFICULTIES

Lewis and Clark Lead the Corps of Volunteers for Northwestern Discovery Across America and Back

VOLUME ONE

An EPIC Story in Two Volumes

By Jeffrey P. Havens

Fraught With Difficulties: Lewis and Clark Lead the Corps of Volunteers for Northwestern Discovery Across America and Back, Volume One

Front and back cover design and photos by Jeff Havens
Logo by Jeff Havens
Map illustrations by Jeff Havens
Interior book design by Jeff Havens

Front and back cover background: map of North America by Nicholas King, ca. 1803, Library of Congress
Back cover images: portraits of Meriwether Lewis and William Clark by Charles Wilson Peale, ca. 1807, Independence National Historic Park
Interior map illustration backgrounds: Lewis and Clark interactive online map, National Park Service

First edition published by FWD, LLC, November 2015

Second printing January 2016

Library of Congress Control Number: 2015913146
International Standard Book Number (ISBN): 978-0-692-49266-6

Published by FWD, LLC

FWD, LLC
P.O. Box 7174
Helena, MT 59604
www.fraughtwithdifficulties.com
lewis@fraughtwithdifficulties.com

Created, researched, written, designed and printed in the United States of America

CONTENTS

VOLUME ONE: 2015

VOLUME TWO: 2016

www.fraughtwithdifficulties.com

DEDICATION

To Mom with love and gratitude for all you did and did not do. Also to, in alphabetical order: Aimee, Bob, Brandon, Dad, Dave, Jacob, Jesse, Jim, Jody, Joe, Liz, Shirley, Troy and everyone else who has made my life worthwhile.

ACKNOWLEDGEMENTS

This book would have never been possible without the generous support of friends and family.

Special thanks to: Robert J. Conboy for his early proofreading and critiques; James R. Havens, my oldest brother for hauling me to visit Lewis and Clark sites in Washington and Oregon during many visits, and for very valuable input regarding design of the book cover and interior; Troy J. List for accompanying me on an extensive vacation trip from Illinois to Montana to see several terrific Lewis and Clark sites in June 2015; Elizabeth A. Temple, a special friend who helped me a great deal in 2010 during my time of great need in the fallout of the Great Recession; Trish who made it possible for me to view the Salmon River in Idaho from the same spot Clark and Old Toby saw it on August 23, 1805; Lisa Palmeno for her editorial and proofreading services; and Jim Murphy for allowing me to borrow his *Wicked Words* book, which added spice to the novel.

I am very grateful to all those who wrote and researched before me on this and related topics, the most notable being: Gary E. Moulton, James P. Ronda, David S. Lavender, and Edward S. Curtis. This huge project was my attempt to stand on their sturdy shoulders in a differing manner. Also, I would like to thank the numerous volunteers who put together the many great Lewis and Clark attractions all along their trail. They were beacons of hope during my time of unexpected unemployment in the wake of the Great Recession. For anyone interested in learning more about Meriwether Lewis, I recommend the book on the topic by Clay S. Jenkinson, *The Character of Meriwether Lewis*.

Finally, I would like to thank Dayton Duncan and Ken Burns who created the entertaining 1997 public television special, *Lewis and Clark: The Journey of the Corps of Discovery*. Without question, their broadcast generated renewed interest in this topic for many people, including myself. Hal Holbrook's narration, combined with Duncan's writing and Burns' many creative skills made viewing it time well spent.

INTRODUCTION

No book will ever be able to capture all the adventure of the Lewis and Clark expedition. However, I have attempted to capture the spirit through many years of research and site visits along the historic trail.

Early drafts of this novel took far too many liberties with facts. But the weight of history and respect for the Corps' achievements compelled me to change trajectory toward history and facts. However, sheer history and facts can be as sterile as the sums, products, and quotients of mathematics, and my aim was vibrancy, truth, and interest. These elements became the building blocks upon which the book evolved.

My hope for the reader is that you enjoy the book as much as I did researching and writing it. Great effort was made to be as historically accurate as possible by using numerous and notable sources and supplementing them with visiting and photographing as many Lewis and Clark sites as possible from Hartford, Illinois to Seaside, Oregon. I hiked parts of the Lolo Trail several times, including the challenging Wendover Ridge in Idaho, and the even more challenging Trail 204 that connects to the section of the Lolo near a site known as the "Smoking Place," especially when there is still snow on the road. I also canoed the White Cliffs section of the Missouri River in Montana, and lived in several places along the trail. However, I did take liberties with history to enhance the story.

As an example, when Captain Lewis first observed today's Sun River in Great Falls, Montana — known to him as the Medicine River — I spelled it "Medisun." I did this to help readers more readily identify the feature, and as a salute to misspellings, which are frequent in their journals, especially by Clark. Similar and known historical liberties are disclosed in the "Story Notes" section of this book.

Work began on this story in the late afternoon of August 10, 2010. This was exactly six months after a financially and spiritually devastating period of unemployment and wrongful home foreclosure in the fallout of the Great Recession, which led me west in search of work. Fortunately, this period also afforded me the opportunity to re-discover Lewis and Clark, after having interest in the topic for many years.

As a consequence of the recession, I was uprooted from my origins in the Midwest, and lived in several tremendous areas along the trail that enabled me to relive the Lewis and Clark adventure — namely South Sioux City, Nebraska; Glendive, Montana; and Helena, Montana. Great proximity afforded many opportunities to visit and revisit sites over several years in an effort to recreate what they likely experienced. More than five years later — and after a great deal of effort — the difficult research and writing adventure was completed for Volume One of this book.

Each page of the story section utilizes space between paragraphs for easier reading. Traditional books do not employ this formatting, but it is used here in hopes that extra space will provide a more enjoyable reading experience — not unlike the vast space the West still offers.

Annotation Notice

Story construction notes and source notes are separated for reader convenience. All story notes are alphabetically superscripted within the body of the text for easier identification. All sources for the story are numerically cited, predominately in order of importance to the story, and by type of source (e.g. hard-copy books, Web pages, commercial compact discs, personal photos, and personal notes, respectively). When appropriate, the numeric source is superscripted within the body of the text, after the story note citation. Also when appropriate, specific topics are declared within commas after the source citation in the "Source Notes" section, starting on page 242.

PROLOGUE

We shall not cease from exploration
And the end of all our exploring
Will be to arrive where we started
And know the place for the first time.
Through the unknown, unremembered gate
When the last of earth left to discover
Is that which was the beginning;
At the source of the longest river

T. S. Eliot, 1942, "Little Gidding"

CHAPTER ONE
INTO THE NIGHT

October 10, 1809
Mrs. Grinder's Inn: 320 miles from the Missouri confluence

I have done the business. That much is certain. And because of it, I am most qualified to reflect on events past. …

The rain that fell finally ceased, and congruently elevated my unpleasant mood. I sat comfortably in a wooden chair on the porch of Mrs. Grinder's inn and watched the blue smoke I exhaled billow up and disperse towards a brilliant setting sun.[A] Smoking tobacco from my pipe had brought me a bit of solace and relief from the troubles I had been experiencing for quite sometime.

However, we need not discuss the details of those problems just now. No. For now, allow me another soothing puff to enjoy this moment with Mrs. Grinder — the owner of this dreary establishment. Of late, I often sought out life's small comforts whenever and wherever possible, if for no other reason than to preserve my sanity. This was obviously one of them.

"Madam, this is a very pleasant evening. A sweet evening, indeed" I commented to her, as I slowly leaned back in her chair, which creaked and groaned under the strain of the ever increasing recline.

"Yes, Captain Lewis. It is a beautiful night," Grinder remarked in a factual tone.

She said this after glancing up from one of her many chores, which, at that moment, included sweeping newly fallen leaves from the porch floor. She looked back down, whisked away the last of the leaves, and turned to enter the inn — confident she had completed the task. Suddenly and dreadfully, I was alone once again with my thoughts.

Even upon my arrival an hour earlier, prospects for comfort were faint. The moment I rode up on my horse and caught my first glimpse of the inn, it didn't much impress me. I thought it to be a gloomy cabin of rather poor construction and design. It should have been much larger if it were to lodge travelers, such as myself. In fact, the entire inn had an aura of despair, desolation, and misery with its constricting, dimly lit rooms that retained a dank, musty odor.

I was there that evening as I reluctantly trekked east to the nation's capitol, to defend my name from spurious accusations, which had been the source of many troublesome days for me. They had weighed heavily on my mind; too heavily to be healthy in any sort of manner.

Several years before, after returning from the westward expedition, I was rewarded an appointment as Governor of the Upper Louisiana Territory by my mentor, friend, and former U.S. President Thomas Jefferson. The appointment was for my efforts exploring the previously unknown, and newly acquired American territory known as the Louisiana Purchase.

As governor and pioneering explorer of that region, I was authorized to allocate government funds for a variety of purposes at a reasonable cost, as I deemed fit. In that case, I apportioned public money to a private company in which my brother, a very dear friend, and eight others had financial interest — the St. Louis Missouri Fur Company.

As an unfortunate consequence of this expenditure, a disagreeable character named Frederick Bates, the secretary of the Territory, accused me of illegally awarding those funds without prior authorization from President Jefferson. To complicate this matter, I was informed I would be held personally responsible to re-pay a portion of these funds, which I did not possess.

Because you now know this much, I'm certain you can appreciate my burden, if not sympathize with my plight. However, I maintained I acted properly because President Jefferson did authorize such expenditures. Of that much I am certain. I just needed to persuade others to listen. This was the reason I was there that evening — to inform those in Washington of my noble intentions.

Now that I reflect on the origins of my worry; one possibility of that worry was the standards I set for myself and others. The aggravations I experienced consumed my waking hours and became an obsession.

I needed rescue. I needed relief. ...

Looking westward that dreadful evening, I found some relief, if just for the moment. I watched the setting sun illuminate the few clouds in the sky. Brilliant reds, oranges and yellows painted the drifting vapors, which offered me temporary respite from my state of anxiety in the extreme.

But rescue would have to come in a different form.

Many times in the past, that rescue took the shape of my good friend and former superior Army officer William Clark. It is with Captain Clark that I explored the interior of North America five years earlier to survey the nation's new territory — vast, expansive, and mostly unknown to Americans. The entire region — 820,000 square miles — was purchased from France in April 1803 for a modest sum of $15 million.

In addition to being one of the partners in the new fur company, Captain Clark was co-commander of our military expedition called on by Jefferson to explore the newly acquired Louisiana territory. The President formally asked me to head the expedition in 1803 because he believed I possessed the attributes required to successfully complete the challenging voyage. In fact, so impressed was he that shortly after the President's inauguration in 1801, I moved into his residence where I worked as his personal secretary. During this time, Jefferson made observations about my character, which he later felt were well-suited for my leading a party to investigate this new territory.

After Congress approved $2,500 for the venture, I happily accepted Jefferson's invitation to lead the expedition. On June 20, 1803, he wrote instructions to me about the undertaking, which included the following passage:

"The object of your mission is to explore the Missouri river, & such principal stream of it as by it's course and communication with the waters of the Pacific ocean whether Columbia, Oregon, Colorado or any other river may offer the most direct & practicable water communication across this continent for the purposes of commerce."

Jefferson's instructions were well-reasoned and accommodating; follow the Missouri River from its confluence with the Mississippi River at the village of St. Louis to its most distant fountain somewhere in the Rocky Mountains, with the hope of establishing a water route to the Pacific Ocean for conducting future trade. This objective also included developing a satisfactory relationship with Indians all along the route. He also instructed me to collect specimens, record observations, and collect latitude and longitudinal data at all remarkable points on the river. This information was to be written in a manner easily understood by others. And, if desired by some of the Indians to which we would become positively acquainted, arrange for influential chiefs to visit Washington. In addition, we were to offer to raise their children in the East, so we might teach them arts and ways that may be of use to them as our newest Americans. He suggested that at such meetings, we should offer gifts. Those presents would hopefully provide us some level of security for safe passage.

The President indicated the mission was to be peaceful in manner, and avoid conflict. The enterprise was to be one of discipline, organization, commitment, and cooperation. To fulfill the President's orders, I needed assistance. I needed someone to enhance my strengths, and compensate for my weaknesses. I needed someone similar, but complementary.

There was only one person I knew who met these criteria, and that person was William Clark. Soon after receiving my instructions from Jefferson, I contacted Clark, and asked whether he would undertake the venture, which we later named "The Corps of Volunteers for North Western Discovery."

Clark accepted my offer to lead the expedition, and for the purposes of demonstrating to you the camaraderie we cultivated, permit me to recount his acceptance letter, which I am certain he would be happy I shared:

Dear Lewis:

This is an undertaking fraught with many difficulties. But my friend, I do assure you that no man lives with whom I would prefer to take such a trip as yourself.

Recalling this letter intensified my understanding of just how critical my predicament had become. I was in dire need of his guidance at this decisive time, as the landscape grew ever darker with the setting sun. I very much needed his help, once again — like I did so many times during the journey.

The light was disappearing, and the evening was turning into what I feared would be a very dark night. As I leaned further back in the chair, my eyes were still cast on the dimming countryside across the horizon where I envisioned Captain Clark coming to my aid — his silhouette slowly emerging over the western landscape where our expedition began more than five years earlier.

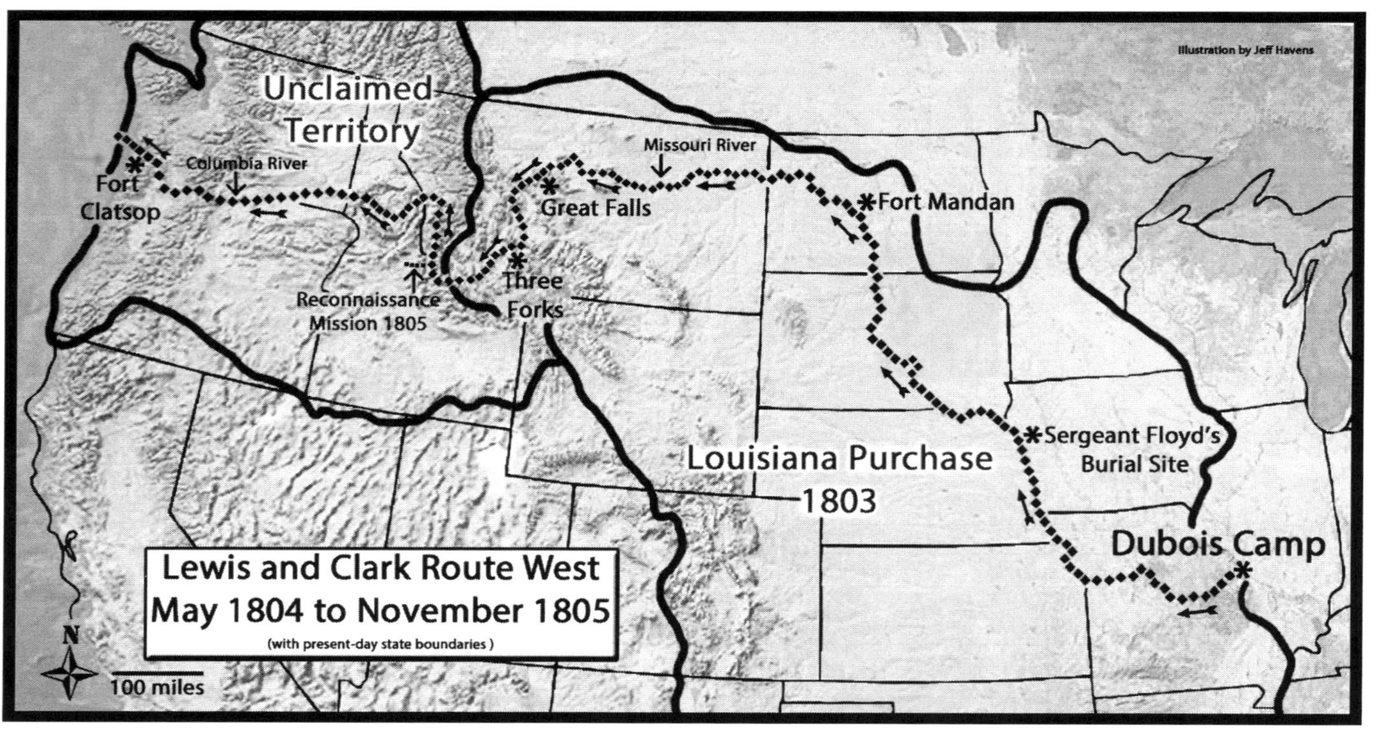

Illustration by Jeff Havens
Unclaimed Territory
Columbia River
Fort Clatsop
Reconnaissance Mission 1805
Three Forks
Great Falls
Missouri River
Fort Mandan
Louisiana Purchase 1803
Sergeant Floyd's Burial Site
Dubois Camp
Lewis and Clark Route West
May 1804 to November 1805
(with present-day state boundaries)
N
100 miles

CHAPTER TWO DEPARTURE

May 17, 1804
St. Charles Camp: 21 miles above the Missouri confluence

"Commence with the punishment, Sergeant Floyd," Captain Clark commanded in a stern voice — standing on the northwestern shore along the Missouri River.[A]

Sergeant Charles Floyd was a young man of much merit at 22 years of age. He was born on the Kentucky frontier and was son of Captain Charles Floyd, Sr., who served a few years earlier in the Army under Captain Clark's elder brother. The qualities I found in Sergeant Floyd were also applicable to others in the corps. This is to say they were healthy, stout, unmarried men, accustomed to the woods and capable of handling bodily fatigue to a considerable degree.

Floyd and 30 other men crowded together in orderly rows and columns to witness how violations of military code would be enforced. I recount with much confidence that they all watched with indignant resignation to discipline and duty as the leathery cords of the cat o' nine tails were drawn back and quickly thrust forward — slashing the evening air.

As the punishing strings of the whip violently advanced, a deep, whirring sound culminated with a high-pitched crack the instant they made contact and broke the skin of the prisoner. With his hands bound and secured above his head to a whipping post, the man winced as jolts of pain raced through his body. After the sting of the initial impact, he groaned loudly, as the red streaks on his bare back oozed crimson with blood.

These were the first of 50 lashes to be inflicted on Private John Collins for infractions that had obvious consequences. This punishment, however unfortunate, was necessary, in my opinion, and in accordance with military code. Captain Clark and I believed such violations must be dealt with in a firm and timely manner in order to maintain control and authority over members of the expedition, which would be crucial in our journey's success.

Private Collins was from Maryland, a fine hunter, but was also a discipline problem during our stay the previous winter at Dubois Camp on the river of the same name in Illinois territory. As an example, there were a few incidents in which he frequented groggeries when he was supposed to be hunting. Collins was a young man who had yet to learn how to conduct himself in a mature manner, especially when imbibing ardent spirits.

He was tried earlier that day after being absent without leave following a celebration held the night before in our honor by the 450 good people of this community. Private Collins was also accused of behaving in an unbecoming manner at said ball, and speaking in a language after his return to camp that tended to bring into disrespect the orders of the commanding officer. After mature deliberation, and in agreement with the evidence, the court was of the opinion that the prisoner was guilty of all charges, with the punishment to be carried out by the sergeant of the guard at sunset, in the presence of expedition members to witness the brutal penalty.

Included in our party of 31 men were Privates William Werner and Hugh Hall. They had their flogging sentences remitted for good conduct, relating to their also being absent without leave after the ball. Other members who witnessed the punishment consisted of 21 privates, three sergeants, and an expert hunter and Indian interpreter named George Drouillard — all who volunteered, and were selected for the long journey.

In addition to these men, there was one man who did not volunteer. His service was compulsory by virtue of his status as Clark's servant — a black slave named York, who grew up with Captain Clark in Virginia and on the Kentucky frontier.

Along with two horses, also in our accompaniment was my loyal, and quite large, Newfoundland dog named Seaman.

At the time the punishment was being administered, Seaman and I were away from camp in St. Louis preparing items to be sent back to President Jefferson. I planned to join the others in three days, before we started the long expedition in earnest.

With the last crack of the whip, Collins groaned once more, but was relieved he endured the excruciating sentence.

"The punishment is complete," Captain Clark proclaimed — devoid of emotion. "Privates, assist the prisoner."

Clothed in formal military-dress uniform, two guards approached; they loosened the straps on the whipping post, and assisted Collins to his quarters for a brief period of recovery.

Clark hung his head and stepped slowly towards the center of the rows of soldiers. He stopped, looked at the group, and spoke directly to our developing unit:

"Corps, I speak for Captain Lewis and myself when I state that we cannot allow insubordinate and unbecoming behavior in the ranks," Clark snapped, as Collins was led away. "Let us not forget this unfortunate incident, and put forth all efforts in the future to prevent such extreme measures. The corps is dismissed to return to your duties."

The group dispersed and made good use of the day's last light. Near the riverbank our three vessels were moored, including a keelboat, which was 55 feet in length, and approximately nine feet in width. Each man executed their orders to re-distribute the tons of supplies and offerings we would need for survival, and gifts for the Indians.

Among those gifts were vermilion paint, colored beads, flags, uniform coats, pipe tomahawks, ribbons, pocket mirrors, spun tobacco, brass kettles, and peace medals. The last were forged in two sizes that featured a handsome profile of President Jefferson on one side of the medallion, and two hands shaking on the other side. This list, I submit to you, was by no means complete. However, it does demonstrate the intent of our undertaking. The soldiers wrapped these, and most of the other supplies, in individually numbered oil-cloth bags, secured with rope, and stored in a series of large cargo boxes that occupied almost the entire body of the boat.

Contained within these boxes were many goods, including: 48 rifles — fifteen of which were new; 400 pounds of lead for ammunition balls; one pneumatic air rifle; one spontoon, which you would recognize as a type of spear; one collapsible iron-framed boat, 36 feet in length, which I named the *Experiment* in Harper's Ferry, Virginia where the metal was fabricated; one portable forge; 150 pounds of highly-condensed soup; six, five-gallon kegs of whiskey; 12 ounces of opium; four pewter penis syringes; one pound of mercury salve; and 50 dozen of Dr. Benjamin Rush's patented mercurous chloride, Thunderclapper pills.

The last item on this brief list was a potent purgative that had the ability to cleanse the body of any ingested material in a rather dramatic, and often times embarrassing manner. Considering this fact, Dr. Rush could not have more aptly named this medicated tablet.

As to the source of the tobacco, I purchased 136 pounds of this comfort from half-brothers René Auguste Chouteau and Jean Pierre Chouteau, not long before we departed. They were influential French merchants and traders, based in St. Louis, and were also the most powerful and wealthy family in that region. As a consequence, we sought to remain in their good graces, despite that France no longer owned the purchased lands west of the Mississippi. But this, by no means, meant they were unoccupied lands. Many thousands of natives had been living there for countless generations, and we were to try and bring them into the fold.

During the course of the following days, the troops continued their work re-organizing our cargo, and I hired the final members of our crew. I chose two privates for the journey, both who were half-French and half-Omaha Indian in ancestry. I was intrigued to learn from these privates that natives in their lineage named themselves during a migration in the 1700s from the lower portion of the Missouri River to the middle section, which translated into the "Against the Current" people.

One of these privates, Francois Labiche, knew several languages spoken by the natives, and I thought this would prove of value during the lengthy voyage. I also believed he would be an excellent animal tracker and good hunter. The other private, Pierre Cruzatte, had worthy attributes as a boatman, fur trader, and violin player. However, the fact that Private Cruzatte could only see with one eye did provide me some pause regarding whether to hire him for the expedition.

I should also inform you that the good eye Private Cruzatte possessed did not serve him well at distances greater than a few dozen feet, which is very apparent now that I have done the business. Employing Labiche was the absolute correct course of action. However, I remained somewhat reserved about Private Cruzatte, if for no other reason than that dreadful misidentification incident I wish could be forgotten.

Prior to employing Labiche and Cruzatte, I also hired 12 French engagés or boatmen to primarily man one of our two accompanying pirogues or open boats. One pirogue was colored red, the other white. The latter was 39 feet in length, and had a mast height of 22 feet from the waterline, while the former was only about two feet shorter, but had a slightly longer mast.

I arrived at St. Charles camp late on the 20th under heavy rain, accompanied by a fair number of very respectable inhabitants of St. Louis. I was happy to find the party in good health and spirits. I also found that those final hires brought the total number in our party to nearly four dozen military and non-military individuals for the start of our journey the following day.[B]

"Is everyone on board and ready, Captain Clark?" I asked; stepping onto the deck of the keelboat, as Seaman excitedly bounded down the pier onto the craft.

"Everyone except you and the dog, Commander," Clark responded in a jovial manner, as light rain soaked his officers' hat, which was high and dark.

The party stood in proper formation ready to depart in the main vessel, while six soldiers manned the white pirogue, and most of the engagés sat at the ready in the red pirogue. A small crowd of men from the village had assembled on the muddy bank of the river, patiently watching the proceedings. I took a final glance to my left and right to survey conditions, and mentally noted the time — it was half-past three in the afternoon. In that instant, I must admit, the fact that we expected many hardships during the next two years caused me some trepidation, but there was no turning back. During the same moment, I felt an exuberance I knew would never recur during my lifetime.

Satisfied we were ready, I shouted the order to cast off over the din of hard rain.

The men, dressed in their work uniforms, fell out of formation. We pushed off from the pier. Twenty soldiers then took their places at the oars, lowered them into the water, and the vessel shifted toward the main channel of the river. A team of 10 men on each side of the keelboat moved the heavy craft, which was loaded with nine tons of supplies. Each of the two pirogues only required a team of six to maneuver the vessels, due to the fact they were much lighter and smaller than our keelboat. Witnessing the movement of the flotilla, the waterlogged gentlemen on the river bank elatedly offered up three cheers to send us off on our venture westward. Whistles and claps ensued for several minutes, until they attenuated at some distance.

Although they had turned silent, I continued to stare at the crowd on the shore as their images slowly turned into smaller and dimmer silhouettes — knowing they represented one of the last semblances of civilization we would have the pleasure of enjoying for several years, if we survived our long voyage. I watched until our saturated, 15-star flag hanging from the stern finally obscured them from view.

After struggling in opposition of the Missouri's strong flow, we traveled upstream three and one-quarter miles before halting for the night. We camped at the head of an island, while a spring rain poured through the evening. Cooks prepared enough lyed corn, grease, and deer for supper that night to sustain us through breakfast and lunch the following the day — a practice to which we adhered for nearly the entire journey. With supper, I commanded First Sergeant John Ordway to issue each man our standard daily gill, or four-ounce allotment of whiskey, which they very much enjoyed after the exertion.

Ordway was born in 1775 in Hebron, New Hampshire, and was one of the few formally educated men on the expedition. Other than the rudimentary, I did not elect to detail more in the written record about Sergeant Ordway or other expedition applicants because the important aspect was whether the candidate was suitable for duty, which I determined through verifiable reference, thorough interview, and astute observation.

Finishing the last of the First Sergeant's spirits, I placed my head on a pillow under the shelter of the captains' quarters on the keelboat. I lay there for hours listening to the rain pummel the canvas canopy and wooden deck of the boat. The constant stream from the heavens drained my spirit. Regardless, I was determined to conquer such melancholy to faithfully execute President Jefferson's important instructions; any and all other challenges be damned. However, I never imagined such a perilous challenge would so quickly levy itself, and impose such a hazardous warning.

CHAPTER THREE
AGAINST THE CURRENT

May 23, 1804
Tavern Island Camp: 47 miles above the Missouri confluence

We set out early and passed a large cavern on the larboard side that was approximately 120 feet wide and 20 feet high with a depth of 40 feet. Clark and I determined this feature must be examined.

"Sergeant Pryor," I shouted from the upper portion of the keelboat.

"Sir!" the 32-year-old cousin of Sergeant Floyd responded, as he quickly twisted his head to focus his attention.

"To the larboard, Sergeant! We need to examine the cave," I said pointing to the left river bank, emphasizing the directive.

"Aye, Captain," Pryor immediately replied.

He subsequently signaled our objective to the crew in the trailing pirogues.

The party slowly pulled to the water's edge, and awaited instructions. After stepping onto the riverbank, I sent different units to explore opposite sections of the shoreline. I also sent a special contingent to study the cave.

"Sergeant Pryor, take McNeal and Shields with you to explore the grotto.[A] We'll meet here in two hours," I said in a forceful manner.

Private Hugh McNeal was an excellent hunter from Pennsylvania. Private John Shields was the oldest member of the expedition at 34 years, and an able blacksmith, carpenter, and relative of a celebrated pioneer named Daniel Boone.

Extending my index finger in the direction of a cliff high above our position, I informed Pryor and the others of my intention to study the bluff. We then separated in pursuit of our destinations. The three dispatched toward the cave, while I embarked on my hike — alone.

With rifle in hand, I laboriously climbed the rock face for a commanding view of the surrounding territory. Somewhat winded, I stopped to rest for a moment, peered through the spring foliage, and was delivered a disappointingly limited view of our landing below. The sight of the neighboring area was obstructed by many barriers, mostly the abundance of deciduous leaves, which had sprouted weeks prior. After a brief reprieve, I collected myself and continued to scale the bluff for a better vantage point. After approximately 30 minutes, I arrived at the pinnacle far above the cave, and lowered my foot onto a small rock, as I prepared to visually survey the countryside.

However, the moment my foot made contact with the jagged rock, the survey was most in question.

My foot touched the stone, and it promptly shifted then plummeted towards the distant water below — its downward and rotational motion accelerating as it fell. For a brief moment, I watched in curious fascination while the rock turned and spun during its descent, as my foot followed its lead. I twisted and fell forward. Instinctively, I released my rifle to break my fall, using both hands.

Before fully comprehending what was occurring, I was chopped prostrate, and began sliding over rubble, which tore at my clothes and skin. With each inch I advanced towards the edge of the cliff, portions of my uniform and flesh deposited on countless projections that comprised the rough surface of the bluff. My shirt quickly rolled up towards my chest, and my exposed abdomen dutifully acquired numerous painful lacerations and abrasions.

My momentum built as I slid sideways towards the overhang. I slipped several more yards before I sensed my speed decreasing, but soon felt my right foot creep ominously over the edge, followed by my right arm. Quickly, I reached with my left hand to grab a sturdy tree sapling, which arrested my imminent demise. My right leg and arm were then dangling 300 feet above the sandy beach. I lay there for a moment to consider my next course of action. Reaching with my right hand, I grabbed my knife handle and unsheathed the blade from my hip. Yanking the knife from its leathery covering, I carved a foothold out of the craggy bluff. [B] Beads of nervous sweat trickled and rolled down the sides of my face, as I anxiously bent my right leg and carefully placed it into the hole. Applying increasing pressure on the opening, I managed to push myself to my knees and crawl away from the precipitous ledge. Cautiously pushing upright, I stood and turned to finally survey the surrounding countryside.

It was a grand sight to behold, but I was certain the compensation was not commensurate with the effort. This was a conclusion to which I vowed henceforth to always remain diligent; the risk must correspond with the expenditure of resources.

Cognizant of the experience, I warily proceeded to the rendezvous, as my heart thumped and pounded — the rushing blood caused my head to pulse with each beat. The expedition was barely two days in duration, and it may have very well ended with my untimely death. But having survived the ordeal, I was then more certain duty and destiny mandated we move forward — up the river, towards the unmapped and unexplored. However, we had nearly 2,000 miles to travel before we reached completely unmapped territory.

Grateful I had not perished, we continued our journey, and two days later arrived at the final settlement of whites on the river at the small, French village of seven homes called La Charrette — 69 miles from the confluence. We moored the vessels about a quarter-mile upriver where Clark and I walked along the shore to pay a visit to a man named Régis Loisel.

He had arrived in St. Louis in about 1793, and had since formed a company and built a fur trading post that Clark and I wished to visit. Loisel established his company in about 1798 when one Mr. Hugh Heney was made a partner. However, by the time we arrived, Mr. Heney had already joined a competing company, and resided upriver.

As we walked toward Loisel's trading post, Clark and I enjoyed viewing the many cows feeding near the river. They casually grazed, as the sun was setting behind a darkening wall of budding trees. While we were observing the cows, Loisel had been observing us from his position on a porch abutting his home. The house was a stout structure constructed of brick and wood – made by the very man who shouted his greeting:

"Bonjour!" he said, reaching out towards us.

"Bonjour, Monsieur Loisel," I cheerfully said, extending my hand in friendship.

"Merci, Capitaine," he jauntily replied, taking me in with a very firm grip.

He offered the same to Captain Clark.

"I also speak English, Captain Lewis," Loisel informed us in a significant French accent.

"That's good, Mr. Loisel because my French is limited," I advised with a smile, as he escorted us into his small post.

"Please, take a seat," Loisel said gesturing towards some chairs and a table in the corner of the tight quarters. "I was informed you were arriving, and am happy to help in whatever manner possible," he said, pushing four pieces of paper across the table in our direction.

"These are introduction letters I wrote my partners. They will help you. ... They are to, as you see," he said, pointing to the upper, left corner of the letter on the top of the pile.

The name read: "Pierre-Antoine Tabeau."

I thumbed through the other three letters of introduction, and they were respectively addressed to: Pierre Dorion, Joseph Gravelines and Jean Vallé. After cursorily examining the Tabeau letter, I gave the stack to Clark.

"If you meet them, give them the letters. ... I just returned from there," he proudly emphasized.

"Excuse me, Mr. Loisel, but I do not know from where you just came," I stated.

"Yes, yes, how clumsy of me — 400 leagues up. We built a fortress. I was there last winter. It is at the island named 'Cedar' among the Sioux nation," he informed. "You will find that Tabeau and Vallé are relations — cousins, to be precise."

I responded: "We are hoping to meet with many Indians to spread the news of the Purchase from France. Can you tell us where you saw Indians?"

Pausing a few seconds to recall events, he replied: "I did not see any below the Poncas, I believe. They are 300 leagues above."

We chatted more and had supper. By nine that evening, we took leave of Mr. Loisel — most grateful for his assistance, and looking forward to meeting his partners far upriver near his fort.

But to arrive at Cedar Island and beyond meant breaking down our entire trip into the careful planning and obedient execution of hundreds of small tasks each day assigned to the most capable. The daily tasks were to become routine and regular to best prepare for the unknown. This system was an effort to maximize order and minimize disorder, even in the midst of chaotic conditions.

Towards that goal, three days later, I issued detachment orders that were recorded in Sergeant Ordway's Orderly Book, which detailed posts and duties for the sergeants who would direct the privates to carry out their commands.

Of the three sergeants, one was stationed at the helm of the keelboat, one in the center on the starboard locker, and the last at the bow. Whenever practicable, campsites would consist of one row of eight tents for the privates, sergeants, and boatmen, with five to six men occupying each tent. At each shelter opening towards the riverside, every man who was provided a rifle would have them loaded and vertically propped against each other for ease of access in case of alarm. Five fires would be lit on the landward side of the tents for illumination, warmth, cooking, and additional protection by means of deterrence. We captains would occupy a separate tent when not aboard the keelboat, and have our own campfire on the flank of travel.

Butchering and latrine areas would be at opposite ends of the camp, approximately 100 feet from the outermost tents. Kitchens were to be located nearest the campfires. Each sergeant was directed to keep a journal of noteworthy events, relieved from the labor of making fires, pitching tents, cooking, and commanding a squad of six to eight privates.

No cooking would be allowed during the day while on the march. Lyed corn, or hominy and grease would be issued to the party on the first day, salt pork and flour the next, and salt pork and cornmeal on the last. No pork was to be issued when fresh meat was available. The sergeant at the helm steered the boat, attended the compass, and kept the quarterdeck orderly. The non-commissioned officer at the center managed the sails, commanded the guard, oversaw the men at the oars, posted sentinels upon landing, and attended to the issuance of spirituous liquors. The sergeant at the bow assisted the bowsman in poling the boat, communicated signals to and from the pirogues, kept watch, and immediately reported river dangers of all sorts.

Similarly, because of their prior experience successfully navigating the Missouri, Privates Labiche and Cruzatte were assigned to also watch for dangers, such as floating logs, sandbars, snags, overhanging tree limbs, sawyers, and other hazards that choked the river. In obedience to this assignment on the following day, Private Cruzatte stood at the bow of the keelboat straining with his good eye to survey the opaque, brown river as far ahead as he could manage — a black patch over one eye, the other looking intently for threatening obstructions.

But as we were shoving off from shore, the only objects to capture our attention were two canoes carrying several men downstream. The men shouted greetings to us as they passed; their vessels loaded with fur and other trade goods. They informed us they had come from the Omaha nation, which they said was about 730 miles above our position. A few hours later, four rafts carrying even more men passed, and were also loaded with similar cargo. This time the men said they had been trading with Indians who lived along the Osage River.

Such friendly distractions made Cruzatte's duties easy for the time being, but that was soon to change, as the river began to test our mettle.

The sun's rays beat down on the water and reflected off incalculable numbers of wave crests, which immediately transformed into thousands of tiny lights that changed in an instant and dispersed in seemingly every direction. The lights temporarily blinded Cruzatte, and obstructed his gallant efforts to spot danger. He squinted to ward off the incessant glare, and placed a hand above his brow to cast a shadow, which increased his limited visibility.

In the shadowy current, Cruzatte recognized the impending menace.

"Driftwood ahead, Sergeant! On the larboard!" Cruzatte shouted to Ordway, as the private turned his head into a massive cloud of gnats, and inadvertently breathed in a large quantity of the tiny beasts.

The one-eyed soldier waved a hand in front of his face to repel the pests, but it was too late. Cruzatte repeatedly coughed and swallowed in a futile attempt to expel the troublesome insects from his throat. He rolled his tongue, sucked in his cheeks, and generated as much saliva as possible to ingest the creatures, while his good eye blinked away the intruders.

By the time Cruzatte sounded the warning, the boat was nearly on top of the floating debris, which was more than 20 feet in length and could have easily breached the wooden planks of the ship.

"Bowsman! Driftwood! On the larboard!" Sergeant Ordway yelled, as he pointed to the large remnant of a giant cottonwood tree.

But Private Gass, the bowsman on duty, had already identified the potential peril long before Cruzatte. He pushed the nearest end of the tree away from the side of the vessel with an iron-tipped setting pole, which was 20 feet in length. The log harmlessly scraped the side of the hull, and safely drifted past the two pirogues, which were following in the keelboat's wake.

Although he had a difficult time expressing himself in writing, Private Gass was a skilled carpenter from Pennsylvania who joined the expedition with Sergeants Ordway and Floyd — all who previously were members of Captain Russell Bissell's military company, stationed in Kaskaskia, Illinois.

While Gass was bowsman this day, Sergeant Floyd was at the helm trying to steer the lumbering vessel with the ship's rudder in a manner that would take advantage of every eddy nearest the riverbank, which assisted our movement upstream. The others laboriously pulled hard on the oars while leaning back and pushing with their legs to gain leverage against the challenging water. But this was only half the taxing chore.

The complete cycle also involved a demanding push and forward lean: pulling and pushing, leaning forward then back, over and over, day after day.

When the wind blew favorably, we dropped sail and traveled as far as 20 miles per day. However, even that option was temporarily annulled when the 36-foot mast on the keelboat was snapped by an overhanging tree branch on the 4th of June.

If the wind proved unconstructive but the water was sufficiently deep, the men rowed. Unfortunately, on such days we only covered half the distance than under favorable conditions. If the water was too shallow for rowing, the expedition members grabbed a setting pole from the hull at the ship's stern and pushed the boat up river, provided the current was not too swift. If the water was too swift, a rope several hundred feet in length was affixed to the mast for the crew to pull on while either walking along shore or — more often — wading through the river. In addition to these tribulations, there were several times the tow rope broke under the immense tension of pulling the heavy vessel.

This remarkable physical endeavor required a vast amount of drinking water, and the river was our only source for satiating our thirst. The men often skimmed the surface with their cups and drank the murky liquid. By June 17, some had dysentery and two thirds had boils or ulcers. After prudent deliberation, I agreed with Captain Clark's assessment that the water was responsible for their afflictions, and urged all henceforth to dip their cups well below the surface when obtaining a drink, which appeared to provide some relief.

At that same time, the engagés complained about not being able to eat more frequently for which I severely rebuked them for their haughty presumption of such a luxury. Time was of the essence, and halting to eat six times a day in the French manner was simply not an option, which is to what they were accustomed and felt entitled. And not quite unlike the hired French boatmen, the ticks and mosquitoes were also becoming quite troublesome.

Each day George Drouillard searched the surrounding countryside for game to hunt, and bagged mostly deer. In the evening at camp on the fourteenth of the month, Drouillard conveyed a tale about a remarkable snake that inhabited a lake five miles below our position. He claimed the Indians informed him that snakes infested those waters, and they had the ability to make gobbling sounds similar to a turkey, which could supposedly be heard for several miles. Astounded by the claim, but lacking in time, I elected to not investigate this alleged phenomenon, with hopes that we might on the return voyage.

Although, we did not have the luxury to confirm or refute this unbelievable assertion, we made time to consume the deer that Drouillard consistently harvested. We ate what venison was needed, and jerked the remainder for later consumption. Our diet was heavily laden with meat, but on occasion we were afforded the opportunity to supplement it with greens. This was the case on June 5, when Clark's servant, York, splashed into the river, and agilely swam to a nearby sandbar to harvest a sufficient quantity of Bog Yellowcress for supper.

The night of June 17, the sultry air was filled with troublesome mosquitoes and gnats that swarmed in numbers so immense they were difficult to keep from invading any opening. But it was the former that were proving to be our mission's plague.

"Goddamn it!" Captain Clark exclaimed in frustration, as he once again slapped at the ravenous mosquitoes on his neck. "They are very bad this evening, Captain," he complained while sitting near the campfire, glancing up from the field desk on his lap.

"How can I finish this if I have to keep smacking these sons a bitches every five seconds? He said, gesturing at the journal on his field desk.

I rummaged through my knapsack on the ground, and removed a metal container from the bottom. In it was several ounces of voyager's grease, which was made from buffalo tallow. I had purchased 300 pounds of this crude insect repellant on June 12 from a group of French traders traveling south.

"Try some of this," I said, tossing the container to him. "It will help."

Clark groaned at my gesture, knowing well what was inside.

"That smells like shit, but it's better than being eaten alive," Clark said, reluctantly removing the lid. "Thank you."

He liberally applied the concoction to his exposed skin, which provided some respite. The campfire made a series of cracking sounds. Clark rolled down his sock, and found a bloated tick attached to his leg.

"While I'm at it, I'm also going to do something about this," Clark said, as he carefully pulled the blood-filled creature from his skin, and examined it. "It's going to be a long trip if these bastards are going to be with us the entire voyage."

He crushed the tiny creature. Blood squirted from its body, and coated a small portion of Clark's index finger and thumb. I smiled in amusement.

"The insects are more of a pain than the rats and rattlesnakes. At least the rats and snakes can't fly or drink your blood," I joked wryly, which prompted a chuckle of agreement from Clark. "Perhaps it will rain soon, and knock down the bugs."

"I hope so," Clark said, wiping the grease from his hands before returning to work on his journal.

I crouched to sit on my heels and stared into the fire, which made another series of cracking sounds. After a short pause and moment of reflection, I shared a new thought with my companion.

"You may smell like shit, Captain, but I'm very glad you're here. I don't think I could do this without you," I commented in a subdued tone, still looking ahead.

"Despite your odiferous remedy Commander Lewis, I know of no one else I'd rather take such a trip, my friend — I'm actually enjoying myself," he added.

"You're a good man, Captain," I laughingly replied, turning towards him. "I'm calling it a day," I concluded, patting him on the shoulder.

"You do that. I'm almost done here," Clark responded, before finishing his work.

In our tent, I reviewed the day's events in my mind.

Rain began to tap at the exterior of our shelter about an hour later. With each drop that saturated the ground, my spirituous mood declined, accordingly. It seemed to have an ability to redirect my disposition and emblazon images in my memory, which I could not escape for better or worse.

In a letter penned nine months later, before leaving our winter fortress, I recalled some of these images for my mother in which I wrote:

"Such is the velocity of the current at all seasons of the year ... that it is impossible to resist its force by means of oars or poles in the main channel of the river; the eddies, which therefore exist on one side or the other of the river, are sought by the navigators, but ... the base of the river banks being composed of a fine light sand, is easily removed by the water ... [and] the banks being unable to support themselves longer tumble into the river with tremendous force, destroying everything within their reach."

During the ensuing days, I often walked along shore while my obedient companion, Seaman, followed his master. I also helped Drouillard hunt, collected plant and soil samples, and made celestial observations. However, clouds prohibited me from making lunar observations to collect data for identifying our longitudinal position on the 27th of June, but I was able to determine our latitude using an observational device known as a sextant.

The last time I had the opportunity to collect such data was earlier that month at the great Osage River. Actually processing the longitudinal numbers was too cumbersome to do in the field, and the plan was to submit the field data to a war department mathematician after the expedition to ascertain the actual location through complex trigonometric formulations.

During my walks, I made it a habit to bring my entrusted spontoon for protection, and as an aiming aid. This metal weapon was about six feet in length and provided my rifle support from a cross-bar for more accurate shooting. At the same time I walked or rode, Captain Clark largely remained on the keelboat, estimating distances for the maps he created, while the crew labored immensely, rowing, pulling or pushing the vessels, and performed well despite their illnesses and afflictions. In addition, Drouillard easily killed several black bears on the 22nd and 23rd, which made for fine meals.

Taking into account the number of trials over which we prevailed during the first few weeks of the journey — from a broken mast to my near-death fall — I surmised the party had developed into a cohesive and capable unit of young soldiers prepared for duty, which included nightly watches. But those watches would test my preconceived notion regarding at what stage of development the party had evolved, and what was required.

CHAPTER FOUR DISCIPLINE

June 29, 1804
Kansas River Camp: 364 miles above the Missouri confluence

The fires burned late into the night and early morning, as Private Collins patrolled the campsite with rifle in hand — his flogging wounds finally healed. Most, including myself, were sound asleep, in preparation for another day of difficult travel. But still awake were Private Moses Reed and Engagé La Liberté who were whispering complaints to each other about how much they hated life on the trail, and questioned the sanity of me and Captain Clark.[A]

As the disgruntled voiced their grievances, Collins' shadow loomed large on their tent, while he paced in the summer humidity, just after three in the morning. He also walked several times past Private Hall who was emerging from a deep slumber in his tent, which was pitched near several wooden containers. All the walking had parched Collins, and he was gradually overwhelmed with an inexorable urge to quench his thirst. Passing between the campfire and shore, the flickering light from the burning logs illuminated the whiskey keg, which captured the soldier's eye.

Seeking to not draw attention, Collins stepped lightly toward the barrel and quietly placed his rifle on the sandy bank. He seized a nearby cup, sat on a cask, and carefully turned the tap in anxious anticipation of the intoxicating liquid. It flowed out to cover the bottom of the metal container, and he kept it flowing until more than a gill filled the mug.

Private Collins carefully lifted the mug in anticipation, brought it to his mouth and tipped back his head. He relished the initial taste, swallowed, and thoroughly enjoyed the burning sensation it caused flowing down the upper portion of his digestive tract. The second sip was even better than the first. Several more followed, and by the end of his sixth sip, Collins had emptied the cup. He expressed his deep satisfaction by noisily exhaling, which stirred Private Hall into consciousness.

Hall wiped the sleep from his eyes, blinked several times then focused on the inebriated sentinel.

"What the hell are you doing, Collins? You're on duty," Hall questioned in a hushed tone.

Private Collins pursed his lips while placing his index finger near his mouth to extinguish Hall's admonishment. He leaned a bit forward and reached out toward Hall, with the empty cup clutched in his right fist. Hall hesitated; recognizing the crossroad of decision, and its possible consequences. Collins quickly responded by repeatedly waving Hall towards him with his left hand and gesturing more forcefully with the cup in the other, in an effort to tip the scale of decision. Hall grinned, silently slid out from beneath his blanket, and the incident was then subdued revelry.

They shared the cup for hours, voiced many thoughts about the mission, and stated plans about after its completion. Each time the drunken soldiers exhaled noxious gasses merged with the stagnant morning air, until an invisible fog hung in the vicinity of the men; an offensive fog that wreaked a strong odor — vile and sickening. Soon, the men passed out not far from where they had sat. A dim light broke the eastern horizon minutes after they slipped into a deep slumber.

Sergeant Floyd awoke and stretched his arms in the early morning light. He glanced to his left and then the opposite direction. His glance transformed into a stare. His eyes widened in disbelief, after observing the odd situation: two soldiers sleeping uncovered on the ground near a keg. He cautiously stepped towards them into the invisible fog, and was ambushed by the disgusting smell.

"Goddamn," Floyd mumbled to himself, after contorting his face, and slightly shaking his head in disgust.

He quickly deduced what had transpired. Floyd ordered both under arrest, and had four troops rouse the men to escort them to the confines of the keelboat, until a court-martial could be convened by Captain Clark.

"You'd think they would have learned, especially Collins!" Clark expressed with outrage about an hour later.

He had just finished breakfast, and was recording facts needed for trying the two prisoners in a court-martial.

"I'm just as baffled as you, Captain. What were they thinking?" I rhetorically asked in dismay.

"They're not thinking. They're still acting like rabble, instead of soldiers," Clark responded in exasperation.

"I don't think Collins' wounds have healed from last month's beating!" I remarked, shaking my head in disappointment.

Resigned to accept the inexplicable, I shifted my focus to an action over which I had complete control.

"Well Captain, since it's such a clear morning I thought it would be best if I took some observations, before the trial."

"Certainly; at least we can achieve something of value today," Clark responded.

The trial began the same day at about eleven that morning. The detail for the court was comprised of six soldiers. Sergeant Pryor presided. Private Collins was charged by Sergeant Floyd with getting drunk while on sentinel by consuming whiskey put under his authority, and urging Hall to draw whiskey from the barrel, which was intended for the party.

To this charge, Collins foolishly pled: "Not guilty."

Hall was accused of taking whiskey out of the keg, which was contrary to all my orders, and the Army's rules and regulations.

To this charge, Hall wisely pled: "Guilty."

After considering all the evidence during mature deliberation, the court was of the opinion that Collins was guilty as charged, and sentenced to 100 lashes on his bare back. Hall was sentenced to 50 lashes for his admission to the crime. Both sentences were to take place at half past three that afternoon in the presence of the party. Promptly at that time, the whip was removed from its bag, and the expedition members grimaced in sympathy each time the leathery tails made painful contact with the prisoners.

Among those soldiers I noticed while the punishment was being executed was Private Alexander Willard.[B] He was a 25-year-old blacksmith from New Hampshire, under the command of Sergeant Ordway. Willard was a proficient hunter, and appeared to cringe more than anyone each time the tails snapped to savagely carry out the penalty.

Although Hall and Collins suffered, they were back at the oars by four that afternoon to help row approximately five miles upstream where we camped near a creek that had a pack of prairie wolves on its bank to receive our arrival.

The day after disciplining Collins and Hall, the midday heat had become routinely insufferable. By June 30, we were compelled to wait out the worst of it before proceeding upriver. The mercury confined in the thermometer that day percolated upward in the stifling summer air to indicate the temperature was a broiling 96 degrees Fahrenheit. The skin and clothes of most of the men became heavily encrusted with bold, white streaks of salt from the enormous quantities of sweat produced in what was a vain attempt to keep cool. Captain Clark observed that the men were becoming very feeble under these conditions, and we agreed to continue the practice of resting the party during the hottest portion of the day for as long as needed.

Also on this day, and for the second time in a month, an overhanging tree limb broke our keelboat mast, which mandated a suitable replacement. Fortunately, our skilled carpenters made short work in cutting a new one on the second of July. Within four hours, during the heat of the day, they had fashioned a suitable replacement from a large tree branch, located on an island of little significance.

The first complete month of the expedition was then past. By the twenty-eighth anniversary of our nation's independence, we started celebrating beginning at sunrise by firing our cannon, which was securely affixed to the bow of the keelboat. The booming sound from the mighty blast radiated in all directions, but had long faded before ever reaching any Indian ears. They were simply not to be found. We were eager to spread the news about the Purchase, and continued on a few more hours, before halting for breakfast at about eight that morning.

"Let's stop there," I said to Sergeant Floyd, as I pointed at a clearing — my other hand on his shoulder.

We moored the vessels, ate a fine meal, and proceeded on. The party rowed, while I walked on the bank in the morning light. As the sun neared its zenith, the heat of the day increased in accordance with its ascent. In response, the men abandoned the oars in favor of the tow rope. They walked barefoot on the searing sand, which soon became too hot. Their soles burned, prompting them to don moccasins for protection. At noon, we again halted to rest and dine on corn, after arriving at a viable creek. This creek we named Independence in honor of our great nation's Declaration 28 years earlier. During this time, Captain Clark and I recorded the names of all people and animals then in our party, which included four horses we had brought and found, my dog Seaman, the original members, and Pierre Dorion — a Frenchman from the middle section of the Missouri who was an associate of Loisel.

Clark and I met Mr. Dorion on June 12 with his accompanying party who were going down river. They were carrying an abundant number of animal pelts and voyager's grease. We wasted no time submitting the introduction letter from Loisel, and hired him after learning he was fluent in the language of the Yankton-Sioux Indians, since his wife was a member of that tribe. Persuasion proved most constructive in no small part because he was positively acquainted with Captain Clark's elder brother nearly 30 years prior, during the Revolutionary War. Our objective was to have Mr. Dorion influence the representatives of that tribe to go east and visit President Jefferson.

Leaving the tributary Independence after our meal, we had traveled a total of 15 miles before deciding to encamp and celebrate on a plain amid the most sublimely beautiful hills, valleys, and prairie we had ever witnessed. This pleasing scenery was diverse with emerald-green grass lowlands, interspersed with copses of timber, surrounded by rolling hills that presented themselves to the river and streams in a manner more striking and handsome than is possibly imaginable. This elegant landscape elevated everyone's disposition in perfect congruence with the surroundings. Reflecting this buoyant mood, Captain Clark ordered an extra gill of whiskey for each man, Private Cruzatte broke out his violin, and we closed the day by firing the cannon once more.

Four days later, the good spirits of that day yielded to another challenge in the form of reigning in a rash of sickness. In response, I issued detachment orders in an attempt to curb what appeared to be an outbreak of foodborne illnesses. This was in addition to the suspected waterborne ailments a few weeks prior. Most recently, six men had been ill, with five suffering from headaches and other maladies. The new orders placed specific soldiers in charge of cooking food and cleaning equipment in each of the three messes. Privates William Werner, John Thompson, and Collins were assigned this task. In exchange for this added responsibility, each was relieved of guard duty, pitching tents, and collecting firewood — a fair exchange.

With the new orders successfully implemented, and nearly two months into the expedition, we still had not met any Indians. However, Clark believed our fortune had turned for the better on the 11th when he spotted fresh horse tracks. Believing these tracks might lead to an Indian camp, he followed them for some distance only to find a single horse grazing along the riverbank. At camp that evening, we concluded the horse was probably lost the previous winter by an Otoe Indian hunting party. Unfortunately, the Otoe were nowhere in the vicinity. We assumed they were likely far away hunting buffalo.

Late that same night, Sergeant Ordway awoke in the final hour of the 11th to answer the call of nature. He threw off his cover, sleepily made his way to a nearby cottonwood tree, unbuttoned his fly, and relieved his bloated bladder of its contents. With the requirement completed, Ordway stepped uneasily through the darkness towards his tent. However, he ceased his advance after hearing a strange noise originating from a significant growth of sedge.

Ordway trod warily in the direction of the intermittent sound. Peering down over the sedge, Ordway recognized the man who recoiled most witnessing the punishment of Privates Collins and Hall. Lying on the comforting bed of plants, Private Willard sensed his sergeant's presence and immediately sprung to his feet, grabbing his rifle in the process.

"You were sleeping!" Ordway loudly accused, as he stabbed Private Willard's chest with his index finger to emphasize the allegation.

"Sergeant! I was just lying down for a minute," Willard lamely protested.

"I heard you fuckin' snoring, you lyin' son of a bitch!" Ordway screamed. "You coulda had us all killed!"

"No, Sergeant! I was resting," Willard reasserted.

"That doesn't make it any goddamn better, Private!" Ordway forcefully stressed, disgusted with both Willard's inaction and explanation. He shook an accusing finger at Willard, and turned to walk back to his tent. Ordway stepped a few paces and mumbled to himself: "Stupid son of a bitch — I sure hope he doesn't have kids."

Like Collins and Hall, Ordway also had Willard arrested and secured on the keelboat, until another court-martial could convene. The penalty, if convicted of the charges, could have been execution by hanging or firing squad. Taking into account the gravity of the offense, and its recurrence, Captain Clark and I presided over the proceedings, which commenced immediately after dinner. Sergeant Ordway charged Willard with lying down and sleeping on his post.

To this charge the prisoner cleverly pled: "Guilty of lying down, and not guilty of going to sleep."

After properly considering the evidence, the court was of the opinion that the prisoner was guilty of every part of the charge against him. This being a breach of the rules and articles of war, as well as tending to the probable destruction of the party had we been attacked, Clark and I sentenced him to receive a total of 100 lashes on his bare back. Twenty-five lashes were to be administered on each of four consecutive nights, with the punishment to commence that evening at sunset, and continue to be inflicted each and every evening until completed.

Private Willard never said to me how he felt about the sentence, but he appeared to reluctantly accept his fate because he realized the significance of the offense. If he did consider it unjust, I never received word from any of the men that Willard thought it unwarranted. After the beatings on the second, third and fourth evenings, I judiciously utilized my medical skills to compassionately treat Willard's seeping wounds, which he appreciated.

During the course of his punishment on the 14th, a strong gust during a storm blew Clark's field notes from the keelboat into the river. He lost details of events that happened the day before, and had to recreate the writings from memory, and reading the sergeants' journals.

Clark could not refer to my own journal of events because I had no such writings during this period, given the fact that Clark and others were recording such events. With the other documentation I was conducting during this time from flora to fauna, and data for latitude and longitude, I did not think it entirely necessary to duplicate our shared experiences, since Jefferson's instructions were to record "other notes" at times of leisure. It was not until the following spring when we entered unmapped territory that I resumed recording events. Paramount in my mind was to have at least one of the leaders of the expedition document daily events, while supplementing them with coordinate data. In addition, this region had already been well-documented by previous explorers, such as John Thomas Evans.

What wasn't lost was the fact that July was not a good month for Willard. On the 29th, in his haste to break camp, Willard forgot his tomahawk. At about noon that day, Willard approached Ordway who was eating:

"Sergeant Ordway," Willard sheepishly said to capture his leader's attention.

"What is it, Private?" Ordway responded studying Willard's face.

"I must report I left my tomahawk at last night's camp," he quietly said.

Ordway dropped his head, shook it, and looked back up at Willard.

"Goddamn, Private. You is dumb as the day is long," he said, before pausing a few seconds. "I'll ask Captain Lewis to delay a few hours while you go back and fetch it. You hear?"

"Thank you, Sergeant," Willard replied meekly.

"Don't fuckin' thank me! Just get it and hurry on back," Ordway angrily said, as he pointed downstream.

Willard quickly turned, grabbed his rifle and possible bag, and hiked more than three miles.[C] He soon arrived at a deep, muddy river named Boyer to access the previous camp. The Private stopped and evaluated the situation for a few seconds before concluding this was the safest point at which to cross. With rifle in hand, he uneasily placed both feet on a fallen tree and began to walk sideways, approximately 15 feet above the surface of the swiftly flowing water. The soldier slowly slid his lead foot, stopped then executed the same move with the other foot, while holding his arms slightly away from his torso. He was about half-way across the log when his center of gravity suddenly shifted forward. To correct the imbalance, he immediately reacted by leaning back, but overcompensated in the process. He then pitched forward and instinctively released the rifle to save himself from falling, and his weapon plummeted butt first into the river, disappearing from view. Willard quickly twisted his body to face the opposite bank, leaned further forward, and grasped the log with both hands, scarcely avoiding the same fate as his rifle. Willard lowered himself to straddle the log, and scooted to the other side of the river.

For a moment, he dejectedly stared at the cloudy water in the vicinity of where the rifle entered and knew if he was sent all this way to retrieve a tomahawk, he must also recover the rifle. Reluctantly, Willard removed his clothes, waded into the river and plunged down, feeling for the weapon in the cold, slimy muck. After repeated attempts that turned up nothing but handfuls of mud, Willard abandoned his efforts to recover the rifle and tomahawk and shamefully re-crossed the river on the log and walked back to camp for help.

Sergeant Ordway was successfully fishing for catfish alongside Private Silas Goodrich when he noticed a dark image approaching.

Goodrich was considered the best fisherman on the expedition, and was a member of Ordway's squad of nine privates, which included the unlucky, but likeable Willard.

Both quickly identified the image as Willard who was empty-handed.

"What the hell, Willard? I don't see no tomahawk," Ordway commented.

"Yes, Sergeant. And you don't see no rifle, neither," Willard added.

Ordway and Goodrich snickered.

"And …" Ordway urged.

"I dropped the rifle in the river tryin' to cross."

Ordway and Goodrich broke into hysterics. Willard could only watch the pair as they bent over at the waist, tears welling up in their eyes. The hapless Private soon grew weary of the joke.

"Are you done?" Willard exasperatedly asked.

Ordway momentarily composed himself to reply, while Goodrich was still giggling, but attempting to contain his amusement.

"Yeah, yeah, we're done … for now."

The pair burst into laughter once more.

After what seemed like an eternity to Willard, Ordway stopped laughing to continue addressing the soldier.

"Okay, okay … We'll send the white pirogue down with a few men. Don't worry, Willard. We'll get your shit back," Ordway assured.

A short time later, a small crew of seven, including Private Reubin Field, had gathered in the pirogue.

Field was related to Captain Clark through marriage, and was the elder brother of Private Joseph Field — both were in Sergeant Floyd's squad. The detail moved downstream, and soon arrived at Boyer River.

"Over there," Willard said pointing to the fallen tree.

The crew rowed the pirogue to the vicinity of a large tree branch, and wrapped a thick rope attached to the boat around the branch.

"Okay, Willard, here's the deal; If any of us find the rifle, you owe 'em your gill," McNeal said.

"That sounds fair," Willard agreed.

"Right, let's go then!" McNeal shouted, before pulling off his shirt and throwing it in a rumpled heap on the bottom of the boat. "I need a bath, anyway."

Willard and four others also stripped off their uniforms and dived into the water. After ten fruitless minutes of searching, Willard and Field swam to the side of the boat and grasped the gunwale for support.

"How about it, Willard; If'n I find it this time, I get your gill tomorrow, too. Deal?" Field asked.

"Deal," Willard replied.

Field took a deep breath and plunged in head first. He swam along the muddy bottom a few seconds, blindly trolling until he felt the unmistakable metal that comprised the barrel of the lost weapon. He resurfaced with the prize in hand and triumphantly displayed it to the group who erupted with laughter and cheers — all relieved the rifle had been recovered.

They continued on, found the tomahawk, and caught the main party by evening. The next day, they were relieved to find that Sergeant Floyd — who had been very ill — was then recovering.

There was not much sympathy for Willard each night he received his punishment, days earlier for his previous offense, and even less after the weapons incidents. When he was whipped the party stood in silence like fence posts, wondering what would have happened had they been attacked that night by an Indian war party.

But confrontation with the natives was contrary to our mission. We were to establish a satisfactory relationship with them for conducting future commerce, in accordance with President Jefferson's instructions. To accomplish this meant finding the natives and cultivating friendly relations, but we had yet to have any meetings. Several of our boatmen predicted this circumstance would soon change after we passed north of the river Platte — where the only trees that could be found were along waterways that broke the vast plains' rolling cover.

CHAPTER FIVE
FIRST MEETING

August 2, 1804
Council Bluff Camp: 680 miles above the Missouri confluence

I sat nervously at my field desk making final alterations to a nearly 3,000-word speech I planned to deliver the following morning to 13 representatives of the Otoe-Missouria Indians, as I fought the nightly battle with mosquitoes.[A] This was the council for which we had sought and anticipated since leaving St. Charles nearly three months prior, and I was nearly incapacitated with anxiety knowing the expectations of the President, and not knowing the reaction of those who were to attend.

In an odd respect, the constant clash with the troublesome insects served as useful diversion from the pressure of the speech. Regardless, I considered the opportunity positive, thanks to the good fortune of our expert hunter, and one of our Indian interpreters, George Drouillard.

Five days prior — the same day Private Willard dropped his rifle into the river — Drouillard was tracking elk on the prairie when he had our first encounter with the natives.

From a distance of a quarter mile, he observed three figures on the same plain between a large hill and stand of trees near a stream. Well aware of our mission objectives, Drouillard wisely used his initiative, and cautiously approached the trio, until he positively identified them by their manner of dress. Then 200 paces from the group, he placed trust and perhaps his life in a constructive Indian response. He ceased advancing. Drouillard set down his gun, waved his arms, and loudly shouted the word, "Dakho'ta" several times, which he understood to mean "friend" in their native language.[12]

Drouillard's gestures were happily received by the three Indians who signaled back for him to join them. The Indians were of the Missouria tribe, and were busy field dressing a freshly killed elk. Their nation had recently allied with the Otoe, after they were almost all killed during frequent battles with more powerful tribes from the Mississippi River region. Although associated with the Otoe nation, their combined numbers were still low.

The group of four communicated several minutes when the Indians generously offered a portion of the elk in exchange for seeing our boats. Together, they hiked back to the river.

One of the natives, whose name was Running Horse, accompanied Drouillard into camp.[B] He informed us that his nation was hunting buffalo, which is why we had yet to meet all the chiefs and principals of the tribe. Before meeting him, we had witnessed numerous signs of their presence. The most spectacular indication being the billowing clouds of smoke from scorching fires that consumed huge sections of prairie grass. Such fires we concluded could have only been artificially ignited.

The following day, July 29, Captain Clark sent an Otoe-speaking engagé named La Liberté on horseback with Running Horse. La Liberté's mission was to meet leaders of Running Horse's tribe, and inform them of our desire to hold a council upriver at our camp. It was there that we had been since July 30, and named the encampment Council Bluff. During our time at this site, Captain Clark noted that the nearby land contained high quality, and large quantities of clay, which would be ideal for making bricks for a new settlement.

We marked the end of July and a few days into the next month at this spot, and still had not met the Indians. But fortune changed for the better at sunset when a group of 13 people finally arrived, along with a Frenchman named Fairfong who traded goods, and lived among the Otoe.

However, for an unknown reason Engagé La Liberté did not return with them. I later suspected he may have quit the expedition, since he was well-acquainted with people of that tribe, and likely found our pay incommensurate with the arduous demands of the work. Since he was not a military member of the expedition, we opted to not send out a tracking party to learn of his fate, but a group of Otoe Indians later volunteered to watch for him.

Along with Mr. Fairfong, Captain Clark and I enthusiastically offered our friendship to the Indian group, which included the six lesser-chiefs and seven principals. Being unprepared for the exact time of their arrival, we were not in our formal, military-dress uniforms during the impromptu reception. However, we shook hands and presented them with small gifts consisting of tobacco twists that were about two feet in length, some minor provisions, and fired the keelboat cannon twice — much to their amazement. In exchange, they gave us several watermelons, which we considered exquisite dining, and a welcomed supplement to the large quantities of venison and fish we consumed each day. After this most auspicious start, we parted for the evening. The Indians camped less than a mile downriver from us.

After supper, by the fire, I made the last changes to my 11-page manuscript, and began making a duplicate copy of the speech for Captain Clark. Gradually, I was overwhelmed with a feeling of nausea from the tension and anticipation of this important delivery. After many hours of composition, I wished to close the message in an encouraging manner, but had trouble choosing the final words. Finally, they came to me. I scribbled the ending on both versions and turned in for the night, shortly after eleven. Except for the sentry on duty, the entire party was asleep. However, sleep would prove elusive for me, as I continually rehearsed the speech in my mind, until I finally rested a great deal of time later — mentally and physically exhausted.

While I struggled to slumber, a thick fog descended in the night to blanket the area, especially in vicinity of the river. Water droplets coated the outside of the tent, and even covered interior sections of the oiled cloths. One droplet near the ridge in Private Shields' shelter had collected enough moisture that gravity began tugging it along the inside of the fabric, causing it to slowly slide downward.[C] With each advancing inch, the droplet absorbed more water and grew in size, until it finally broke free of the side. It was airborne a few feet before splashing onto the bridge of Private Shields' nose, which wrested him awake. He wiped away the water, blinked a few times, and saw the sun had already broken the horizon. Deciding further sleep was not possible, Shields peeled off the moist, woolen blanket, put on his dress uniform, and carried out his assigned morning duties, in expectation of the great meeting.

The sun burned off the last of the enveloping fog and mist shortly after eight that morning. I anxiously paced back and forth in close proximity to our tent practicing my address and re-reading the most crucial parts of the final product. Confident my preparation for the speech was complete, I spent the next 25 minutes pumping air into a small, metal cylinder for demonstration of my pneumatic rifle. This specially made weapon was a repeating air gun, which could shoot 20 balls from a tubular magazine in a minute through a target at about 50 paces. The unit also housed an air cylinder in the butt of the rifle, which contained 800 pounds of pressure per square inch.

Nearly a year earlier, I demonstrated the power and accuracy of this novel weapon to a group of gentlemen at Bruno's Island near Pittsburgh. A man named Blaze Cenas was so enamored with its features that he begged for the opportunity to shoot the gun. To satisfy his curiosity, I handed him the weapon, and he subsequently discharged the piece by accident. The ball rapidly hurtled through the air in the direction of a group of people standing about 40 yards from him. It found its way through the hat of a woman, and grazed her temple. Blood began to gush down the side of her face, as others watched in horror. Members of the group rushed to her aid, while we sprinted to check her status. After several unnerving minutes, we determined the wound was not mortal, and she would be fine. Providence shielded us from tragedy, and the gun certainly proved its potential, which solidified its usefulness for our expedition.

While I laboriously filled the gun's chamber with air, the men finished breakfast, and were soon busy erecting a large awning made from our mainsail, which would be used as shade for hosting the council.

Nearby, Private McNeal worked digging a small hole with a hand spade near the riverbank. He cleared a few feet of soil to form an opening approximately three inches in diameter. The Private grabbed the object of his efforts and carefully lowered one end into the hole, at an angle slightly less than perpendicular. He straightened the object and used his foot to kick in soil around a wooden staff, which was about seven feet in length. After compacting the earth about the staff, McNeal stepped back to inspect his work. With his hands placed on his hips and a satisfied smile on his face, he stared at our young country's flag, which was secured to the upper part of the pole. It assertively fluttered in the mid-morning breeze, boldly proclaiming dominion over the new territory and Indians, as the hot August sun blazingly illuminated the Stars and Stripes.

Meanwhile, Captain Clark supervised gift preparation, which included the unwrapping of bundle number thirty. Enclosed in the numeric bundle were sewing threads and needles; striped, silk ribbons; broaches; metal rings; brass wire; breech cloth; assorted colored beads; sewing cloths; pocket mirrors; earrings; vermilion body paint; American flags; peace medals; ruffled, calico shirts; and printed commission certificates for each principal. The certificates were worded in recognition of their status, and gave assurance that they would be protected by their new Great Father in the east. The specific name of the certificate recipient was to be hand-written on the document at the time they were awarded.

The unanswered questions were how well these gifts and my speech would be received and understood by our newly adopted children.

Under the awning, Captain Clark and I sat on two of 18 wooden boxes that were arranged in a circular fashion. The boxes served as makeshift stools for the Indians and our interpreters — Mr. Fairfong, Labiche and Drouillard. The remaining members of the corps assembled near the awning, awaiting the natives. Shortly before ten that morning, they arrived on horseback, dismounted, and approached. Captain Clark ordered the men into formation; complete with rifles in hand. I quickly marched out to meet their advance, stopped a few feet in front of an Indian who appeared to be leading the group, and extended my right hand in alliance, as I placed my left hand on his opposite shoulder.

"Welcome! Welcome!" I cheerfully exclaimed to the principal named Big Horse. I believed he was an Otoe subordinate to grand Chief Little Thief — the leader not in attendance because he was with his people hunting buffalo.

I shook hands with our guests and escorted everyone to the council site. There, I formally introduced Big Horse and the others to Captain Clark and our three sergeants: Floyd, Ordway and Pryor. The rest of the corps observed the proceedings from a short distance. Standing outside the awning after introductions, I deduced the time had finally arrived, and gleefully launched into the beginning of my speech I had committed to memory:[7]

"Children. It gives us much pleasure to meet you here this day in council. We salute you as the children of your Great Father and Great Chief of the 17 states of America. It will please your Great Father when he is informed of the readiness with which you have assembled yourselves to hear the good council, which he has commanded us to give you."

The interpreters did their best to accurately translate my words, which appeared to be understood.

I continued: "As a part of this command, we are compelled to demonstrate that we come from a mighty nation of wealth, discipline, duty, and justice. Sergeant Floyd, commence with drill."

"Captain! Yes, Sir!" Floyd immediately responded, saluted, and executed an about-face movement with expert precision, despite his recent pain and illness.

Directly addressing the men, Floyd barked out his order: "Platoon! Attention!"

The men stood tall and simultaneously drew their rifles with bayonets close to their right legs. Floyd then led the men through a series of ceremony drills, including marching in step, and firing a volley in unison on command, which was most impressive. However, it was difficult to determine exactly what impact, if any, the parade had on the Indians. They stoically sat observing the soldiers.

After the military review concluded, the Indians and our interpreters were directed by Captain Clark and me to seek shade under the awning to cultivate favorable conditions for the council. Members of the expedition huddled around the sail, and I moved to the center of the assembly to deliver my speech, which I forcefully read aloud, in earnest, and with much conviction:

"Children. Now, open your ears to hear the Great Father's words, and dispose your minds to understand. We have been commissioned and sent by the Great Chief of the 17 Great States of America to inform you that a meeting was held between this Great Chief and your old fathers, the French and Spaniards. In this meeting, it was agreed that all the white men on the waters of the Missouri and Mississippi rivers, should obey the commands of the Great Chief who has adopted them as his children, and now form one family with us."

I paused to establish eye contact with each of the Indians, provide the interpreters an opportunity to convey my words, and observe their reaction to this astonishing news. This information was translated into French by Labiche and from French to Otoe by Mr. Fairfong. Not sensing any response in either the affirmative or negative, I pressed onward:

"Children. Your old fathers — the French and Spaniards — have gone beyond the Great Lakes toward the rising sun and never intend on returning. You must live in peace with all the white men, for they are his children; neither wage war against your neighbors the red men, for they are all equally his children, and your new Great Father is bound to protect them. Injure not the persons of any traders who may come among you, neither destroy, nor take from them their property, for they visit under the protection of your Great Father's flag."

I again paused and surveyed all. Everyone, including the expedition members, was intent on listening.

"Children. This Great Chief has commanded us to undertake this long journey to clear the road, and make it one of peace between himself and his red children. Do these things the Great Chief has commanded and you will be happy. But should you bring upon yourself the displeasure of your Great Father, he will destroy you and your nation, as the fire destroys and consumes the grass of the plains."

Cognizant of the power of this immense threat, I again stopped to gauge reaction, as the warning was communicated, but to no avail. The Indians still sat stoically, giving no indication of sentiment.

No longer in need of reading directly from the manuscript, I concluded with the positive message I penned the prior evening by reciting the words from memory, while turning to address each man in the group:

"Children. In this final message, follow the councils of your Great Father and the Grandfather Spirit will smile upon your nation, and in future years will make you to outnumber the stars in the night sky."

With the lecture concluded, I carefully examined their faces for a response, as the interpreters relayed the message. The Indians' gestures and expressions indicated it was well-received, which was of great relief and comfort. I immediately directed the sergeants to distribute the gifts, which included six peace medals to the lesser-chiefs, commission certificates to the other seven, and the additional gifts contained in bundle thirty. We then anxiously awaited their reply with much anticipation.

The Indians began speaking among themselves and appeared to be primarily addressing Big Horse who glanced to his left and right, listening to brief comments from members of his party. He faced Mr. Fairfong and expressed himself in a convincing manner, while others in his party motioned agreement. Mr. Fairfong attentively listened, collected his thoughts for a moment, and conveyed the points to Labiche.

"Captain Lewis, Big Horse said he promises to follow the good advice in your speech, and is pleased to know the Great Chief is reliable," Labiche announced. "He also said the Spanish and French traders were never so generous. They never gave them as much as a knife."

Hearing the agreeable news, I smiled broadly and gladly nodded my approval, looking at Big Horse. The other 12 men followed Big Horse's lead by also expressing their intention to honor the pact, and acknowledging President Jefferson's word. But each Indian also articulated that they were at war with their neighbors to the north, and in need of goods to fight their enemies. They specifically expressed the want of whiskey, rifle ammunition, and gun powder to which Captain Clark responded in the affirmative by giving the group a bottle of whiskey, 50 ammunition balls, and a canister of powder. They appeared pleased we met this request.

For purposes of not only inspiration, but intimidation, I then astonished our guests with an exhibition of my air gun. I set the target at 25 paces, stepped back, and repeatedly fired round after round into the mark. Big Horse and the other Indians said they could not comprehend its shooting so often and without powder, which made the time that morning invested in pumping the 1,500 strokes of air into the reservoir well worth the effort. We also tried to impress our guests with a demonstration of items aboard the keelboat, including a magnifying glass, magnet, and telescope.

Our merriment continued with each of us consuming a dram of whiskey with dinner, and smoking tobacco from the pipe tomahawks. I closed the council by giving a copy of the speech to Big Horse for transfer to his leader, Chief Little Thief, along with a peace medal, flag, and calico shirts. My request was for their leader to attend a meeting in Washington with President Jefferson, upon our return from the western ocean the following spring. I also asked that Little Thief attend a future council upriver. In exchange, the natives gave us more watermelons to supplement our diet. With the business concluded, we bid farewell, prepared to cast off, and set sail at about three in the afternoon.

With a gentle breeze to push us upstream, we traveled five miles north and made camp beside the river, before a violent storm descended upon us for two hours. Once again, my spirituous mood gave way to a squall, which was an unfortunate harbinger for coming days.

CHAPTER SIX
CONSEQUENCES

August 4, 1804
Snag Camp: 685 miles above the Missouri confluence

For more than a month Private Reed had been thinking about his late night discussion near the end of June with Engagé La Liberté, and decided the time to act had arrived late on August 3, after we made camp: [A]

"Sergeant Ordway," Reed nervously called out to draw the attention his immediate commander.

"What is it, Private?" Ordway responded, glancing up from his supper.

"My knife. I'm sorry to report I left my knife at last night's camp."

"You what?" Ordway questioned in astonishment with a mouth half-full of partially eaten venison and hominy. He chewed a few more times and swallowed. "You sure?"

"Yes, I'm sure. I searched everywhere," Reed replied.

"Seems strange that you and Willard are afflicted with the same condition," the irked Sergeant observed.

"Yes, Sergeant, I apologize. I'd like your permission to recover the knife."

"That's good because I'd be sendin' your ass back to fuckin' get it, if you hadn't volunteered." Ordway chomped a few more times. "Permission granted … Are you goin' tonight or in the mornin'?"

"Early morning, Sergeant … I will try to catch up by mid-afternoon."

"Fine," Ordway said, shoveling another spoonful into his mouth. "Do you need a guard?"

"No, I can manage on my own," Reed deceptively replied.

"We'll expect you back by evenin', then," Ordway remarked.

"I'll catch up as soon as I can, Sergeant," Reed promised again to close the tense and foreboding exchange.

Reed was overwrought, and quickly made way to his tent. Beads of anxious sweat rolled down his forehead. He trembled with apprehension, as he removed all his clothes from his knapsack. He turned his head numerous times to watch for witnesses, as he stuffed all his provisions into a possible bag. With the valuable goods tucked away, including ammunition and gun powder, he headed south of camp about a half-mile downstream, carefully hid the stolen items in a wooded area near the river, and returned to camp for the night to divert suspicion. Early the next morning on the 4th of the month, Reed grabbed his Army-issued rifle, broke camp, and left his knapsack behind.

As of that evening, he still had not rejoined us. On the 5th of August — suspect of his motives — Captain Clark ordered Sergeant Ordway to examine the contents of his abandoned sack and concluded he likely deserted with inspiration, no doubt provided by a combination of Willard's lost tomahawk and La Liberté's unexpected exodus near the small Otoe village. Piecing together fragments of information from the recent and distant past, we believed Reed was probably among the Otoe where we also expected to find our missing engagé.

When Reed failed to return August 6, we were certain he had deserted, and ordered a search team to bring him back dead or alive.

To that team, Captain Clark and I assigned Drouillard, Reuben Field, Labiche, and Private William Bratton who was a 27-year-old blacksmith and gunsmith from Virginia. They were commanded to kill Reed, if he refused to return peacefully. In addition, they were instructed to bring back La Liberté if he was found to fulfill his contractual obligations, return the stolen horse, and invite the Otoe chiefs to attend a council upriver, provided they made contact.

The objective of the second Indian council was to mediate peace between the Otoe-Missouria and Omaha people. These groups had been at war for some time for reasons we did not entirely understand. The Omaha lived just north of the Otoe, and had long demanded costly tribute from Spanish and French traders in a manner not unlike the Teton-Sioux nation. The Teton lived further north of both the Omaha and Yankton-Sioux.

At one in the afternoon on the 7th, the capture or kill team set out on horses to complete their assignment.

During their absence, we continued traveling along the plains when the bowsman observed a curious phenomenon the following day. Far ahead in the distance, Private Cruzatte was disturbed about what was in our path and called me from the keelboat cabin to the bow. Alarmed about his tone of urgency, I walked briskly past the men who continued to row with their backs towards the oddity in the August heat and humidity. Cruzatte and I peered out several hundred yards and saw the entire river strangely turned from its characteristic brownish hue to a vibrant white, as if covered with a layer of ice and snow.

"What should we do, Captain?" Cruzatte asked.

"Keep rowing," I replied with trepidation — staring into the distance.

We advanced to within 50 yards of the curiosity and still could not determine its origin.

What is it, Captain? Is it ice?" Cruzatte questioned with a great deal of concern.

"I'm not sure. But how could it be ice in this heat?" I responded, as we both fixed our gaze on the bizarre sight.

We drew closer not knowing whether a harsh collision with the object was imminent. Tension increased as we both surveyed the water. The front of the boat made contact, but there was no impact sound or jostling of the vessel. Seconds later the entire ship was surrounded by a sea of white. I looked directly down, examined details of the oddity, and began to laugh.

"Feathers! They're feathers," I exclaimed with great relief.

I continued to chuckle at my naiveté and Cruzatte joined in, as I placed my hand on his shoulder. The boat rounded a bend in the river. On a large sandbar at the head of an island, huge numbers of white pelicans preened themselves. It was their summer molting season. The birds' discarded feathers covered every part of the land, and were blown into the water by a gentle breeze from the northwest. Later that day, Private John Dame shot one of the pelicans for an experiment, and I was amazed to learn the bladder-like pouch attached to its bill had a capacity to hold three gallons of water. The beast also had a wing span in excess of nine feet.

In addition to recording scientific observations such as that of the pelican, we continued with our efforts to learn more about the natives, which brought us to the burial site of a great Omaha Chief on the 11th of August. The morning began with a storm that lasted six hours, after which a strong, southerly wind remained. This enabled us to hoist the sails and move rapidly upstream.

From the river, Mr. Dorion spotted a sacred pole atop a large hill that rose 300 feet above the water. He said this was the grave site of Chief Blackbird who had presided over a large village eight miles north called Tonwantonga. He said this is where they once grew thriving crops of beans, corn, melons, and squash. A few years earlier, the community had about 1,100 residents who occupied approximately 300 earthen lodges, before a devastating outbreak of smallpox killed more than a third of their population, including Blackbird in 1800. So in fear of this unknown force reigning death upon their people, the Indian patriarchs reportedly and preemptively killed their wives and children in hopes they would be taken to a better existence before the horrifying force claimed their lives and, perhaps, their spirits.

According to Mr. Dorion, the deceased chief attained a portion of his notorious reputation through his alleged powers of sorcery, by vanquishing his enemies using poison obtained from unscrupulous traders. It seemed that whenever Blackbird wanted to kill Indian rivals, they were invited to a feast and offered arsenic-laced food, which resulted in their deaths within days of consumption. After eradicating his enemies, he triumphantly sliced open their foreheads with his tomahawk, pried his fingers between the under part of their skin and skull and ripped the scalp from their head as a war prize. To me, this seemed to pair the cunning of Machiavelli with the vengeance of Vlad the Impaler.[B]

Legend described this steep knoll in which he was entombed as Blackbird's favorite vantage point to observe river travelers. Prior to his death, he asked his followers to bury him astride his horse facing the great waterway to enable him to continue his watch over the area in the afterlife.

Captain Clark and I decided to pull ashore and bring ten others to pay our respects to the fallen chief, which we hoped would win us positive favor with the Omaha people. We ascended the hill, and saw the grave was a mound about six feet in height, and 12 feet in diameter, crowned with an eight-foot pole to which were attached the many scalps the Chief had acquired — securely bound atop the post. The scalps waved in the wind, as gusts raised and twisted them about the pole. Captain Clark and I climbed the mound and saw close to its base were offerings of food, his shield that was decorated with eagle feathers, a peace pipe, and a fringed tobacco pouch. Near the vertical center of the pole we affixed a white pennant that had a red-white-and-blue-colored border. We hoped this tribute would honor the former leader and please his survivors.

After paying resects to the fallen chief, we sailed north, and traveled 18 miles before halting to encamp.

Two days later on the 13th, Sergeant Ordway and a squad of four men were ordered back downriver to explore Tonwantonga, which we passed the prior day on the larboard side. They were instructed to invite Blackbird's survivors to a council, but found an unoccupied community. Like their Otoe neighbors, we speculated the Omaha were also out hunting buffalo.

Up to this point, we had not the opportunity or need to kill buffalo, which was especially true during the five days we stopped at a site we aptly named "Fish Camp" to await the Indians for a another council. On the 15th, Captain Clark and 10 men, including an ailing Sergeant Floyd, constructed a brush drag comprised of willow branches woven together, and stretched it across Omaha Creek. Using the flexible wooden net, the soldiers caught 318 pike, bass, perch, trout, and catfish. Clark jokingly boasted of his catch to me, and we agreed to a gentlemanly wager that I could double his total — the winner receiving the other's whiskey ration. The following morning, 12 men and I did just that and more, by trapping 709 fish.

While we enjoyed our bounty of aquatic species, Drouillard, Field, Labiche and Bratton were already making their way north to our camp.

In the days before, they had tracked Reed's path and arrived within a quarter-mile of the temporarily vacated Otoe village. As leader of the small party on the evening of the 13th, Private Field motioned for the group to halt. They dismounted their horses and hid them in a thicket where they discussed a plan to capture the malcontented deserter.

"I reckon we'll likely find him in the village, so double-check your weapon," Field stated. "Remember, we're here for Reed — Let's split up and flank the village. I'll do the talkin'.

"Who's going with who?" Labiche asked.

Field paused: "Drouillard, you come with me on the left. Labiche and Bratton, you swing right. Keep within shoutin' distance, and don't shoot unless you have to. And for God's sake don't shoot each other ... Give him a chance to surrender. Understood?"

The men nodded in agreement.

"Let's go, then."

Cautiously, the two teams quietly closed in on the perimeter of the village — stalking their would-be prisoners. At about 25 paces, Field could clearly see Reed and La Liberté tending a campfire, and a horse tied to a projection from the exterior of an earthen lodge. Both teams maneuvered ever closer by repeatedly running and hiding behind lodges on both sides of the runaways, until they were within a few paces. Field raised his weapon and aimed at Reed. From his line of sight, Field could also see a portion of a rifle barrel poking out from behind a wall, which indicated the others were ready.

"Reed! It's Reubin Field. You're surrounded. Give up peacefully and I won't kill ya!"

Upon hearing the familiar voice, Reed was stunned and incapacitated with fear. La Liberté suffered no such condition. He bolted for the horse, untied it, and quickly rode off in a southwesterly direction — leaving his discontented companion behind. No one even thought of shooting the fleeing man in the back, despite his abandonment of the expedition. Capturing the engagé was optional. The primary duty was to apprehend Reed. The deserter looked to his left and saw a tense Field, then glanced right to see a sweaty Labiche, and knew he must surrender or die in the process of resisting.

"Put your hands in the air, Private!" Bratton ordered, as he stepped from behind Labiche with his rifle pointed at the captured man's torso.

Reed uneasily obeyed.

"Now, lay flat on your belly."

Reed dropped to his knees and sprawled out on the ground near the campfire. Bratton slung his rifle onto his shoulder, approached from behind, and removed metal wrist cuffs from his shot pouch.

"You shouldn't have left, Reed," Bratton said, as he grabbed the prisoner's right wrist. Bratton twisted Reed's right arm back and clamped the cuff around Reed's wrist — repeating the process for the other.

With the deserter easily in custody, the successful team decided to spend the night and all the following morning in the village — in hopes of meeting the Otoe before returning to our camp. Private Field tethered himself with rope to Reed who was to remain cuffed and tied until his trial. The team slept comfortably, and shortly after the morning dew evaporated, Labiche used a magnifying glass to light the prairie on fire, which generated smoke to summon the Otoe. The message was received. By early afternoon, Big Horse, Chief Little Thief, and seven warriors all mounted on horses arrived and brought with them buffalo supplies. Drouillard and Labiche combined their efforts to communicate our desire to mediate peace between the warring Indian factions at a second council, which was gladly received by Little Thief.

Wasting no time, the Indian delegation and Field's team headed north, with Reed on a forced march, instead of riding a horse. Less than four days later, Private Labiche reached our site at Fish Camp in late afternoon on the 17th —just ahead of the others in the group who were expected to arrive the next morning. He reported to Captain Clark and me, not only the arrest of Reed, but successful contact and persuasion of Little Thief and the others to attend peace talks. Labiche also learned Big Horse was actually a Missouria chief, not an Otoe subordinate to Little Thief.

We were delighted.

The joyous mood lasted all of a few seconds before realizing there was no one with whom to make peace. The Omaha were still out hunting buffalo. Incensed at the irony, I ordered Sergeant Pryor to set the prairie ablaze to signal any Omaha who might be in the area. Pryor's entire squad walked about a mile inland; separated over a distance of about 500 paces and ignited a huge fire in which thick, dark clouds of smoke billowed up from the plains for several hours before extinguishing itself near sunset.

Darkness produced a cool evening, and still there was no response to our signal. The chill of the evening turned to night, and then sunrise — no Indians. Captain Clark ordered the keelboat cannon fired as an auditory signal, and dispatched Private Joseph to meet his brother, Private Reubin, and the coming Otoe. After dispatching Private Joseph, Captain Clark sat down to record the charges for Reed's court-martial, and prepare for the trial.

Shortly after ten that morning on the 18th of August, both Field brothers, Bratton, and the nine Otoe-Missouria Indians arrived, with Drouillard escorting Reed who was still cuffed, roped, and on foot. Captain Clark and I welcomed the Indian delegation and shared dinner with them under the awning near the keelboat. But before conducting the second council, we were obliged to commence with the soldier's court-martial. This unfortunate procedure was held beneath the mainsail by Captain Clark, Sergeant Ordway, and me. Ordway charged Reed with desertion, stealing a public rifle, shot pouch, powder, and ammunition. The Indians and expedition members bore witness. Reed sensibly confessed his guilt, and asked for leniency in his punishment.

After several minutes of mature deliberation, Captain Clark and I accepted his admission. Rather than shoot him dead, we sentenced him to walk a gauntlet four times, which meant he was to pass through two lines, each consisting of 16 soldiers. Every soldier was to be armed with a bundle of nine willow switches. This amounted to 1,152 lashes, which were to be administered in great earnest or members of the party too could suffer the same fate, the men were warned. In addition, we ruled that Reed be immediately discharged from the permanent party, surrender his assigned rifle, and take La Liberté's place as a laborer in the red pirogue. He was also to be sent back to St. Louis at some future date.

When the sentence was translated to the Indian leaders, the three principal chiefs in attendance immediately advocated for a pardon in objection to our use of corporal punishment. According to the chiefs, they would never inflict such an excruciating penalty and public embarrassment on one of their own, and believed the same custom should be rendered by their new Great Father and his representatives. However, we reluctantly denied their request. Through our translators, Captain Clark and I carefully explained the severity of the injury our party suffered through Reed's deception, and the importance of establishing and maintaining discipline in the ranks. This explanation appeared satisfactory to them, if not wholly accepted.

Consistent with the other court-martial sentences, we enforced swift punishment. Thirty-two enlisted men were ordered to each cut switches from willow trees near the river, and were to whip Reed when he walked past. Acting as observer, Sergeant Ordway made Reed remove his shirt and wait until the troops were in line. Two rows of 16 men spaced approximately six feet apart stood at the ready. Reed boldly accepted his fate and marched forward, at the command of Ordway. Privates McNeal and Shields were the first to draw back their arms and flog the deserter without abandon. Reed cried out in agony, but was shown no mercy.

He completed the first gauntlet, dropped to one knee, and began to weep from the pain and humiliation. Quickly regaining his composure, and determined to atone for his crime, he wearily rose to his feet and proceeded through for a second round of whirring, snapping, and cracking sounds, which were savagely indicative of the shredding of his back. Blood from his wounds soon saturated the bright blue cloth that comprised the upper-rear portion of his pants, which changed color to a shade of deep maroon. Reed resolutely struggled through two more passes and the ugly duty was finished for everyone.

It was difficult to conclude exactly what impressions the natives had of this display of our military custom, but I believed the punishment was consistent with our traditions, which we had to apply in the Great Father's new land.

With the business complete, we sought to end the day more productively by inquiring why the Otoe-Missouria were at war with the Omaha.

Little Thief and Big Horse explained that two Missouria warriors residing in an Otoe village had raided an Omaha community one night the previous spring to steal horses. The two men were killed during their efforts, which necessitated a similar retaliatory strike against the Omaha. The group also reported they had cultivated a tempestuous relationship with the Pawnee for stealing their corn supplies when they were absent from a village the previous summer, and were in fear of murderous revenge.

These were the type of reprisals I deplored, and would rather not had to address, in light of the grand vision we presented them. They were talking of stealing horses and corn, and revenge killings, while I offered them future trade with one of the most promising economies in the entire world. I simply could not comprehend such pettiness.

This being my 30th birthday, Captain Clark and I wanted to set aside these troublesome problems for the remainder of the evening. We shared our supper with the Indians, and ordered an extra gill of whiskey for each man to toast this special occasion. Private Cruzatte broke out his fiddle, tuned it, and began to play the Virginia reel to which the men happily danced, even though there were no women for accompaniment. They merrily skipped, turned, and side-stepped to more reels and jigs until eleven that night.

I turned in contentedly anesthetized and pleased with how the difficult day concluded. Such a drunken diversion was needed after the unfortunate trial, and before a challenging second council with the Otoe-Missouria who camped less than a half-mile upstream.

CHAPTER SEVEN
CHANGES

August 19, 1804
Fish Camp: 874 miles above the Missouri confluence

Captain Clark was about to eat breakfast when he noticed a shadowy shape moving through the morning mist, just north of camp. The shape slowly changed into a more lucid figure that appeared to be someone on foot.

With a plate in one hand and fork in the other, Clark continued to observe the figure as it closed in, growing larger. He scooped up his food, took a bite and started to chew, planning the day in his mind and calmly wondering who was walking toward camp. Soon, he was able to identify the figure and suddenly spat out his food at the startling sight.

Big Horse — the Indian we had best come to know — was going to attend the important second council nude.

Captain Clark stared and shook his head in disbelief, as the Chief walked directly to him. Not knowing exactly how to react, Clark offered him breakfast and silently questioned the obvious. But the answer would have to wait.

"Captain Lewis, Captain Clark, come quickly!" Private McNeal breathlessly called out while running toward us in a panic.

"What is it, Private?" I asked, turning to him.

"It's Sergeant Floyd, Sir. You must help him. He's very ill!"

Grabbing my medical bag, Captain Clark, York, McNeal and I hurried to Floyd's tent where he lay on his side, eyes shut, next to a small pool of vomit. He was coughing weakly, and in a great deal of pain. Sensing our presence, Floyd feebly opened his eyes and looked towards us. Even this small act appeared most difficult for him. I dropped to one knee, placed my bag on the ground, and gently put my hand on his shoulder.

"Tell me what's wrong, Sergeant."

Floyd coughed once more and swallowed.

"My stomach. Nothing stays on my stomach. I got it coming out both ends, Sir," he said in a barely audible voice.

I carefully thought for a moment about a diagnosis: "Bilious colic," I surmised, as I glanced up at Captain Clark.

I reached into my bag and grabbed a Thunderbolt tablet.

“Give this with some water and thoroughly clean him,” I said, handing the pill to York who took the tablet.

My expectation was the intrepid sergeant would recover like he did several times during the past month. I left Floyd in very capable hands.

Despite his dire condition, we had to finish preparations for the second council. The council was to be similar to our first meeting with the natives. Shortly before nine, the Indian delegation arrived, including Big Horse and eight others. Under the awning, I delivered the same speech I gave 16 days prior, but there was a much different reaction to the message.

After Labiche translated my words directly into Otoe, Little Thief was the first to respond by saying his father instructed him to always be friendly with white people, and he honored this command. What was of most value to his people was not from whom goods were obtained, but the superiority and value of the goods to be traded, regardless of the suppliers’ nationality.

This was not satisfying news to me or Clark. For whatever reason, they did not appear to understand my speech. Eventually, there would be no more Spanish, French or English traders — only merchants and agents working under their new Great Father’s flag. As a courtesy, I elected to wait for a more appropriate time to re-emphasize that point.

In addition to the topic of trade goods, Little Thief also asked us to broker a truce between his people and the Omaha to which I replied would not be possible. The Omaha had not responded to our signals, and we could no longer wait for them to return. This too did not appear to be well-received by our guests. Little Thief closed his speech by requesting that Private Labiche and Mr. Fairfong travel south to negotiate a treaty between his people and the Pawnee. We reluctantly had to refuse this request, also.

Big Horse then explained the motive for his nudity. The Chief said he wanted to dramatically emphasize his destitution, and feared he would depart in the same condition — destitute. He too wished for peace, but to grow the seeds of tranquility, he would need goods and whiskey to replace the prizes of war and conflict. If peace was to be honored, the young men in his village would need resources to give their families and community. They would need to gain status through different means. However, until goods could be secured, he emphasized a generous supply of whiskey would be the most useful tool for his men to wage peace. The other members of the delegation communicated similar sentiments, but we refused to give anything more than token amounts of whiskey and goods.

I again tried to explain that we were not there to trade, but to open the road for future trade. In hopes of changing the anemic tone of the meeting, Captain Clark and I ordered the sergeants to distribute gifts of tobacco twists, face paint, and beads for everyone. Now that I was aware of Big Horse’s chiefly status among the Missouria Indians, I awarded him a larger medallion equal in size to that of Little Thief who was given a similar pendant weeks earlier, after our first council. In addition to the other presents, the seven warriors were given paper certificates that proclaimed them a friend and ally of the United States. A warrior named Very Big Eyes examined the certificate, and a puzzled expression grew on his face.

With the gifts issued, I invited Little Thief to Washington to meet President Jefferson next spring. The Chief listened to Labiche's translation, looked down, and turned to study other delegation members for a few seconds. He noticed Very Big Eyes was intently peering at the certificate, but Very Big Eye's expression changed from bewilderment to anger. Meaning to make a favorable impression and advance his people's interests, Little Thief announced his acceptance of our invitation, much to my pleasure. But the pleasure was short lived. Discontentment had emerged.

Hearing this declaration, Very Big Eyes stood and curtly gave his certificate to Captain Clark who was taken aback at the warrior's harsh action. Clark and I exchanged curious glances. Once I processed what had just transacted, coupled with other misunderstandings, I severely admonished the Indian for insulting us, our nation, and an official document. This brief, but stern rebuke apparently changed the warrior's opinion and he requested Clark give back the certificate, which he flatly denied. Little Thief recognized then that this was his delegation's time to decrease tensions, and calmly requested Clark return the certificate to Very Big Eyes. Clark stood and walked toward the great leader.

"Chief Little Thief, I ask you to bestow this important document to the most worthy of your warriors," Clark solemnly requested, as he handed the Chief the certificate.

After Labiche translated the message, Clark went back to his seat under the mainsail. The Chief pondered his next move and returned the certificate to Very Big Eyes who happily received the article. In silence, Captain Clark and I grudgingly accepted the Chief's judgment, and changed the topic by offering them dinner with a dram of whiskey.

During the meal, the delegation informed us that not far upriver there existed a large hill. They claimed this hill was inhabited by great spirits who were fiercely guarded by devils who stood only about 18 inches in height and possessed remarkably large heads. They were supposedly armed with sharp arrows that had a huge range at which they could kill any and all who approached this hallowed mound. According to one warrior named Brave One, the Otoe-Missouria, Sioux, and Omaha all believed this tale, and never advanced towards it for fear of being slain or bringing misfortune onto their people. Apparently, these devils killed three Omaha warriors several years earlier from a great distance. Little Thief said this conical formation was known as the "Mountain of Little People" or "Spirit Mound," which we planned to investigate at the first opportunity. The tale was even more appealing than gobbling snakes.

After dinner, I demonstrated the air gun, and later brought our guests aboard the keelboat to show the group the magnet, telescope, compass, and magnifying glass. Big Horse begged for the latter. He too wanted to use the sun to light fires. Again, I had to reject yet another request, which was a disappointment for all.

Although the meeting fell far short of everyone's expectations, both sides could claim some success when the council closed. At the request of the chiefs, we agreed to remain another night at our camp, which also allowed us time to focus attention on the ailing Floyd.

He was much weaker and no better, which prompted me to try bleeding him of toxins. I suspected toxins were causing his illness, and hoped bleeding him would balance the four humors that comprised fluids in the body. Floyd was too fragile to do anything more than weakly writhe during the procedure. The procedure involved making a small incision into his wrist with a sharp knife, and allowing blood to flow into a copper bowl, which was received by a circular drainboard. Captain Clark and York stayed with him through the night; they gave him water and food, but nothing would stay a moment on his stomach.

In the morning, Ordway, Pryor, McNeal, and Shields gently carried Sergeant Floyd on a blanket to the white pirogue, which ferried him to the keelboat. The group entered the keelboat cabin and set him on a bed, which was a rope-woven mattress, covered with a woolen blanket. With Floyd aboard and as comfortable as possible, we set sail under a gentle breeze from the southeast, and passed two small islands. By noon, we had traveled about four miles before halting for dinner near a bluff on the starboard side, and to prepare a warm bath for our sickly patient. He was not recovering.

Floyd lay motionless next to Clark, who was seated on a cask next to him.

Floyd slightly opened his eyes, and with a great deal of effort, cleared his throat, before whispering in a barely audible tone: "Captain."

Clark dropped to one knee and lowered his head, until he could feel the dying man's breath on his ear. "Yes, Sergeant," Clark whispered back.

Floyd lay in silence, re-gathering strength for his next words. Images of his mother, father, brother and two sisters flashed through his mind, and brought him solace from the excruciating pain he had been enduring for weeks. In an instant, he relived countless fond memories, and his pain suddenly dissipated.

With newfound composure, Sergeant Floyd summoned the remnants of his power to convey a final message: "I — I'm going away — I want you to write me a letter."

Clark immediately glanced up and saw dictation materials on a desk near the end of the bed weighted down by the Floyd's pipe tomahawk.[2] Before standing to obtain the writing implements, Captain Clark looked to his left to see Floyd's facial complexion change color, as the last signs of life drained from his body. It was shortly before one in the afternoon. Realizing a great threshold had just been crossed, Clark dropped his head into his hands, as tears welled up in his eyes. He stayed in the same position for a moment, took a deep breath then wiped away his sorrow with each shirt sleeve. Clark slowly stood up and heavily sighed before exiting the cabin to announce the passing to Floyd's cousin, Sergeant Pryor, the three other soldiers on deck and York. The four military brethren entered the cabin, wrapped Floyd's body in the blanket, and transferred the remains to the white pirogue. All climbed aboard, and together silently rowed ashore to meet the rest of the expedition. The news was a shock. Many wondered how many more would perish before our long journey was complete.

The body was moved onto a makeshift cot in a tent where York carefully removed Sergeant Floyd's clothing, and dressed him in his formal uniform in the most dignified manner possible. Lying in state with his hands neatly placed across his chest, all members of the expedition visited to pay respects to their deceased brother. As the wake proceeded, Captain Clark wrote a short eulogy for me to read at the memorial service, and gave Floyd's tomahawk to Private Shields for constructing grave markers.

With memories of Chief Blackbird's magnificent burial site in mind, Captain Clark and I thought a similar bluff would be a fitting tribute to our late sergeant.[A] Private Gass built a fine wooden casket, while Private Shields cut and carved a marker from a red-cedar post, using his own tools and Floyd's tomahawk. At the same moment, four privates volunteered for grave-digging detail. Within three hours of his death, the tomb, post, and coffin were ready for the funeral on a spectacular vista overlooking the river.

With the manual labor and visitation complete, the soldiers changed into their dress uniforms for the formal service. Shields retuned the tomahawk to Clark. In the tent, Pryor, Ordway, Gass, and Corporal Richard Warfington each grabbed a corner of the blanket and lifted Floyd's corpse from the cot and slowly lowered it into the casket, without saying a word. Pryor reached down to cover his cousin with the blanket then placed the wooden lid on the coffin, with assistance from Gass who started nailing it closed. He pounded away at the solemn task, while he and onlookers struggled to hold back tears. Outside, soldiers stood at attention in two columns. The engagés, Drouillard, Mr. Dorion, and York observed the sad display.

Captain Clark placed an American flag over the coffin, and on my order we led the funeral procession up the bluff in silence. Behind us, Ordway, Pryor, Gass, and Warfington carried Floyd. They were followed by the military members of the Corps who marched in formation followed by the others. At the top of the hill, the casket was placed immediately to the north side of the grave, which was several feet in depth, with the footing towards the west. Next to the casket, the soldiers faced the coffin in two columns parallel to Floyd. They stood in reverse-arms formation. Their rifles were turned upside down with barrels resting on their left feet. On the butt of their rifles, the soldiers folded their hands on which the men rested their foreheads.

I read the eulogy, which closed with words written by Clark:

“This man at all times gave us proof of his firmness and determined resolution to do service to his country and honor to himself. We, therefore, proclaim this hill be known henceforth and forever as ‘Sergeant Floyd’s Bluff.’”

Equal to the number of states in the union, I ordered 17 men in the first column to fire a salute to Floyd, which went off with a thunderous sound nearly equivalent to that of our keelboat cannon.

Ordway and Warfington removed the flag from the casket. They properly folded it, and the Great Symbol was handed to Captain Clark who presented it to Sergeant Pryor for delivery to Floyd’s family sometime in the future.[B] Privates McNeal, Shields, Whitehouse and Bratton paired up and took the ends of two ropes, slipped them below the wooden box and gently lowered the casket into the ground. The post was hoisted upright by York and Captain Clark and placed at the head of the casket. A long shadow was cast in the late afternoon sun by the post on which the following words were carved: “Sergt. C. Floyd died here 20th of August 1804.” York steadied the marker, and the privates took turns shoveling soil into the grave until the last portion of upturned earth was shoveled on his final resting place. The service was complete.

We proceed downhill and upriver approximately one mile from the monument where we encamped on the same side at the mouth of a small waterway that we named “Floyd’s River” — about 30 yards wide. It was a beautiful evening.

CHAPTER EIGHT
ADVENTURE AND MISADVENTURE

August 22, 1804
Elk Sign Camp: 906 miles above the Missouri confluence

Near the campfire the night of Sergeant Floyd's passing, Captain Clark and I discussed at great length a proper mourning period and decided how to best proceed. We left his position vacant all the following day, and on the next had the men elect a successor at a location that showed signs that a great number of elk were in the vicinity — the most obvious being abundant hoof prints in the fine, light sand that comprised the gently sloping riverbanks along the mighty Missouri River.

Shortly before lunch, Clark asked three soldiers whether they would accept being nominated for the opportunity. The candidates all gladly agreed. Clark selected Gass, Bratton, and Private George Gibson who was born in Pennsylvania and reared in Kentucky. Gibson was a good hunter, sign language interpreter, and occasionally played the fiddle when Cruzatte was in need of a break. All were terrific candidates.

After briefly interviewing the men, Clark announced to the party that he was ordering an advisory election. As commanding officers, we could have simply appointed Floyd's replacement, but we believed nurturing democracy in the new territory was an important step towards advancing our nation and successfully completing our mission. By holding the election, we hoped to inspire confidence that we were committed to cultivating liberty, even in undeveloped regions. To ensure a level of anonymity, the enlisted men were asked to form a single line to our left about 25 paces from Captain Clark and me.[A] One by one, the soldiers were asked to step forward and voice their preference for the replacement sergeant. Clark inquired, I recorded the vote, and the soldier was instructed to form a new line an equal distance away on the right. In the end, Private Gass received 19 of 31 votes, while Bratton and Gibson split the difference — each with six. The men appeared pleased with this approach of blending military and democratic protocol, which marked the first election in the new territory.

Sergeant Gass was then in charge of seven privates in his squad. He was assigned to keep a written journal and rotate duties with the other two sergeants, which included dispensing supplies, guiding the keelboat, and posting camp guards. With Gass then vacating his former position, the other privates were expected to incorporate his old duties into their own workloads.

Later that afternoon, Gass was proudly steering the keelboat while I walked along shore. To the starboard, I noticed a magnificent bluff, which showed indications it contained significant quantities of what appeared to be an unknown metal ore. Seeking to advance the scientific discoveries for the expedition, I hiked partially up the slope and extracted small chunks of a mineral with a pick axe. Using a mortar and pestle, I crushed the constituents into a fine powder, and was nearly overcome by the fumes, but I still thought it prudent to sniff and taste the substance for positive identification. I barely made it back to the keelboat before I fell violently ill with stomach cramps, vomiting, and diarrhea. In great pain, I administered myself doses of purgative salts in the form of magnesia, cream of tartar and sal glauber to neutralize the poison. Captain Clark believed the ore was a combination of arsenic, alum, copper, cobalt, iron sulfate and sandstone, and my illness was attributable to arsenic poisoning.

After a very difficult and nearly sleepless night, the new day arrived shrouded in mist, but did bring me some relief.

While I was recovering, Private Joseph Field prepared for the day by loading his rifle and possible bag with ammunition and supplies for hunting on the prairie. After breakfast and performing chores, he broke camp, and walked about an hour inland under a warm August sun. He eventually came upon a bare spot on the plain where the underlying soil was exposed among a sea of short, green grass. In the dirt were numerous crescent-shaped imprints. They were immediately adjacent to each one, several inches in length, and mirror images of each other. Private Joseph recognized that they could only be from buffalo hooves. He followed the tracks for several hours. Shortly before eleven, he came upon newly dropped scat at the base of a large hill. Field determined the direction of a slight breeze and hiked downwind from the area he anticipated seeing a herd in the valley on the opposite side of the hill. The soldier cautiously approached the crest of the hill, dropped to the prone position, and crawled to the top. Poking his head above the grass, he could see thousands of buffalo leisurely grazing in the heat and humidity on an expansive plain.

At the bottom of the mound, Field observed two, young bulls jousting in practice for future bouts to determine prominence in the herd. Back and forth the beasts shoved each other with their disproportionally large heads. Field pushed himself up to fire from a kneeling position, aimed, and squeezed the trigger. The gun powder exploded with a loud crack, and the ammunition ball was launched down the rifle barrel and rapidly found its mark in the animal's head. The bizarre noise caused a panic in the herd. Suddenly, a stampede of movement opposite the sound was in motion. Thousands of hooves pounded the terrain that resonated like thunder. The injured buffalo stood motionless for a moment then fell heavily onto its side. Its nostrils flared as it exhaled one last time and then expired. Blood oozed from the entry point to soak the animal's dark fur, giving it a glossy sheen under the late summer sun.

The successful hunter paced down the hill to examine his trophy — the expedition's first buffalo kill. Field made his way back towards the river and notified the party of his triumph. Overjoyed with the news, I was well enough to follow Field and lead eleven other men to the site where it fell about a mile from the river. The men field dressed and butchered the beast, while a pack of prairie wolves intently patrolled the area for any opportunity to forage. We obliged them by leaving the innards and hide on the ground for the scavengers. With great effort, we hauled thirteen huge pieces of meat back to shore. We set aside a sufficient quantity for supper. The remainder we salted and made jerky for storage in two wooden barrels. Our evening was quite satisfying until a light rain arrived as an unwelcomed guest who remained through the better part of morning the next day.

After the rain finally departed, Captain Clark, and Sergeants Gass, and Ordway visited a very curious formation that emanated a tremendous amount of heat, consistent with volcanic activity. A tall, conic-shaped bluff about 180 feet in height arose from an eminent plain, which appeared to be comprised of blue clay. The mound also had immense quantities of coal, cobalt and sulfur. Water vapors and a strong, disagreeable odor radiated from its surface, which was too hot to touch for any length of time. Despite investigating this phenomenon, we were at a loss to explain the origin of the heat. After recording relevant notes about this odd feature, we continued on, and encamped near mouth of the White Stone River where the Yankton-Sioux Indians reportedly obtained minerals for painting various objects.

On the 25th of August, I, along with Seaman, Captain Clark, York, Drouillard, Ordway, Shields, Joseph Field, Labiche, Bratton, Warfington, Privates Robert Frazer, John Colter, and Engagé Cann traveled a short distance downstream in the white pirogue, and secured the boat to a tree along the shore. Under a cloudy sky, shortly after breakfast, we set out on foot to investigate the fearsome mound that the Indians said was inhabited by spirits who were protected by small devils. Bringing up the rear of our intrepid group were Cann, Frazer, and Colter.

Colter was 29 years of age, born in Virginia, raised in Kentucky, and a gifted hunter. Although a very valued member of the expedition, Colter defied Sergeant Ordway last winter during our stay at Dubois Camp when he and Collins got very drunk at a local groggery, after being ordered to not visit the establishment. Since then, he had developed into a courageous and obedient soldier. As to Frazer and Cann, I didn't know much about either, other than that they were both fine members of the Corps.

Without fear of being attacked, we began what I anticipated would be a trek of at least several miles inland towards the mysterious mound. After hiking more than two hours, the usual morning humidity hadn't dissipated. The clouds lifted and enabled a burning sun. Stifling heat and humidity added to the burden of our trek, and proved to be the greatest challenge. At four miles, we crossed a large creek, and continued into an extensive valley, which was flanked by gently sloping knolls covered with thick grass. This beautiful scene starkly contrasted with the oppressive heat, which drained every one of essential fluids and minerals. Six miles into the hike, Seaman was laboring immensely — incessantly panting to cool off, but his thick, black coat of fur prevented any such relief. He struggled to keep up with us. Captain Clark and I decided to send the dog back to camp with York. To be frank, I was not in much better condition than Seaman, due to my bout with the unknown poison.

By half-past eleven, the mound was clearly visible to the northwest rising some 70 feet from a vast stretch of flat land devoid of trees. By noon, we arrived at its base, after a nearly nine-mile walk. The perimeter of the hill was oval-shaped, and much more pronounced in height on the northeast end. This gave the mound a conical shape where a large number of birds hovered above its crest. In our thirsty state, we stopped to drink from a small creek less than a quarter mile from its summit. Captain Clark and I briefly discussed whether the origin of the mound was natural or constructed by man, and concluded it was natural. This assessment was based upon the many loose pebbles and other substances that comprised the hill, and its resemblance to the ground along the creeks. Our group of eleven topped the hill. Hovering birds at the summit did not fly off until we were within a few feet of them. They were capturing and feeding on a type of flying ant whose numbers were enormous on the leeward side of the mound. Since this was the only shelter from the wind for miles, Captain Clark speculated the insects may have been seeking refuge at this place, which attracted the birds.

Looking out from the peak, we saw hundreds of buffalo and elk in every direction grazing on an abundance of tall and short grasses on the plains below. We could view a great deal, but nowhere to be found were the feared devils. The worst that happened was flying ants bit our necks, if they were not quickly swatted. After an hour of recording observations, we descended the mound and detoured three miles southeast, following the small creek in order to allay our great thirst. Traveling towards the White Stone River, I guessed the temperature was close to 90 degrees when we stopped for about a half hour at a spectacular grove filled with two types of plums, and the largest and most delicious grapes we ever consumed.

On our trek back, we set the plains ablaze in two areas to signal the Yankton-Sioux Indians to attend a conference. Several miles upriver, Sergeant Pryor saw the smoke and ordered Private McNeal to also set a fire near their new camp, which was on the south shore of the river. By sunset, we retrieved the pirogue and determined to spend the night at the same location as the previous evening. We were separated from the main party by only five miles — where we hoped to overtake the keelboat the following morning. This is also where Private George Shannon killed his first elk.

Shannon was the youngest member of the Corps at age 19. He was not known for his hunting skills. In fact, Shannon was regarded as weak hunter, at best, which made his bagging the elk all that much more remarkable. He was from Pennsylvania, joined the expedition in Kentucky, and was part of Sergeant Pryor's squad. I considered him to be a promising young soldier, but his future status would be in serious question during the coming days.

By nine the next morning, we caught up with the main party, and were informed that during the night, two of our three remaining horses wandered off — most likely frightened by thunder and lightning during a brief storm, or perhaps they went in search of better pasture for grazing. Regardless of the reason,

Captain Clark ordered Pryor to dispatch someone to accompany Drouillard in returning the missing horses.

"Shannon!" Pryor shouted, as he quickly stepped toward the soldier.

Shannon was helping others preserve the elk meat he had successfully harvested the day before by transforming it into jerky, and placing it into casks. Meanwhile, the hide was being cut and braided into a tow rope.

"Sergeant Pryor," Shannon responded in acknowledgment, turning his head towards his commander.

"Since you seem to be on a lucky streak, I want to try your luck huntin' down them two horses. Get your things and go with Drouillard," the Sergeant insisted.

Shannon made haste to grab his gear, and within minutes, he broke camp with Drouillard. They soon started searching for the wayward animals. Walking together, they headed in a southerly direction away from the river until Drouillard spotted hoof prints.[B] Drouillard believed the prints belonged to the runaway horses. They continued to track the prints over several miles of rolling hills. The further out they advanced, the more difficult it was to spot signs of the horses. Eventually, the tracks disappeared on a ridgeline. Standing on top of the crest, the two stopped to discuss a strategy:

"Well, what do you think?" Shannon asked, as both men slipped their rifle from a shoulder and placed the butt of the weapon on the ground.

Drouillard paused a moment: "You go west for about an hour, and I'll head east. Then head back towards the river. Follow the bank, and we'll meet back where we started. How's that sound?"

"That sounds like we should be able to find them," Shannon confidently replied, eager to show his competency and zeal for being selected for this important duty to return such valuable commodity.

"Damn right! We'll rendezvous in about four or five hours. If you're not back by sunset, stay put and I'll come look for ya. If you get back, and I'm not there, report to the captains. You got that?"

"Understood," Shannon responded.

"Good. Let's eat," Drouillard suggested.

The men ate an adequate meal of dried elk meat with water, and went in opposite directions. Shortly before he was due to turn north, Shannon discovered more tracks that appeared to be those of the missing horses. In his youthful fervor to find the beasts and please his superiors, he kept following the tracks, which led him further west. Hours passed. Suddenly, he noticed the sunlight decreasing. Shannon looked above and didn't see any clouds. His gaze turned west.

"Goddamn it," Shannon thought, disgusted with himself, as he looked to the horizon and saw the sun was about to set behind a wall of clouds. Realizing he should have turned back much sooner, he made his way to the bottom of a large hill where he decided to stop for the night on the leeward side of the knoll. The Private hadn't eaten or drunk since he separated from Drouillard. He pulled the last of the jerky from his possible bag and consumed it for a late supper. Shannon slept under the shelter of a light coat he had brought, while Drouillard walked and shouted through the night in search of his lost comrade. At about two in the morning, Drouillard abandoned his search, headed towards the river, and followed the larboard shore until he reached the main party's camp just before sunrise — without Shannon or the horses.

At the same moment, the lost soldier awoke after a restless and worrisome night under the stars. He sipped the last water from his canteen and walked nearly four hours before intercepting the river where he dined on a small number of wild grapes, and re-filled his canteen. Slightly rejuvenated, the Private moved farther upstream in hopes of catching up with the main party, not knowing he was actually miles ahead of us. After Drouillard apprised us of his unsuccessful search, we sent Shields and Private Joseph to catch up with Shannon and return the horses; but the two would have a difficult task surpassing Shannon's pace to overtake him before dark.

Just before dinner, Clark and I ordered the prairie set afire three miles above a cobalt-colored bluff. The signal worked. At about two in the afternoon, a young, Yankton-Sioux Indian named "Little Bear" appeared on the north bank and swam to the white pirogue. We pulled ashore near a grove of cottonwood trees on the starboard side where two more Indian boys appeared, and said their people were camped upriver along a nearby tributary. Hearing this promising news, we sent an advance party consisting of Sergeant Pryor, an Engagé Peter Roi, and our interpreter, Mr. Dorion, to invite their great chiefs to attend a council at a bluff. Stopping at this spot for the night was welcomed, if for no other reason than to avoid the persistent afternoon wind that barraged us with small particles picked up from the riverbanks and sandbars.

While we set up camp for the evening, Shannon spotted horse tracks and followed them west for a mile where he finally found the missing horses. One of the horses was quite weak and appeared to be quickly failing. Regardless, it was a triumphant moment for the Private, despite his feeling ill for the want of food. At the same time, Field and Shields hadn't made much progress overtaking Shannon. However, his path was easy to follow. The pair continued on until they reached the spot where Shannon found the horses, but it was then nightfall. They decided to rest before heading back downstream in the morning. The lost soldier was still several miles and hours ahead of them.

In the morning, Shannon started his day by taking two shots at several rabbits, but badly missed each one. Having taken 20 rounds of ammunition when he left, the soldier decided to ration his supply of balls to three per day, which he was sure would be sufficient until he rejoined us. But our hopes of catching him this day were unexpectedly delayed when we were forced to travail through an underwater forest of fallen trees. One log in particular awaited our arrival.

It lay almost entirely submerged beneath the rippling waves, whipped up from a strong wind from the south. The strong wind allowed us to hoist the sails, and provided welcomed relief from the taxing chore of rowing, pulling, and poling. We had already made five miles by noon when the keelboat and white pirogue both passed the massive log without incident. The rotted tree had a long branch that extended six feet from the trunk and came to a sharp point just below the water's surface. A gust suddenly pushed the red pirogue sharply to its larboard side where the broken limb easily punctured the hull of the boat. Water poured into the vessel, soaking cloth bags that were filled with many goods. In a panic, the men attempted to plug the hole with a bag, which could only slow the water's overwhelming progress. Four men each grabbed an oar to push free of the snag. Others then lowered the sail, and steered the boat to the riverbank before the boat had a chance to sink, but the damage was done. Some of the cargo was ruined.

The crew relayed message of the mishap to men in the other boats. After learning of this latest misfortune, Clark and I immediately decided to stop on the south side to wait for the Indians and to repair the hole. We also needed time to recover from another mysterious ailment that Captain Clark and I had somehow acquired. A short while later, Shields and Field returned to inform us that Shannon had found the horses, but they could not overtake him.

Shannon moved even farther ahead, while we camped near the bluff for the next four days.

Well aware of the Private's developing hunting and navigation skills, Captain Clark and I again ordered someone to find Shannon. Sergeant Ordway chose Private Colter for the job. Colter took provisions for both of them. He hiked at a brisk pace for several hours until a fierce squall raged in from the northwest at about eight that evening. Both Shannon and his rescuer would have to endure the storm under makeshift shelters, while we prepared for a third meeting with the accomodating Indians.

CHAPTER NINE
WARNINGS

August 29, 1804
Calumet Bluff Camp: 984 miles above the Missouri confluence

Rain poured through the night and did not cease until early morning. Private Colter uneasily slept in damp clothing under an oiled cloth, and tiredly awoke before first light to continue his search for the wayward teen.

Approximately 40 miles to the west of our new camp and 30 from Colter, Shannon weakly went further upriver following tracks he mistakenly believed were imprinted by our party. He failed time and again to procure food to satiate his ever-growing hunger. Before eight that morning, he had already used his daily allotment of ammunition for hunting with nothing to show for the effort. Instead, he meagerly dined on grapes. Shannon moved at a slightly slower pace than his rescuer. And though his trail was relatively easy to follow, Colter was too far behind to ever make significant progress catching him, in no small part because he kept killing almost every animal that crossed his path for food for himself, Shannon, and the remainder of the party. What he didn't immediately consume, he placed on crude, wooden drying racks he constructed that kept the food several feet off the ground, just out of predatory reach.

Back at camp, and at my request, Captain Clark spent most of the day re-writing the 11-page speech I had given to the Indians earlier that month.[A] I conveyed to him the need for a different perspective, and was confident he would improve the message.

Late that afternoon our advance party of Sergeant Pryor, Mr. Dorion, and Roi appeared on shore opposite our camp. They were accompanied by five chiefs and 70 other members of the tribe. Astonished at the size of the response and obviously successful outcome, I sent Sergeant Gass and Private Warfington across the river in the white pirogue to ferry our men back to us. I watched intently as they moved closer — details of their hazy images slowly emerged until I could clearly see the perspiration soaking portions of their clothes.

"Well Sergeant, I take this was an agreeable venture," I remarked.

"Yes, Captain. They wanted to carry us into camp on buffalo robes," Pryor excitedly reported. "They thought we owned the boats."

Interrupting, Mr. Dorion emphasized that he informed the tribe that they did not own the boats, and were not worthy of being carried. He also informed the chiefs how to identify the rank of expedition members by their manner of dress.

Sergeant Pryor nodded agreement and continued, "They lodge in very handsome shelters. They're conical and made of buffalo hides and wood. Outside they paint the hides different colors. Each one houses about 10 to 15 people."

Only much later did I understand that what Pryor was actually describing was known as a "tipi," or leather lodge. As was their custom, such lodges were situated facing east toward the rising sun, which they believed was the source of all life.[15] In addition, each support post represented the role members of the family performed for the community.

Captain Clark and I listened with curiosity.

"What about cooking?" Clark inquired.

"Each lodge has a place for cooking. The lodges are arranged around a central fire. For food, they gave us a fat dog … and it was damn good!" Pryor exclaimed.

Hearing this, Clark turned toward me and teasingly grinned.

Cutting off his words before they were spoken, I shook my head several times and said: "No, Captain. That's not going to happen. That will not happen."

Of course, he was jesting that I should keep a careful watch on Seaman — lest my faithful companion meet the same fate as the Indians' dog.

We sent the group back with gifts of tobacco, corn, and cooking kettles. They were instructed to inform the natives that we would prefer to meet the next day. The group departed, delivered the items, and returned to say the council was set. During the night, another very thick fog descended on camp and finally lifted not long before our meeting was to commence.

Shortly after ten in the morning, Mr. Dorion, 70 warriors, and five chiefs arrived at our camp. The chiefs were clad in ornamented buffalo robes and elaborately decorated in face paint, porcupine quills, and feathers. They greeted Clark and me with a solemn handshake, while four Indian musicians danced, sang, beat drums, and shook rattles. It was quite a sight. We responded in kind by firing two rounds from the keelboat cannon. The chiefs' accompanying warriors were dressed with leggings, moccasins, and brought their bows and arrows.

After nearly two hours of greetings and exchanging stories, I led everyone towards a large oak tree under which we assembled for the meeting. Nearby, our flag was again affixed to the wooden staff. Similar to our first meeting weeks before, we provided 18 wooden boxes for seating, which were arranged in a circular fashion for me, Clark, chiefs, interpreters, and ranking members of the tribe and expedition.

I delivered Captain Clark's version of my speech in the usual manner. In addition, Clark's version stated the Yankton-Sioux should make peace with the neighboring tribes: the Otoe, Omaha, and Missouria.

During the speech, I noticed one chief had his face painted differently than the others. I assumed he must be the head chief, since he was adorned all in white, while the others were each painted with three colors — red, gold and blue. After concluding my speech, I asked the head chief — whose name was Shaking Hand — if he would plan on bringing four or five members of their nation to Washington the following spring. My hope was that like Chief Little Thief, they too would agree to meet President Jefferson to discuss future commerce. I explained we did not need an answer that day, but soon would, well before our departure on the next day.

Chief Shaking Hand acknowledged receiving the message, after Mr. Dorion translated my words. He was then presented with a red-laced coat, large peace medallion, military hat, red feather, white shirt, certificate, and American flag. The lesser chiefs were given smaller peace medals, which appeared to be gladly received by all.

Afterward, I astonished our guests with another demonstration of my air gun. This time I rapidly shot 20 balls into the trunk of a cottonwood tree. They shouted aloud each time the trigger was pulled, and once more after ceasing fire. Many ran to examine the resulting damage in obvious fascination.

With our interests of the day concluded at about four in the afternoon, we agreed to attend a celebration that evening at the Indians' camp. They were situated just north of our location, and across the river. Shortly before dark and immediately after supper, most of the expedition ferried themselves to the Indians' camp. The remainder of the men who did not attend guarded the boats and our possessions.

We were greeted warmly by young warriors who also insisted on demonstrating their marksmanship, but with bows and arrows. In return, we gave them colored beads in appreciation of their efforts. There was no doubt this demonstration was a direct response to my air gun exhibition.

After sunset, three fires were lit. I gave Shaking Hand a deer skin to stretch over a half-keg, as a drum. Their women wore petticoats and white buffalo robes, while the men were dressed in festive regalia. At each fire, two warriors beat on a drum — while eight to ten others shook small bags filled with beads or pebbles. The balance of the men and women happily danced around the fires to the rhythm of the musicians and singers. Their voices were in unison for every song, and they began and ended each one with a loud whoop and holler.

During breaks, a warrior would rise with his weapon and boast of his actions in war, how many warriors he killed, and what war prizes were in his possession. Similar to the other tribes, it was apparent the men of the first nations acquired their status through feats of bravado, which I concluded involved violence and theft. In stately fashion, the chiefs watched, listened, and appeared very much pleased with what they had heard and observed.

It was very late when the festivities ended, and still neither Colter nor Shannon had returned. They were still somewhere on the plains; Colter searching for Shannon, Shannon searching for us, and the expedition far behind them, exploring lands inhabited by our newly adopted children. The night was peaceful and thankfully uneventful.

We were to meet once more with the natives the following day to hear their answer to our pleas. Not long after eight in the morning, and after all had eaten breakfast, the chiefs and warriors assembled in a row for another brief council.

Some warriors attended the event with very large bear claws strung on necklaces, which were proudly worn, as additional evidence of their courage and exemplary hunting skills. Much to our amazement, a few of the claws were approximately three inches in length, which we recognized could have never been obtained from the black bears we knew in the east. After inquiring about where they obtained such large ornaments, they reported such animals were common upriver; most ferocious and much feared. They respectfully called these fearsome beasts, "White bears," after the brilliant color of their sharp teeth, which were often exposed during confrontations.

Captain Clark and I wondered how immense this grizzly creature must be, but had great difficulty believing the Indians' claims about its viciousness, given the doubts of credibility we developed after investigating Spirit Mound. Even if this creature's temperament was as reported, we were confident our weaponry could easily neutralize this terrible and dreaded predator.

At the conclusion of the meeting, we sat down in front of an elegantly carved and painted peace pipe. According to Indian legend communicated to them by the Great Spirit, the red stone comprising the pipe bowls were made from the flesh of their ancestors, and the stone was never to be used for any other purpose.[14] The Great Spirit also said the stone belonged to all tribes, and the ground where these rocks could be found was sacred.

Through our interpreter Mr. Dorion, the chiefs replied to our requests while others listened. Confidently sitting, Chief Shaking Hand addressed us first, and spoke at some length, as we listened with great attention:

"I am glad to hear the word of my Great Father. All my warriors and men about me are also glad. I see my two fathers here and heard what you said. I believe — and all my people believe — you would take pity on us this day because we are poor. We have no powder, ball, knives, or whiskey milk.

"My Great Father and his two sons: You see me and the rest of the chiefs and warriors. We are very poor. The women and children at the village have little clothes, and wish that my Great Father's sons would be charitable enough to give us some things or give permission to stop a boat to trade with us.

"We will do as you advise and make peace with the Pawnee, Omaha, and other tribes. We will also bring chiefs from each nation to travel towards the rising sun next spring to visit the Great Father. But before that, I wish you would consider giving me something for our women and brothers."

After hearing this appeal once more, Captain Clark and I explained to Shaking Hand that we were not traders. We were here to open the road for traders who would soon be following us. They would supply their needs and wants on better terms than they ever had from the French, British, or Spanish. We also requested they not stop boats, and allow them free travel up and down river.

Shaking Hand appeared to appreciate our position and concluded: "We are very sorry our women are naked and our children have no clothes. I understand you do not want me to stop the boats. But I wish Mr. Dorion would stay to help with traders, and bring peace between all Indians … I have your word and promises, and am glad of it."

Chief White Crane gave a short statement in support of Shaking Hand:

"Listen to my words. I am a young man and inexperienced, and cannot say much. What the Great Chief said is as much as I could say. I wish you to take pity on us for we are poor. Offer us ball, powder, and some whiskey milk."

Chief Struck by the Pana followed; He reached to grab the pipe at his feet and held it above his head:

"The pipe I hold in my hand is the pipe of my father who would want me to listen to your wise counsel. I am poor, as you see. Take pity on me. I believe what you have said. The great medal you gave my Great Chief pleases me, as does the small one you gave me. This gives me the heart to go with him in the spring to see my new Great Father. What the Great Chief said is all I could say."

A warrior named Tar-ro-mo-nee gestured toward Shaking Hand and spoke:

"When I was a young man, I heard the Spanish, and did not like their sayings so well as yours. I am very glad you have made this man our Great Chief. The British and Spaniards also acknowledged him, but never clothed him. You have clothed him. And soon he will go see our Great Father. We do not wish to spare him, but he must go and see the new Great Father.

"Along with the clothes and flag, give him some of your milk, powder, and ball. These things we need. We have horses, bows, and arrows. But we want a little powder and ball to kill buffalo. This is because our horses are poor this season, and cannot run after them as before.

"I will not go to war, and take your advice. I will bury my tomahawk and knife in the ground, and go with my old chief to see my Great Father."

The last to speak was Chief Arcawechar. He echoed the others, but spoke in a prophetic tone:

"I do not speak very well. I am a poor man, and am glad you have made my old chief a fine and a great man. I have been a great warrior, but now I hear your words of peace. I too will bury my hatchet, and be at peace with all, and go with my Great Chief to see my Great Father. I am glad my Great Father sent you to visit the red people on this river, and that you gave us a flag — the shade of which we can sit under.

"We want one thing for our nation very much. We have no trader and often want goods. We would like Mr. Dorion to help with this. My fathers — I am glad — as well as all around me — to hear your word. We open our ears, and I think our old friend, Mr. Dorion, can open the ears of the other bands of Sioux. But I fear those nations upriver will not open their ears, and you cannot, I fear, open them."

Upon receiving this message, Captain Clark and I glanced at each other and knew we could not react to this claim. As disturbing and reliable as it sounded, we again had credibility doubts, and believed cultivating favorites among our red children should not be permitted. Instead, we joined the chiefs in smoking from the peace pipes. To fulfill at least part of their requests, we followed this ceremony with the distribution of additional gifts, which consisted of knives, tobacco, and corn. This appeared satisfactory to them, despite our having obviously rejected their requests for gun powder and ammunition.

Afterward, most of the warriors went across the river to their encampment on the opposite shore, but the chiefs remained with us. Chief Arcawechar informed me a baby was born earlier that day, and I expressed my desire to see the child in the morning — a suggestion to which he was most receptive.

At dusk, we sent a bottle of whiskey with Mr. Dorion and the chiefs for them to take back to camp. Dorion agreed to stay with the Yankton-Sioux until someone from our party returned the following year. During the interim, he was to persuade as many chiefs as possible to meet President Jefferson, and to also broker peace between the Sioux and their neighbors.

Before departing the next day, I visited the parents of the baby boy who they named Struck by the Ree.[B] I took with me a flag, and Captain Clark's written speech. We entered the tipi where the baby was clad in a small buffalo robe. I reached down to take him in my arms, and quietly cooed, as he appeared to smile and laugh at my babbling sounds and facial contortions. Pulling the flag from my coat pocket while holding him in my other arm, I wrapped the infant in the flag, and declared him an American.

I gave Shaking Hand one last gift, which was the paper on which Clark inscribed our speech. He graciously accepted the document.

I only knew at a much later date that it was later given to an Otoe Chief named Big Ax, and believed it was a gesture of peace between the Yankton-Sioux and Otoe, which Mr. Dorion helped successfully cultivate.

But peace would prove a premium commodity, if Chief Arcawechar's assertion about the next band of Sioux upriver was correct, and we were anxious to discover the truth.

CHAPTER TEN
CONFLICT

September 3, 1804
Ancient Fortification Camp: 1,002 miles above the Missouri confluence

A clear sky provided for a spectacular sunrise when we set out from camp, accompanied by crisp, cool air, which was yet another strong signal that summer was transforming into the tremendous challenges of fall and winter on the shelterless and expansive Great Plains. Adding to this concern was the fact that we were nowhere near the headwaters of the Missouri. By this time, Captain Clark and I hoped we would at least observe indications we were in proximity to its source, but this was certainly not the circumstance. The waters still flowed murky; the river was still broad, and its depth was still conducive to maneuvering our heavy keelboat, despite the increasing number of sandbars. Regrettably, we were still on the map of areas previously explored.

However, on this day we encountered one significant unknown: Captain Clark reported seeing wild goats on the prairie — nimble and graceful. Short horns; stout necks; thin, powerful legs capable of carrying them at great speed, even at a very young age; and bold, red fur set against a white backdrop were the noteworthy characteristics of these extraordinary creatures. They were extremely shy beasts that fled even the most subtle threats as an entire herd. To be afforded the opportunity to witness this flight was to be honored with a truly great demonstration of nature in one of its most regal forms.

As we proceeded beyond the herd, there were many signs indicating that Colter and Shannon were ahead. But it was readily apparent that Colter had not overtaken Shannon.

The youngest member of the Corps aimed, fired and again wildly missed his target. Frightened of the rifle sound, the object of his aspiration quickly scampered up and over a hill — out of Shannon's sight. The Private had just expended the last of his ammunition, and one of the two horses he recovered was then too ill for travel. The animal lay in an open field too lethargic to move, and oblivious to its surroundings where it soon died. Shannon climbed on the surviving stallion and continued upriver. A few hours later, Shannon dined on more grapes near the riverbank.

His would-be rescuer endured no such adversity. In Colter's wake, we found stand after stand of animal meat that he left on wooden racks near the river — most of which was unmolested by competing creatures, such as prairie wolves.

Two days later Shannon was refilling his canteen at the river while his horse also drank nearby when a lone, bull buffalo wandered into the area for the same purpose. Shannon and the bull exchanged stares at a distance no greater than 10 steps. Shannon marveled at the bull's huge eye, which was embedded with many red streaks, giving the outer portion more of a vermillion tint than white. The Private could do no more than stare at the great beast in complete frustration.

“Goddamn it!” the Private whispered to himself, glancing at his rifle on the riverbank, and then back at the buffalo.

The bull leisurely lowered his enormous head to the water, casually drank his fill, turned, and lumbered back toward the herd on the plains.

“Go ahead! Leave, you son of a bitch!” Shannon yelled in exasperation, as he watched the buffalo’s rear end slowly disappear over the horizon. “I’ll find somethin’ else to eat,” he concluded in a hushed manner, after realizing his expression was largely dependent on ammunition, which had been depleted.

His initial optimism had also then disappeared into the wilderness with the bull.

At the same time, and a great distance south of Shannon’s position, Colter determined to abandon his rescue attempt of the starving soldier. He turned back and rejoined the main party the next day, after a lengthy hike through the night and early morning, in a fruitless, but honorable effort to find our man.

On the 7th of the month, Shannon suddenly awakened with inspiration. He hurriedly found a dead tree branch and snapped off a stick, which was slightly smaller in circumference than the barrel of his weapon. After sharpening one end, he jammed the stick into the rifle, and loaded the weapon with powder. He quickly located a jackrabbit feeding a short distance from the river. The soldier aimed at the little target and fired. The stick was launched, and pierced the torso of the rabbit — instantly killing it. The Private was to eat his first meat since he was lost 10 days prior.

Meanwhile, 30 miles to the southeast, Private Shields also had a successful quest for food. He brought the small animal back to the boat for Captain Clark and me to dine on in the evening. Shields informed us there were many such animals in a valley about a mile inland at the bottom of a large knoll. Private Labiche examined the creature. He said the French called these animals “petit chien,” or “small dog,” which we called “barking squirrels.”

Captain Clark and I followed Shields’ instructions about where to find the barking squirrels, and ascended a rise of 70 feet. At the bottom of this rise was the barking squirrel village. The community spanned about four acres, and contained numerous holes, which were each surrounded by a gradually sloping mound created from earth the animals laboriously excavated from their tunnels. The barking squirrels much resembled squirrels back home, but smaller with a much shorter and narrower tail. When assessing danger, these small mammals sat erect atop the mound near their tunnels. If alarmed, they chattered and produced a high-pitched, whistling noise to signal others of threats. We decided to try capturing one of these creatures alive to send President Jefferson for more formal scientific examination.

While I observed the animals, Captain Clark went back to the boats, and summoned four men for duty. They each grabbed a shovel, and Private McNeal also took the wooden flag staff. For more than an hour, we unsuccessfully tried to extricate one of these creatures from its burrows. First, we dug six feet below grade, and found we had yet to reach their lodge. After abandoning further excavation on our part, McNeal repeatedly drove the staff in and out of several tunnels, but the barking squirrels still eluded capture.

Leaving two men to guard the boats, we ordered the rest of the party to the site with 30 barrels of water to pour into their burrows. After emptying five barrels into a single hole, one of the animals exited, and ran straight into Sergeant Ordway's coat, which he had strategically held in place to catch the specimen should it emerge. A makeshift cage was quickly constructed, and the squirrel was perfectly unharmed in his new confine.

Two days had passed since we caught and caged the barking squirrel, and Shannon was then too weak to walk. Although his improvised ammunition proved useful, his aim had not been enhanced, especially in his famished condition. Although exhausted and ravenous, he summoned enough strength to mount the horse. His plan for the day was to ride further back from the river on the high hills that lined the river in an attempt to view any passing boats. No boat was seen that day, and he spent the night among a grove of trees near a cluster of grapes where his horse grazed on an abundance of leafy plants.

Unknown to us at the time, we were then only 20 miles from Shannon when we passed two small islands. Just below the second island, at the top of a high point in a bluff, Private John Newman was hunting and noticed the fossilized skeleton of a monstrous fish.

Newman was from Pennsylvania and often spoke with Moses Reed — the man who was discharged from the expedition several weeks prior for desertion. Newman was a few months older than Shannon, and displayed an ever-growing, ill temperament and disposition, not unlike Reed.

Regardless, Newman was proud to inform us of his valuable find, which measured 45 feet from head to tail. In addition to a complete head and backbone, the fish fossil also had ribs and teeth. Similar to the barking squirrel, we decided this specimen too must be sent to Washington. For several hours, many hands heavily labored to exhume the precious remains, which were then carefully packed into several wooden crates.

The following morning was cloudy, and we set off in the dim light just before sunrise. At the same time, Shannon re-mounted his horse to repeat his effort from the previous day by riding on the high hills.

At the head of the first island we passed that day, Captain Clark, Sergeants Ordway and Pryor, along with Private Gibson, hunted on the starboard side of the river, hoping to easily kill game.

After taking a few animals, Ordway decided to climb a steep hill on the west side, as his red flannel shirt whipped in the wind. From the crest of the ridge, he could clearly see 16 buffalo facing him in the valley below casually grazing on lush prairie grass. They had not yet detected his presence. The Sergeant slowly descended the hill. The buffalo continued feeding. Ordway arrived at the bottom, and surveyed the group for his best shot. He paced sideways moving parallel to the group, hoping to flank them for a better angle. At that moment, a bull sensed the disturbance, raised his head, and turned his head slightly. Ordway continued his angular pursuit, and the bull stepped toward the movement. Ordway panicked, fired at the bull's head from an awkward position, and the ball ricocheted off the bull's thick skull. The bull immediately turned to flee, and the others instinctively followed his lead. They retreated a short distance away, and soon resumed feeding.

Ordway, Clark, Pryor, and Gibson continued hunting on the same side of the river, while we enjoyed a favorable wind to push us upstream. At the same time Ordway had his encounter with the buffalo, Captain Clark was close to the river opposite an island on the larboard side obtaining barking squirrels as specimens.

A short distance from Clark, a shifting figure captured the gaze of Sergeant Gass from the keelboat. His initial glance changed into an intent stare, as he tried to identify the shape, which appeared to be descending a high hill toward the river. Gass thought he recognized features.

"Captain Lewis!" Gass shouted from the deck.

"Yes, Sergeant!" I responded from the keelboat cabin.

"We should investigate this," he said.

I exited the cabin, and climbed on deck to join Gass. He pointed at the figure.

"Yes ... send the white pirogue over," I remarked.

Gass relayed the message to the men in the boat, which included Private McNeal. Together, the soldiers rowed toward the figure. Details gradually became visible, as the distance between the pirogue and the figure diminished. McNeal studied the silhouette. Suddenly, he identified the figure, which was much more than a silhouette. It was a man on horseback.

"Shannon! Shannon! It's Private Shannon!" McNeal hollered, as he pointed toward the riverbank.

Shouts of joy erupted from the men in the pirogue who promptly helped him into the boat to recover. McNeal took charge of the horse, and went downriver to inform Captain Clark of the good news. Shannon was ailing and gaunt. Back on the keelboat, everyone welcomed the teen who said he was soon to slaughter his horse had it not been for our timely rescue. After providing Shannon a light meal, the crew listened intently as he spun his tale of woe, and how it was that the poor soul became lost.

Had Shannon not been so weak, I'm sure he would have wept with joy at our sighting. In total, the young soldier was missing 16 days, and had nearly starved in a land of plenty — an irony not lost on most of the party.

During the next five days, Shannon quickly recovered, and we continued to observe vast herds of deer, elk, buffalo, and wild goats in every direction in numbers so large it is difficult to convey — all grazing on the lush, verdant plains, which seemed to have no boundary.

On the 14th, Captain Clark killed the curious-looking goat that had eluded us for many days. He had slain a male, which was the first antelope we were able to observe at close range. The beast was approximately three feet in height at the shoulder and resembled a deer in many aspects, but with hooves and horns like a goat with patches of fur that were reddish, white, and brown. Like many other plant and animal specimens, this animal too was skinned, preserved, and packed for shipment to President Jefferson.

Between the 10th and 15th of September, rain fell often, which soaked our baggage. On the 16th, we unloaded them to dry for two days. We also transferred heavy baggage from the keelboat to the red pirogue, due to the increasing numbers of sandbars in the river. Transferring the cargo would allow the keelboat to ride higher in the water, thus decreasing the numbers of scrapes the vessel would experience with the troublesome obstacles. Since we were nowhere near the Missouri headwaters, we then determined to keep all the boats until spring to ensure the keelboat and its supplies advanced as far west as possible before sending it back to St. Louis. This decision meant we were abandoning our original plan, which was to send specimens and journals back that year in the pirogues. In addition to drying provisions, this layover allowed the men time to wash and mend their smelly, tattered clothes. Many were already fashioning new clothes and deerskin moccasins.

Before sunrise the next morning, I determined to set out with six of our best hunters, and amuse myself viewing the interior of this rolling country. We hiked over the river bluff and well inland where my objective was to kill a female goat, since Captain Clark had already procured a male.

After several hours, we regaled ourselves on biscuits and jerky, which we had placed in our possible bags. We also stopped to drink from a small pool of water that had collected on the plain. Afterward, we pursued several herds of goats for hours, which led us about eight miles from camp. We found the goats extremely timid with acute senses of sight and smell, which meant we were unable to fire a shot worthy of our labors. However, the trip was still of great value, for we had the opportunity to witness the great agility and superior fleetness of this magnificent animal, which was truly astonishing.

Moreover, this scenery, already rich, pleasing and beautiful, was still further heightened by immense herds of buffalo, deer, elk, and antelope we saw everywhere feeding on the hills and plains. I do not think I exaggerated when I estimated that 3,000 buffalo could be simultaneously viewed in a single glance.

Detaching myself from this grand spectacle was difficult, but we returned to camp, unsuccessful in our attempt to kill a female antelope.

The following morning, we packed our belongings and proceeded on. Three days later we stayed the night on a sandbar that buttressed the shoreline, which rose some 15 feet above the surface of the river. Shortly after one in the morning, Sergeant Pryor alerted us in a panic that the land had fast eroded above and below our site. We watched by moonlight in horrified fascination as tons of sand and silt washed and tumbled into the river all around us. Captain Clark immediately ordered all to abandon camp and move the boats. Had we delayed much longer, the smaller vessels would have certainly sunk, and may have been lost, under the collapse of the adjacent bank.

Barely avoiding a burdensome setback, the following day we observed signs Indians were in the area. Captain Clark and I hoped these were the Teton-Sioux. More than any other nation, President Jefferson emphasized that we were to establish a positive relationship with them because of their great influence in the middle section of the Missouri River.

Also known as the Lakota or Brulé, the Teton-Sioux migrated from the upper plains west of Lake Superior onto lands formerly occupied by the Omaha and Arikara Indians in the early 1700s. French and Spanish boatmen often had negative encounters with them, during which they charged outrageous tolls for use of the river. We were warned by Chief Arcawechar and prospectors back east that the Teton were fierce, treacherous, cruel and particularly hostile to white men. The neighboring tribes were also wary of the Teton because they were very aggressive, mastered the use of rifles, and often prevailed in violent conflicts, with the exception of when they fought the Rocky Mountain, or Crow nation. The Crow were formidable opponents not easily defeated.

According to Mr. Loisel, Teton legend indicated that if an Indian could grab and hold a mooring rope, the vessel and its cargo could be claimed as a war prize.[A, 8]

While we continued our journey, our hunters searched the high ground for game, and returned to complain that acidic minerals, weathered shale, and numerous prickly pears destroyed their moccasins. I investigated these claims and found some of the land too acidic to support the same lush growth as its surroundings. The prickly pears were also as reported, with needle-like spikes that could easily puncture skin or pierce tough animal hide. During this same period, Captain Clark estimated a great bend in the river was almost a complete circle, 30 miles in length, but only about a mile across from our camp the night before last; a Grand Detour that consumed precious time.

Shortly upriver from the Grand Detour, we, at last, came upon Loisel's trading post at Cedar Island. As one might expect, the post was constructed of cedar planks, and was approximately 1,500 square-feet in area, designed for commerce with the Indians. Surrounding the fort were tipis, horse stables, and a high, wooden picket fence nearly 14 feet in height. At each of two opposite corners of the post fence, were sentry boxes situated above the walls for added security — protection they certainly needed from their unfriendly neighbors.

After paying a brief visit to the fort, we moved further upstream, and on the 23rd of September, observed great plumes of smoke to the southwest. Soon after landing to camp, three Indian boys swam across to advise us that 80 Teton lodges were close to the next river mouth, and sixty more were above that village.

Upon seeing our boats, the boys set the prairie afire to signal others of our imminent approach.

We gave the boys two tobacco twists to give their elders. However, we had difficulty asking them to convey the message to their chiefs that we wished to speak with them soon. This was made difficult because Mr. Dorion was no longer with us — having left him with the Yankton-Sioux. Instead, Private Labiche spoke to them in the Omaha language, which was a complete failure. I dearly hoped this would be our last such failure.

The following morning, Colter and his horse waded through a shallow portion of the river to a large island in pursuit of elk. He dismounted the mare, secured the reins to a tree branch, and set off on foot — leaving behind one of his two supply pouches. Approximately three hours later, he successfully killed two elk and a deer, and was dragging the last one to the riverbank for pick-up when he heard his horse whinny loudly. He looked upriver about 75 yards to see two Indians stealing his horse. Both warriors climbed onto the mare, re-crossed the river, and quickly headed north toward their village.

Colter futilely ran after the pair, screaming obscenities as sand kicked up from the soles of his moccasins. He slowly eased his useless chase, and stopped near his supply pouch to watch the group scurry into the distance. Colter crouched to inspect the contents of his bag, which was missing a container of salt.

"Goddamn Indians!" Colter cursed to himself. "Thieving sons a bitchs!"

Alarmed and angry, he rushed two miles down the riverbank to intercept us coming upstream. He shouted for the pirogues to come ashore for the game at the opposite end of the island, and informed us of the stolen horse. Later in the afternoon we observed five Indians on shore, and stopped about 100 yards from them. Labiche, Captain Clark, twelve others and I took the pirogues to visit the group who were taking a break from hunting. Armed and ready for any possible altercation, we approached with caution, but greeted each with handshakes and gestures of friendliness.

"Ask them who their grand chief is," I instructed Labiche.

The Private did his best, but most of what was said was lost in the incompatible translation. However, we did learn the principal was a leader named Black Buffalo. Through Labiche, I told the group we were sent by their new Great Father, and that two of their warriors stole our horse. I said if they returned the animal, we would speak with their leaders the next day. If they refused, we would not meet with them. After a brief time, it was apparent none of the information was understood because of the language barrier.

Despite that failure, the Indians indicated they wanted to travel on the keelboat, to which we were receptive. All climbed aboard, and we sailed four miles to the mouth of large tributary we named the "Teton River," which is where we anchored offshore — situated less than two miles south of the larger Brulé village.

From the keelboat, we observed that several Indians had gathered on the bank. I decided to take a small party to meet them, plan a council, and air our grievance, once more. Having no success using Labiche as a translator, Captain Clark and I decided to employ Private Cruzatte's crude knowledge of the language. Clark and I took a small group and landed near them. We soon learned that one of the Indians was a chief named Buffalo Medicine who claimed he was not aware of any stolen horse, but would be willing to make reparations, if the deed was perpetrated by his people. We exchanged handshakes, gave them tobacco, and smoked from the peace pipe. Despite having not procured the horse, we agreed to meet the village principals the next day on a sandbar in the mouth of the river, and allowed the group to lodge for the night on the keelboat.

In the morning, we halted 70 yards from a sandbar, and ferried the five Indians to the riverbank. They quickly went back to their village, and we prepared for the council in the usual manner. The soldiers set up the mainsail as an awning, and hoisted the flagpole. Cognizant of Chief Arcawechar's dire warning and unlike the previous Indian meetings, we commanded most of the party to stay on the keelboat during the council.

At eleven that morning, Lakota flocked to both sides of the river, and appeared in numbers reminiscent of the great buffalo herds. The three chiefs and 30 warriors on horseback rode through the shallows, onto the sandbar and dismounted. Accompanied by Captain Clark and Cruzatte, I quickly rushed out to meet 33 grim faces. Even during the greetings, it was evident the interpretations were troublesome. Cruzatte said the third chief was named Partisan, or Tortohongar who was flanked by chiefs Buffalo Medicine and Black Buffalo.

They offered us about 300 pounds of buffalo meat, some of which was spoiled. In return, we gave them cut pork, which was stacked in alternating layers of salt and meat contained in a wooden cask. We then gathered under the awning, sat on wooden boxes, and smoked from their pipe, before I delivered my speech.

All seemed to be going well with the much-feared nation. However, that quickly changed after I noticed Cruzatte was having great difficulty communicating my words. Drouillard was unfortunately experiencing the same using sign language. In frustration, I opted to truncate the speech, and move on to the ceremonial parade and drill, which did not appear to impress them.

Thinking a more forceful exhibition was in order for this audience, I demonstrated my air gun, showed them the magnifying glass, and allowed the chiefs to peer through my telescope — none of which had a great impact. They appeared to want goods, and goods were what we gave them. Among the gifts were tobacco, knives, rings, brass wire, bells, earrings, cloth, ribbons, thread, shirts, fire strikers, scissors and fish hooks. To the first chief, Black Buffalo, I gave a large medal, red military coat, and cocked hat. To one warrior of merit, I awarded him a certificate that indicated he was a friend and ally of the United States. His name was Makoshika, which meant "bad earth" in Sioux language.[B, 12]

Black Buffalo, the other chiefs, and Makoshika glanced at each other with puzzled looks, and did not express any overt gratitude for the gifts. Recognizing the dissatisfaction, Clark invited the chiefs and Makoshika to visit the keelboat. We rowed out, and they stayed three hours observing items, such as our camping supplies, forge, scientific instruments, navigational equipment, and weaponry, which included three, mounted artillery pieces — the swivel cannon, and two pivoting guns. The guns were mounted on opposite sides of the upper deck, and the cannon was secured to the bow.

From a nearly empty bottle, Captain Clark poured each in the group several ounces of whiskey into four drinking glasses. Clark inverted the bottle, and the last drops splashed into a glass. He handed the whiskey to the Indians. All four grinned in anticipation. Nearly simultaneously they tossed the whiskey back in one large gulp. Shocking members of our party, Chief Tortohongar went to the empty bottle, and deeply inhaled the intoxicating aroma. He tried to suck vestiges from the container. The men in our party refrained from expressing surprise and disgust with such a pathetic display. His mannerisms then took a turn for the worse: Tortohongar began to feign drunkenness, and became belligerent. It was then we decided the group must return to shore before the situation devolved into something even more dismal. With great effort on our part, and much reluctance on theirs, we were able to get the four back into the pirogue, along with Captain Clark and seven soldiers.

We closely observed them row to shore — hopeful nothing worse would occur. In the pirogue, the chiefs spoke among themselves planning their next actions. The party coasted into the shallows and Captain Clark, five of the seven expedition members, and three of the four Indians stepped out of the boat to wade towards shore. At the behest of Chief Tortohongar, and consistent with the war-prize legend, three warriors immediately seized the pirogue mooring rope in hopes of glory, while Makoshika tightly hugged the mast.

Tortohongar explained to Cruzatte that they were poor and wished to keep the pirogue and its goods, since they believed the quality and quantity of gifts given to them were inadequate. He added that we should not leave, until such payment was rendered. Based on past skirmishes with Indians on the Kentucky frontier, Clark reached his capacity to absorb insolence, and slowly drew his sword from its scabbard — then pointed the sword in the direction of Black Buffalo. The sword brightly glittered under the afternoon sunlight.

With seething rage in the tone of his voice, Clark bellowed an order and signaled all hands under arms. The seven expedition members reached into their supply pouches to load their weapons. Observing the alarming situation on shore, I commanded all on the keelboat to the ready. The men scurried to collect their rifles and ammunition, and took positions behind cargo boxes, which occupied the body of the boat. They lifted the hinged lids to use them as shields, and rested their rifles atop the box covers. Corporal Warfington loaded the swivel guns with buckshot, while I quickly loaded the cannon on the bow with 16 musket balls and lit a taper — ready to ignite the cannon fuse.

Along the riverbank, dozens of warriors aimed their rifles while others notched arrows in their bows.

Black Buffalo surveyed the escalating incident and understood that many women and children could be casualties if battle ensued. The Chief and captain traded steely stares. Clark menacingly glared, and gestured with his sword at Black Buffalo's chest to emphasize his intent. Clark maintained his stern appearance. Black Buffalo broke the standoff by turning his head to Makoshika, and motioning for the warrior to leave the boat. The chief then took the rope from the three who seized it, and instructed them to retreat further up the riverbank. Chief Tortohongar followed them.

Black Buffalo clarified that all they wanted was the opportunity for their women and children to see the keelboat, since they had never observed a vessel of that size and grandeur. Upon learning of this modest request, Clark glanced down at his scabbard and calmly sheathed his sword. He then said through Cruzatte that he would happily grant their wish. Black Buffalo responded by releasing the rope and letting it drop onto the riverbank.

Still wary of their actions, Clark ordered the two soldiers in the pirogue to return to the keelboat for 10 additional troops.

"Private Cruzatte, tell the chief we must and will go on, and that we are not women, but warriors."

Hearing Clark's words, Cruzatte somehow successfully relayed the message. Black Buffalo angrily reacted, complete with gestures.

"He said they too have warriors, and if we go on, they will follow and kill us," Cruzatte reported.

Clark countered with more incendiary words: "Private, tell him we were sent by their Great Father, and if they misuse us, we will destroy all of them. Tell them we have more medicine on board that will kill twenty of their nations in a day."

While Cruzatte translated, a dozen soldiers returned from the keelboat in the red pirogue to reinforce Clark's small squad. Reacting to the growing numbers of troops, the chiefs withdrew further up the bank to confer with each other, while Clark stood at the water's edge observing the group — silently collecting his thoughts. His assessment of the situation concluded, Clark slowly approached the trio, and offered his hand in reconciliation to Black Buffalo who just stared down at Clark's open hand. Clark then motioned in the same manner to Buffalo Medicine who also refused to take Clark's hand.

Angry once more, the Captain tersely executed an about-face maneuver, waded through the water and stepped into the boat. Black Buffalo abruptly ended the conference and he, Makoshika, and another warrior called Running Deer slogged in after Clark. Standing in water up to his knees, Black Buffalo requested the trio be allowed to stay the night on the keelboat. Clark reluctantly agreed, and we proceeded on about a mile where Sergeant Gass dropped anchor near a small island we called "Bad Humored," since we were all in an exceedingly bad state, having narrowly avoided a bloodbath.

Fortunately, the near calamity of that day was not repeated the next. We set out early, traveled four miles, and stopped at the Chief's request to enable their women and children to see the boat. Along the way, the south riverbank was lined with Indians of all ages. I went ashore with five soldiers for more than three hours to tour the village, which had about 900 people living in approximately 100 tipis.

Captain Clark became uneasy during my long absence, and sent Sergeant Pryor to check on our status. By then, the natives were preparing for an elaborate celebration that evening by adorning themselves with items, such as hawk feathers, porcupine quills, and many colors of body paint. Shortly before five in the afternoon, our group returned to the boat to allow Captain Clark to see the village. As he and other members of the expedition landed on shore, Captain Clark was met by six warriors who insisted on carrying him on a bison robe to Black Buffalo's tipi where he was asked to sit on two special buffalo hides that had been previously painted white.

After exchanging uncomfortable pleasantries and smoking, Clark walked through the village and saw what I had already observed. He noted that the women appeared quite healthy, had fine teeth, and high cheek bones. They dressed in buffalo-skin petticoats, and did all the laborious work for the community. It was our impression that they were perfect slaves for their husbands who frequently had several wives. Often, the additional wives were widows of warriors who had been slain in battle.

Under the close escort of our Teton hosts, we also saw several Omaha women and boys in a tipi. We were informed they were war prisoners taken earlier that month when the Teton destroyed 40 Omaha lodges, killed 75 men, and captured 48 prisoners — all women and boys. This was the same nation, if not the same village members, we searched for near Sergeant Floyd's grave, and discovered they were out hunting. After observing the Omaha, Clark returned to Black Buffalo's tipi to advise the chiefs to make peace with that nation, and release the prisoners, if they intended to follow the words of their Great Father.

Soon after Clark strongly recommended release of the captives, eight warriors carried me into the tipi where I sat next to Clark. An old man asked for pity and more gifts, which we politely declined. The Chief then signaled it was time to exit, and assemble around the fire for a feast and dancing. Before the festivities, they offered our party more cooked and dried buffalo meat, which I estimated at 400 pounds. After situating ourselves around the fire, Black Buffalo rose to his feet and began a sermon, while holding a peace pipe above his head. He stated the words in the most earnest and sincere manner possible — offering his remarks to the heavens and four corners of the earth.

Only much later did I understand Black Buffalo's prayer.[13]

He turned to the setting sun and said: "Great Mystery, this pipe enriches life. Lend us another of your good days that this nation may live. This pipe I raise to the heavens for you. Let there be no adversity that the nation may live."

He turned north to begin addressing the creatures that hold dominion over the remaining quarters of the world: "This day all creatures are with us. Spotted Eagle — most powerful — lend us this day, one of your good days. This pipe will enrich the life of its people. One of your feathers I borrow. Lend us one of your good days. May the nation live, and may there be no adversity. Before the north, let the nation live."

To the east he faced: "Sunrise, all creatures may be mentioned. Woodpecker, your day is good. Lend me this day, one of your feathers. This pipe will enrich the life of its people. Lend me a good day. Let there be no adversity that the nation may live."

Pivoting to his right he said: "South, all creatures may be mentioned. Mallard, your day is good. Lend me this day, a good day. Your feather I borrow. This pipe will enrich the life of its people. Let us have a good day. May there be no adversity that the nation may live."

To the zenith, he looked up: "Heavens, all may be mentioned. Great Mystery, you were the first to exist. This earth you created and placed here. Above it you raised the Indian. Now, I am rejoicing the arrival of our visitors and pray our race may grow strong in numbers because of the promise they bring. I pray there may be no more adversity. Great Mystery, you are mighty. Pity me, so our nation may live. Lend me a day. This pipe will enrich the life of its people. Great Mystery, help me. Help me with a good day."

With the prayer concluded, tobacco was lit, and the pipe was passed around a circle of people for all to smoke, which we did until dark. This was when the main course of the grand meal was served, which were roasted dogs. The party had become particularly fond of consuming this animal, since first partaking of it with the Yankton-Sioux. In addition, we ate prairie turnips, and pemmican, which is a dried, pulverized meat mixed with animal fat.

Afterward, several highly decorated men with tambourines and rattles began to sing and beat drums. To encourage warriors in their conquests and acknowledge victories, women then came forward and danced around the fire with 65 Omaha scalps secured to the tops of wooden poles. They danced until eleven that night.

When the celebration concluded, Black Buffalo offered us very handsome women for our amusement, which we also politely, but grudgingly declined in no small part because were Virginia gentlemen, and believed we should act as such at all times in deed and will.[C,3] We also did this on behalf of the safety of the party — wary of the negative complexities that could arise from such interludes.

Near midnight, we returned to the keelboat with Black Buffalo and Chief Tortohongar whom we warily consented to lodge on board. A few hours later, Private Cruzatte quietly entered our quarters and gently wrested me awake from a sound sleep on my bed:

"Captain Lewis," Cruzatte whispered, as he nudged my shoulder. "Captain Lewis, wake up."

I looked up and focused on the black patch over his left eye.

"What is it, Private?"

"I must report something," he said.

By then, Captain Clark was also awake. From across the room, he turned to us, and propped himself up on his right elbow.

"During our visit yesterday, I gave several prisoners some trinkets. They informed me the Teton plan to plunder and end the expedition, since they were not satisfied with the gifts we gave them," he stated in a distressed tone.

After a brief discussion and given Black Buffalo's comments, we had little doubt about the validity of the Omaha's assertions, and agreed to not show signs we knew of the villainous plan. As a result, we were highly guarded the remainder of the night and rested poorly.

The morning of the 27th was clear and pleasant. At the Chiefs' request, we reluctantly determined to remain another day. After breakfast, we gave Black Buffalo and Chief Tortohongar the blankets on which they lay, for that is what they expected by custom. They also received a peck of corn. Most of the party went to the village during the day — five or six at a time. In return, the chiefs and their sons came aboard, and dined with Captain Clark and me.

In the afternoon, Sergeant Gass, six men, and I went to the Indian village. The women were employed dressing buffalo skins for clothing and lodge coverings. I must admit the Teton were the friendliest people I ever saw up to that time, but they would also pilfer, if given the opportunity. In a curious tradition, when friends of these people passed on to the next world, survivors inserted small arrows through their flesh above and below their elbows, as a testimonial to their grief. Another scalp dance was performed in the evening, during which nine in our party stayed until after midnight. Again, we were offered women for amusement, but decided it best to not partake for our party's safety.

Afterward, Captain Clark boarded the red pirogue with six of our men, while I stayed on shore with a guard.

Through the neglect of the helmsman, the pirogue rounded the front of the keelboat with the current, and the pirogue's bow became entangled in the keelboat's anchor rope. With the pirogue then pivoting around its own bow, the current pushed the pirogue, and it violently smashed broadside into the keelboat, causing both vessels to tip. There was a loud thump on the side of the pirogue, and the rope snapped causing both ends to hurl in opposite directions, as the immense tension was released. The anchor sank to the bottom of the river, and the keelboat was then adrift.[D] Captain Clark shouted for all hands to attach a new rope, and tow the keelboat ashore. Men scurried about the deck then leapt into the water to retrieve the severed rope, hoping to save the keelboat from floating downstream. Within minutes, the men affixed a new cable to the front of the keelboat, and secured the rope to the trunk of a cottonwood tree on the south shore near another threatening and eroding overhang.

Hearing the commotion and not understanding its meaning, Chief Tortohongar called his warriors to arms, believing an Omaha counter-attack was underway. He erroneously suspected the counter-attack had been initiated through our collusion with the Omaha. Indians began firing their guns to alert others. Soon more than 200 fighters lined the shore ready for action. After they realized there was no attack, and understood the cause of the ruckus, most went back to their lodges. But some stayed near us for the remainder of the morning.

All this made for another night of little or no sleep, especially for Captain Clark and me, as we suddenly awoke after each strange noise.

By sunrise, Sergeant Gass had examined the red pirogue, and found the hull had been punctured near the waterline on the starboard side by an unknown object. We speculated the object may have been the anchor. Gass corked the hole and found the damage minimal. With the fix complete, Clark employed the pirogues in a search for the lost anchor. After dragging the river bottom for almost four hours, we abandoned the mission for breakfast, by which time many armed and unarmed Teton were on the bank, which we took as an ominous sign.

We finished eating, and were about to cast off when the three chiefs on horseback rode from the crowd and asked, once again, for us to stay another day, and welcome them aboard. We allowed them onto the keelboat.

Captain Clark conferred with Black Buffalo in the cabin about traveling with us farther upriver, while we prepared to leave. As Clark and Black Buffalo communicated through Cruzatte, three of Chief Tortohongar's warriors on shore seized the keelboat's mooring rope, in a move similar to the altercation just three days prior. One of the warriors holding the line was Makoshika — the man who hugged the mast in the previous incident. From the cabin window, Clark saw the recurring act and complained angrily to Black Buffalo both with words and gestures. Black Buffalo recognized the degenerating situation and he, Captain Clark, and Cruzatte rushed from the cabin onto the deck.

The Chief tried to reassure me that all the three men on shore wished for was tobacco before we departed. Even this trifle seemed outrageous to me, given everything we had already paid in tribute. I informed Cruzatte to tell the Chief I refused to give them any toll, regardless of its form or value. Infuriated by Black Buffalo's request, I ordered all hands to prepare to head off, and raise the mainsail. I then instructed Private McNeal to take in the mooring line.

McNeal jumped into the river and waded through the water. He gave the three warriors an irate stare as he boldly bypassed the trio on his way to the tree. He swiftly untied the rope, and started back to the keelboat. Once again, McNeal and the group exchanged uneasy glares, as he passed them. In response, Makoshika looked down at the rope in his hands then turned in the direction of the tree. He suddenly released the rope, strode to the tree, and retied the cable to the trunk.

Meanwhile back on the keelboat, Chief Tortohongar said he too wanted tobacco and a flag, as terms for leaving. Upon hearing this, I angrily commanded him and Buffalo Medicine escorted off the boat.

Captain Clark turned to throw open a cargo container lid, and tersely grabbed a tobacco twist. In his outstretched hand, Clark showed the good to Black Buffalo, and shook it in his face.

Enraged, Clark screamed.

The veins in his neck pulsed with blood: "You said you are a great man with great influence! Take this, and show us your influence! Show us by making your men let go of the rope!"

Clark flung the tobacco on shore at the feet of the trio, and stormed to the bow of the boat to light a firing taper next to the cannon. With taper in hand, he slowly and deliberately turned the cannon towards the Indians on shore. Upon seeing Clark swivel the cannon, terrified women and children began to flee the scene of escalating hostility.

Black Buffalo countered. He said he too was angry that we would allow our relationship to breakdown over such a small request.

Following Clark's lead, I grabbed two additional tobacco twists from the box and threw them on shore in disgust. With a twist for each warrior then on shore, Black Buffalo walked towards Clark at the bow, and pulled once on the rope. The warriors let go, and Makoshika untied the knot that secured the boat to the tree. Everyone, including the Indians, was quite anxious.

The second confrontation was done, but tensions remained.

We finally departed with Black Buffalo still on board. Our hope was to broker a more stable peace between the Teton and their neighbors to the north who were called the Arikara. Black Buffalo agreed to be a part of this mission. The Arikara resided about 100 miles from our location at that time. Since the Teton occupied land further south, they had the first opportunity to charge traders and merchants a toll to advance upstream, which meant the Teton had an ample supply of weapons and ammunition. However, the Arikara had many agricultural commodities, and access to horses the Teton needed to thrive. Together, the two often traded goods, even though they occasionally killed each other in disputes, and competed for natural resources and power along the river.

Shortly after taking on Chief Black Buffalo, we landed to encamp for the evening. At camp, the men made a new anchor, which was constructed from rope wrapped and tied around very large stones. Free once more, we aptly named this place “Liberty Camp” with hopes that other nations above were much more hospitable, which we were going to need to survive an uncertain winter on the Great Plains.

CHAPTER ELEVEN
TRANSITION

September 29, 1804
Liberty Camp: 1,299 miles above the Missouri confluence

The cold night provided time to reflect on the disastrous incidents that avoided bloodshed, but mortally wounded hopes in converting the Teton into allies. I speculated that from the Teton perspective they were merely collecting appropriate payment for the natural resources we had been harvesting without permission since we entered their territory. However, this did not annul the fact that our nation legally purchased this land, and it was our duty to enlighten and persuade the savages to become partners. Regardless, since the encounters were finished and could not be recalled, I resolved to focus on keeping the expedition moving forward, endure the winter, and avoid similar disasters in the future.

After considerable analysis, I was still not certain how the adverse events could have been averted, even if Mr. Dorion had been present to better convey our messages, especially in light of the rope seizure legend.

Sunrises were coming noticeably later, and with it came frost that coated short grasses. The ice feebly clung to the blades and sheaths for a few dark hours, only to melt with the advancing morning, by which time we had proceeded on to observe Chief Tortohongar, Makoshika, and Running Deer on shore. They signaled they too wished to visit the Arikara. We refused, but grudgingly took Black Buffalo's advice to ferry them in a pirogue to the opposite shore, and provide them additional tobacco.

With the trio transported to the opposite riverbank, the pirogue caught up with the keelboat, which was slowly moving north toward the Arikara villages. Corresponding with smallpox outbreaks that decimated the Omaha years earlier, the Arikara also suffered the same, during which 75 percent of their original population of almost 30,000 perished. Before the outbreaks, they lived in a series of villages on a 150-mile stretch of the Missouri between the Cheyenne and Cannonball rivers — the latter of which took its name from the many stones that resembled this artillery piece.

The Arikara gained their name by adorning themselves with animal bones and horns. Surviving members of this nation were primarily farmers who occupied three villages on a large island near the mouth of the Grand River. Similar to the other tribes below, manual labor was mainly performed by women, while men supplemented their diet by providing buffalo, elk and deer. These women toiled in fields cultivating crops of corn, beans, squash, watermelon, pumpkins and tobacco with farming implements constructed of wood and skeletal parts from animals. The most prominent implement was a hoe made from a buffalo shoulder blade attached to a wooden pole. Excess crops were used as trade commodities for items, such as rifles, ammunition, and gun powder.

Before breakfast on the last day of September, Makoshika appeared on shore again — this time on the starboard side. He informed us that another Teton encampment was above, and it was customary for visitors to stop and meet them. Clark advised Makoshika that we had no intention of stopping, and did not wish to hold council with them. With the abrupt exchange concluded, we set off with the wind, and a few hours later observed 200 Indians on the eastern shore watching us sail to a nearby sandbar. Warily, we dispatched the white pirogue to pick up two Teton warriors who wanted to join us for breakfast on the sandbar, which was situated some 100 yards opposite their village.

The pair said they were friendly, and only wanted us to come ashore to exchange pleasantries, eat and smoke. Cruzatte referred them to Mr. Dorion, and explained our reticence to meet, due to our mistreatment by the band below. However, we graciously accepted their friendship, and buttressed these words by offering each chief and principal a tobacco carrot, which was happily accepted.

An easy morning transformed into an aggressive afternoon when the wind suddenly shifted, blowing from the east in a most unpredictable manner. With each gust, waves acquired white-capped crests with deep troughs, which violently rocked the keelboat, as it swiftly plowed through the choppy surface. Pitching and swaying, the vessel tilted from side to side, nearly foundering. The crew brought her under control by partially rolling up a sail to reduce its surface area. Despite this action, the wind blew so hard that the rocking continued, and the keelboat was propelled at a speed that greatly frightened Black Buffalo. He anxiously requested that we immediately pull ashore. The Chief wanted off the boat. He said our boat was "bad medicine," and would travel no farther with us. Before taking leave of our guest, Captain Clark and I gave him a blanket, tobacco, knife, and other goods to give his nation. Whatever hopes of brokering peace between the Teton and Arikara went with Black Buffalo that afternoon.

On the first of October, we saw our first evidence of the Arikara in the form of an abandoned village near the mouth of the Cheyenne River. The village consisted of numerous earthen lodges that were protected by circular walls, comprised of dried mud and wood to deny raiders easy access, and provide shielding from enemy arrows and musket balls. They were beautiful structures.

After landing to camp for the evening, a white man on the opposite shore called to us in French, and Engagé Francois Rivet shouted back for him to join us for the night. He brought his canoe, and introduced himself as Jean Vallé — another associate of Régis Loisel. Around the fire that evening, we provided him the letter from Loisel, and Vallé gave us a wealth of information about the surrounding territory. Vallé said the Cheyenne River split into north and south forks about 100 miles to the west. About 200 miles beyond the north fork, Vallé said he wintered the previous year in a region known as the Black Hills. To our astonishment, we learned some of the mountain peaks west of that area retained snow throughout the summer. He also informed us there were large numbers of bears, elk, pronghorn, and sheep with big horns that lived among pine trees.

More importantly, Vallé claimed many Teton were about 75 miles upstream at one of the Arikara villages named Sawa-haini, which had about 700 Indians living in 60 earth lodges. This was unfortunate news, for we had hoped to have seen the last of the Teton until our return.

Vallé went back to his camp the following morning. This is when we started north, once again. The day was routine until shortly afternoon when a group of Teton warriors were noticed on a hill. One of them came down, fired his gun, cried out for an unknown reason, and drew our attention in a very certain manner. Clark ordered all hands to be at the ready for a possible confrontation, while we continued to proceed. The Indian followed us for some time, as Cruzatte and the warrior exchanged curt shouts. Cruzatte referred him to Mr. Dorion, and informed us the warrior wanted the party to come to his village, which consisted of 20 tipis. Ignoring his request, we passed an island Captain Clark named "Caution," and again encamped on the safety of a sandbar. The Tetons were proving to be much more troublesome than expected to the extent that all hunting was suspended until need or security prevailed.

As a result of the tensions, Private Newman reached his breaking point. Near his tent that night, the constant fear of death, and physical demands of daily work had driven him to plan his abandonment of the party.[A, 2]

Stoking Newman's resentment was Moses Reed — the convicted deserter: "I'm telling ya they ain't fit to command," Reed emphasized. "They damn near got us killed at least twice this week."

Newman nodded agreement. "You're right, we shoulda turned back."

"Sons a bitches are playin' with everyone's lives," Reed responded with contempt. "We need to go back before we get killed."

"Okay ... How ya reckon we do that?" Newman asked.

Reed paused: "Well, the way I figure is, we're gonna need two more guys to make it past the Teton."

"Two is gonna be hard." Newman assessed.

The pair paused to think of alternatives.

"What about the Field Brothers? You're friends with them. Maybe you could convince one and the other would folla," Reed said.

"That's good. They're both good hunters, too."

"Okay then, we just needs to wait for the right time." Reed concluded.

With a plan for escape conceived, Newman continued to work in the squad, under the command of Sergeant Gass. The following day he and others thoroughly searched the boats for mice, and assessed the damage the rodents inflicted on articles in storage. The men caught several dozen, and found they chewed through a number of bags, fed on corn, and used paper and clothing for nesting material. Our prairie campsites on shore were often among the pests, which numbered in the hundreds running along well-worn paths through the grass.

While the mice were preparing for the change of season by searching for new food supplies, large flocks of geese flying south did the same, which served as reminders that the time for navigation would soon be coming to a close. As the temperatures dropped, washing clothes, and comfortably bathing was becoming a greater challenge. There was no time to waste, and the daily encounters with the Teton were doing just that.

The 4th and 5th of October were similar to the preceding days insomuch as we had more Indians asking us to land and meet. We also passed more abandoned Arikara villages.

In one of those villages, we found crude boats constructed from willow branches and buffalo hide. The boat was shaped much like a very large basket or crate. The vessel had a wooden frame in the form of a hemisphere on which bison skin was stretched and secured. The bullboat, as we called it, was light enough to be carried by a single person, but large enough to accommodate two, if needed.

At the mouth of the Moreau River on the 7th of the month, the party marveled at the size of tracks imprinted by the white or grizzled bear. The fore print was more than a foot in length, and about the same in width. The tracks had tremendous claw marks, which suggested they were at least four inches in length, and could not have been imprinted by a Black bear. To our amazement, these claws were even larger than the ones worn by the Yankton-Sioux chiefs.

The next day in the late afternoon, we passed Sawa-haini, as dozens of Arikara Indians watched from the shoreline of a large island. We halted to make camp a mile north of the island on the opposite shore. Shortly afterward, we were joined by Joseph Gravelines — a partner of Loisel, like Vallé, and Dorion. He spoke fluent French, English, Sioux and Arikara, and had lived among the latter for more than a dozen years. While Captain Clark prepared camp for war or peace, I obtained tobacco to smoke with the chiefs, and rowed to the village with Gravelines, Drouillard, and Private Joseph. Mr. Gravelines informed of us about Arikara life, and volunteered his services to communicate with the tribe. The visit was brief, but cordial during which Gravelines said the Arikara were friends, and they were delighted we had arrived. I remarked that we would return in the morning for further discussions.

Back at camp, Gravelines tempered his enthusiastic message with a warning. He cautioned that in addition to arms, trade goods and smallpox, European merchants also inadvertently brought venereal disease to many women in the villages. He explained this was relevant because local custom called for men to offer their wives for intimate encounters, which was similar to the Sioux practice we resisted. According to Gravelines, Arikara women were also known to initiate sexual contact with non-Indian men for a variety of economic reasons, rather than just recreation. Moreover, he said the deed was viewed as transference of power to Indian men from non-Indians who had special medicine.

The next day was stormy when three village chiefs, Lightning Crow, Eagle Feather, and Pocasse visited our water-soaked camp. They were accompanied by a Pierre-Antoine Tabeau who was also a colleague of Loisel, and had been living with the Indians for many years. Mr. Tabeau offered more enlightenment with regards to Arikara customs and politics. One item he shared was that some jealousy existed between the chiefs as to whom we might deem the Grand Chief. Aware of this information, I gave each chief an equal amount of tobacco, and agreed to meet for a council the following afternoon near the keelboat.

On the 10th of October, the chiefs arrived and everyone assembled under the awning and flag in the usual manner. The Indians were awe struck by the presence of Clark's servant, York. Many gawked, pointed, and looked on in curious, but silent fascination, as the council proceeded. The ceremonial parade commenced, and was followed by my speech, gifts for all three leaders, and an offering of whiskey.

Captain Clark reached into a wooden box, uncorked a whiskey bottle, and gestured with it to Lightning Crow. The Chief observed the bottle, glanced at Clark, and turned to Mr. Gravelines who explained in Arikara what was in the bottle. Lightning Crow listened and grew a disapproving appearance on his face. He replied to Gravelines.

"The Chief said he is surprised his new father would present a gift that would make them fools," Gravelines reported.

Clark hung his head in ignorance and nodded agreement. The offering was an error. "Tell the Chief he's correct, and I apologize for the mistake."

Gravelines explained, and all appeared satisfactory.

Lightning Crow then went on to tell the legend of the stone idols through Gravelines: "He said you will see three large stones about 20 miles upstream at the Spring River. These stones are sacred.

"Many years ago there was a young couple who were madly in love. The man was named Sun Walker who had a faithful dog. Each day he prayed to the Great Spirit that he would meet a woman worthy of his affections. Filled with the Great Spirit, the next day his dog went on a mission to a nearby rival village, and befriended a woman called Night Wanderer.

"Despite an ongoing dispute between the competing villages, the woman followed the dog to Sun Walker, and the pair was immediately enchanted with each other. They became lovers, but their relationship was forbidden by members of both villages, especially their parents. Distraught about his inability to marry Night Wanderer, Sun Walker went to the confluence of rivers to pray to the Great Spirit that he be forever united with his lover or turned to stone. His dog looked on.

"The Great Spirit answered Sun Walker's prayer by turning his feet into stone, and inspired the dog, once more. The dog hurried to the village and coaxed Night Wanderer to the site. She embraced Sun Walker, and all three gradually turned to stone — forever united on this landscape.

"This, the Chief said, you will soon see," Gravelines concluded.

Although certainly entertained by the fable, I assigned it as much credibility as the devils inhabiting Spirit Mound and gobbling snakes,. I then quickly changed the topic to gifts for the leaders. Each chief was given an equal portion of goods, which included a flag, red coat, cocked hat, feathers, medal, paint, and tobacco. In return, they offered much-needed corn, beans, dried pumpkins, and squash. With gift giving and other formalities concluded, we adjourned to the air-gun exhibition, which had the desired impact. By this time, Captain Clark and I developed a confident impression of the Arikara, and agreed to the Chief's suggestions that the party visit all the villages that evening. The men separated into small groups. Several soldiers were left behind to guard the camp and boats.

Captain Clark, York, and four expedition members arrived at Sawa-haini. Again, the natives stared at York, unsure what to conclude about the meaning and origin of his very dark skin. Through Gravelines, Clark explained that York was the Captain's servant, and had been with him almost his entire life. The Indians said they had never seen a black man.

Sensing the opportunity to amuse himself, exploit the naiveté of the Indians and spin his own tale, York expanded on his owner's remarks.[B] A gathering crowd of children maintained a safe distance.

"A long time ago, I used to live in the woods," York began his tale.

The Indians marveled at his rich baritone voice and immense height and weight. He crouched to eye level with the children.

"I used to eat all sorts of things," he said. "But my's favorite was people. Yes, sir! I loved eatin' people, especially young'uns likes you all! Mmmm, Mmmm! Mighty tasty them young folks was."

He paused to allow Gravelines to translate and enjoy the reaction of the children.

As Gravelines finished, puzzled and fearful looks appeared on the children's faces. York grinned and began to chuckle. Known to the youngsters, but unknown to York, was that sometimes the children's fathers partook in ritualistic cannibalism to gain strength, after vanquishing their enemies in battle.

York concluded: "Don't you worry none. I give that up after Captain Clark caught and tamed me. Now, I just plain love young'uns. You needn't be afraid," York assured, as he stood up to tower above the crowd.

Resuming our stroll to Chief Lightning Crow's lodge, some braver youth walked behind and to the side of York. He began to playfully chase them through the village and demonstrated feats of strength, such as lifting heavy rocks, and snapping tree branches. The adults were so astonished that they believed he had special spiritual power and nicknamed him "Big Medicine."

While the natives were impressed with York's color, stature, and strength, Sergeant Gass was equally impressed with the Arikara's skillful construction of the earth lodges, which were made without modern tools. Being a carpenter by trade before the expedition, Gass had a unique appreciation of the workmanship.

As an outer wall, forked posts were vertically erected — each stood five or six feet in height, and was arranged in a large circle. The circle was about 30 to 40 feet in diameter. On top of these posts were smaller poles, situated horizontally between the forks. This comprised the skeleton of the outer wall. To this skeleton, willow branches were woven together, and covered with grass and mud to complete the wall.

In the center of the lodge were four additional vertical and horizontal posts arranged in a cubic manner that supported the roof, which was also comprised of poles, branches, grass, and clay. On the floor of the cube was a fire pit that emanated smoke through a hole in the roof. Around the interior perimeter of the structure were six beds for the family, spaced almost equally from each other. The building was even large enough to corral several horses near the doorway. Entry and exit was through a single passage, above which a buffalo skin was hung as a door.

Similar to Omaha earth homes, the north half of the lodge was occupied by people of the sky, and the south by Earth: The latter were in charge of securing the tribe's physical welfare; the former were responsible for the community's spiritual needs.

After greeting the Indians and observing their living quarters, we parted for the night, and arranged to meet again the next morning to hear their answers to our requests. We also took leave of Engagé Peter Roi who wished to remain with our hosts.

Before dinner on the 11th, Lightning Crow arrived, thanked us for the gifts, and promised that his people would honor our appeals for trade, peace, and travel to meet President Jefferson.

Specifically, he stated, "My heart is gladder than it ever was before to see my fathers. If you want the road open, no one can prevent it. It will always be open for you. We do not think closing the road was wise by the nation below.

"Can you think of anyone here who would dare put their hands on the rope of your boat?

"No! No one here would dare! When you get to the Mandan, we wish you to speak good words with that nation for us. We wish to be at peace with them, as you advise. And we want to trade.

"It gives us pain that we do not know how to best trade the beaver, for we know of their value. Instead, we will make buffalo robes the best we can for trade.

"When you return, if I am living, you will see me again the same man. The Indians on the prairie know me, and listen to my words. When you return they will meet to see you. We shall look at the river with impatience for your return."

We happily received the Chief's friendly words, and set off in early afternoon — traveled 11 miles, and camped on a sandbar below the next Arikara village. As we landed, an uproarious cheer went up from the men. We were surprisingly greeted by an American flag flying atop a lodge. This was the same flag I had given Chief Pocasse the previous day.

As darkness fell and the day's duties were complete, rotating teams of our men were granted liberty in the village. The soldiers requested leave to partake in the warriors' offering their wives for intimate encounters, which we had been without since leaving St. Louis. As the deed was transacted, a warrior guarded the entry to the lodge until the couple re-emerged.

York was especially in demand.

Now that the business is done, I learned it was customary among western Indians who returned from success in battle to paint themselves in charcoal before returning to camp. As a consequence, many Indians believed York's appearance was an extension of this success, and assumed he was the bravest among the party.

Once again, Captain Clark and I resisted such invitations, but our resolution was dissolving among the numerous temptations. Through the night, I thought of one woman who had captured my imagination, and the possibilities kept me from sleeping well the entire night.

With the men's confined energy released, they returned to sleep in the safety of their tents at our camp.

In the morning, many Indians were on shore anxious to trade with us, which was likely catalyzed by the liaisons the men enjoyed the previous evening. The Indians mostly wanted red paint for articles, which we were happy to provide. With the trading complete, Captain Clark, a small group, and I went to the village to listen to Chiefs Pocasse and Eagle Feather response to our meeting.

Chief Pocasse spoke first:

"My Fathers, I am glad to see you this fine day. I am glad to hear your good council, and talk the good talk. I see our Grand Father has sent you to open the road. By sending you, our Grand Father wants you to take pity on us.

"Our Grand Father sent you with tobacco, and to make peace with all nations. I hear the first village recommended the road be clear and open, and you have directed all nations to open and clear the road. We wish you to tell our Grand Father that we also wish the road to be clear and open. I expect the Chief in the village above will tell you the same, and believe the Sioux told you the same.

"We see you here today, and you see we are poor. Our women have no knives to cut meat. Take pity on us. When you return, you come here. You direct us to stay home, and not go to war. This we shall do. We hope when you get to the Mandan you will tell them the same. No one dare stop you. You go when you please. You tell us to go down, and see our Grand Father to receive his gifts. When we go our people will look for us with the same impatience that our Grand Father looks for your return.

"If I am going to see my Grand Father, there are many bad nations on the road. I am not afraid to die for the good of my people," Pocasse paused, as many around him cried out upon the possibility of losing their leader.

The moaning ceased.

Pocasse continued: "The Chief by me will go to the Mandan, and hear what they will say. The moment we set out, all on the open prairie will see me part on this great mission to see my Great Father. Our people hunting shall be glad to hear of your being here, and will wait for your return.

"We are poor. Take pity on our wants. The road is for you all to go on. After you leave, many nations may come to make war against us. We wish you to stop their guns and prevent it, if possible," Pocasse concluded.

Chief Eagle Feather spoke next, while Gravelines continued translating:

"My fathers, we believe your words. I will see the Indians above to see their heart with you. The nations below — the Omaha and Otoe — have a good heart. But one nation — the Sioux — does not have a good heart.

"I look at the other chiefs, and will go when they go. When I return maybe I can give my people knives, powder, and ball. We do not go for nothing. If my Great Chief wishes to go, I wish to go, also.

"When I go see my Grand Father, I wish to return quickly for fear of my people being uneasy. My children are small and perhaps will be uneasy for my safety. When I return my people will be glad. I will stay at home and not go to war, even if my people are struck. We will believe your word, but I fear the Indians below will not believe your word.

"What did the Sioux tell you?" he asked.

Through Mr. Gravelines, we informed Eagle Feather of the Tetons' treachery, and injury to our party. Eagle Feather expressed disgust.

By noon, the meeting was finished, and we were on the boat where Captain Clark complained of rheumatism in his neck. After a brief examination, I determined to treat his ailment that evening by heating a stone, wrapping it in flannel, and applying it to his neck.

Feeling jovial at the generous hospitality of our hosts, we proceed on while Cruzatte played the fiddle, and others sounded horns. As we rowed, great numbers of women were seen toting wood across the river in their ingenious bullboats. By four in the afternoon, we traveled ten miles, and halted for the night on the eastern side of the river. Sunset came quickly, and fires burned. Through the darkness, an Indian on the opposite shore continually shouted at us, until he saw Sergeant Gass, and five soldiers take to the white pirogue to investigate the disturbance.

While Gass and the others visited the Indian, Privates Newman and Reed decided the time had finally arrived to execute their mutinous plan. They approached Private Joseph who was busy sewing himself a new flannel shirt. Field was working alone near one of the fires at the far end of camp. The movement of Newman and Reed caught Field's attention. Suspicious of their intent, he stopped sewing, and warily watched the pair advance, knowing something was amiss. His resentment of Reed grew with each step.

"Joseph!" Newman exclaimed in a friendly manner, as he dropped to one knee.

Newman lightly placed his left hand on Field's right shoulder.

"Can you break? We want to discuss something with you." Newman said.

"What you need?" Field asked, annoyed by their presence.

"Moses and I been thinkin'that things haven't been goin' too well."

"What you mean?" Field distrustfully responded.

"I mean we damn near been killed a few times already. Moses and I ain't gonna take more chances," Newman said.

He paused to study Field's reaction.

"We want you to come with us back to Saint Louie," he announced. "We need your help gettin' there. The captains ain't fit to lead."

Field looked intently at Reed, and shifted his eyes to observe Newman.

"I ain't doin' it. I signed up for what I signed up for. You two best leave right now before I get in trouble for even talking to ya."

Newman restated his case, this time including Field's brother as a desired participant. Again, Field curtly rejected the logic. Newman and Reed persisted, but Field refused, and angrily yelled for them to leave.

The pair made a hasty retreat. Field returned to stitching his shirt. The Private stopped midway through pulling on a long piece of thread, and thought it best to immediately report the incident to his commander, Sergeant Gass who was still investigating the disturbance across the river. Unable to locate Gass, Field informed Sergeant Ordway of Newman and Reed's plan. Ordway reported the incident to me, and I immediately ordered eight men to confine the pair on the keelboat, until a court-martial could convene the following day.

After investigating the disturbance, Gass and the others returned to the boat with a warrior and both his wives. The warrior wished for Captain Clark and me to enjoy their company for the night, so he could obtain some of our medicine. Having imbibed a moderate amount of ardent spirits, we decided to accept the invitation in the most discrete manner possible. This also served as a pleasant diversion to the stressful task we knew awaited us in the morning.

With the trial imminent, we proceeded on in the morning. Eventually, we passed the stone idols at Spring Creek, which were the subject of the Indian lore. However, we did not stop until we found a suitable site for the court-martial. It commenced at noon. Newman was charged with uttering repeated expressions of a highly criminal and mutinous nature. His expressions had the potential to not only destroy every principle of military discipline, but also alienate the affections of soldiers for their officers, and disaffect them from the service to which they had been sacredly and solemnly engaged.

To the charge, Newman pled: "Not guilty."

In an absolute rejection of his argument, all nine members of the court found him guilty, and sentenced him to 75 lashes on his bare back. They also banished him from the expedition.

Captain Clark and I approved the sentence, and directed the punishment be executed the next day, on the 14th of the month, between the hours of one and two in the afternoon. We further directed that Newman join Reed as a laboring hand in the red pirogue and, in the future, execute any and all drudgeries, as deemed proper by the guard on duty.

On a sandbar the next day in the midst of light rain, we halted to carry out the punishment. Newman was compelled to strip off his shirt, and secured to a post. Sergeant Gass removed the cat-o-nine tails from a bag, and began to beat Newman. He grimaced, but remained silent.

After the second strike, Chief Eagle Feather cried out loudly, and motioned for Gass to cease. Captain Clark and I rushed to the Chief, and asked Mr. Gravelines to explain the reasoning for the penalty. The Chief responded that he too thought consequences were necessary, but such punishment was never carried out against anyone in his village, regardless of the infraction. Gravelines went into more detail, and the explanation appeared adequate, if not altogether accepted by Eagle Feather.

The last Arikara village was visited the subsequent day where the men again benefited from their hospitality customs and moved on. During a walk on the 19th, Captain Clark reported seeing numerous conical mounds, hills, and buttes of various sizes — one of which was 90 feet in height. All of them were comprised of dozens of layers of exposed soils, which each had a differing shade of yellow, brown, red, or white. Along the sides of the unusual formations, deep furrows were carved from incalculable numbers of years of water erosion. Each layer was several inches to a few feet in thickness, and majestically appeared from the flatness of the surrounding plain. It provided a spectacular contrast to the grass of the plains, which were still painted many hues of green, despite being late in the season.

Walking north, the one-eyed Cruzatte went out to hunt the next morning. At a distance of about 30 paces, Cruzatte observed a fuzzy silhouette along the river of a very large figure he concluded could only be that of the grizzled bear the Sioux and Arikara had referenced. He carefully aimed and squeezed the trigger. The ball found its mark in the bear's shoulder. The animal became immediately agitated, reared up on its hind quarters, and roared loudly. Cruzatte was stunned; the animal had not dropped over dead in an instant. He was even more shocked at the deafening roar of the great beast, and its threatening actions. The frightened Cruzatte quickly dropped his tomahawk and gun in disbelief, and swiftly ran downstream in the opposite direction of the bear. He fled two miles before meeting our boats. Under the security of our group, Cruzatte directed the white pirogue back to the area to retrieve his weapons, and informed everyone of his encounter with the fearsome beast.

The tracks indicated the bear moved north when Cruzatte ran south. However, after an extensive search, we deduced the animal had merely been wounded by his shot. Signs suggested the bear went inland. But we decided to pursue no further, knowing we must not delay in finding a site to lodge for the winter, before the river turned to ice.

Ice not only meant ceasing our travel by water, but likely meant destruction of the boats, if they were not pulled from the river. Light snow the following day reminded us of this fact, and accentuated the first signs of the Mandan Indians. As we passed, many abandoned villages were visible from the boat. The Mandan nation — similar to their Hidatsa neighbors — lived much like the Arikara. They occupied earthen lodges, and were primarily farmers who grew crops of corn, beans, squash, and tobacco. They also supplemented their diet by hunting deer, elk, and buffalo. The Mandan occupied two villages northwest of our position at that time, while the Hidatsa resided in three villages, north of the Mandan.

The Hidatsa were known by the French as the Gros Ventre of the Missouri River. They were commonly referred to by white traders as the Big Bellies — the name of which was acquired from sign language. The motion of one's hands and arms during the signing suggested the appearance of a large stomach. However, we had no reason to believe the Hidatsa had any bigger abdomens than any other people. That nation of Indians was separate from another tribe who lived northwest of the Hidatsa, known as the Gros Ventre of the prairie, rather than the Gros Ventre of the river.

Regardless of the size of the Hidatsa or Mandan, in this warrior culture, men conducted raids on other Indian villages, in addition to hunting game. Hidatsa war parties often traveled as far west as the Rocky Mountains to invade Shoshone and Flathead Indian villages to take goods and capture prisoners. Mandan warriors showed battle experience through the adornment of feathers on their head: Notched feathers indicated the cutting of an enemy throat, and taking his scalp; painted feathers represented a variety of achievements from suffering an arrow wound to killing a rival.[12] Similar to other western Indians, four combat feats were needed for a warrior to become a war chief: Lead a successful war party, touch a living enemy, steal an adversary's horse, and take a rival's weapon.[17] In addition, after the men prevailed in conflict, women would celebrate the victory by dancing and singing near a fire.

On the 24th of October, we met a Mandan hunting party at noon, and visited with them for several hours. After exchanging pleasantries, we proceeded on to the lower end of an island at a sharp westerly bend in the river. Here we camped for the night. Also camping on this island were five Mandan Indians from the nearby Matootonha village: Chief Big White, a second chief named Little Crow, and three warriors. We were cordially greeted by the group, and they offered to smoke from a peace pipe with us. As the conversation concluded, I agreed to accompany the leaders a short distance upriver. With us went Mr. Gravelines and Chief Eagle Feather. The objective of the trip was to discuss peace terms between the Mandan and Arikara who had been in a feud for many years, regarding a topic I had yet to learn.

The peace discussions progressed well enough that Eagle Feather stayed with the Mandan that night. The next morning, we advanced 11 miles upstream, and were met by huge numbers of Indians on foot and horseback, lining both sides of the river — singing and shouting greetings. In the evening, several Indians came to visit, including the son of a Mandan chief who recently died. The former Chief's son was a warrior named Big Hawk. Like the Sioux, the Mandan also had a curious custom of self-mutilation to demonstrate grief. After the death of his father, Big Hawk cut off the smallest finger on each hand, and pierced himself numerous times with small arrows.

We set out early the next morning, and traveled a short distance to another Indian hunting camp. There, we met a Scottish goods trader named Hugh McCracken from the North West Company. McCracken was there to trade beaver pelts with the Mandan for horses and buffalo robes. McCracken was based at a North West Company post, located 150 miles to the northeast on the Assiniboine River in British Territory.

The following day, we met another goods trader from British Territory. His name was René Jusseaume. I found him an assuming and discontented character, but likely useful as an interpreter with the Mandan and Hidatsa. Jusseaume also told Captain Clark that he had been a spy in Illinois for Clark's brother during the Revolutionary War.

We moved on, and halted to camp just below the first Mandan village called Matootonha, or Mitutanka. We were then 1,598 miles above the Missouri confluence, and an unknown distance from the source of this great river, which was somewhere in the yet unseen mountains far to the west.

Although we were nowhere near the Rockies, at this point, I still had every reason to believe there was an easy portage over the mountains. Geographers indicated that travel down the Columbia River should have been as moderate in character as that of the Missouri had been to that point. Basis for this assumption was largely upon the written accounts of one, Alexander Mackenzie whose adventures I shall detail for you at a later time. But for now, it should be stated that Mackenzie said his portage over the great, shining, rocky mountains in the year 1793 was a mere 817 steps, which posed no significant difficulty. This was obviously an encouraging testimonial.

Late in the morning on the 29th of October, four of the five village chiefs, and their immediate subordinates assembled under the awning for our requested council. The meeting had already been delayed an entire day by strong winds, which continued on the 29th. However, we decided to wait no longer. The wind was exceedingly violent, and we stretched sails around a portion of the meeting site to shield us from the gale. Behind this shield, I delivered the usual speech, asked them to answer our requests the following day, and encouraged the Mandan and Hidatsa to make peace with the Arikara. Afterward, we distributed the typical gifts, and also offered to the Mandan a special present: A small, steel mill for grinding grains. All the gifts were gladly received by our hosts.

The day went well, but the evening was unusual.

Chief Eagle Feather informed Captain Clark and me that he wished to return to his nation, since he was uneasy being around so many enemies. Clark asked him to stay at least one more day to enable us to hear the Mandan and Hidatsa answers to our questions about travel to Washington, peace, and future commerce. Clark gave him a string of wampum, as compensation for his patience. The Chief agreed to stay to listen to their replies.

With the crisis averted, a new one emerged in the form of a fast-moving prairie fire, fueled by a powerful wind. The origin of the fire was not known, and claimed the lives of a man and woman who could not escape the deadly flames. Another family survived, but not without suffering burns to their arms, as they crouched to protect themselves from the consuming inferno. One boy — who was reported to be half-white in ancestry — was spared injury through the actions of his mother. The woman threw a buffalo skin over the youth, and the fire passed around them. This same fire passed our camp at about eight that evening in a most tremendous manner.

But rather than crediting the courageous actions of the mother, some Indians claimed the boy was saved by the Great Spirit because he was filled with medicine from his white father. Captain Clark and I thought this was another exhibit of ignorance. It was increasingly apparent that intervention of a deity was too readily used to explain unknown phenomena without first exhausting rational reasons, a charge to which our ancestors would also be guilty, but I still found disturbing.

The following day, I awaited the natives' reply, while Captain Clark took eight men to find a suitable location on which to build a winter fortress. The prospective site was approximately a mile north of the upper-most Hidatsa village. During Clark's exploration, most of the Indians did not arrive to respond to our inquiries. However, we were visited by Chief Big White of the Matootonha, or first Mandan village, who could not attend the previous day, because his bullboat was unable to negotiate the windswept current. After Clark and the men returned, they reported that the visited area was devoid of timber and game, and determined to look for a better location.

On the last day of October, Captain Clark and four soldiers went to a nearby Mandan village to receive a gift of corn, at the invitation of the village chief who was named "Black Cat." The Chief had sent two other tribe leaders to deliver the message. They came from their village, which they called Rooptahee, but we referred to it as the second or upper Mandan village. The secondary chief who delivered the message was known as "Raven Man." The upper Mandan village had about 50 lodges, with at least that number of inhabitants, after a devastating smallpox outbreak in the year 1781.

With much ceremony, Clark was seated on a buffalo robe next to Black Cat, and the meeting went well. Black Cat promised to go to Washington, and no longer wage war on the Arikara. Like Eagle Feather, Black Cat too looked forward to the day when his people could hunt and work in the fields without fear of being attacked by an enemy.

With the meeting concluded, Clark and the men returned to camp where he found me finishing a letter for Mr. McCracken to deliver to Charles Chaboillez, senior executive of the North West Company. In light of my unfamiliarity with details of existing international treaties at that time, I felt compelled to explain the purpose of our mission and presence in this area to prevent possible accusations that the United States was in violation of any agreements. The letter also invited Chaboillez to visit us that winter. Soon after I finished the correspondence, Mandan leaders and their entourage paid a visit. The chiefs were dressed in the clothes we had given them, and requested our men dance for entertainment. We were happy to grant the request.

Cruzatte played the fiddle. The men reeled and jigged, locked elbows, and spun to the delight of the natives. We hadn't danced in such a manner since my birthday in August.

McCracken left for the North West trading post at first light the following day. With him went the letter I wrote and a copy of my British passport, which detailed the nature of the expedition, and asked all subjects of His Majesty, King George III, to allow me to pass and render protection and aid as needed.

At ten that morning, the chiefs from the lower Mandan village visited our camp again, this time to respond to our council.

Chief Big White stood and said: "We have heard your words, and our wish is to be at peace with all. We will smoke and make good peace with the Arikara. The Arikara know we did not begin the war. They always begin. We sent a chief with peace pipe and men to the Arikara, and they killed them. We struck back and killed them like birds. We killed enough of them. We do not wish to kill more. We will make a good peace."

Changing his focus, Big White asked: "Are you going to stay above or below our village this season?"

I answered through Jusseaume that we planned on traveling downriver a few miles towards the Chief's village, since we could find no proper place above the Hidatsa.

Big White appeared pleased and continued: "We were sorry when we heard of your going up, but now you are going down, and we are glad. If we eat, you shall eat. If we starve, you must starve, also. Our village is too far from here to bring corn, but we hope you will call on us as you pass."

With the conference concluded, the two chiefs returned to their village. Satisfied with the disposition and motives of the natives, shortly after dark we descended nine miles towards the most promising area for construction of our fortress, which would be our home until the rivers flowed freely once more sometime the following spring.

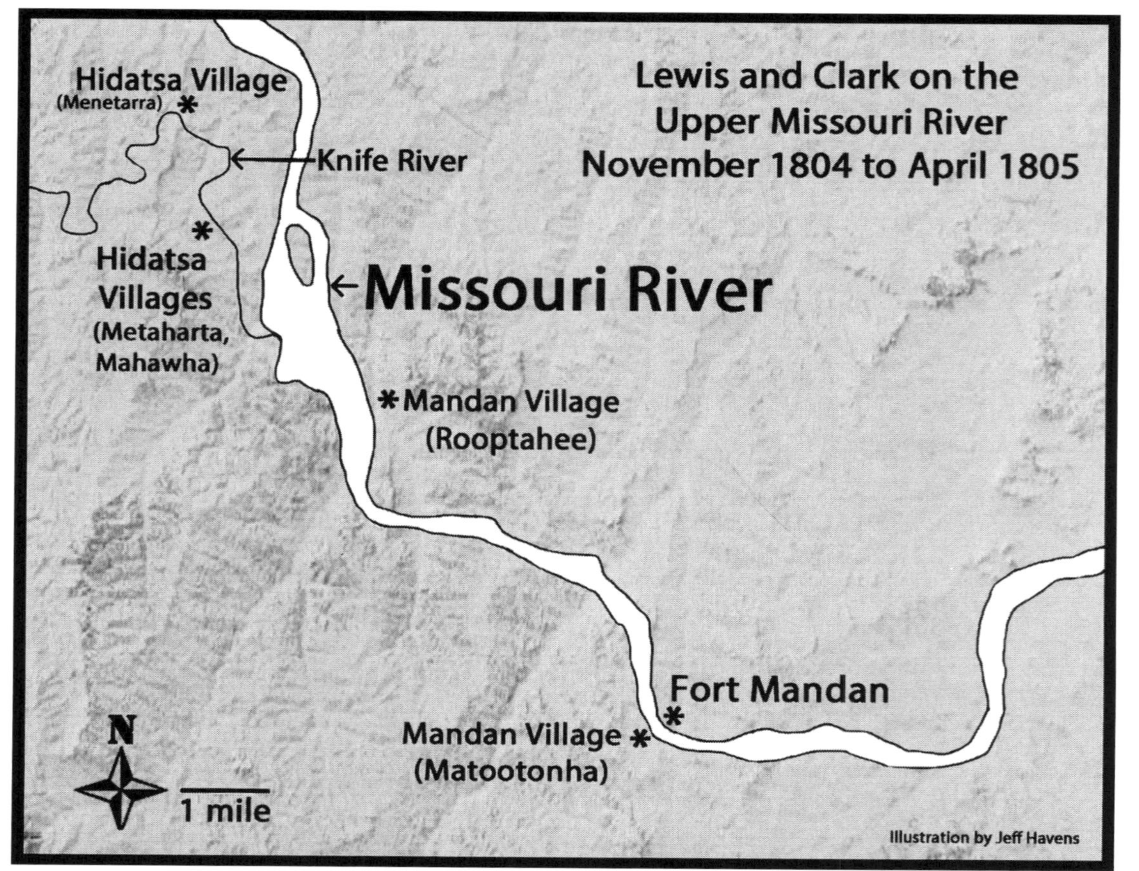
Lewis and Clark on the
Upper Missouri River
November 1804 to April 1805
Hidatsa Village
(Menetarra)
Knife River
Hidatsa
Villages
(Metaharta,
Mahawha)
Missouri River
Mandan Village
(Rooptahee)
Fort Mandan
Mandan Village
(Matootonha)
N
1 mile
Illustration by Jeff Havens

CHAPTER TWELVE
MANDAN

November 2, 1804
Assessment Camp: 1,603 miles above the Missouri confluence

Soon after breakfast, Captain Clark and four soldiers took the keelboat down three miles to a grove of cottonwood trees on the northeast bank across the river from the lower Mandan village. After a brief assessment and chance meeting of an Indian hunting party, he found the area suitable for building our winter quarters, pitched tents, and began felling trees with axes and saws for the foundation. In honor of our welcoming neighbors, Captain Clark and I named this place "Fort Mandan," which was 1,600 miles above the Missouri confluence. The location of our fort would provide easy access to the villages for trade, game for hunting, and wood to fuel our fires.

Given our resources for the garrison and possible attack, Sergeant Gass, Captain Clark, and I determined the best shape for the structure was an equilateral triangle. Both legs of the triangle were each to be 56 feet in length, while a portion of the base would serve as the entry and exit gate. Contained within each leg we planned four adjoining rooms — each room 14 feet in length and width, with ceilings seven feet in height, capable of comfortably housing five or six men. Inside every room would be a sleeping loft, and shared, stone fireplaces for heat and cooking. Considering the likelihood of Teton invaders, we decided the appropriate height of the outer walls should be 18 feet, which was nearly twice that for Dubois Camp — our fort in Illinois Territory the previous winter.

While Clark and his crew began constructing the fort, I took several men to visit the lower Mandan village, and called upon Chief Big White. He offered 11 bushels of corn for which we were grateful, and happily took back to camp. After our return, we bid farewell to Chief Eagle Feather who departed in a dugout canoe to return to his village. The Chief was accompanied by three Mandan warriors who planned to winter among the Arikara — a positive sign that peace had been successfully brokered. The canoe in which they were to travel was about 20 feet in length, and three feet in width with an equal number of seats. The vessel was made from the trunk of a large cottonwood tree whose center was painstakingly hollowed out using axes and adzes. This effort was backbreaking labor that consumed a fair amount of time, but was better than a bullboat for a long journey.

The following morning, I discharged the 10 engagés from further duty, and paid cash for their nearly six months of service. Five engagés soon commenced in constructing their own dugout in which they planned to eventually return to St. Louis sometime the following year.

One Frenchman named Jean Baptiste Lepage was hired to replace the discharged Newman. Lepage was a fur trader living among the Hidatsa and Mandan who explored the Black Hills and Little Missouri River regions of the west in previous outings. Although a man of no particular merit, his experience in these areas I thought might be of value when we resumed our journey. Two other boatmen elected to stay the winter at our fort, and the other three stayed with the Mandan.

On the 4th of the month, as we labored, a white man approached Captain Clark, me and other expedition members, including Private Labiche who was to my left. The man was dressed in flannel and deerskin, and appeared unusually well groomed for the occasion. Clark and I stopped work to observe him striding towards us.

"Salutations, Capitaine!" the man cheerfully said in an heavy French accent, as he reached out to offer his hand to me.

"Greetings to you too, Sir," I replied, gripping his hand firmly and shaking it for a moment.

He met my handshake with a limp response. His handshake suggested he was not a man of rigor or integrity. He said something in French. I turned to ask Labiche for help interpreting.

The strange man offered the same limp gesture to Captain Clark. Labiche ceased work and began to interpret for the man.

The two exchanged words, and Labiche reported: "Captain Lewis, he heard of your arrival and plan to explore the mountains next year. He wants to know if this is correct."

"Oui," I responded, nodding in the affirmative. "Private, kindly ask him to state his business," I said suspiciously.

Labiche conversed with the man, and relayed his response: "This is Toussaint Charbonneau. He is fluent in the language of The Gros Ventre … ahh … the Big Belly and French. He comes to offer his services as an interpreter, and that of his wives. His wives are Shoshone — or — ahh — Snake Indians from a village in the mountains near the river of the same name. He believes they could be of great service to us. … They know the language of the Big Belly and Snake Indians to the west."

As Labiche spoke, I examined Charbonneau and took mental notes about his arrogant smirk that distorted a puffy face, and accentuated his bulbous nose. His appearance was soft. Charbonneau was middle-aged, cowardly and had a conniving look and air about him that was disagreeable. However, I provided the benefit of doubt, and again extended my hand in friendship. I watched as his smirk transformed into a contrived smile designed to persuade. Regardless of his uninspiring appearance and character, I knew his offerings might prove of value, if they were as he claimed.

"Well?" I asked turning to Clark.

Tacitly agreeing with my initial assessment, Clark looked at the ground for a moment, and then glanced up at Charbonneau to further examine him before voicing an opinion.

"I reckon," he said in a quiet tone. "We'll probably need horses to get over the mountains. It would help to have an Indian interpreter for gettin' em. But I'm not sure about bringin' two women. One is more than needed. Two gums up the works for everyone."

I didn't think long before I responded: "Agreed."

I immediately turned to address Labiche: "Tell Mr. Charbonneau we would like to hire him, but he must perform labor as commanded, stand watch, limit the provisions he brings, and is not permitted to leave until we release him from service … He may also only bring one wife, and we must verify his credentials. If he agrees to these conditions, we are receptive of his application."

Labiche relayed the message. Charbonneau balked at the terms. They talked a few more seconds.

"Mr. Charbonneau wishes to bring both wives, and lodge in the fort this winter. He has one wife who is six months with child," Labiche explained.

I thought for a time and concluded it best to acquiesce, but added another condition: "This is fine provided Mr. Charbonneau understands he must honor the conditions, and not speak ill words to the Indians about the United States or any of its citizens," I demanded.

Charbonneau reacted positively to the terms.

"Merci, Capitaine. Merci — Au revoir," he said, as he used both hands to shake again with Captain Clark, Labiche, and me before he returned to his camp.

I later learned from Jusseaume — who was assigned the task of verifying Charbonneau's credentials — that Charbonneau frequently worked for the North West Company as an interpreter. Hidatsa Indians confirmed Charbonneau's' claim that both his wives could speak the Snake language, which secured his employment. Jusseaume said Charbonneau purchased his women about seven months prior to that date from Hidatsa warriors who captured them as war prizes. The warriors had taken the two girls four years earlier during a raid on a village near the headwaters of the Missouri. The pregnant teen was then close to 16 years in age, and was called "Bird Woman" or "Sacajawea."[A,13,37] Charbonneau's other wife, who was named "Otter Woman," was approximately as old as Sacajawea, but not pregnant.

The following day we continued our work on the buildings. Approximately 100 yards outside the fort, four men dug a latrine, which was about 10 feet in depth. This would provide for proper disposal of our waste, and create healthy conditions.

On the sixth of November, Gravelines, two French choreboys who came with our hired boatmen, and Engagés Paul Primeau and Jean Baptiste La Jeunesse slid their newly constructed dugout canoe into the water, with plans to winter among the Arikara. We thanked them for their service, instructed Gravelines to escort Chief Eagle Feather to Washington the succeeding year, and bid them farewell. Many of our men stopped to watch the group, as they floated quickly downriver in the light of the late afternoon. The cloud-filtered sun illuminated their backs, until they disappeared around a southerly bend in the river.

Later that night, Sergeant Pryor awoke Captain Clark and me to witness a magnificent display in the form of the northern lights. Brilliant, waving streaks and floating columns of green, violet, and white lights danced vertically and horizontally about 20 degrees above the horizon. This was truly a privilege to be given an opportunity to observe such a grand phenomenon of nature. As I watched, I was overwhelmed with curiosity as to what could be the source of this impressive exhibition. However, there was but little time for such contemplation. More pragmatic issues were before us, which included procuring rocks and stones that would comprise our chimneys for the fort.

Five days passed since the nighttime display, during which much progress was made toward completing the fort. However progress had a price: Privates McNeal and Shields inadvertently cut their legs with axes while chopping notches in logs. Soon after I treated their wounds, Charbonneau arrived at the fort with both his wives. He also brought four buffalo robes for me and Captain Clark, as a gesture of gratitude for his being hired. We exchanged pleasantries, and the trio went back to their camp with the Hidatsa.

The following day, my medical skills were again called into action. Three men fell ill with symptoms consistent with venereal disease. The afflicted said the symptoms included a burning sensation when urinating, accompanied by a white discharge. For this ailment, I distributed an ointment for topical application, which contained a salt of mercury. I had little doubt the men had acquired the malady during their sexual interludes with the Arikara women.

Half past ten in the evening on the 12th of November, Captain Clark returned from the latrine to report that ice was forming in the river. The temperature had dramatically fallen 42 degrees Fahrenheit in six hours, from 60 in the afternoon to 18 by the time Clark took notice. Nature had delivered a dire warning that our expedition should advance no further this season, lest we risk being trapped in a more inhospitable environment. However, given the climate and remoteness of this location, I could not imagine a worse place any sane person would choose to reside for any length of time during the year. Why the Indians chose to live here was a mystery to me, despite my knowledge of facts regarding the matter.

The following day, Chief Black Cat brought with him a chief and seven other members of the Assiniboine nation. Captain Clark learned that they were related to the Teton-Sioux, and their disposition was just as unseemly. The Assiniboine resided primarily in British territory, but often traveled south to trade and hunt.

Given their surly behavior, fondness of whiskey, and relation to the Teton, Clark and I later determined to avoid these fellows when we resumed our long journey in early spring.

Regardless of floating ice in the river, and my most charitable opinion of this area, the same day Clark met with the Assiniboine, I took six men in the white pirogue upriver to obtain more stones for completing our chimneys. We loaded hundreds of pounds of material into the boat. Upon our return, the sheer weight and swift current caused our vessel to run aground on a sandbar. We labored two hours in icy waters before extricating ourselves, while our feet and lower legs began to freeze. After arriving back at camp, we revived the men with an extra ration of whiskey, while I treated Private Hugh Hall's feet for frostbite. I could only hope Private Hall's experience would be the last of this season, but knew the worst of the frigid weather was yet to come.

Three days passed, and we awoke to fog that froze in the night. It coated all the trees and grasses in a significant layer of frost and ice. I had never experienced such conditions in the States, and was fascinated with how such an icy environment muffled sounds, slowed the pace of life, and simultaneously provided visual delights with uneasy comfort. Especially in this wilderness, the same surroundings that offered such visual wonders could just as easily extinguish life with its cold embrace, if not respected with adequate preparation and sensible judgment, combined with a bit of good fortune.

During the ensuing days, we worked toward completion of the fort, and prepared for winter. The men began daubing the walls with clay to seal chinks between logs, and placed the roof on the smokehouse. On the roof, we installed a temporary platform on which the sentry could walk and observe the surroundings from more than 20 feet above ground. At opposite ends of the platform, we mounted the two swivel guns we had removed from the upper deck of the keelboat. In the center of the courtyard, we secured the cannon to a large tree stump.

While this was occurring, the hunting party returned from its two-week absence with significant numbers of game: 32 deer, 12 elk, and one buffalo. Upon arriving, these animals were immediately skinned and hung up in the smokehouse for cooking and preservation. Their hides were to be made into clothes by our tailor-in-residence, Private Joseph Whitehouse. By this time, many of the men's clothes and shoes they were issued in May were in need of replacement or repair. The animal hides and sheets of flannel we brought fit this need.

With most of the fort construction complete by the 20th, Charbonneau abandoned his home among the Hidatsa. He, Otter Woman, and Sacajawea loaded their belongings and some buffalo meat onto four horses, forded the river near the village, and made their way to our garrison.

At the same time they moved into their new hut, Captain Clark and I completed setting up ours, which is where we welcomed three chiefs from the upper Mandan village that afternoon. They reported bad news. The chiefs informed us the Teton moved north of the Cheyenne River near the Arikara villages to enable them to stage raids against the Mandan that winter. Apparently, the Teton were displeased with the fact we brokered peace between the Mandan and Arikara. We allayed the Mandan chiefs by pledging to assist in their defense against the Teton at whatever cost to the expedition.

This disturbing knowledge about Teton movement made us understandably apprehensive of a possible attack. It also fed our alarm late on the 22nd of November when Private Shields alerted us of a developing incident: A Mandan warrior from the upper Mandan village was threatening to kill his wife with a very large and intimidating knife.

Shields was the sentry on duty when his patrol led him to investigate a disturbance that was about 60 yards from the fort at Jusseaume's camp. After quickly assessing the startling situation, Shields raced to notify Captain Clark and me. Clark immediately dressed and went to the site.

On his arrival, he looked on in horror when he saw a badly beaten woman who was bleeding from three stab wounds on her hands and right arm. She was cowering behind Jusseaume, and his Mandan wife, Talking Crow.[B] Clark spoke with Jusseaume and learned the terrified woman was named "Radiant Day." She had come to his camp to seek refuge from her enraged husband, and gain access to the hut in which Sacajawea and Otter Woman resided. According to Jusseaume, Radiant Day said her husband was incensed that she had a sexual encounter with Sergeant Ordway soon after our arrival. As a result, the couple had a bitter argument, and the woman left to lodge with women belonging to Charbonneau and Jusseaume. Upon her return, the argument resumed, which led her to flee once more.

Clark was already aware of Ordway's nocturnal interlude. The Captain looked at the husband with dismay and turned to Jusseaume: "Inform him who I am and ask his name."

Clark said this as he turned his eyes back toward the jilted husband. The husband tightly clutched a large knife in this right hand, which was partially covered in blood.

Jusseaume exchanged words with the Indian.

"He said his name is Two Bears, and if the Sergeant wants his wife he would give her to him."

Clark disapprovingly shook his head. "Tell him we do not want his wife, but I will order Sergeant Ordway to give him some goods."

The tension on Two Bears' face eased somewhat upon hearing the news. But the Indian said nothing. He continued to breathe heavily, as he glared at his wife standing behind Jusseaume and Talking Crow.

Clark followed up the offer with additional remarks: "Tell him that not one man of this party touched his wife except the one he had given for the night, and he did so in his own bed, not Two Bears'."

Jusseaume paused to glance at Clark, and give the Captain an opportunity to reconsider his remarks. Clark was certain.

"Please tell him, Mr. Jusseaume," Clark said, as he gestured with his hand.

Jusseaume relayed the comment. Two Bears appeared puzzled. Before he could react, Clark had more words for the husband. The Captain placed his hand on Jusseaume's shoulder, as Clark continued to eye the confused Indian.

"Tell him no one in our party would touch a woman, if they knew her to be the wife of another man. Also, tell him that I will issue an order that no man of our party will have intercourse with this woman again under penalty of punishment."

This message further calmed Two Bears, and Clark offered to shake hands with the man. The warrior switched the knife to his other hand, and reached out to meet Clark's gesture of conciliation.

"Two Bears, go and live happily together in the future," Clark said with conviction and certainty.

At that moment, Chief Black Cat emerged from the darkness, after being apprised of Two Bears' assault on Radiant Day. The Chief scolded Two Bears, reminded him that we were gifted with medicine, and urged the couple to return to the village. The unhappy pair departed, but Black Cat stayed with us.

The incident demonstrated the many complexities of building relationships with the Indians at all levels, and we had yet to master any. Considering these intricacies and given Ordway's ordeal, Captain Clark and I vowed to not have any additional sexual interludes with women, regardless of our desires.

Adding to these complexities was the fact we had yet to confer with the Hidatsa. As a result, I decided to pay a visit to Chief Serpent at the Menetarra village. On horseback with me went Jusseaume and Charbonneau, while six soldiers took the white pirogue up the Missouri. To meet us at the village, the boat made its way northwest, and turned into the Knife River where we greeted them, as they coasted ashore. Despite some time and effort, we were unable to locate Serpent, and instead attempted to meet with another chief named Horned Weasel. Upon arriving, we were curtly informed by one of his warriors that the Chief was not home. This was most surprising and suspect because I was aware that these exact words were used by Englishmen when they did not wish to receive unwelcomed callers. Given the circumstances, I did not believe this inhospitable reception was coincidence. Despite this, the whole of our party were welcomed into another lodge for the evening by an empathetic family.

At the same time we were experiencing our peculiar reception, Captain Clark was incongruously greeting two Hidatsa chiefs at the fort — one of whom was named "Red Shield." With both interpreters with me and unable to verbally communicate, all Clark could do was offer a few small gifts. However, all this was unknown to us at the time, since we were about 20 miles from the fort.

In the morning, we traveled from Menetarra to the Metaharta village, which was approximately two miles south. Concerned about his wives, and not in need of his services, Charbonneau requested to return home, which I granted. As we proceeded without Charbonneau, we happened upon a Mr. Charles McKenzie — a French-and English-speaking clerk from the North West Company. He worked under Francois-Antoine Larocque, and was heading north on an errand for Larocque, as we were heading south.

The North West Company, along with Hudson's Bay Company represented competition for the natives' allegiances, and I was suspect of their motives. They were based about four to five days travel northeast from Fort Mandan, near the confluence of the Assiniboine and Souris rivers. Because of the United States' acquisition of land in the Louisiana Purchase, I believed the companies continued business and political activity in this region was illegal because such activity was not addressed in the Jay Treaty of 1794. The treaty allowed traders from Great Britain and the United States to work in each other's territory, provided they adhered to stipulations of the host nation. Regardless, I understood that President Jefferson's policy was to allow such international trade, if it did not threaten United States' interests.

We exchanged pleasantries with McKenzie, and informed him of the purpose of our stay. He responded by saying Larocque was below at Metaharta, and would like to introduce him to us. McKenzie turned his horse, and we went to the village. There, I invited McKenzie and Larocque to attend a council I planned to hold with Chiefs Black Moccasin and Little Fox.

Mr. Larocque appeared to be in his early twenties, was well-educated, and affable. He had recently arrived at the village, and was eager to prove his worth to superiors. Although not as tall as his boss, Mr. McKenzie was very similar to Larocque in manner and behavior.

In Black Moccasin's lodge, I gave the usual speech, and offered them clothing, medals and flags. However, not all the Hidatsa accepted the gifts. This too struck me as strange, and I had a difficult time understanding the origin of their resistance. But the chiefs did pledge to not conduct further raids on the Snake Indians. Through Jusseaume, the Hidatsa then expressed discontent with our very presence. I silently attributed these feelings to irreconcilable jealously, in no small part because we chose to locate our fort near the Mandan instead of the Hidatsa. Similar to my dealings with the Otoe the previous summer, I chose to pursue further discussions with the leaders of this village at a later date, rather than risk additional confrontation. As an entertaining diversion to astonish and intimidate, I suggested the group witness a demonstration of my air gun, to which they heartily agreed.

Recognizing a break in the activity, Larocque asked me for Charbonneau's interpretation services for his negotiations with the Indians. Charbonneau had previously performed such work for North West workers. I reluctantly agreed, and reminded him that Charbonneau was then under our employ, and his duties for the United States took precedence over any and all British interests. Despite my acrimony toward the British, I invited him to meet Captain Clark and me at the fort for supper the next day.

In need of salvaging what was an evolving diplomatic disaster, later in the day we traveled to the third Hidatsa village called Mahawha. There, I was able to convince Chiefs Big Stealer and Calumet Bird Tail to provide us lodging for the night, and visit the fort in the morning. My belief was that a change of venue might have a more positive outcome than the one of that day. The chiefs also wished to bring with them a man of considerable regard whose name was Two Eagles.[C] Our hosts treated us well, which provided for a comfortable night.

Early the following day, all five of us were astride our horses plodding toward the fort where nearly all the men were busy chopping and placing large picket logs around the buildings. The wall construction crew included the six men from the pirogue who preceded us by several hours. Upon viewing the fort, cannon, and guns, the chiefs and Two Eagles did not express any impression. I escorted the Indians into our hut for the council, and soon learned why our visit to the big Hidatsa village was met with enmity.

Jusseaume conversed with the group for a minute. He then turned toward me.

"Big Stealer said he and the others were alarmed to learn that you joined the Sioux. They think you plan on killing them sometime this winter."

My eyes widened in surprise at this astonishing news. I shook my head in disbelief. I glanced at Captain Clark who sat there, stunned. I collected myself and replied.

"Who said this?" I asked incredulously.

"They said the Mandan," Jusseaume replied.

With his mouth agape, Clark blankly stared and listened as our interpreter continued:

"The Mandan also said if any Hidatsa visited the fort, you would kill them. They claimed this is why Mr. Charbonneau and I moved our families from their village to the fort. This is why they had not come to visit sooner," Jusseaume concluded.

Shocked, I thought for a moment about the disputes between the other tribes on the lower section of the Missouri. Despite my best efforts, many natives unfortunately had yet to embrace President Jefferson's grand vision of commerce. In this case, the most logical explanation for the Mandan's words was they hoped to limit the Hidatsa's opportunities to acquire goods from us and future merchants.

"Tell them these reports are obviously not true, otherwise they'd be dead by now," I said, exasperated.

"We are here not to trade, but to open the road for other merchants. Future trade depends on peace between all Indians, including the Mandan and Hidatsa. Soon, the best, and most, goods will come from the south, not the north. They must understand this," I remarked.

Jusseaume relayed the message to the three Indians who appeared to appreciate my words. They spoke in hushed tones among themselves for a few minutes, and soon responded.

"The chiefs said this is enough talk for today. They heard of your dancing, and want to see for themselves."

Before we could grant their request, the arrival of seven North West Company members was announced, which included Larocque, McKenzie, and Jean Baptiste Lafrance.

Mr. Lafrance had accompanied Jusseaume to this area in 1793, and was a regular visitor to the Mandan and Hidatsa. Similar to Charbonneau, Lafrance also served as one of the North West Company's interpreters.

To properly host our guests, I initiated more greetings, discussed additional issues, and shared our supper with them. With the meal complete and to satisfy the chiefs, the men entertained our visitors by dancing much of the evening, while Cruzatte tirelessly played the fiddle. In accordance with the festive atmosphere, former Engagé Francois Rivet upstaged everyone by demonstrating an amazing feat of upper-body strength and agility: He stood on his hands, danced around the room, and spun on his head.

During the course of the evening, Captain Clark and I discretely learned from Chiefs Calumet Bird Tail and Big Stealer that Mr. Lafrance had previously asserted the best deals and goods could only come from their company. The chiefs also claimed that Lafrance said America could not supply or fulfill their material needs. Shortly after hearing this, Clark and I patiently waited for a time we could ask McKenzie and Larocque to step outside for a brief discussion. The time quickly came and we exited. Standing in the snow, Clark and I confronted the pair about their interpreter's unfavorable comments, and advised them to cease and desist or suffer the consequences. Larocque and McKenzie acknowledged the warning, but said nothing as to whether they would address our grievance with Lafrance. Satisfied the notice was delivered, we went inside to close the evening with a drink of reconciliation.

The following day, after the North West representatives had departed for the Menetarra village, Mandan Chief Black Cat arrived with his entourage. We gave the Indians arm bands, handkerchiefs, paint, and tobacco. On our parting, after a positive meeting, we learned from the chiefs that during travels throughout this area, North West Company representatives routinely awarded medals and flags to esteemed chiefs. I quickly determined that this activity could not be further allowed by any foreign company on American soil, especially the British. This was much more than gifts or exchange of goods; this was a foreign nation designating leaders, and an attempt to usurp a developing American policy. We advised the chiefs not to accept such symbols, if offered, or risk incurring the displeasure of their Great American Father.

After the chiefs departed, and a nighttime storm that dumped 13 inches of snow, Larocque and McKenzie visited the fort late on the 29th of November to inquire about the use of Charbonneau's services, again. Fortunate this was, for we had just dispatched Sergeant Pryor to summon Larocque to answer questions regarding the awarding of flags and medals. In our hut with Charbonneau and Labiche, we confronted the pair, once more.[D]

"Please, take a chair," I cheerfully invited Larocque and McKenzie.

They sat down next to the fireplace. Seaman inspected each by rubbing his wet nose on the men's hands. I focused my attention on them.

"The United States does not plan on forbidding you to trade with the Indians. However, I understand you want to recognize chiefs with medals and flags," I stated in a serious manner.

Larocque and McKenzie's eyes repeatedly shifted between Captain Clark and me — hoping to detect any breach in unity.

"This cannot stand, and I forbid you from continuing this practice," I ordered with the utmost conviction.

Larocque paused for a moment, glanced at Clark, and replied in a conniving manner: "Captain Lewis, we run no risk of disobeying your command, since we carry no such objects," he insisted. "Rather than an adversary, I ask that you consider having me accompany you next spring."

I paused for a strategy, and to increase pressure on the young businessman. Larocque perceived my reticence, and hurriedly interjected to break the tense silence and save face.

"I came mainly to request the services of Mr. Charbonneau," he added, as a diversion to the discussion.

I quickly gathered my thoughts and responded: "Mr. Charbonneau may continue to work for you, provided our previous agreement stands, and he does not utter a word to the Indians that may prejudice them against the United States or any of its citizens. This applies even if you order him to do so. Agreed?"

Larocque processed the proposal. "Oui, Capitaine."

"Do you understand this, Mr. Charbonneau?" I asked, examining the expression on his rotund face.

Labiche translated the words from English to French for Charbonneau who responded: "Oui," while nodding acknowledgement.

I purposely avoided answering the question of whether we would allow Larocque to accompany us, knowing I had no intention of allowing a goddamn Brit go with us the following spring. Regardless of whether he went, I hoped this would be the last of uneasy diplomatic issues we would have to deal with for a time. With the confrontation complete, I suggested we adjourn for whiskey, food, and more pleasant discussions to reconstruct our frayed relationship, to which they were receptive.

However, despite my want of tranquility, a much greater predicament arose the next day. This occurred soon after Larocque, McKenzie, and Charbonneau had departed to conduct business.

The early sun lit Chief Big White's figure as he exited his lodge and trudged through deep snow towards the riverbank. As the Chief plowed through the powdery substance, each time Big White exhaled large plumes of opaque vapor emanated from his nose and mouth and dissipated into the 17-degree morning air. A long trail of compacted snow lay in the wake of the distraught Chief who was wrapped in a large buffalo robe. He stopped at a small cliff near the river and began to shout in the direction of the fort, which was some 100 yards away. Between the worried chief and fort, the water flowed. Numerous chunks of ice of varying size and shape floated before him, as he urgently yelled to capture someone's attention.

Private McNeal was the sentry on guard. He was pacing back and forth on a wooden runway situated on top of the smokehouse roof when he reacted to the origin of the noise. In the distance, he saw the silhouette of the Indian calling to him. McNeal scurried from the roof, down a ladder, and across the courtyard to alert me, Captain Clark, and Jusseaume of the disturbance. We rushed from our quarters, and hurried to the shoreline. Jusseaume said Big White had news to report. He requested that we cross the river. Captain Clark quickly put together a small detail of men to ferry the Chief to the fort in the white pirogue. We greeted the Chief, and escorted him into our hut. Big White had a solemn appearance, as he addressed his words to Jusseaume who relayed the urgent message to us.

"Big White said five of his men were ambushed yesterday about 20 miles southwest of here, while they were hunting. One man was killed, two were wounded, and nine horses were stolen," Jusseaume reported.

The two exchanged more words, while the Chief emphasized his points with dramatic hand gestures.

"He also expects they will soon be attacked by an army of Sioux," Jusseaume said with urgency.

Clark and I exchanged concerned looks.

"Tell the Chief we thank him for alerting us. We need time to develop a plan," I replied in great haste.

Big White listened. We shook hands again, and he returned to his village.

About an hour later, Captain Clark had assembled 23 men on the opposite shore, including Jusseaume, to reconnoiter the woods along the river south of the first Mandan village. Clark led the armed contingency. They marched in battle formation plowing through 18 inches of snow, among the leafless trees. Seeing no Teton, the group turned north toward the village. The intimidating force slowly paced out of the river bottom, up a rise, and onto a plain to arrive within sight of the lower village — having then traveled nearly six miles.

A few villagers observed the unknown unit, gradually approaching, far off in the distance. In a panic, runners alerted others. Warriors gathered their weapons, and women rushed children to the lodges for protection. Dozens of fighters and Big White formed a human wall to shield the village. As they watched the tiny silhouettes advance, the Indians boldly stood facing the advancing group — ready to fend off an attack. Soon the tension was relieved when Big White recognized the uniforms and faces of Captain Clark and Jusseaume. The Chief shouted to his men that the party was not hostile, and walked out to meet Clark under the noonday sun. Big White invited the Captain into his lodge to discuss a plan of action and for the soldiers to stay and eat in any lodge they chose to visit. Clark sat down on a buffalo robe, along with Jusseaume.

"Tell the Chief we have come here to assist in chastising the enemy of our dutiful children," Clark said to Jusseaume.

Big White seemed quite puzzled.

"The Chief doesn't quite understand, Captain," Jusseaume remarked.

"Ask him to repeat the circumstance of the Sioux attack, as it happened," Clark replied.

Jusseaume and Big White exchanged words, which were communicated to Clark. The Captain nodded in understanding.

"Ask him to send runners to the other villages and gather warriors. We want to punish the Sioux."

Big White and Little Crow conversed between themselves for several minutes, considering how best to react. Big White turned to Jusseaume.

"The Chief says they know you speak the truth. They are impressed you were ready to protect them and kill those who did not listen to your councils. The Arikara and Sioux spilled Mandan blood and went home. The snow is deep, and it is cold. The horses cannot travel under these conditions. If you go in the spring after the snow is gone, they will assemble all the warriors and brave men in all the villages to go with you," Jusseaume explained.

Clark thought for a moment and remarked: "We understand their situation, and wish to assist in defending them at anytime during our stay. The Arikara vowed to be at peace with you and the Sioux. Please do not to get angry with the Arikara, until you are certain of their involvement in the attack."

The Chief reacted favorably. He also offered to share a meal with Clark and Jusseaume, before they, and the rest of the men departed. After enjoying satisfying food with the Chief and his family, Big White suggested the group return to the garrison on a stable layer of ice. Taking the Chief's advice, the party crossed the river on foot, less than a quarter-mile upstream from the village. Soon after their arrival, I refreshed them with a generous amount of tafia rum I procured for just such an occasion. This invigorating liquid was in addition to the whiskey and brandy I also brought for the journey. The men were very much pleased and surprised with the inebriating gift, which seemed an appropriate reward for their dauntless bravery.

This delightful indulgence eased our transition into a month of the most brutal cold any of us had ever experienced.

Captain Clark arose at sunrise on the first of December to sleepily make his way to read the thermometer hanging from a post outside our door. He focused on the column of mercury encased in glass, widened his eyes in disbelief, and recorded the value in his weather log; one degree below zero. Although this was the first day the temperature was below zero that season, all hands were soon engaged in working on the outer wall, despite the frigid weather.

In the evening, a competitor of the North West Company paid a visit. His name was George Henderson of the Hudson's Bay Company. Henderson said he was sent to trade with the Big Bellies, and had learned of our arrival after his appearance at one of the villages. He had a pleasant disposition and keen knowledge of the area.

Since receiving its business charter in 1670, Hudson's Bay Company had been in the region searching for the Northwest Passage — an easy water route connecting the Atlantic and Pacific Oceans — and in the process discovered the abundant furs and pelts in the region that they acquired for trade and shipment back east and to Europe.[16] Finding the Passage meant the potential for great wealth. It represented future commerce along the entire route, and prosperity for inhabitants living along its path. More recently, since 1795, Hudson's Bay had been trading regularly with the Mandan and Hidatsa for pelts and horses.

By mid-morning the next day, Chief Big White came to the fort to inform us that buffalo were making their way from the prairie to the riverbanks. Apparently, these animals searched for grasses and tree buds in areas near the river when snow became too deep on the plains. With such easy targets amassing so close to the fort, I gathered 15 men to hunt in comfortable conditions, with temperatures in the mid-30s. Within three hours, we shot 10 buffalo, while the Mandan killed 50 of the beasts. As the men processed the meat in the smokehouse later that afternoon, several Mandan chiefs visited. They brought with them four Cheyenne Indians who occupied land near the source of the Platte River in mountains far to the southwest of our fort. They arrived with a peace pipe, and we gave them a flag, tobacco, and a copy of the speech I gave to our new Arikara friends.

On the 5th of December, Sergeant Gass laid the permanent platform upon the smokehouse roof for the sentinel walk. On the 7th, the river froze solid in front of the fort to a depth of nearly two inches. Amazingly, it did this within a few hours during the night, after the air stayed below 20 degrees for 36 hours.

Unfortunately, this also meant our boats were then completely encased in ice, and easily removing them from the river was no longer possible. I had not anticipated such an occurrence would happen that early in the season, and thought we had another month before the boats needed to be removed.

At sunrise, the temperature was again one degree below zero. Shortly afterward, Chief Big White arrived at the garrison to tell us the buffalo were heading to the river, once more. This time I took 12 men out, and we shot 11 buffalo, while the Indians took 40 of the burly beasts.

The natives had their horses trained to advance within a few feet of the fleeing buffalo. At that time, the warrior shot his rifle or arrow, and the action alerted the horse to abruptly turn perpendicular from the wounded buffalo to prevent a counter-attack, which I thought to be a terrific feat by man and horse.

As the hunt continued, one by one, prairie wolves gathered to scavenge for whatever they could forage. After spending several hours in zero-degree weather, three men were badly frostbitten on their feet and ears, which I later treated with cool water, and an extra half-gill of whiskey for the effort.

About five miles upstream during the night, a small herd of buffalo headed from the plain down to the riverbank. Without hesitation, the lead bull stepped onto the thin ice, followed by eight others. The group was oblivious to the sudden cracking sounds, and continued to follow the male, as he stepped toward the center of the river. Water began bubbling up in huge quantities from the many fissures. Suddenly, a huge section gave way with a thunderous snap, and all nine buffalo plunged into the frigid Missouri. The cold water surrounded the animals, and the dramatic temperature drop shocked the lead bull, despite his thick hide. The bull instinctively gasped for air, but instead inhaled the cold waters of the river. His legs frantically kicked to swim, while he repeatedly turned his gigantic head from side to side, up and down, searching for air. Rather than rescue, the current swept the great beast under the ice where he soon expired, after a great effort to save himself. The flow pushed him a short way downstream where he was snagged by a submerged tree. Here, he would stay the remainder of the season until the spring sunshine released his carcass from winter's clutch. The bull's eight followers quickly met a similar fate, not far from the hopeless bull.

As the buffalo remained under the ice as perfectly preserved meat, above, the morning air was very cold and heavy with an icy fog. At 12 below zero, it was more frigid than I had ever known it to be in Virginia. This day was Captain Clark's turn to lead the men on the hunt. During the outing, the men observed a curious phenomenon, but not nearly as wondrous as the northern lights; the sun appeared to have a bright and distinct halo. The outer reflection made it appear as if there were a large white ring around the sun.

As the sun began to set, Clark and the men returned to report that they had killed eight buffalo, but they also regretted to report that three more men had frostbitten feet. York got the worst of the weather; not only were his feet frostbitten, his penis had also frozen.[E] This burly man was reduced to tears — crying in the fetal position. He lay on his bed for more than an hour, while it slowly and painfully thawed. York may have been Clark's servant, but all of us were men, and could not have been more understanding of his predicament. Listening to his tormented groans was excruciating for everyone, which made enjoying the extra ration of rum impossible.

On the 10th of December, the temperature at sunrise was 10 degrees below zero, and 11 above at four in the afternoon. Captain Clark and I agreed to relieve the night sentinel every hour whenever conditions became this cold. We also issued a capote blanket to those who wanted this long, hooded coat. The following day was even colder. We determined it too bitter to hunt at twenty-one below, and did the same on the next when the thermometer dipped to thirty-eight below. We did little of anything, but struggle to keep our fires lit and bodies warm in these most brutal winter conditions we had ever known.

Despite the air being barely above zero on the 15th, several chiefs and warriors were outside at play. They were engaged in a gambling sport called "chungkee."[20] To describe this physical game with words is an exercise of great difficulty. However, chungkee is best summarized as an amusement of immense beauty, which was also fine training for the heart and mind.

Between the earthen lodges, at a distance of about 50 yards, two men from opposing parties ran abreast on a smooth surface. One man rolled a stone ring, which was about three inches in diameter. At the same time, the other slid a stick after the ring. The stick was about six feet in length, and affixed at even intervals with leather strips along its body. The objective of the game was to situate the stick and its leather strips as close to the ring as possible or in the ring. Warriors made bets, and the chiefs held the stakes.

The following day was also frigid at 22 below. However, this did not deter Mr. Hugh Heney of the North West Company from delivering documents from his senior supervisor, Charles Chaboillez.

Unlike business partners Gravelines, Tabeau, Dorion, and Vallé, Heney was not a former associate of Régis Loisel — the fur trader based in La Charrette, some 1,500 miles below.

The documents carried by Heney were in response to the letter I had sent Chaboillez the previous month. Chaboillez provided information about our planned route west, expressed a great desire to serve us in any manner possible, and described the country between the Missouri and Mississippi rivers. While Chaboillez expressed his support, Mr. Heney described a root from the Echinacea plant that he believed might be very useful in treating maladies we may suffer, such as toothaches, snakebites, and insect stings. Accompanying Heney were Larocque and George Budge, a clerk with Hudson's Bay Company. They gave us tobacco and remained the night, correctly thinking it too cold to search for alternate lodging.

Soon after sunset, the thermometer mercury dropped below zero, and continued its dramatic plunge to a cold we had yet to experience. Each hour, the new sentry dreaded having to leave the warmth and comfort of the hut, to endure the frigid weather for an hour of guard duty. Meanwhile, the sentinel on duty waited with great anticipation for his opportunity to thaw on this hoary night, before he too became another frostbite victim.

"God … ddddamn, I'm haaapppy to sssee you," Private McNeal stuttered, as he shivered uncontrollably. He anxiously watched his relief climb the ladder to the smokehouse roof. "It's cooolder than ahhh witch's teat."

"Well, wish me luck then," Private Shields replied in a despondent tone, as he reluctantly stepped onto the walkway, his rifle slung across his shoulder. "It's so goddamn cold I doubt this thing will even work," Shields remarked to himself, as he examined his rifle. "Who the hell would be out here, anyway?" he questioned himself.

McNeal happily, but carefully, stepped down the ladder, and made his way across the courtyard on the compacted snow. His feet were nearly frozen. Before entering the hut, curiosity captured the best of him. Under the moonlight, he could not read the thermometer through the ice crystals frozen to his eyelashes. He removed his fur-lined mittens, and reached up to pinch his eyelashes between his thumbs and forefingers. The ice melted. With the frozen obstructions removed, he leaned forward and focused. In disbelief, he glanced once more at the thermometer, while his teeth chattered and his mind comprehended the intense chill he felt throughout his body — 45 degrees below zero. He could scarcely believe what he saw.

We thought it best to remain indoors all the next day. We played backgammon, and learned about the Indians far to the west from Mr. Heney. The men also constructed sleds on which we could haul meat.

By the 21st, there was a break from the intense cold, and Two Bears brought both his wives to the fort. This was the man who had stabbed Radiant Day the previous month. He showed great anxiety, and said through our interpreter that he begged for Sergeant Ordway to forgive him for his wicked behavior. Ordway reacted favorably. Two Bears was much relieved. Along with Two Bears and his wives, came a woman named Standing Elk who brought with her a child.[F] The child had a severe abscess on the lower portion of his back, which was swollen and red. In exchange for my medical skills and treatment, she offered as much corn as she could carry, which we gladly accepted.

On the 22nd, the outer wall was nearly completed. As the soldiers worked setting up the picketed logs, a large number of women, and Indian men dressed as women, arrived with a huge amount of corn and beans for trade. Although back east homosexual, male transvestites were an oddity worthy of scorn, here, they were an accepted part of the culture as conveyors of great spiritual power.[9] We curiously accepted the group, and offered them old shirts, awls, knives, looking glasses, beads, buttons, and other articles pleasing to the eye in exchange for their food. By this time, the food was greatly needed.

Christmas Eve finally arrived, and the men had completed the outer wall. The only construction that remained was to lay the wooden floors in the interpreters' hut and blacksmith shop. Captain Clark requested the natives not visit the fort the following day to enable us to celebrate completion of the fort, a belated winter solstice, and provide the men of Christian faith time to honor their Messiah on their holy day.

On Christmas morning, Privates Colter and Shields loaded the courtyard cannon with powder just before sunrise, while the rest of the soldiers filled their rifles with the same. Upon Sergeant Pryor's order the swivel gun was fired, which went off with a thunderous boom. The deafening sound wrested Captain Clark and me from a deep slumber. That sound was followed by another from all the men's rifles being fired simultaneously. Soon afterward, the swivel gun was fired once more for a boisterous start to a special day.

"Well, we should do this right, if we're going to celebrate," Captain Clark remarked with a mischievous grin.

He finished pulling on his boots, walked to the whiskey cabinet, and reached in to grab a bottle. I followed his lead by placing a cup for each man on a table situated near the center of the room. He began to fill each cup with two ounces of the delightful treat.

"Hell of a breakfast, Captain Clark," I laughed.

"It's the least we can do for the spirits," Clark replied.

"Indeed — spirits for the spirits!" I joked ineffectively.

Clark smiled and nodded. He poured the last drink, set down the bottle, and grabbed two mugs. Reaching out, he gave me one.

"Merry Christmas, Captain Lewis," he said, raising his mug in toast.

"And a happy solstice to you, Sir," I responded, as our cups clunked together.

I drank all the whiskey in one big gulp, while Clark opted to sip. He then exited, and informed the men where they could obtain their intoxicating present.

At ten that morning, we raised the flag and fired the swivel gun three more times, and gave the men another round of whiskey. We then cleared one of the rooms of furniture for a dance. Half the men were sent to hunt, while the other half began dancing to the violins of Privates Cruzatte and Gibson. At one o'clock, the swivel gun was fired again to signal the hunting party that dinner was ready, which was complete with rum, instead of whiskey. A little more than an hour later, Private Colter lit the fuse to the gun one last time, which notified all to assemble for the dance. This was truly a delightful day. The only women in attendance were Sacajawea, Otter Woman, and Talking Crow who did not dance, but appeared to thoroughly enjoy watching the festivities, which ended at eight in the evening.

During the final days of December, the Indians were much impressed with our forge-and-bellows method of making iron tools and other metal sundries. The forge itself was heated with charcoal, and operated by Privates Shields, Willard, and Bratton. Meanwhile, Sergeant Gass finished the floors in the smith shop and interpreters' hut. So awed were the natives with the work of Shields and Willard, they brought their cutting axes and kettles to fix in exchange for corn, beans, and squash.

In total, there were 16 days in December in which the thermometer was below zero at sunrise. However, we all knew January would prove worse. I tried not to contemplate this, and what better diversion than another party for the New Year.

The following day, Privates McNeal and Shields loaded the swivel gun, lit the firing taper, and ignited the fuse to the gun. The burning cord loudly hissed, as the men watched and listened. It fizzled away becoming shorter with each second, until the gun powder caught fire and exploded with a tremendous booming noise. At that same moment, a shock wave burst through the air, pushing past the men. McNeal, Shields, and the rest of the soldiers could not contain their juvenile glee. They laughed heartily at the whole affair.

"Hold on! Don't fire! … Let's do this one more time!" McNeal shouted, as he re-loaded the gun for the same effect.

After the second firing, the troops followed up with a round from their rifles, at Sergeant Pryor's command.

"Happy New Year!" Pryor exclaimed.

The elated soldiers reacted by offering up a hearty cheer, accompanied by whistling and clapping. As if on cue, I then gave each man a cup of whiskey for breakfast, which was received with more cheers and hollering. We adjourned to eat. Captain Clark served up another round of drinks before preparing for the trek to the lower Mandan village.

In the closing days of 1804, the Mandan had requested that we dance for them sometime soon. We agreed it would be done on our New Year. At about ten that morning, Jusseaume and 15 men crossed the river to the lower village carrying a fiddle, tambourine, and sounding horn. On entering the village, the soldiers fired their rifles, and began to play. They marched to the center of the town, and fired another round, under the watchful eyes of the villagers. Chief Black Cat then escorted the men into his lodge for the dance. Much to the amusement of our hosts, the men danced until dinner was served. Rivet again showed up everyone by dancing on his hands and head.

In the early afternoon, Captain Clark and three more men departed for the village, including York. Having not had much opportunity to view York up to that time, the natives took a curious fascination with this very dark-skinned man. Sensing the opportunity to further amaze our hosts, Captain Clark then ordered York to dance for their entertainment. The Indians were amazed that a man of his large stature could nimbly and quickly move and jump in synchronization with the music.

They performed in lodge after lodge all afternoon, until they had visited all but two homes. The remaining lodges were not visited because Clark received word from Jusseaume that the leaders of those residences compared us to northern traders, and uttered other unfavorable expressions. The chiefs later explained that what was said was strictly in jest, and not to be taken seriously. By then, the sun was low on the horizon. Clark gave permission for many of the men to stay the night in the village to further partake in Mandan hospitality. Those who decided not to partake followed Clark back to the fort where I greeted them with another cup of whiskey.

The following day was the remainder of the party's opportunity to amuse themselves with the Mandan. After the men returned from the lower village in the early morning, I led the soldiers to the upper village for more dancing, which was thoroughly enjoyed by all. We returned in the evening, which is when the lower village held their own special ceremony known as a "Medicine Dance."

During this dance, elderly male members of the community sat in a large circle smoking from a pipe, which was passed to each man by young warriors who were elaborately dressed for the purpose. The wives of these young warriors stood around the seated men, and were clad only in a buffalo robe. After the smoking ritual, a young warrior approached an elder, singing in a whining tone, and asked that he take his wife for intercourse. The woman then escorted the old man to a convenient place to conduct the transaction, which was supposed to convey power and wisdom to succeeding generations. I was informed that this transaction also served the purpose of beckoning the buffalo near the village.

We learned of this dance the morning of the 4th from Little Crow, and sent Sergeant Pryor to witness the event that evening. He was offered, and happily accepted, four women for the occasion.

On the 7th of January, Chief Big White and his warriors returned from hunting and visited the fort. The Chief dined with me and Captain Clark, and helped us sketch on paper the country to the Rocky Mountains, including the region around the Yellowstone River, or Roche Jaune, in French. According to Big White, close to the source of the Yellowstone there existed a spectacular canyon where the riverbed contained large quantities of yellow rocks, which inspired the name of this immense waterway. He said the region also had huge numbers of beaver that inhabit very hilly country, which was covered with timber. In contrast to this landscape, about 800 miles immediately to the west of our fort, he said there was the Great Falls of the Missouri, in the midst of expansive plains and rocky coulees in a climate akin to a desert.

Two days later at sunrise, the thermometer was 21 below zero. At mid-day, the temperature had only risen two degrees when Privates Peter Weiser and John Potts reluctantly went out on foot to hunt.

Weiser was born in 1781, and raised in Pennsylvania. He was a discipline problem the previous winter at Dubois Camp, but had since developed into a fine soldier worthy of the Corps.

Potts was a 28-year-old German immigrant who was a former miller, and a good friend of one of our best hunters, John Colter. However, unlike Colter, neither Potts nor Weiser was an accomplished hunter. Nonetheless, we were in need of game, and it was their turn to hunt.

Sometime before sunset, the pair lost each other in the midst of violently blowing and drifting snow. Potts returned at about eight in the evening with a frostbitten right foot. Realizing he was too far from the fort to return for shelter, Weiser spent the night near the river, where the temperature plunged from nineteen below to minus forty. At the same time Weiser struggled to survive, not far away an Indian boy named Little Buffalo did the same in a thicket nearby.[G]

Earlier that day — like Potts and Weiser — a group of Mandan went to hunt buffalo. Among the group was Little Buffalo. After several hours, the boy tried desperately to keep pace with the rest of his hunting party, as they trudged through nearly a foot of snow on the wind-swept plain. The wind howled as Little Buffalo fell slowly farther and farther behind. He gradually lost enough circulation in his feet that they then felt like two wooden blocks. With each step, his feet felt very heavy, and a pain raced from the sole of his foot to the inner portion of his leg, lodging itself in the pelvic area. Tears of agony and terror streamed down the boy's face, and almost froze to his cheeks, as he watched his party abandon him over the distant horizon. The half-dead boy made his way to the river to implement the survival skills he had learned from his elders and peers. With half-frozen hands that shook uncontrollably, he broke tree branches and twigs to cover the snow for a bed. He lay down and wrapped himself in a buffalo robe. He had only antelope-skin coverings over his legs and buffalo-hide moccasins on his feet. As the temperature continued to drop, ice crystals formed in the circulatory system of his feet, which swelled them to grotesque proportions. He curled up to shiver under his inadequate robe.

Nearby, Weiser tended to a fire through the night, which allowed him to avoid the same unfortunate fate as the boy.

Sunrise came but provided little relief from the cold. Five men prepared to search for Weiser, but he had already found his way back to the fort by eight that morning, before the team departed. Two hours later, an Indian rescue team brought Little Buffalo to the fort for treatment of his feet. I immersed them in cool water, and offered him gum opii to relieve his pain. I watched the boy, and wondered if I would have to amputate his frozen feet.

The cold would not relent. A few days later, the temperature was still well below zero. At dawn, it was 34 below and only warmed to 20 below during the day. Regardless, Charbonneau, and one of our former boatmen returned that day from one of the outermost Hidatsa villages, which was about 70 miles west amid what was known as the Turtle Mountains.

Upon their arrival, both men's faces were so badly frostbitten that a great deal of their skin had blistered and peeled off in large chunks. Despite the pain on his face, Charbonneau told us he learned that North West Company representatives planned to construct a garrison near the Hidatsa villages north of our fort. He also said George Budge of the Hudson's Bay Company had been speaking unfavorably about us. These developments would not go unanswered, but we decided to wait for the correct time to address these unfortunate plans.

On the 14th of January, the toll of the frostbitten continued its ascent; Private Whitehouse and five others went to hunt in ten-below weather. Like Little Buffalo, after a few hours, Whitehouse collapsed and could not walk. Also like Little Buffalo, the men were forced to leave their ailing comrade on the snow-covered plains. However, they soon returned with a horse to carry him to safety. After treating Whitehouse, I also gave aid to men who again displayed venereal disease symptoms, which I treated with a mixture of medicinal solids and liquids, placed in a penis syringe.

Two days later, Mandan women carrying corn arrived for more blacksmith work on their farming implements and cutting axes. Later, a young Hidatsa war chief named "Seeing Snake" helped us draw a map of the Missouri River to the west. He also informed us of his intention to wage war on the Shoshone in the spring to acquire horses. Captain Clark and I advised Seeing Snake against such a plan, lest he suffer the displeasure of his Great Father, and not receive his protections. We also stressed that other nations had listened and adhered to the words we delivered. Seeing Snake responded that he did not wish to displease his Great Father, and decided he had enough horses.

The cold sufficiently broke on the 22nd so all the men attempted to cut the boats from the ice for fear of their incurring irreparable damage. The pirogues were nearly buried in hard snow and thick ice, up to the gunwales. After chopping away with axes for nearly an hour, a few men succeeded in breaking through some of the numerous alternating layers of water and ice. From the holes, water gushed and prevented them from continuing their work. During the remainder of the month, we repeatedly failed, day after day, in getting the boats out of the ice. We even employed iron spikes, pry bars and heating rocks of different compositions, but they shattered and broke in the fires as the embedded water expanded in the hot stones. This was very tedious and back-breaking labor, which proved fruitless but at least kept the men busy.

At the same time the men worked with the boats, Privates Willard and Shields were strangely not busy tending our once-thriving forge business. They had evidently repaired all the metal tools the Indians deemed in need of such service. We had previously refused work making war and battle axes for fear of encouraging violent conflicts. However — like the Indians — our meat supplies from November and December were nearly exhausted, and finding game was almost impossible near the fort.

The conflicting sides of this dilemma weighed heavily on my mind:

Manufacturing war axes could be viewed as providing the Indians with offensive killing tools. However, the counter-argument was that we were providing them weapons with which they could defend themselves against the Teton. But by the end of January, the demand for war and battle axes versus the need for food proved a force too powerful to resist; we began manufacturing axes in earnest on the 26th. Hunger trumped aspiring virtue. In exchange for making these weapons, we received much-needed corn to supplement our then-meager diet.

The following day I took action to save Little Buffalo, after I bled a man to relieve his pleurisy.

Little Buffalo's father — whose name was Yellow Wolf — walked into my hut carrying the boy in his arms.[H] I signaled for him to lay the boy down on my bed. Little Buffalo's feet were covered with moccasins, and I carefully removed them. I was disheartened to see five toes on one foot had blackened with gangrene. Knowing what must be done; I went to my supply cabinet, grabbed gum opii, and encouraged the boy to take the pain reliever with a cup of water. After waiting an half-hour for the opii to take full effect, I opened my medical bag and removed a coping saw. I explained to Jusseaume the procedure, and why the saw was needed. He relayed the message to the boy and Yellow Wolf, and they both bravely accepted the remedy without question or hesitation.

I walked to the bedside and glanced down at the boy and offered him a broad smile. He responded in-kind. Little Buffalo's father held the boy's hand, and I stepped to the end of the bed where Private Shields held a pan to catch the falling toes. After bracing the sole of his foot on the bed frame, I pressed down hard on the top of his foot with my left hand, and used my right to cut through the tissue, tendons and bone. The sharp blade made the amputation short work. It was done in seconds, almost before Little Buffalo could react. The boy moaned and grimaced, but did not cry or scream. Private Shields made eye contact with Yellow Wolf who peered at the toes in the pan and motioned to the fire for proper disposal. Shields tossed them into the flames where the lost digits burned into their constituent components. I cleaned and bandaged Little Buffalo's foot and urged Yellow Wolf to allow him to stay among us for the duration of his recovery, which he also respected.

On the 13th of January, Mr. Larocque paid us another visit, and we respectfully declined his prior request to accompany us west. Unspoken to Larocque, we had no intention of providing an opportunity for the British Crown to further enrich itself at the expense of the United States. The people of this nation sacrificed a great deal during the Revolutionary War to gain independence from the same agents and monarchy who then wanted to accompany us on an American expedition. We had no purpose or reason for changing the mission into an international endeavor, especially with the goddamn British.

One of the few matters that could readily distract my attention from my hatred of the British was the ongoing cold weather. By any standard, the month of January was brutally frigid with 21 of 31 days below zero at sunrise — the coldest of which was 40 below. In contrast, December only had 16 days below zero. I am confident in speaking on behalf of everyone that we did not wish to endure another winter in this harsh and despicable locale on our return. We had endured the worst of the cruel weather, and had only to wait a short time for signs the season was to end. But it wasn't coming soon enough.

With food supplies almost depleted, and despite a ten-below temperature, Captain Clark and 16 men set out to hunt east of the fort on the 4th of February. The purpose was to not only procure food for the rest of the winter, but build a stockpile for our voyage in the spring. Clark and his group walked 25 miles on river ice that had sharp projections to a place called Mandan Island. There, they encamped in an abandoned Arikara village named Maakoti. By the time Clark and his team arrived near sunset, the men's feet were battered and blistered.[I]

As they hunted during the following days, I continued my writing and leadership duties. On the 7th, Sergeant Ordway alerted me to a serious security breach, which he had just learned had been recurring for more than a month. Sacajawea, Otter Woman, and Talking Crow habitually unlatched the fort gate to allow their Indian guests entry, at all times of the night. In response, I ordered that a lock be placed on the latch, commanded the gate be shut from sunrise to sunset, and no Indian be allowed in the fort after dark, except those attached to the garrison.

Despite this stern order, an even more critical breach occurred just two days later by one of our very own.

I had given liberty to Private Thomas Howard to visit the Mandan for the evening, where he enjoyed their hospitality and whiskey. Upon his return, and unbeknownst to Howard, he was followed by three warriors who wanted to visit the fort. Rather than requesting that the sentinel unlock and open the gate, the drunken Howard walked around to the back of the fort, and easily scaled the wall in the area of the rooftop walkway above the smokehouse. He strode past a surprised Sergeant Ordway who was the sentry on duty, pacing around the courtyard. The two exchanged curious glances, and Ordway watched as Howard entered his hut.

After the door closed, Ordway turned his head to look across the courtyard. Above the walkway he noticed a pair of hands grasping the interior portion of the pickets. Within seconds, a warrior made his way onto the platform and was climbing down the ladder where he was intercepted by Ordway's rifle and bayonet. The Sergeant shouted an order to the warrior, which was not understood in words, but was easily comprehended through the soldier's action and tone. The other two Indians peered over and decided it best to not follow their Indian brother. Ordway escorted the warrior to my hut.

"Captain Lewis! Captain Lewis!" Ordway shouted, as he urgently banged on the sturdy wooden door.

"Enter, Sergeant," I responded, sitting at a table near the fire.

"Captain, Private Howard, and this Indian just climbed the fort wall," he said in a stressed tone, as he hastily closed the door.

"The wall?" I rhetorically asked in shock, as I stood up — pushing my chair back against the timbers of the wall.

"Yes Sir, just now," Ordway replied.

"Get Jusseaume and meet me in the privates' quarters," I ordered, as I angrily threw open the door to race across the courtyard.

I walked into the hut where Howard and others had assembled around the fireplace. Ordway and Jusseaume followed, not far behind. The men were smiling and laughing, but all fell silent after they took notice of my austere expression. I made steely eye contact with Howard, and he immediately realized the grave error of his judgment. Observing my presence had the desired effect; I turned my glare to the Indian and summoned Jusseaume.

"Tell this man he was nearly killed for scaling the wall," I said in an authoritative manner, while maintaining eye contact with the Indian.

Hearing Jusseaume, the young fellow appeared much alarmed at learning this information. I could see the look of regret and terror on his face. Sensing I needed to soften the admonishment, I grabbed a small tobacco twist from a nearby table and gently placed it in his hand.

"Go and never do this again," I said with compassion. "Sergeant, escort this man through the gate."

Jusseaume relayed the message, and the Indian and Ordway departed in silence. The men also remained quiet, as I slowly stepped toward Howard to emphasize my disapproval. I glared at him, and stopped a few feet from where he stood.

"Sergeant Pryor, take this man into custody," I ordered in a dejected voice. "Jail him in the blacksmith quarters until his trial."

Without any resistance, Howard went with Pryor.

The court-martial was held at noon the next day. He was found guilty of setting a pernicious example, and sentenced to 50 lashes at sunset. However, the court recommended the punishment be remitted because Howard was unaware of the Indians' watchful eyes, and there was not a prior order that forbade such entry. I agreed with the recommendation — confident the lesson was communicated.

In the evening, Charbonneau returned with Rivet from a hunting excursion. Charbonneau informed me that he had left three horses, two men, and a significant quantity of meat downstream that was procured for transport back to the fort. He said it was not possible for the horses to walk on the ice without shoes, and I determined to send six men with two sleds early the next morning to retrieve the much-needed meat.

About the same time the men departed for the food cache, Sacajawea went into labor, which lasted throughout the day. This being her first child, the ordeal was painful and tedious. Many hours passed, and she had yet to bring forth. Fearing she might die in the process, Jusseaume requested to enter my quarters, shortly before five in the afternoon. He asked if I had the skin of a rattlesnake. Searching through my animal specimens, I found the object, and he indicated that only the rattle portion was needed. Jusseaume said in the past he frequently administered this to laboring women, which he assured never failed to produce the desired effect.

He left quietly and returned to his hut where Charbonneau and Otter Woman were desperately trying to comfort Sacajawea, who lay in agony on the bed. Jusseaume had Charbonneau and Otter Woman carefully prop up Sacajawea's head. He then crushed two rings of the skin between his fingers and gently fed them to the ailing teen, along with a small quantity of water to wash it down. Approximately ten minutes later, Sacajawea made a final push to give birth to a healthy boy, whom the father named Jean Baptiste Charbonneau. Like so many other myths on the plains, I highly doubted the rattlesnake skin was the reason for her bringing forth. However, I could not summarily dismiss its purported effects, and thought it at least worthy of future consideration. Regardless, I was relieved to learn that mother and child were both doing well, after the difficult delivery. It was a happy occasion.

Shortly after dark the following day, Captain Clark and the men arrived with a huge quantity of buffalo, elk, and deer meat. Clark and his team made a very difficult 30-mile march on ice, along the riverbank and through snow that was nearly to their knees. Unfortunately, much of the meat brought back was so meager it was unfit for consumption. According to Clark, a considerable portion that was of value was taken by prairie wolves, which were in great abundance and harassed the party the entire trip. They brought what they could, but again left a significant cache about 20 miles below. In great need of this reserve, we planned to send four men back in the morning to retrieve the meat.

Shortly after first light, Drouillard, Privates Frazer, Goodrich and Newman set out early for the food with three shoed horses and two sleds. They followed the river 18 miles, and halted near the riverbank at an opening in the ice to water their horses. As they patiently waited for the animals to drink their fill, more than 100 Teton warriors on horseback emerged from an adjacent grove of trees. They thundered toward the startled group — shouting and hollering war cries. The warriors quickly surrounded the men, and two young leaders demanded three horses, a tomahawk, and three knives, as minimum payment for passing through the territory. Greatly outnumbered and afraid for their lives, the men reluctantly paid the toll, and six leaders deliberated a short time to determine the fate of the surrounded men.

They debated several minutes, and the majority wanted to kill the men, Drouillard had overheard. However, two of the elder leaders opposed the decision, and suggested the more appropriate payment was to set the group free, and only take two horses and two knives. The other Indians acquiesced. One of the chiefs returned the tomahawk, horse and knife. Drouillard responded by giving the Indian a loaf of cornbread, as a token of appreciation for the ill-gotten items. With another overwrought Teton incident concluded, the warriors quietly headed south toward the Arikara villages.

Their lives still intact, the four men trod in the opposite direction without the supply of meat, two horses, and an equal number of knives.

Approximately six hours later — at about ten that night — the men arrived to report the robbery. I immediately asked for 20 volunteers to avenge the theft, and punish the Teton. Aware of the dangers and risks, 24 men bravely wanted to make the treacherous journey the next day. We remained awake the better part of the night in preparation, which included recruitment of Mandan fighters.

Shortly after first light, we set out on foot with 24 soldiers, and a dozen Mandan warriors in pursuit of the Teton. We marched about 18 miles before stopping to eat unclaimed meat from our previous outings. By then, only four Mandan remained with us. Despite this disappointment, we proceeded on another six miles to the Maakoti village where we were expected, but did not encounter the

Teton.[41] Like Captain Clark's team, all the men complained of sore feet from walking nearly 30 miles on rough, jagged ice.

Regardless of the pain, I led our slow march when we resumed in the morning. We walked in two columns for several hours, and advanced another 12 miles when we arrived near another abandoned village. Raising my right hand, the soldiers recognized my signal and ceased marching. I turned to face the men.

"Listen! I need a private to scout the village," I stated.

The soldiers hesitated and looked at each other. Seeing no one was in a hurry to volunteer, Private Colter bravely raised his hand.

"Good man, Private." I commended, as Colter walked towards me.

I placed my hand on his shoulder. Pointing in the direction of a rise opposite the shore of the village, I suggested a safe route that would likely provide him the best vantage point for viewing. About one half-hour later, Colter returned to report seeing smoke but no overt signs of Indians.

"Alright, listen men," I yelled to the group. "We will execute a double-flanking maneuver in two columns. I will lead one and Sergeant Ordway will lead the other. … Sergeant Ordway's squad will take the left flank on the landward side of the camp. My men will follow me along the river. … At the sound of the horn, both squads converge on the campsite with all due speed. Be ready to fire. Is that understood?"

"Yes, Sir!" the soldiers shouted in unison.

"Right, let's move out!" I ordered.

We crossed the river to the east bank, split into our separate squads, and cautiously marched toward the smoke. Sergeant Ordway was nervous, as he clutched the sounding horn in his right hand. He steadfastly placed one foot in front of the other. All were silent, as we walked. The only sound was that of the ice and snow crunching under the weight of our feet. I signaled for the men to halt once more, and climbed the riverbank to stealthily peer into the village. I could distinctly see smoke, but did not see any signs of life. I took a few deep breaths, and watched my exhaled vapors disappear into the crisp, afternoon air. Seconds later, Ordway sounded the horn loudly in three forceful blasts. We swiftly ran towards the fire without shouting or yelling. It was soon apparent the Teton were not in the vicinity. In their wake, they had set lodges afire, burned Clark's cache of meat, and left a wide trail in the snow, which extended south along the river.

Realizing further pursuit was unwise, we opted to change our focus from vengeance to hunting. During the next few days, we harvested 2,400 pounds of meat, which we loaded onto sleds and delivered on the 21st of February.

That same day, Chief Big White visited our garrison and said several of his principals and warriors had gone to consult their medicine rock.[38] The rock was located on a hill about 80 miles southwest of our fort. Based on his description, the rock was likely a large boulder with paintings and carvings, used as an oracle. They claimed the rock foretold important events, so they visited it each spring, and occasionally in summer. We were not invited to see this oracle, and I did not ask to visit, given my low opinion of such dubious lore.

Two days later the temperature rose to the lower 30s, and all hands were again employed in cutting boats from the ice. Using axes and iron spikes attached to poles, we discovered the alternating layers of water and ice had increased during the month. The boats were then in imminent peril of being damaged. In the early afternoon, we finally succeeded in freeing the 5-ton, white pirogue by using enormous timber levers set on log fulcrums. With great effort, we pulled and shoved the boat onto the top of the ice and turned her on her side. Not wasting anytime, we then focused our exertions on freeing the keelboat and red pirogue. Hours passed, and the day closed.

We finally ceased work when Yellow Wolf arrived at the fort to take Little Buffalo back to the lower village. The boy's foot healed quite well, but not enough to walk. Yellow Wolf carried his son from the hut, carefully placed the boy on a sled, and pulled him home into the twilight.

On the 24th, we continued freeing the red pirogue and keelboat. As the pry bars hoisted the pirogue above the ice, the cork installed by Sergeant Gass the previous fall was torn from the hull. Water flooded the boat for several minutes, until we could replace the cork. An hour later, the red pirogue laid on her side near its sister vessel. All that remained was to free the keelboat.

The following day Sergeant Gass, Captain Clark, and I decided the best plan to pull the heavier boats onto the bank was to construct and utilize a large hoisting device. This device — known as a windlass — was comprised of customized wood and a great amount of rope.[39]

To begin, we selected a large tree within 50 feet of riverbank that had a significant, horizontal branch. The branch extended about 10 feet from the trunk, and an equal distance from the ground. The tree and ground would serve as the frame for the device.

To aid in moving all three vessels, 17 soldiers went to work felling small trees. All but one of the trees was to be used to construct a road made of timbers on which the boats would be transported by rolling on top of the tree trunks.

The last tree for the device was to be the vertical shaft for the windlass, which would be situated between the ground and horizontal branch. In addition to this work, two other men were busy using augers to drill a hole into the horizontal branch and the frozen ground.

While this was occurring, Indians had gathered to watch Sergeant Gass build a spindle drum for the windlass. Using a cross-section of log, he drilled six holes into the wood: Four were equally spaced around the outer edge of the cross-section, used for inserting four dowels as push arms. The other two holes were located in the center of the cross-section, above and below the unit. Into these holes, Gass secured separate dowels, which would form the vertical spindle for the ingenious device.

After the components were ready, the men assembled the windlass, and a road of logs was placed on the ground. One end of a heavy, elk-hide rope was affixed to the spindle drum, and the other end was tied to the white pirogue. One man then pushed on each of the four dowels, the spindle rotated, and the rope wrapped around the drum. The windlass easily drew the white pirogue off the ice and onto the bank. Weighing two tons less than its sister vessel, the red pirogue was light enough that all she required were the rollers — no windlass was needed.

The same was certainly not the case for the keelboat. During our initial attempts, the rope proved too weak, and snapped twice under the tension of pulling the 12-ton barge. On the third try, we doubled-up the rope, got her out of the water, and onto the rollers. By this time, darkness fell; we were exhausted, and abandoned the effort for the day.

Not long after sunrise, numerous Indians had already assembled around the keelboat in anticipation of our resuming work. Having heard of the activities the day before, the Indians were anxious to witness the windlass and rollers in action, and were not disappointed. The remainder of the day, we slowly moved the barge — pushing and pulling a few inches at a time. It was a long, slow struggle. Within minutes of getting the stern off the river, a very wide and long crack in the ice formed parallel to the bank. The crack was about 100 yards in length, several feet in width, and would have certainly impeded our efforts, if not for our good fortune. But with luck in our favor, and darkness coming on, we left her to rest on the rollers a few yards from the outer wall of the fort. The job was complete — much to everyone's delight and satisfaction.

With the boats safely on the bank — on the last day of February — our attention turned to constructing canoes. These would transport us west in a few weeks when we planned to send the keelboat in the opposite direction to St. Louis. Sixteen men were assigned the task of searching for suitable trees to construct four canoes. They traveled six miles upriver where they found prospects for the job, and started construction there on-site.

During their absence, Mr. Gravelines, and former Engagé Peter Roi arrived from the Arikara villages to deliver an urgent and disturbing message. They said Mr. Tabeau had learned that a few days earlier, the Teton had declared war against the Mandan and Hidatsa, and planned to kill every white man they encountered in their pursuit of the Mandan and Hidatsa. They also boasted of robbing our men of our horses and articles.

In better news, Gravelines and Roi also said the Arikara reaffirmed their commitment to peace, and desire to settle among the Mandan and Hidatsa to unite against the Teton.

Regardless of Teton threats, Captain Clark and I still planned to carry out our mission, but we were very concerned how well the return party might fare in the keelboat. Given the Teton would likely be traveling north on land when the keelboat was floating south through water, we guessed our return party would likely pass safely through their territory in a day or less without incident.

Later that night, my thoughts changed from troop safety to further documenting our trip for President Jefferson. Towards that end, I continued to describe the geography of the areas we had been, and were to encounter all the way to the Northwest Passage. I also informed him of our plan to explore the Yellowstone River on our return journey, and took great care in detailing animal, botanical, and mineralogical discoveries, while Clark processed information from the Hidatsa about what landmarks were ahead.

The Hidatsa had been as far as the Rocky Mountains, but traveled mostly by land between the Missouri and Yellowstone rivers, not by waterways. Regardless, we were confident there were no large gaps in our knowledge of the area, given the maps we obtained from President Jefferson before our departure, combined with Hidatsa accounts of the region. Indian testimonials supported Alexander Mackenzie's assessment that the mountains dividing the Missouri River and Columbia River drainages were easily crossed. According to our maps, on the western side of that dividing ridge, a watercourse likely gave rise to a river that flowed from the southeast to northwest. If it existed, this was the south fork of the Columbia River, which would lead to the Pacific Ocean.

We hoped the conjectural watercourse on the map was the fabled Northwest Passage.

Explorers had been searching for this route for more than 200 years, but it had eluded all, including Mackenzie. Finding the Passage meant a more direct trading route to the Orient, which translated into tremendous wealth for the entire nation.

February faded into March, and a distinct sign spring would soon be upon us was when the Hidatsa torched the plains. They set fires in hopes of stimulating an early crop of grass, which would entice the buffalo nearer the villages for hunting, and provide feed for their horses.

While the plains burned, our men continued their work constructing the four dugout canoes, using adzes and axes.

George Shannon was stooped over one of the boats with his feet spread wide to offset the swinging adze he clutched in his hands. He swung the tool upward and forced it back down. The sharp edge sliced off a chunk of wood. He repeated the process several more times. On the last swing, the blade missed its mark, skipped on top of the wood, and cleanly cut open Shannon's moccasin and left foot, which began to profusely bleed. He and several other men quickly rowed back to the fort where I stitched the wound together, and applied a tincture of benzoin to aid its healing.

Nearly a week had passed after Shannon's mishap when Captain Clark and I decided two additional canoes would be needed to transport our people and provisions. This was because we did not have enough space to transport 34 people with supplies in just four canoes, and two pirogues. Each canoe, we calculated, could comfortably carry three or four people, and still have ample room to store supplies.

We issued the order for more canoes, and shortly afterward, Charbonneau delivered disappointing news. He knocked on the door of our hut, entered, and requested the services of Labiche to interpret for him. Captain Clark sat at his desk sketching a map, while I wrote a description of the area Clark was mapping. Labiche and Charbonneau spoke for several minutes, until Labiche shook his head, and fell silent.

"Captain Lewis, Mr. Charbonneau wishes to report that he has reconsidered the terms of his employment and withdraws his verbal agreement to go west," Labiche said with surprise.

Captain Clark and I looked at each other in disbelief, but did not to express any outward signs of shock.

"Would you please ask Mr. Charbonneau if he would indulge our curiosity? I would like to know what terms he felt were objectionable," I replied in a calm and steady voice.

The two exchanged words. Labiche turned back to me.

"He does not wish to labor, as ordered, or stand guard. He also wants to return whenever he pleases, and take with all the provisions he deems necessary," Labiche reported.

"Tell him the original terms stand, and they have not, and will not change. However, we will allow him at least the night to reconsider his decision, before we hire a new interpreter," I responded.

Charbonneau listened. He shook his head in rejection and exited. Clark and I discussed our options, and decided to offer the position to Jusseaume, if Charbonneau did not change his mind. Given the negative activities of the North West and Hudson's Bay companies that winter, we were certain someone from at least one, or both those businesses had corrupted Charbonneau against us.

The following morning, Charbonneau said he could not accept the terms, and commenced moving his belongings into a makeshift shelter outside the fort.

Five days later, Charbonneau took down his shelter, and moved all his possessions across the river. After watching him complete several trips, I asked Labiche to call on Charbonneau for a meeting. Labiche and the Frenchman entered our hut. The pair talked for some time, as Clark and I watched in curiosity. The two fell silent. Labiche turned to face us.

"Captain Lewis, Mr. Charbonneau wishes to apologize for his foolishness, and is ready to accept the terms as you stated."

I looked down at the floor. I fought back a smile and expression of glee. After composing myself, I looked at Charbonneau who appeared nervous. He was sweating heavily from hauling his belongings. He looked every part of the buffoon he was proving himself to be.

"Just a moment, please," I said, gesturing with my right hand.

I walked toward Clark who was behind me. We turned our backs to the men, and conversed for a moment. Knowing we did not have a suitable Shoshone interpreter, there wasn't much to debate. We adjourned to address Charbonneau and Labiche.

"Inform Mr. Charbonneau we would be happy to hire him, again," I cheerfully announced for all to clearly hear.

Labiche communicated the message, and Charbonneau's worried grin grew into a relieved smile. He stepped toward us.

"Merci, Capitaine, Merci!" Charbonneau exclaimed, as he reached out to limply shake my hand.

He repeated the process for Clark. Finally, we had come to terms. He left and moved back into the fort within a few hours.

By the 26th of March, winter was complete. Warmer weather arrived, along with large flocks of geese flying north. The dugout canoes were also finished without further injuries, other than minor blisters. Although it was warmer, the ice on the river had not yet broken and obliged the men to drag the canoes six miles downstream to the fort. There, the remainder of the party was busy preparing for resumption of our voyage.

Two days later the temperature reached a welcomed 64 degrees, which further melted the ice, but had yet to break winter's frozen grip on the river. Another two days passed, and the grip was finally released — the river flowed once more, but with many chunks of ice, which varied greatly in size and shape.

The Missouri was then a slow-moving threat of treacherous ice, and the plains was again a sea of fire. With the free-flowing ice chunks, came dead buffalo. The beasts that had fallen through the ice during the winter were then drifting with the cold current. The water preserved the animals, and made salvaging the meat a sensible, but risky endeavor for Indian warriors. They skillfully maneuvered the buffalo to shore with spears, after agilely jumping from ice chuck to ice chunk without falling.

Approximately 200 miles west and several feet underground in a hillside comprised of clay-loam, a grizzled bear stirred from its winter slumber, after more than four months of hibernation. The young male crawled eight feet from the chamber, down a narrow tunnel, and emerged into the bright light of day. The 300-pound creature was famished, and like the Mandan, went to the river to catch and feed on dead buffalo. The beast waded into the cold waters of the Yellowstone River, opened its mouth wide, and clenched down hard with its huge incisors, which penetrated deep into the buffalo. With the animal secured between its teeth, the bear swam towards shore, and easily dragged the carcass onto the bank. Swiping its giant claws, they tore through the hairy hide to expose the rich, muscle tissue. The bear was able to feast for the first time since the previous November. With its appetite satiated, the bear moved downriver on a path that was likely to intersect our own.

As March closed and April set in, the river was nearly free of ice. By the 5th, we had the keelboat back in the water, and her crew was ready to set sail for St. Louis. In addition, members of our permanent party were also ready.

However, because of the complications we anticipated if we took more people than necessary, we had persuaded Charbonneau to leave Otter Woman among the Hidatsa. This meant Sacajawea and Jean Baptiste were to accompany us west. Taking Sacajawea and Jean Baptiste would mean most of Charbonneau's family could stay intact, while utilizing her additional knowledge of the Snake Indians, should it be needed. Bringing them also meant that the presence of an infant with his mother among us would signal to hostiles that ours was a mission of peace, not war.

With much anticipation and thrill, I later recorded the following in my journal of what lay ahead,

"... we were now about to penetrate a country at least two thousand miles in width, on which the foot of civilized man had never trodden; the good or evil it had in store for us was for experiment yet to determine, and these little vessells contained every article by which we were to expect to subsist or defend ourselves."

On the 6th of April, we hoped to depart.

However, I learned early from a Mandan warrior that the whole Arikara nation arrived at one of their abandoned villages downstream, and an advance party was then moving toward the lower Mandan village. As a result, we delayed in order to greet them. I sent Gravelines and three other men down to verify the report of their imminent appearance.

That evening, 10 Arikara Indians arrived at the fort. They promptly restated their commitment to peace, and agreement to meet President Jefferson. Knowing this, we were finally ready to embark on the second leg of our long journey; give our remaining horse to the Mandan; and send sundries, samples, specimens, and information back east to Jefferson. How much time the return trip would take our men was a topic of curiosity for me that I knew would remain unanswered until I returned — if I returned.

Just as I found the men when we began our long voyage the previous spring, all were in good spirits and anxious to at last explore the unknown. Finally, after five difficult months of waiting, I would soon be in unmapped territory, and was in a most joyous mood for having been provided the prospect.

CHAPTER THIRTEEN
RESUMPTION

April 7, 1805
Fort Mandan: 1,600 miles above the Missouri confluence

Before entering unmapped territory, much of the following day was exhausted conducting diplomatic duties, and making final preparations. By four that afternoon, every arrangement necessary for our separate departures was complete. Captain Clark and I bid Corporal Warfington farewell, along with his crew of eight men, which included Moses Reed and John Newman — the pair who were discharged from the expedition the prior year. Although small in number, Warfington and his party vowed to fight to the last man should they be attacked by the Teton or any other hostile Indians.

With that assurance, and a firing of the swivel gun on the white pirogue, I turned to catch one last glimpse of the keelboat as it turned with the current. I intently watched it float downstream, just for a moment. Within seconds, Clark, and our party of 33 people once again began the Herculean task of struggling against the murky flow, to the source of this immense waterway. We departed in six dugout canoes and two pirogues.

For a brief time from my vantage point on the bank near the fort, I was able to observe both flotillas parting in opposite directions. I must confess that knowing the keelboat was heading towards the comforts and safety of home, family, and friends gave me pause about moving further west. However, the thrill of discovery and call for duty was a far greater enticement to resume our quest. I turned on my heel, and contentedly stepped toward the late afternoon sun, hiking to our next campsite, which would be some four miles upstream.

This moment of departure I esteemed to be the happiest of my life.

The expedition then consisted of myself, Captain Clark, William Bratton, John Collins, John Colter, Pierre Cruzatte, George Drouillard, Joseph Field, Reubin Field, Robert Frazer, Patrick Gass, George Gibson, Silas Goodrich, Hugh Hall, Thomas Howard, Francois Labiche, John Baptiste Lepage, Hugh McNeal, John Ordway, John Potts, Nathaniel Pryor, George Shannon, John Shields, John Thompson, Peter Weiser, William Werner, Joseph Whitehouse, Alexander Willard, Richard Windsor, York, Toussaint Charbonneau, Sacajawea, and her infant son, Jean Baptiste Charbonneau.

As the sun rose the following day and heated the landscape, the wind correspondingly increased to dramatically slow our progress. This only added to our great burden in advancing upstream. Once again, I walked along the shore where large numbers of Indians had assembled to watch us travel slowly against the current. By mid-morning, I arrived to visit Chief Black Cat at the upper Mandan village where Captain Clark later joined us. We smoked, as was their custom, exchanged goodbyes, and Black Cat gave Captain Clark an excellent pair of moccasins, as a parting gift. I waved, and proceeded on four miles, while Clark waited for the party.

Word soon made its way to Clark that one of the dugout canoes was in distress from water overtopping the gunwale. Strong winds generated large waves, which overwhelmed the vessel. Clark returned to find everything in the canoe was soaked, including biscuits and 30 pounds of gun powder. Six men pulled the heavy craft onto the riverbank, removed its cargo, and turned her upside down, dumping the water onto the sandy shore. The men carefully untied rope that bound the cloth together, which contained a supply of gun powder. Private Shields neatly spread the powder on the cloth to let it dry in the afternoon sun while he and the rest of our party prepared dinner.

"That oughta work," Sergeant Pryor remarked, looking down at the dried powder about one hour later. "Load her up and let's go."

They re-packed, and we moved on to our encampment — 14 miles from the previous night's stay.

During the evening, a Mandan warrior named "Soaring Raven" expressed interest in accompanying us to the mountains since he was acquainted with the country.[A] With him was a handsome woman who had also been to the mountains. Moreover, the woman had a deep affection for Private McNeal. We refused his request to bring the woman, and immediately sent her back, but happily accepted Soaring Raven's offer. By morning, Soaring Raven changed his mind and planned to return to his village — no doubt his change was because of our refusal to bring the woman. This was a disappointment, but not a significant setback.

Much like the previous fall, the country through which we passed had miles of rolling, treeless plains beyond the river as far as the eye could see, on which grazed endless numbers of deer, elk, buffalo, and antelope. However, the terrain along the water was changing: High, irregular bluffs lined the banks — some about 100 feet in height. They were comprised of multi-colored, horizontal strata made of clay and sand, which varied in thickness from one to five feet.

With the days growing increasingly warmer, mosquitoes started to plague our morning and evening activities. Despite their troublesome presence, this did not prevent Sacajawea from utilizing a sharp stick to unearth wild artichoke tubers from the soil. After stopping to make camp each evening, in less than an hour, she was able to procure a great many of these starchy roots to complement our pleasing suppers, which were based on fresh meat.

On the 10th, we overtook three French fur traders who set out from Fort Mandan a few days before we departed. Since that time, they had already trapped 12 large beavers, and processed the pelts for shipment back east. The following day, Captain Clark and Drouillard walked along shore hunting. Clark extended his right arm to stop Drouillard.

“Look,” Clark said in awe, as he pointed.

He and Drouillard were mesmerized by the sight: Giant imprints in the soft riverbank they knew were from a formidable beast.

Clark crouched on his heels to get a better view of the tracks. He leaned over, reached out with his arm, and spread his fingers as wide as possible. The track dwarfed his open hand, which hovered just above the imprint.

“It’s huge,” Drouillard responded, shaking his head with equal impression.

The track was more than a foot in length and the same in width. The imprint had tremendous claw marks several inches in length, which meant they could have only been left by the much-fabled bear.

“Let’s hope they aren’t as fearsome as the Indians claim,” Clark said looking up at him with great concern.

We continued upstream, and on the 12th of April reached the mouth of the Little Missouri River, which flowed in from the south. There, we halted to camp, and discovered mice had chewed through several bags of corn and parched meal. We reluctantly unloaded all the vessels, and killed as many of the pests as possible in hopes of eradicating the problem.

Beyond the mouth of the Little Missouri, we were informed by the Hidatsa that there was a high range of hills to the south, known as the Turtle Mountains. Given the Little Missouri River was very similar in character to that of the Missouri, I deduced the land through which the Little Missouri passed must have been comparable to the land along the Missouri.

For as long as we had been in this region, I still found it difficult to summon the words that can accurately portray the sublime beauty and grandeur of the surroundings. This statement applies to the landscape, sky, and creatures that inhabited this gifted province. Of course, the price for such beauty was a heavy toll indeed, paid through enduring harsh winters, searing summer heat, and constant winds — the latter of which were proving to be most troublesome, along with mice and mosquitoes.

The wind shifted to our favor the following day, and we were able to hoist the pirogue sails. This allowed us to make significant progress, with the dugouts following in the boats’ wakes.

Early in the afternoon, Charbonneau was at the helm of the white pirogue when a sudden gust jolted him from his lull. He panicked. Partly because of his inability to swim, Charbonneau became alarmed. He was fearful of nearly everything over which he had little or no control, and wrongly steered the boat sideways to the wind. The result was high waves battered the side of the vessel, which only exacerbated the danger.

"Drouillard!" I shouted from the red pirogue. "Drouillard! Take the rudder and sails!" I ordered with urgency, waving my right hand to emphasize the point.

After quickly rolling up both sails, Drouillard disgustedly pushed the pathetic Frenchman aside, and righted the boat. Had the pirogue capsized, Sacajawea, her son, and three men who could not swim would likely have been drowned in the cold and choppy water. Charbonneau was proving to not only be a buffoon, but a threat to us all. Realistically, the toll of the dead in that boat could have been in excess of a dozen.

With the calamity averted, we proceeded on and passed the remains of 43 Assiniboine tipi camps. They were sighted along with innumerable buffalo carcasses — more victims of the brutal winter. The unlucky animals also drowned when they fell through fragile ice. Near the carcasses were many tracks of enormous white bears who had feasted on the dead.

According to the Hidatsa, happening upon this great brute, the bear more often attacked rather than flee an encounter. Except for Cruzatte, all of us were quite anxious to meet these bears to confirm their ferocity. The Indians said they never dared assail these beasts unless they pursued in parties of six to ten of their best men. Even then, the hunters painted themselves as if in preparation for war. Frequently, they lost one or more men to the bear. I attributed their losses to attacking with bows, arrows, and indifferent guns furnished to them by disingenuous French or British traders. To their great misfortune, such firearms were not worth a damn beyond short distances.

Two more Assiniboine encampments were passed on the 14th of April that had been recently abandoned. According to sources back east, no other nation on the Missouri above the Teton had more of a passion for spirituous liquor than that of the Assiniboine. Supposedly, they bartered with traders for small kegs of rum, and often drunkenly reveled with friends and relations. Women and children also indulged on such occasions and equally imbibed to the point of intoxication. Despite such alleged misbehavior, it was a testimony to the men's great skill and industry as hunters that allowed them to so frequently procure such expensive intoxicants.

Our good fortune and avoidance of these fellows continued, as I walked west of vacant Assiniboine camps. This is where I happened upon a meager elk, took aim and killed the animal where it grazed.

At the same moment, a pair of white bears not far in the distance was startled by the unfamiliar sound of gunfire. They quickly scurried up and over several steep hills with tremendous ease, and at great speed. This was near an area where Captain Clark had been collecting river data. After assessing these incidents, I was left to conclude that contrary to the Indians' account of this great beast, our experiences with these bears up to that time did not correspond with their testimonials. Rather than being a ravenous creature, they appeared much more wary and shy than we were led to believe. However, Cruzatte was steadfast in his account of the bears' ferocity, given his terrifying encounter the previous year.

Morning seemed to swiftly age into afternoon, which is when a steady breeze from the north dramatically transformed into a violent wind. It blew with such power that we were forced to the south shore for several hours. During that time, we anchored the pirogues along shore, and secured the canoes to the pirogues. Wave after wave crashed into the sides of the canoes and topped the gunwales, splashing into the vessels. We were compelled to continuously monitor the situation and bale water before they were overwhelmed.

Circumstances did not change much the following day, and we thought it prudent to remain in the harbor where we had camped the prior evening. I did not wish to contemplate the outcome if we were to suffer many more such setbacks. Cognizant of this possibility, we departed on the 20th at about seven in the morning against another steady breeze from the northwest. Fighting the wind and current day after day was a constant test of everyone's mettle, but especially true for laborers in the boats who struggled to paddle or pull our lumbering vessels upstream.

Being expedition leader and itinerant scientist, I was fortunate to be relieved of such physical duty, unless absolutely necessary. My obligations were elsewhere, which included recording observations about the surroundings and people. To that end, I again walked along shore with Seaman, and discovered additional remains of Indian hunting camps. Near one camp was a wooden scaffold, about seven feet in height, comprised of many small tree branches secured together with willow rope.

The scaffold was intact, but the purpose for which it had been built was compromised. At the foot of the structure lay a large bundle of buffalo skins in which the remains of a prominent Indian had been recently placed. It had been atop the scaffold, and had fallen in the not-too-distant past. The custom among the Assiniboine, Mandan, and Hidatsa was to honor the deceased by constructing such a shrine, and placing items with the remains they believed would be of service to the departed in the land of spirits. This method of homage was reminiscent of Chief Blackbird's burial mound we had visited the previous fall. However, it appeared that with these tribes the body was always faced toward the setting sun, which was symbolic of death, and indicated transition to their spirit world.

Along with the deceased Indian were two dog sleighs, with an equal number of harnesses, the rotting carcass of a dog, and small bag. I bent down, reached for the bag, and examined its contents. Inside the bag were many sundry articles including: A pair of moccasins; red and blue rocks; beaver claws; various tools for dressing buffalo skin; dried roots; grass; a dead blue-jay; and tobacco. Not wishing to further molest the site, I closed the sack, placed it where it had been, and re-directed my attention to the dead dog. Seaman panted at my side. His warm breath enveloped my right hand. I patted Seaman and shook my head in sadness at the fate of this poor dog whose reward for obedient service was to have his life cut short at the hands of a mourner.

Along with such death rituals as scaffolds and sundries, sacrificing a favorite horse or dog for the deceased was obviously another custom. Fortunately, I saw no evidence of similar sacrifice involving humans.

Through the night and into morning, the thermometer slowly dropped from 42 to 26 degrees Fahrenheit, just before sunrise. Near the campfire were eight wooden buckets filled with water from the river. The firelight flickered on the sides of the buckets, as water crystals began forming near the interior perimeter of the containers. The formation of one crystal catalyzed the formation of others, and soon a lattice began changing the cool liquid into a frozen solid. This made breaking the ice layer one of the first chores of the day, before it could be used for drinking, cleaning, and brushing teeth. After morning chores were completed, we loaded the buckets onto the boats, and proceeded on with much difficulty against a challenging wind.

Captain Clark and I walked together along shore much of the day. Toward evening, a frightened buffalo calf appeared from a thicket, and readily attached itself to me by walking at my side nearest the river. Not far behind, Seaman bounded from the same grove in pursuit of the calf. Rather than continue the chase, the dog lost interest and ran ahead, following another scent trail. The calf continued at my heels for some time, and I felt it appropriate to affectionately name it "Stumpy." Knowing what was best for the animal, I gently prodded the beast with my spontoon back toward the plains.

Stumpy wandered over a hill, and finally re-joined the herd. He found his mother near the edge of the group. They watchfully grazed for the better part of an hour when all of the beasts suddenly bolted south in a raging stampede. Thousands of hooves pounded the ground with a thunderous roar, as the herd moved in unison. A short distance behind, eight wolves flanked the fleeing animals, intent on procuring their next meal. Stumpy and his mother valiantly ran for nearly a mile, but the calf was tiring. The young buffalo slowed its pace, and the mother momentarily decelerated, but soon resumed flight speed. The gap between parent and progeny increased. The wolf pack had then successfully singled out a target for their survival. Sensing victory, the wolves continued their relentless chase, while Stumpy frequently changed directions to throw off his pursuers. Glancing up to assess the movement and location of the herd, the calf put its head back down and ran as quickly as its compact legs could carry it back to its mother.

A wolf to the right of Stumpy leaped and pounced on the young bull. A powerful bite to a hind leg swiftly subdued the calf, and the two crashed and tumbled to the ground in a billowing cloud of dust. Despite the collision, the wolf steadfastly maintained its grip on the calf. Stumpy lifted his head off the ground and loudly bellowed several times. At the same time, two more wolves on each side of Stumpy sank their teeth into the neck of the doomed animal. The calf cried out one last time for his mother. His desperate call would go unanswered. The herd indifferently moved on, and the pack moved in to share an infrequent triumph.

At camp that night, Clark shared this interesting observation after witnessing this curious and fascinating event.

Nature being forever engaged, took another shape during the succeeding days in the form of a violent wind. This incessant wind meant we were unable to travel any significant distance. In addition, sore eyes began to be a common complaint among the party. The malady originated from immense quantities of wind-blown sand that insistently pelted us the better part of each day. So fine and light were the particles that clouds of it traveled many miles from its source. From afar, the thick clouds of sand particles took on the same appearance as wafting smoke from adjacent prairie fires. The troublesome particles deposited on every item, and we were unwillingly compelled to eat, drink, breathe, and taste this unwelcomed additive.

On the 25th of April, it was apparent that the country in which we were entering near a beaver's hill was much drier than that of the region near Fort Mandan.[B] This was evident in the changing flora and terrain, which included less hearty and lush plants, more rocky, broken ground, and layers of bare earth adjacent to the riverbanks. Reports from our hunters indicated the river ahead was more twisting and winding, which indicated we must have been near the mouth of the Yellowstone. Having not received any relief from the wind, and anxious to view the Yellowstone River, at eleven that morning I set out on foot with Ordway, McNeal, Drouillard, and Private Joseph to explore the area near the confluence of these two great waterways.

Traveling eight miles on the south side of the Missouri, we ascended a high hill from which our group had a pleasing view of a wooded area surrounded by great valleys. I surmised a wooded area concealed the confluence, but not concealed were the large number of buffalo, elk, and antelope in the grand basin below. Having satisfied our curiosity and adequately appraised the situation, we marched into the valley, and passed buffalo that were unconcerned with our presence. This allowed us to easily kill a bison calf and three cows — two of which were too meager for meat. Instead, they were harvested only for their delicious tongues and marrow.

With much effort, we carried the food a short distance to the confluence. There, I instructed Drouillard and McNeal to remain until Clark's arrival, further dress the buffalo, and hang the meat out of the wolves' reach. Meanwhile, Private Joseph, Ordway, and I hiked another two miles below to camp on a beach among a timber copse. Trees in this area included elm, cottonwood, and ash. Our camp was below towering bluffs, hundreds of feet in height, which appeared to contain bits of glass of varying colors.

Prior to our departure from Fort Mandan, the Hidatsa had informed us that the Yellowstone was navigable nearly to the Rocky Mountains. They said it passed within a half-day's march of a navigable part of the Missouri. This was supposedly near an area where the Missouri acquired three forks. The Hidatsa also reported that the mountainous country from which the Yellowstone originated was well-timbered, while the middle section flowed through fertile country, surrounded by timber but interspersed with immense fields. Finally, they asserted the lower portion of the Yellowstone consisted of fertile plains and meadows, accentuated with naked bluffs lining the riverbanks. This was where we found ourselves that evening — below a bluff with a shiny appearance.

The morning of the 26th was clear and crisp. Not long after sunrise, I ordered Private Joseph to go up river and explore the Yellowstone as far as possible, and return before evening. While he ventured out, Ordway and I hunted, and surveyed the area, which included making celestial observations at nine in the morning and noon — at which time Clark and the rest of the party were greeted at the confluence by McNeal and Drouillard.

Upon their arrival at this long-sought junction, they promptly set up camp, and fired their guns at buffalo calves. Even though we were miles away, I could distinctly hear their shots in the distance. Having reached this landmark confluence with great difficulty, an air of levity and joy filled the party, as they happily began constructing camp.

Meanwhile, Captain Clark carefully took measurements, and found the Missouri was 330 yards wide at this point, and Yellowstone only slightly less broad. They were two remarkable rivers, wild, untamed and beautiful.

With camp established, Drouillard grabbed his rifle, and approached Clark.

"Captain!" Drouillard yelled to capture his attention.

Clark kept his head down for a moment and recorded the last distance traveled. Adding up the mileage, Clark estimated we were then 1,885 miles from the mouth of the Missouri at St. Louis. He looked to turn his attention to Drouillard.

"Captain, I would like permission to inform Captain Lewis of your arrival," Drouillard urged.

"Certainly — should have thought of that sooner. Thank you. Thank you for reminding me," Clark replied with sincerity.

"We'll be back by evening," Drouillard said, before departing upstream.

Within an hour, Drouillard joined Ordway and me in hunting. By the time we were done, we harvested a good number of buffalo, antelope, and deer. We also had time to catch several small fish. Even Seaman successfully took an antelope when he swam after a herd that was crossing the river, and was able to drown and drag the animal back to shore.

At about four that afternoon, Private Joseph returned with a buffalo calf restlessly pacing at his heels. Like the one that followed me, this one attached itself to him about four miles upstream, which was half the distance he was able to explore that day.

The Private then reported his findings, after sending the calf toward the plains:

"Well, the river is crooked, and the valley is four to five miles wide," he stated, as we carefully listened.

While he talked, I scribbled notes in my journal.

"For the most part, the current is mild, and the bed has many sandbars," Field said, rubbing a hand over his chin.

"About five miles up there's a big island covered with timber. Three miles beyond that, a large creek dumps into it from the southeast. At that spot, a high bluff has layers of coal. It's beautiful country. I walked to the bluff, and as far as I could see were plains, just like the ones on the Missour'ah. That bluff is where I found this," Field said, as he reached out to show us a large, curved horn.

It was from wild sheep that inhabited the region. He gave me the horn, and I placed it in my possible bag for closer scrutiny at a later date.

"Thank you. Very well, then. Anyone want to walk back to get a pirogue for the meat and baggage?" I asked looking at each man.

"I'll go," Drouillard quickly responded, always seeking new challenges.

"We'll meet you back at camp," I said, grateful for his enthusiasm.

He left us, and we remained to guard the meat, which also allowed me time to record my last celestial observation for the day. After documenting the observations, I walked down to the confluence and joined the others. They were all in good health and spirits, and much pleased at having arrived at this grand spot. To add pleasure to our little community, Captain Clark and I ordered a dram be issued to each person, and Cruzatte produced his fiddle. He and Gibson took turns entertaining everyone. That evening was spent in much hilarity, as we danced and sang, despite the past toils, and those we knew were yet to come.

The morning welcomed us with a temperature slightly above freezing. As the day progressed, the wind once again stopped us from advancing much further. But the afternoon allowed us to explore a region several miles up that looked promising for a future settlement. Clark and I agreed that with an available supply of limestone in the vicinity, a good prospect for a community was a low plain in an area just east of the confluence.

On the 29th of April, we set out at the usual hour. I walked along shore with Drouillard for some time when I suddenly spotted a pair of white bears about 100 yards in the distance that had yet to detect our presence. I stopped and silently extended my arm to cease Drouillard's advance. I quietly pointed in the direction of the bears.

"I'll shoot the one closest to the water. You shoot the other. Wait for my order," I whispered to Drouillard.

We raised our weapons and carefully aimed.

"Ready! Fire!" I said in a voice loud enough to be heard, but not enough to alert the bears and provoke a premature attack.

The command was immediately followed by a booming noise that echoed off the bluffs adjacent to the river. Both animals were hit, but neither fell. The bear wounded by Drouillard quickly turned and fled over a hill away from the river. The other reared up on its hind quarters, roared, dropped back on all fours, and began charging towards us. Drouillard and I hurriedly re-loaded, while the bear's pace dramatically slowed from the severity of his injury. In great pain, the bear was still able to advance within 20 yards of us before we both able to fire again. The balls found their target, and the bear finally expired. We loaded once more and monitored the situation before approaching. Seeing no signs of life, Drouillard and I cautiously stepped toward the downed animal. Observing the great beast up close, I marveled at its enormity, and knelt down on one knee to at last closely examine the fearsome predator.

It was a young male, but still about 300 pounds. His legs were somewhat longer than those of a black bear, as were his claws and incisor teeth. The fur was thick and yellowish-brown in color with fine, individual hairs. The bear's eyes were small and black. Contrary to my initial impression, and consistent with Hidatsa reports, this animal was much more furious and fearsome than a black bear. It obviously would pursue a hunter, even when wounded. I found it astonishing to witness the damage they could endure before dying.

Regardless of this encounter, I concluded that the Indians may have justly feared this animal, being equipped with only bows, arrows, and pitiable rifles, but in the hands of skillful marksman equipped with an apt weapon, they were by no means as terrifying or dangerous as they had been represented.

We field dressed the bear, and when the boats arrived, we loaded the flesh and proceeded on.

Late that morning, we passed bluffs that were greater in height and width than we had ever encountered to that point. Like the bluffs we had seen in the past weeks, they too had many colored strata, but some layers were as thick as six feet. A group of us, including Drouillard, Clark, York, Charbonneau, and Sacajawea climbed to the top of one immense bluff and saw more of the sheep Private Joseph had seen a few days prior. Through Charbonneau and Drouillard, Sacajawea informed us that these creatures were also commonly found in the Rocky Mountains still to the west of us.

The winds that beleaguered us in April plagued us in May, but with greater vigor and challenge. For most of the month, paddling proved impractical, and this option was dropped in favor of the tow ropes. However, picking up the ropes meant walking along shore, which created new problems in the form of wet sand, mud, large stones, or some combination of those difficulties. Towards the end of the month, even walking on the bank was no longer an option when the river cut through the surrounding cliffs and bluffs, which rose nearly perpendicular to the water.

Before overcoming those challenges, we passed through more Assiniboine land. It was there on the second of May, the party observed signs of Indian activity. In the morning, Private Frazer shot and killed an Indian dog that had been following us for several days. The wayward dog had stolen cooked meat at every opportunity, and we were left with no alternative but to kill the beast. In the afternoon, several hunters found several pieces of red cloth at an old Indian camp. Through our interpreters, Sacajawea said the red cloths were an offering of humble gratitude to the Great Spirit for providing them a wonderful place to temporarily reside for however brief the period.

Throughout the month, mornings were cool, afternoons warm, and hunting game was feast or famine, without much in between the further we penetrated the increasingly dry climate. Upon encountering buffalo, they scarcely gave way for one to pass. In some cases, the men pulling on tow ropes resorted to throwing sticks and stones to drive them out of the way, as the soldiers walked on shore towing the vessels.

As the climate grew more arid, the flora and landscape expectantly changed in congruence with the lack of moisture. Most of the naked bluffs had great furrows carved in them by centuries of erosion from wind and water. White, yellow, brown, and black strata comprised predominately of sandstone and clay had rocks of varying sizes embedded in nearly every layer. Away from the river, short grasses, prickly pear, and scrubby pine covered the ground, which was not nearly as robust and fertile as the soils back east.

One the 5th of May, Captain Clark and Drouillard killed an even larger white bear, almost twice the size of the one I had killed six days earlier. The pair shot the animal with 10 balls — five through the lungs — and the beast was still able to swim to a sandbar, which was more than half the distance across the river. It did not die for 20 minutes — all the while the beast repeatedly roared a most frightening call. Later we measured, skinned and boiled him for oil, which we stored in two casks. As a result of that encounter, I found our party's curiosity with regards to this animal was pretty well-satisfied.

With our military-issued clothing evermore tattered and torn, and the party's questions about the bear fulfilled, we began killing more elk not only for clothing, but for skins to cover the collapsible, iron-framed boat I brought for use when other vessels became less practicable. I estimated this 36-foot vessel would carry up to 8,000 pounds, and could easily be assembled and dismantled as needed, unlike our other boats. At that time, the iron frame lay in a neat pile wrapped in cloth on the bottom of the white pirogue.

While the iron-boat frame laid in the pirogue, it passed a river that had a peculiar whitish hue on the 8th of the month. Captain Clark and I concluded this was the river the Hidatsa called: "The River Which Scolds All Others." Because the waters resembled tea with a considerable amount of milk, we thought it proper to name this the Milk River. The Indians claimed this river had origins in the mountains west of our position, and it flowed through many miles of broken country, which had woodlands and prairies. Near this confluence, Captain Clark ascended a very high point from which he said he could see at least 50 or 60 miles in all directions. He reported that the country was level and beautiful, with large herds of buffalo, but did not see mountains.

Despite not viewing the peaks we sought, I deduced that we must be getting closer, since the Missouri was becoming shallower and less turbid, which was a considerable change from its character the 2,094 miles below. Had it not been for this fact, I should have begun to despair of ever reaching its source. We were all extremely anxious to view the mountains, and wondered when that day would finally come, but expected it soon.

Although there were significant differences in the river this far up, one similarity with the lower section was the fragile banks also collapsed into the river, which again endangered our flotilla. Immense masses of earth fell with tons of force that could have easily crushed both people and boats. Fortunately, we passed through these geologic threats without incident, but could not report the same about other serious incidents that were growing in numbers and severity:

His footsteps pounded the ground as he raced across the plains along the river for the safety of our party. Clutched tightly in his right hand was a rifle. In the distance, he saw the silhouettes of our eight vessels slowly advancing upstream. He began to yell and wave his left arm to capture our attention, while his legs carried him towards us at top speed. The man was breathing very hard. Perspiration dripped from his face. Sweat obscured his vision, as he focused his efforts on outrunning his pursuer.

Hearing an odd noise from behind, I stopped to investigate the disturbance. A person was running towards me on the same side of the river, but I was too far away to discern who it was, and they were obviously in distress.

Turning to face the flotilla, I shouted: "Sergeant Ordway! Sergeant Ordway!"

Ordway looked in my direction, from his position at the rudder in the red pirogue, which was slowly moving upriver.

"Bring the boat ashore!" I yelled.

Ordway waved acknowledgement of the command, and began to maneuver the pirogue to a landing spot.

I glanced back downriver. As the person drew closer, I could see it was Private Bratton whom I had permitted to walk on shore, due to soreness in his left hand that made paddling and poling inadvisable. Bratton slowed his pace to a walk, bent over, and placed his hands on his knees to catch his breath, and disclosed the reason for his flight.

“Bear,” he said between breaths, still doubled over.

“Big bear,” Bratton added a few seconds later. He stood, and began telling a tale very similar to Cruzatte’s account the previous fall.

“About a mile-and-a-half back I … I shot a bear … through the lungs. He didn’t drop. He came after me and I ran,” Bratton exhaustedly said.

“I didn’t even bother looking back. I shot him while he was eatin’ in a bottom.”

“Right,” I responded. “Sergeant Ordway!”

“Sir!” Ordway replied, snapping to attention.

“Bring five men with us to find a bear.”

Within a short time, we found a bloody trail and tracked the bear a mile to a thick brush of rose bushes and willow. Although wounded, the bear was still able to dig itself a bed two feet in depth and about five feet in length and width. Two balls through the skull finished off the bear, but even that seemed an uncertainty given the amazing strength of that animal.

I concluded there was no other way to kill these beasts but with a single shot through the brain. Nonetheless, this proved difficult because of two large muscles that covered the sides of the forehead, and a rather thick skull, which had a sharp projection at its center. The fact that these bears were so difficult to kill intimidated us all. I did not like these gentlemen, and would have rather fought two Indians than one bear. Regardless, I felt myself an equal match with theses brutes near the water or woods when equipped with my rifle and spontoon, but was much less certain if I were on an open plain. Therefore, I resolved to only act from a defensive position on the plain. I shared these observations with the men, and they thought them astute.

The evening of the 14th of May, men in two of the rear canoes, which included Colter, McNeal, and Shields, discovered a huge grizzly lying in the open about 300 paces from the river. They decided six of them would try to bag the animal. Taking advantage of a small hill nearby for concealment, the group was able to get within 40 paces of the beast, which was resting in a meadow below. There, they separated into two groups — one with four who would shoot first, while the other pair would provide supporting fire, if needed. From the point on the ridge, the four primary shooters took aim. Almost simultaneously they shot, and each ball found its mark in the torso of the animal. In an instant, the bear charged up the mound at the four — growling and snarling. The two that reserved firing then discharged their pieces, missed, and the bear changed direction towards the stunned pair. Unable to re-load before being overtaken, all six fled towards the river. Two made it to a canoe, and the others split up to hide in the willows, which provided them time to re-load their rifles.

The angry brute paced up and down near the riverbank still roaring. When the opportunity presented itself, the men in the willows shot several more times — all but two missed. Private McNeal finished re-loading, and nervously poked his head above the brush and fired. Although the ball found its target, the ammunition only served to re-direct the bear's attention to McNeal's concealment, and it pursued him in earnest. Terrified, McNeal tossed aside his rifle and supply pouch, and sprinted for the river. Without hesitation, McNeal raced to the water, even though he was well aware that between him and the river was a fall of 20 feet. Reaching the edge of the cliff, McNeal pushed off with his right foot to generate as much force as possible to clear the bank below. His forward momentum carried him past the shore, and he plunged feet first into deep water. Pushing aside the murky liquid with both arms and kicking frantically, McNeal soon resurfaced, took a huge gulp of air, and forcefully threw his head sideways to fling the water from his face. He looked to his right and left, gained his bearings, and began swimming to the opposite shore.

During this time, the bear shifted its attention to Private Shields who fired to protect McNeal. The result was the same. Shields followed McNeal's lead, but this time the wounded animal was so enraged it followed the fleeing soldier over the cliff.

Down the pair fell and soon splashed into the river, with Shields slightly ahead of the grizzly. Colter emerged from his hiding spot, and finished the beast off with a shot through its skull as it swam toward Shields. The carcass rolled on its side, and the current carried the bear to shore. The men butchered the monster on the riverbank, but harvested only its pelt since the flesh was advanced in age, and of little value. A total of nine balls passed through the bear from varying directions, but only the shot through the brain was able to stop its ferocious and unrelenting attack.

While this extraordinary ordeal was taking place, an even greater trial was unfolding farther upriver, due to the incessant wind, and our buffoonish Frenchman who could not manage a boat:

Drouillard was walking along shore with me and Captain Clark, rather than manning the rudder in the white pirogue. This left the task to Charbonneau. At the tiller, the going was easy enough that the Frenchman began to whistle "Malbrough s'en va-t-en guerre."[19] At the same time, Cruzatte was at the bow looking upstream when he glanced a short distance to the northwest to see a cluster of very dark clouds had moved in, which brought with them prolonged and violent winds. A sudden gust snatched the clew rope from Private Hall's hand, and blew the square sail 45 degrees to the larboard. This also brought a swift end to Charbonneau's happy tune, as he panicked once again, and mistakenly turned the boat perpendicular to the breeze, rather than tacking the vessel into the wind. Immediately, the boat started to tilt, and the 10 passengers onboard were thrown to the larboard side of the vessel, which exacerbated its peril. Over the boat went until its capsizing was ceased by an awning that had been rigged for shade. Watching in shock, Captain Clark and I responded by firing our guns to capture the crew's attention.

"Cut the halyards and take in the sail!" I shouted from shore.

The crew did not react, and the larboard gunwale slipped under the surface of the cold, murky water — soaking passengers and articles on board.

Charbonneau began weeping and crying to his God for mercy.

"Cut the halyards and take in the sail, goddamn it!" I screamed once more, but was not close enough to be heard, being some 300 yards from the group.

Determined to act in some manner, instinctively I dropped my gun, threw my shot pouch, and frantically started unbuttoning my coat before thoroughly considering the possible consequences of my intent. My objective was to swim to the pirogue to save it from foundering, but by the time I got to my fifth button I realized the folly of such an attempt, and could only stand there helplessly watching with Captain Clark and Drouillard.

Sergeant Floyd's carefully folded coffin flag and several bagged articles began floating in the turbulent waters filling the boat. The flag drifted out of the pirogue, soon became saturated, and sank below the choppy surface. Recognizing the value of the articles, Sacajawea calmly reached out and repeatedly grabbed the remaining goods before the current swept them downriver. She bravely did this while Jean Baptiste was safely secured in a cradleboard strapped to her back. Soon afterward, Cruzatte and Hall took in the sail, which righted the boat, but it was then filled with water to within an inch of the gunwale, and seconds from calamity.

Waves washed into the boat with each gust, while Charbonneau stood near the bow weeping and praying, despite having been ordered by Cruzatte to take back the rudder. Tears streamed down his blubbery cheeks, and his bottom lip quivered, as he cast his eyes to the heavens. He slowly pulled his hands down his face at his feelings of despair and fear. Disgusted and infuriated with the Frenchman's inaction and paralysis, Cruzatte repeated his command, but Charbonneau again ignored the order. Cruzatte angrily unslung his rifle, and swiftly placed the rifle butt against his shoulder. Cruzatte pointed the weapon at Charbonneau and threatened to shoot him dead, if he did not immediately take the tiller and perform his duties. Without uttering a sound, the Frenchman gradually turned his eyes to stare at the angry Cruzatte. For a tense moment, the only sounds that could be heard were the wind blowing against the awning and waves crashing into the boat. Charbonneau studied Cruzatte's face, which was overwrought with rage. He thought for a moment, and silently waded through the water to take his place at the other end of the vessel. Cruzatte lowered the rifle, and ordered Privates Willard and Hall to throw water out of the boat with two kettles, and for two other men to row ashore.

The boat gradually moved through the water with its gunnels only a few inches above the surface. After the pirogue slid onto the riverbank, the crew emptied the vessel of all the water, and removed every article for drying. Considering that tragedy was avoided, we thought it proper to cheer the party's spirits with an ample provision of grog.

Had I executed my plan to swim to the pirogue, I estimated my probability of success was perhaps one hundred to one. But if I paid for the effort through the forfeiture of my life, and saved the pirogue in the process, I would have deemed the price worthy of the exchange. Charbonneau endangered the lives of nearly a dozen people, including his wife and son. In addition, the danger extended to the potential loss of vital notes, books, medicine, trade goods, gun powder, scientific instruments, and our journals. Charbonneau was perhaps the most timid waterman in the world, which was the most charitable conclusion applicable to this man, besides being a good cook.

Now that I have done the business, I recount the following to provide you a better understanding of our Frenchman:[20]

According to the journal of one John MacDowell, in November 1793, Charbonneau set out with four other men, traveling with supplies and trade goods through British Territory. On May 30, 1795, Charbonneau was stabbed in the back with an awl by an old woman. Apparently, the woman did this to stop Charbonneau who was allegedly in the act of raping her daughter in the village of Portage la Prairie, south of Lake Manitoba.

Wrote MacDowell: *"... a fate he highly deserved for his brutality — It was with difficulty he could walk back over the portage."*

Despite his loathsome character, Charbonneau was the patriarch of a family needed for the success of our enterprise, which made our tolerance of his cowardice and cruelty a priority.

Putting that most recent incident behind us, we proceeded on, and faced the usual trials.

Three days passed since the incidents when we experienced a similar occurrence to the one the previous fall when the riverbank collapsed. During the late hours, we were awoken by the sentry, and informed a large tree over our tent had somehow caught fire. We hurriedly dismantled the tent, and a few minutes after moving our shelter, a large branch crashed to the ground, which would have certainly crushed us in our sleep had we not relocated.

Two days later Drouillard shot and wounded a beaver. As usual, Seaman jumped into the water to retrieve the animal. However, the beaver was able to avoid being taken by diving under Seaman and biting him through one of his hind legs. The dog loudly yelped, and swam back to shore where I saw the wound was very serious. The bite had severed an artery. Only with great difficulty was I able to stop the bleeding. At that time, I was still uncertain whether the injury would prove fatal to my faithful companion.

Shortly after caring for Seaman, Captain Clark returned from his scouting mission, and informed me that from the top of an adjacent hill, he saw a large watercourse we concluded must be the river Musselshell. The Hidatsa said this river flowed through broken country and originated in a little belt of mountains, which was no great distance from the Yellowstone River. And — at long last — Clark also reported viewing a range of small mountains to the northwest, 40 or 50 miles from this spot. About five miles below the mouth of the Musselshell, we later discovered a handsome river about 50 yards in width, which we named Sacajawea in honor of our bold interpreter — the Shoshone woman — who saved our valued articles from being claimed by the great Missouri.

The confluence of the Missouri and Musselshell were approximately 2,270 miles from St. Louis, which is where Corporal Warfington and his crew safely arrived in the keelboat on the 22nd of May. With him were Gravelines, Arikara Chief Eagle Feather, and Otoe Chief Little Thief, along with the live barking squirrel, fossilized skeleton of the monstrous fish, and many other plant, animal, and mineral specimens for President Jefferson. Warfington reached St. Louis in a little more than a year after our departure from Dubois Camp, and had managed to travel from Fort Mandan to the confluence in only 46 days — covering an average of 35 miles per day. By contrast, this same voyage upstream took us 156 days to traverse in 1804.

Thousands of miles northwest of St. Louis in the high country, we continued our battle against the violent wind and immense clouds of sand and dust. At camp, we found ourselves so enveloped in particles we could not cook, eat, or sleep. Finally, we were compelled to move our lodge to the foot of an adjacent hill where we were somewhat shielded from the wind. In addition, several loose articles were blown overboard and lost to the churning waters.

The land in which we had been traveling for many days I surmised to be a continuation of what the Indians and French boatmen called the Black Hills. Regardless of its name, this tract where we were at was almost a desert — devoid, barren, with a collection of irregular hills and short mountains. But despite this vice, the region contained air so pure that earthen formations and other objects appeared closer than their actual distance.

During Captain Clark's walk on the 25th, he reported seeing at least three isolated mountain ranges, including the mountains he had viewed six days prior. He said the others were to the northwest and southwest. I was overjoyed with the news, and waited with great anticipation for my opportunity to view this striking site the following day.

I climbed out of the river bottom and spotted one of the highest points in the region, and laboriously hiked for an hour to what promised to be a commanding vista. My efforts were compensated upon viewing the grand spectacle. Although distant, I could see that the mountains were topped with snow, even though it was greater than 70 degrees Fahrenheit where I stood. While I beheld these stunning objects, I took additional pleasure in finding myself so near the headwaters of the heretofore endless Missouri. But upon contemplating the difficulties these snowy barriers would prove to be on our passage to the Pacific, and the sufferings and hardships we would likely endure crossing them, the initial joy I experienced was neutralized by the impending toil. I had always held it a crime to anticipate such evils, and therefore believed it to be a good and comfortable road, until compelled to differently believe.

Although the mountains were still covered with snow, evidence showed it was melting without abandon. The creeks and rivers flowed high, and with them articles were found not far from our camp on the 28th. One of the articles was a lodge pole that was significantly worn on one end, as if dragged on the ground, likely by horses or dogs. Also found was a football comprised of elk skin. I was informed that such balls were used in a game played by many tribes on the plains. No doubt the lost ball was property of the Minnetares Indians of the prairie, or perhaps Blackfeet Indians whom we had not met, but were close to their homeland.

Knowing our proximity to potentially hostile Indians, we were much alarmed early morning on the 29th when a disturbance rousted us from sleep.

From the opposite shore, a large bull buffalo had crossed the river and climbed over the white pirogue to gain access to the riverbank near our camp. The bull darted from the water straight toward our campfires. The raging animal was inches from the men's heads as they lay sleeping. Realizing what was occurring, the sentry yelled several times, and frantically waved his arms to re-direct the path of the buffalo, which subsequently turned to charge toward our vulnerable tent on the edge of camp.

The men were all much alarmed and grabbed their rifles, as the sentry repeatedly screamed: "Buffalo! Buffalo in camp!"

Seaman — who survived his ordeal with the beaver — saw the buffalo closing in and raced out to confront the huge beast — barking the entire time. The bull changed its path again, and headed northeast away from camp. I could do nothing short of crediting Seaman for saving our tent, if not our lives.

After panic subsided, we happily found no one injured. The following morning we discovered the buffalo had crushed York's rifle, which he had carelessly left in the boat, instead of propping it up with the others near the fires. In addition, the bull snapped the spindle pivot attached to the blunderbuss on the boat. Given that incident, and others involving the white pirogue, I then wagered the boat was attended by an evil genie bent on delivering harm at every opportunity.

Putting yet another near tragedy behind us, a short way from camp Captain Clark and I separately explored a clear, handsome river to the south. The river was about 100 yards wide, and had a bed comprised of gravel, mud, and sand. More importantly, there were no large stones or rocks to obstruct navigation. I originally called this the Big Horn River, after the numerous sheep in that region through which it traversed, but Clark thought better. Considering the attractiveness of this waterway, and the fact that Clark ventured further upstream than me, he thought it more proper to name it Judith's River, after a 13-year-old girl named Julia Hancock who had captured Clark's romantic thoughts.

Exploring this river, I observed evidence of 126 Indian lodges, which appeared to be no greater than 12 to 15 days in age. York, Sacajawea, and her son accompanied Clark in his examination of the river, and found moccasins the Indian woman identified as that of tribes north of her homeland — possibly Blackfeet or Gros Ventre of the prairie Indians.

Later that day, and back on the Missouri, about nine miles upstream, we passed the rotting carcasses of more than 100 dead buffalo along one riverbank. They appeared to have been driven over a nearby cliff, which was about 120 feet in dizzying height.

According to the Indians, an entire herd of buffalo could be slaughtered at once in part by disguising oneself in a buffalo skin, and leading the herd over a precipice. A young warrior, selected for the act, adorns himself in buffalo skin, pretends to be a bison and situates himself between the herd and cliff. Other warriors surround the herd opposite the decoy, and drive the animals toward the lure, who hopefully jumps to safety before the buffalo stampede tramples him to death. If completed as planned, one after the other, the bison run over the edge and tumble to their fate onto the shore below. In honor of this ancient practice of procuring food wholesale, we named the nearby stream "Slaughter River."

On the last day of May, we encountered more riffles and mild rapids, as the river became shallower. The rocky obstructions were such that in some areas the only way to advance was for the men to plunge into the cold water up to their chests, and pull the boats with rotting and fragile tow ropes. The men spent approximately a quarter of their time in the water in many places where their moccasins had to be removed to enable them to slog through thick mud and walk on slippery stones. The stones had originally tumbled from the high cliffs adjacent to the river. As the men pulled the white pirogue through a particularly gravelly section, the decomposing rope snapped under the great tension. The swift current quickly swung the boat against a large rock, and was again in danger of capsizing when the men saved her by retying the line, and pulling it to safety. I feared the evil genie who appeared to possess this craft might one day win, and send the boat and her cargo to the bottom of the drink.

Further on, the land and cliffs along the river transformed into contours that took on a most romantic appearance.

The white, sandstone bluffs varied in height from 2 to 300 feet, and in most places rose nearly perpendicular to the water. Beyond the bluffs, the earth was comprised of dark, rich loam that extended a half-mile, and gradually ascended to meet bold, rolling hills, covered with short vegetation and prickly pear. Through the eons, the water and wind removed the soft and hard substances to differing degrees to forge cliffs and rocks into thousands of grotesque shapes and attractive figures. With a bit of imagination, some of the figures were the ruins of stone buildings and gothic churches, with buttresses, walls, and columns in various states of decomposition. A few of the figures had their columns intact — others had just a base — and more appeared to be remnants of toppled walls made of large dark bricks a few feet thick. Some white cliffs looked as if they were the cemented outer walls of a giant, impenetrable fortress. Many shapes looked as if they were narrow walls only a few feet in width, ranging in height from a few to hundreds of feet, towering above the river, which mirrored the shimmering images into ever-changing similes. Niches and alcoves of various forms and sizes were observed — some of which had globular nests attached to the rocks that industrious swallows utilized as well-protected homes.

At camp that evening, I penned the following in a futile endeavor to accurately summarize what we witnessed this day:

"As we passed on, it seemed as if those scenes of visionary enchantment would never have an end; for here it is too that nature presents to the view of the traveler vast ranges of walls of tolerable workmanship."

Beyond the white cliffs, we proceeded into a new month, and past the region I believed to be the Black Hills. From there, I could see handsome mountains to the northeast and south, and a more subdued and modest terrain nearest the river. The mountain range to the north was of no great distance, while the ones bearing south were much further, but still quite visible.

With the changing terrain, again came white bears, seeking easy feeding grounds in the vicinity of fish, elk, and other animals.

Charbonneau was busy on shore searching for edible plants when a bear spotted him, and decided to investigate the curious sight. Lumbering towards Charbonneau, the bear caught the attention of the Frenchman who immediately screamed, turned to run, and fired his rifle into the air. Charbonneau rounded a slight bend in the river, and ran past a puzzled Drouillard who turned his head to watch him disappear into a thicket where Charbonneau wept and trembled with fear. Not far behind, the bear followed, and a startled Drouillard scarcely had time to run. He raced up shore about 100 yards, and stopped after sensing the bear's pursuit had ceased. Turning to assess the situation, Drouillard had time to aim and fire a ball into the head of the curious creature. Wobbling for a few seconds, the bear dropped dead onto its side. Water splashed up, and began to soak its fur.

As the sun was setting that same day, we arrived opposite the mouth of a very large river, which appeared much like the Missouri. Having traveled 18 miles, and unsure which branch was the Missouri, we decided to encamp at this location, which was situated at a remarkable confluence.

“Well Captain, what do you make of the fork?” I asked, as we sat near our fire.

Pausing for a moment, Clark thought and wiped the sweat from his forehead with a long pull of his shirt sleeve.

“I’m not sure,” he replied in a somber tone. “It’s odd.”

“Yes,” I quickly responded, glancing toward him. “I don’t recall the Indians referencing this fork.”

“No. I don’t either,” Clark said, shaking his head.

I looked up into the night sky and sighed heavily.

“Then we don’t have much choice but go up both tomorrow.”

Clark grinned at the comical dichotomy of the circumstances and nodded. “Sure, but let’s worry about that in the morning.”

He then threw back a cup of whiskey, and stood to make his way to the latrine.

Watching him step into the darkness, I raised my cup in satirical toast: “To all forks big and small,” I yelled to him, as he disappeared into the shadows.

I gulped my whiskey and retired for the evening. The night proved mostly sleepless. During the early morning hours, I repeatedly wrestled with the fact that I could not understand why the Indians did not mention this fork. Moreover, I concluded after much deliberation that to choose the wrong stream this late in the spring would very likely cost us the whole of the traveling season, and depress the party to the extent that an incorrect decision may altogether defeat the entire expedition.

About eight the next morning, we broke camp to move to the other side of the river to a point formed by the confluence of the two great waterways. From there, I ordered Sergeants Gass and Pryor to each choose two men to accompany them upstream. Their mission was to make observations about the character of the river, including width, depth, turbidity, and turbulence and return by evening. Pryor was to ascend the north fork; Gass the south. In addition, I assigned the Field brothers to go by land up the south fork. In the meantime, the remaining men guarding camp made elk-skin clothes, and tended to their sore, bruised, and cut feet from walking barefoot on rocks and stones those days past.

While the men made clothes, Captain Clark and I decided to survey the land between the forks, and discovered a vast plain occupied by a large number of prickly pear and innumerable herds of buffalo, with a few wolves and antelope. Many snowy mountains were also seen jutting above the plain, which abruptly terminated to the southwest. Behind these mountains was a belt of more lofty ones, much greater in the distance, and also topped with snow. On our walk back to camp, Clark and I discovered a striking river less than two miles from camp, which discharged into the north fork on the larboard side. We agreed to name this the Tansy River, after a yellowish flowering plant we found in great abundance along its banks.

Back at camp, I recorded several additional celestial measurements, and deduced we were at 47 degrees, 24 minutes, and 12.8 seconds north latitude. Soon after entering the data into my field notes, the first of the three teams began arriving, separated by less than an hour. After supper, I ordered a council to discuss our findings. Surrounding a large fire, the entire party was aware of the gravity of the decision that was before us, regarding which fork to pursue. We gathered to talk, listen, and ponder the results. Some sat on logs, while others stood at ease.

"Sergeant Pryor, you go first," I suggested, standing near the center of the whole party, as the campfire burned.

"Well, we went up the north fork about 15 miles. It's a lot like most of the Missouri. It's muddy, and the bed is mud with a little gravel. Its shallowest section was about five feet. ... It appears slower than the south fork. ... That's about all we saw," Pryor stated in a calm, but loud voice.

Looking at the ground, I took a few steps and glanced up.

"Sergeant Gass, please report your observations," I said, turning in his direction.

"We also went about 15 miles, and found the south fork perfectly clear the whole way. There were many islands, and flat and round stones in the bed ... not much mud."

"How deep, Sergeant?" I asked.

"The shallowest part was about six feet," Gass responded.

I analyzed the statements and added my own: "And Captain Clark measured the width of the north fork at 200 yards, and south at 372 yards."

A moment of silence was followed by quiet discussion, as everyone processed the meaning of the reports, and translated for those who did not speak English. After a lull in talking, I resumed my inquiry.

"Private Joseph, what did you find?"

"We saw a lot of rolling hills. We only got seven miles before we had to turn back. ... I can't tell you much more than you already know," Field said.

"Captain Clark, what say you?" I said directly facing him, as he sat comfortably on a small piece of driftwood.

"The Indians did not mention a river like this falling in from the south. ... The north fork can't be 'The River Which Scolds All Others' because we passed that a long time ago." Clark stopped and examined the group. He collected his thoughts and continued: "I would expect the Missouri to be getting more rapid, clearer, and shallower coming from mountains, not muddier and slower."

After quickly assessing his logic while pacing about, I announced my conclusion: "I agree. ... The north fork must acquire its appearance from soil particles in the water. This could only come from passing through many miles of open plains. I suspect it originates on the eastern side of the Rockies somewhere in British Territory, rather than flowing through the first range of mountains to the southwest. Therefore, I am confident the route to the great waterfall and Columbia is the south fork, not the north."

I paused to plan the next course of action, and resumed my message: "With that said, I am interested in hearing everyone's opinion who wishes to offer one. ... We are in this together, so feel free to express yourselves."

Most of the men voiced their concerns, and were not persuaded by our analysis. They felt the true Missouri was the turbid north fork, not the clear south fork. Given this dispute, and the fact the decision affected the whole party, I sought to continue building unanimity.

After briefly conferring with Clark, I voiced our intentions: "I respect your views, and want to alleviate your apprehensions. Early tomorrow we shall send two squads by land up each fork. I will lead one. Captain Clark will lead the other. We will go at least a day and a half up each. Hopefully, one of us will find the falls. This should settle the question."

Clark decided to take the south fork with York, Gass, Shannon, and the Field brothers. For my squad, I selected Drouillard, Pryor, Shields, Windsor, Cruzatte, and Lepage.

With the council concluded, we refreshed the men with a generous allotment of whiskey. Later that evening in our tent, and for the first time as an Army officer, I prepared a knapsack to carry the supplies I would need for the three-or-four-day trip. Carrying such provisions was usually a duty of enlisted men, rather than officers. However, I felt it important to lug my own gear in demonstration of my commitment to building consensus for this critical decision.

The morning sun was draped behind a wall of clouds, as Captain Clark's team and mine separated. Quite early it was apparent the path on which my group was traveling was a huge, continuous plain that appeared to extend to the foot of the mountains far in the distance. The soil appeared dark and fertile, yet the ground was covered with anemic grass and vast numbers of prickly pear that readily pierced moccasins, and proved extremely troublesome. Despite these immediate problems, our eyes were saluted with a majestic sight in the distance of a square-looking mountain that took the appearance of a gigantic barn.

On the 5th of June, we observed a similar vision in the form of a large conic mountain adjacent to others northwest of our position. Along the river, great furrows were cut into the banks from eons of water flowing from the plain, down the bank, and eroding the earth to create intimidating ravines that would be daunting to even the most intrepid hiker.

Having progressed about 60 miles by the 6th, I was convinced that fork was too far north to originate near the southern headwaters of the Columbia, but still dispatched Pryor and Windsor with orders to proceed up to a commanding eminence to further apprise our position.

While the pair searched for a prominent landmark, the remainder of our squad was busy constructing two rafts on which we planned to float back to camp. Through great effort, we procured five elk skins, and had wrapped them around wooden frames when the idea was abandoned after we determined the crafts to be too narrow and small to facilitate safe passage. With the weight of each man and his provisions and weapons, the bottom surface area of the raft was simply not large enough to displace enough water to stay afloat. We had no other option but to return by land, which was disagreeable in no small part because the weather had taken a turn for the worse. Rain began to pour from the sky toward evening. Our situation was made even more uncomfortable, since we had no shelter for camping.

The depressing shower continued through the night and into the morning, which congruently not only had a gloomy effect on my disposition, but the other men. Nonetheless, we marched forward on remarkably slippery ground that accumulated and clung to our boots and moccasins, making our trek very difficult. This soil was heavily laden with clay that was hard to saturate and equally difficult to yield its moisture once absorbed. Walking was not unlike stepping on mushy soap. With each step, the gumbo clumped and covered our footwear to make subsequent steps that much heavier and unsteady.[C] Going was slow and treacherous.

In hiking along the face of one of these steep bluffs, I slipped at a very narrow pass, which was about 30 yards in length, and a few feet in width. But I made a quick and fortunate recovery by means of my spontoon. Had I failed to execute this maneuver, I should have suffered significant injuries, if not perished during a fall down a craggy precipice of about 90 feet, and into the churning river. I scarcely reached a place on which I could safely stand before I heard a voice behind me scream out from above the din of the rain,

"God! God! Captain! What shall I do!"

With anxiety in the extreme, I spun to find Windsor facing me, prostrate near the center of the pass, and the men behind staring in shock. His right arm and leg were dangling over the slanted precipice, while his left fingers dug into the oozing gumbo, searching for something solid on which to grasp. Windsor's rifle lay a short distance away farthest from the ledge. His predicament was quite tenuous, and I expected him slip over the edge at any moment. Although much alarmed, I disguised my anxiety to assure him he was not in danger.

Recalling my near-death fall a little more than a year earlier at Tavern Bluffs, I calmly instructed Windsor:

"You're … You're fine. Remain calm, and we'll get you out."

"Yes … Yes, Sir," Windsor responded in a terrified, but low voice.

"Remove your knife with your right hand, and dig a hole for your right foot," I instructed, over the sound of the rain.

Windsor unsheathed the blade from his belt. He was able to reach down and carve a small foothold, after slicing through inches of wet and dry clay. He slowly raised his leg, applied pressure on the hole, and was able to push himself to his knees, as large amounts of gumbo flowed up around him.

"That's good, Private! Now, carefully take off your moccasins and crawl towards me."

He slipped the coverings off his feet, and cautiously advanced — knife clutched in his right hand, rifle in his left. With Windsor to safety, and his moccasins where he left them on the pass, I ordered the other men away from the pass and back to the river at the bottom of the bluff where we would meet them.

Realizing that returning by the plains was not possible because of the imposing bluffs and ravines obstructing our access, we had no option but to wade through chest-deep waters and mud along shore. In areas where the water was too deep, we cut footholds in the bluffs to advance. We continued our disagreeable march through the rain and cold, and covered only 18 miles by evening. With great relief, we discovered an abandoned Indian stick lodge, which offered much-needed shelter, after the most uncomfortable day we had yet experienced. Having killed six deer for supper, we ate heartily, and retired for the night to dry and cordial conditions.

By late morning the following day, the sky had cleared, which made travel much easier. We moved swiftly, and were able to reach the confluence by early evening where Clark had been waiting all day.

"Welcome back. We were about to send a search party if you didn't return," Clark greeted us with much relief.

"Thank you. When did you get back?" I asked.

"Yesterday. I take it you had problems."

"More than you can imagine. … Tell me what you found," I responded.

"We got up about 45 miles, but did not see the falls. The river curves southwest. … Private Joseph was nearly caught by a bear on the 4th. We shot at it, and yelled. Thankfully, the bear took to the water. Other than that, the river was as Gass reported," Clark said.

"We didn't see the falls either. We got up 60 miles. I'm convinced the fork is too north to be the Missouri," I replied.

Later, we held another council, and again failed to persuade the men that the south fork was the true Missouri. Convinced otherwise, and following Clark's lead, I named the north fork after my lovely, young cousin, Miss Maria Wood, and called it "Maria's River."

Watching Clark plot the rivers' paths on a map that night as I sipped whiskey, I became more suspect of the veracity of instruments carried by one Peter Fidler — a surveyor for the Hudson's Bay Company. More accurately, I suspected Mr. Fidler himself was the problem. I understood that Fidler claimed to have traveled in this area, south to the forty-fifth parallel, yet the British map based on his observations had no details about any waterfall, and the Missouri River only flowed east on the map, originating in mountains north of 45 degrees latitude. I was puzzled, but confident I understood what likely happened.

Now that I have done the business, I understand that while exploring the area near the Blackfeet nation, Fidler obtained his information in 1801 from a Blackfeet Chief named "The Feathers" who drew him a map about the headwaters of the Missouri, and drainage network of the upper Missouri along the eastern Rocky Mountain front. This information was eventually communicated to London cartographer Aaron Arrowsmith who created a detailed map in 1802, which was obtained by Jefferson.

In preparation for of our journey, Jefferson assigned Secretary of the Treasury, Albert Gallatin, to find an American cartographer who could create the best map possible for us. For this task, Gallatin worked with Nicholas King who combined information from nine explorations, including ones led by George Vancouver, Alexander Mackenzie, and David Thompson. On his 1803 map, King drew the Mandan and Hidatsa villages at approximately 46 degrees north latitude, and 101 degrees west longitude. He also drew a remarkable mountain called the "Boars Tooth" at the same latitude, but west at about 114 degrees longitude amid a single chain of mountains comprising the Rockies. We were then within 100 miles of the Rocky Mountains, and I had already determined we were at 47 degrees latitude. Therefore, I deduced that the river must turn south somewhere between the Missouri and Maria confluence, and the foothills of the mountains. This meant I believed the Missouri entered the mountains a great deal north of 45 degrees — not even remotely close to where Fidler claimed.

On the 9th of June, many were engaged in dressing skins for clothes when we determined to cache all our heavy baggage, and store the red pirogue for the return voyage. We made this decision because we would soon be entering the mountains, and needed to provide some relief to the men hauling the boats.

Because Private Cruzatte was well-acquainted with constructing caches, I left him to supervise the project. He chose a location on a high plain about 40 yards from a steep bluff, located on the northern side of the south fork.

To build a suitable cache, sod was carefully removed, and a hole was excavated that was about 20 inches in diameter and seven feet in depth. As the hole became deeper, the men increased its diameter, which gave it the appearance of being a subterranean kettle. Once excavated, the sides and bottoms were lined with sticks, branches, dry grass, and animal hides. If properly completed, I was assured the stored items would keep perfectly for several years. Traders on the Missouri — particularly those engaged in trade with the Sioux — were obliged to utilize this method to avoid being robbed.

At the end of that day, we held another meeting in which Sacajawea strongly argued in favor of the south fork. She and the Indians informed us that water at the Great Falls was nearly transparent, and this was certainly the case for the south fork. Still, most of the party was not convinced. This was because Cruzatte had declared the north fork to be the true, genuine Missouri, and could be no other, due to its murky flow. The men had a great deal of respect for Cruzatte's integrity and knowledge of the Missouri, and were understandably grappling with the issue of who was correct.

Regardless, the party reaffirmed their commitment to our leadership by very cheerfully indicating they were ready to follow us wherever we led them, but still felt the south fork would terminate in the mountains far from the Columbia. Finding them married to this belief and wishing to correct ourselves should we be in error, we decided by the end of the council to send a scouting party by land far up the south fork to search for the falls, or enter the mountains.

With the meeting completed, Cruzatte pulled out his violin, and the men passed the evening dancing and singing. All were in good spirits.

Daybreak arrived, and Private Shields endeavored to repair the main spring on my air gun, which had somehow broken since the time it was last used the previous fall. On many occasions Shields had been of great service to the party through his ingenuity — making tools, artisan work with metal and wood, and skills as a waterman and hunter. After inspecting the newly repaired gun and placing it in my tent, I hiked to inspect the cache.

It was sight a to behold. Before sealing the cache with buffalo hides, soil, and turf, we stored two axes, one auger, blacksmith bellows, hammers, tongs, one keg of flour, two kegs of parched meal, two kegs of pork, one keg of salt, chisels, tin cups, two muskets, three bear skins, beaver skins, sheep horns, and superfluous baggage of every description. However, we still had many more goods to deposit, and decided to build a second cache the following day.

With the second cache site under consideration, we then started the process of securing the red pirogue. Similar to the manner in which we hauled the boats out of the river the previous winter, we constructed a log road, and pulled and pushed the red pirogue to the middle of a small island at the entrance of Maria's River. There she was secured to trees to prevent floods from carrying her off. Near the boat, I built a small fire, heated my branding iron, and burned my name and title into several trees, which then read: "U.S. Capt. M. Lewis." After imprinting the trees, we covered the pirogue with brush to shelter her from the negative effects of the elements.

At camp that night, I felt ill, as did Sacajawea, but was determined to leave early and travel up the south fork. Accordingly, I issued orders to Drouillard, Private Joseph, Gibson, and Goodrich to accompany me in the morning. During our absence, Clark agreed to complete the second cache, and then follow by water.

Stress and anxiety were growing to find the falls before the season aged and recovery was not possible in avoiding another brutal winter in the wilderness. Should that have proved to be the case, our lives would surely have been in great peril, given our diminishing supplies in a yet unmapped section of the nation.

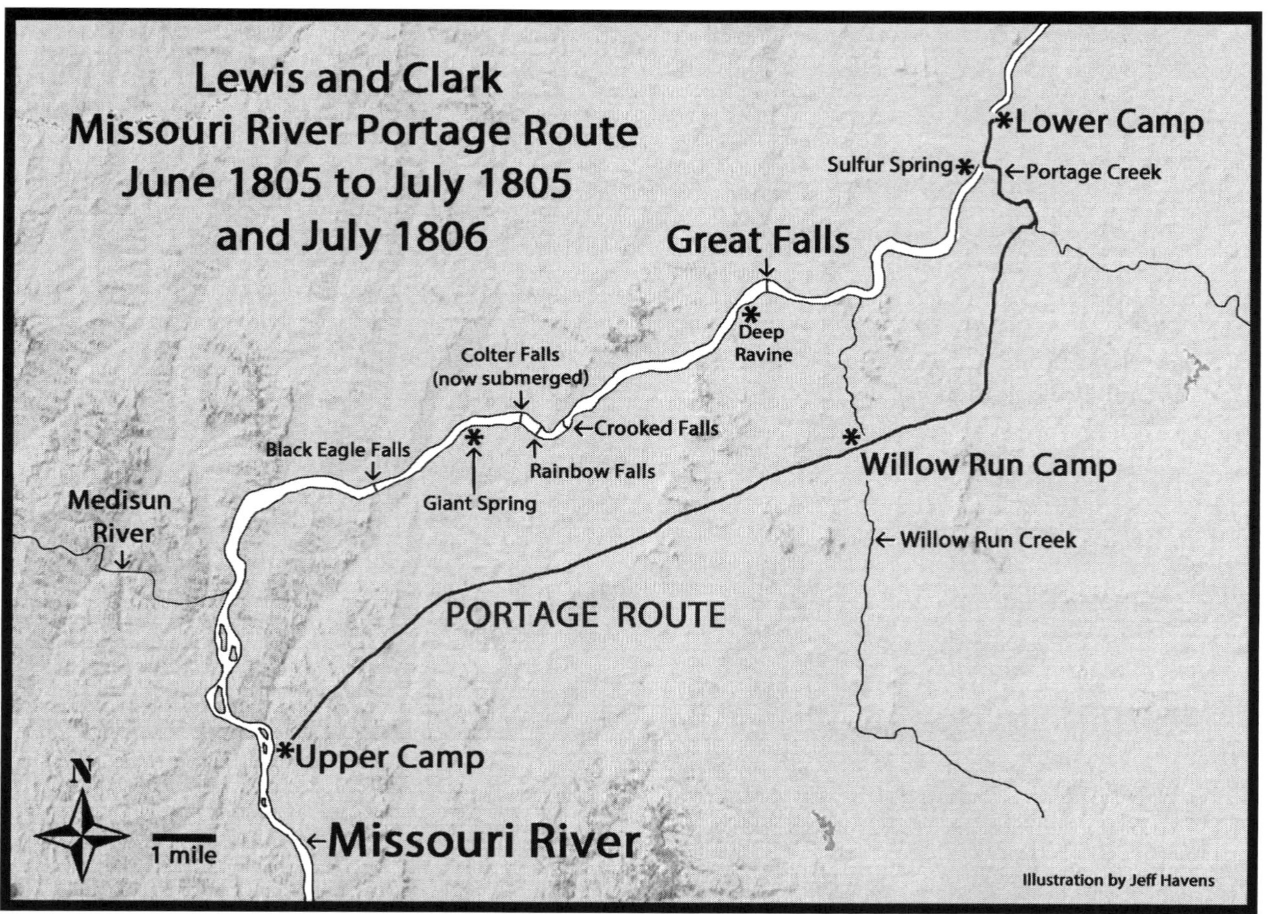

Lewis and Clark
Missouri River Portage Route
June 1805 to July 1805
and July 1806
*Lower Camp
Sulfur Spring*
←Portage Creek
Great Falls
Deep Ravine
Colter Falls
(now submerged)
←Crooked Falls
Black Eagle Falls
Rainbow Falls
Giant Spring
Willow Run Camp
Medisun River
←Willow Run Creek
PORTAGE ROUTE
*Upper Camp
N
1 mile
←Missouri River
Illustration by Jeff Havens

CHAPTER FOURTEEN PORTAGE

June 11, 1805
Expectation Camp: 2,521 miles above the Missouri confluence

Dawn was ushered in by clear and pleasant weather, and shortly after eight, I led my squad by land in hopes of finding the falls, despite being weakened by my disorder. The overstuffed pack on my shoulder jostled, as we hiked the vast plain where elk made themselves easy targets for several meals. After killing four elk, and the men consuming their fill, we hung the excess in trees for the remainder of the party.

Despite the bounty, I could not partake. Even before the meat was cooked, I was overtaken with such violent and inexplicable abdominal pain I found it impossible to eat. While the cramps raged, we slowly marched several additional miles until I was unable to proceed, after a high fever added to the pain. The group remained with me, and we camped, having traveled only nine miles. Wishing to alleviate my suffering and not having brought any medicine, I experimented with the twigs of a chokecherry plant for relief. I stripped the leaves, cut the twigs two inches in length, and boiled the strands in water, which yielded a dark, astringent, and bitter concoction for drinking. I repeated the process every hour until ten that night when I was completely relieved of my affliction, which permitted me a refreshing slumber through the early morning.

As I struggled to hike further into the unknown that day, Sacajawea was also very ill with symptoms similar to my own. Captain Clark bled her, which appeared to be of great service. While Clark aided our interpreter, the men completed the cache whose construction consumed the whole of the day.

Buried in this cache were: Two powder canisters; a lead bar; a keg filled with salted pork; two kegs of parched meal; blacksmith bellows; tin cups; one Dutch oven; hand mill; pelts of buffalo, bear and beaver; axes; auger; keg of flour; cask of salt; chisel; two muskets; beaver traps; and different animal horns. After fitting the last piece of sod on top of the hole, the group spent a final night at Maria's River Camp before proceeding on the following morning — a half-day behind us.

Anxious to view whatever might be ahead, my squad set out at sunrise — after I drank one more dose of my therapeutic concoction. We hiked away from the river to avoid steep ravines, until the heat of day necessitated our moving back to the river to allay our great thirst. By ten that morning, we advanced 15 miles when we happened upon two white bears near the river, and promptly killed both. Like the elk the previous day, we hung the leftover meat and skins from trees, which is where I penned a note informing Clark of our progress, and secured it to a stick with ribbon.

Climbing the bluffs and hiking on the plain once again, we were able to travel another 12 miles before stopping for the night. During the hike, we were afforded a spectacular view of many snow-covered mountains spanning from the southeast to northwest. Several separate ranges comprised these mountains in succession, rather than being one continuous range, as our maps suggested. To my amazement, each succeeding range rose higher than the previous one, until the most distant peaks were shrouded in clouds far to the west.

This landscape was a stark contrast to the single range of mountains depicted on the maps, and offered me concern about the difficulty that likely lay ahead. At camp that night, I once again could not help but sense dread knowing we must soon travel up and over those formidable barriers to reach the ocean. However, where and when was still a mystery, despite having the maps and information from the Indians. Should the area in which we were to pass over these mountains be similar to the ones I was observing, this would only serve to increase the importance and role of our interpreter, Sacajawea, to aid us in negotiating for horses with her people. But I still trusted that the learned geographers' assessment that the Northwest Passage should be a tolerable road, which would minimize or perhaps even eliminate the need for horses. The King and Arrowsmith maps suggested this was the case, and the range that separated the east and west flowing waters was pyramidal in shape, offering an easy portage to the south branch of the Columbia River, which flowed to the sea.

Towards that end, on the 13th of June, my squad ascended the bluffs once more, and again walked the plain, which was perfectly flat and rolled on for at least 50 or 60 miles before terminating at the horizon. The entire area was covered with more buffalo than I had ever witnessed in a single view. Tens of thousands of the beasts cautiously grazed on the short grass, which was a deep, emerald green. After walking about a dozen miles, we observed two odd projections, separated by a short distance. They were square in appearance, jutting up hundreds of feet perpendicular to the plain; regal spectacles with profound grooves on their sides that gave one the impression that these were immense fortresses, built by giant overlords for supervising this enormous plain.

We stared in wonder at these mountainous forts, and I soon brought the team's attention back to more urgent concerns. With Field and Goodrich on my right, and Drouillard and Gibson on my left, I ordered Field, Gibson, and Drouillard to hunt for our next meal. Afterward, they were to meet Goodrich and me upriver.

I proceeded on with Goodrich far behind, while he plucked prickly pear needles from his moccasins and feet. Passing a spring that had the odor of sulfur and visual signs of iron, I filled my canteen, moved on, and gradually heard a faint rumbling in front of me — wondering if this was a stampeding herd of buffalo. I picked up the pace, and soon my ears were saluted with the unmistakable sound of not buffalo, but water cascading over a great precipice. I anxiously hurried forward to verify what I anticipated with unspeakable joy. I could see what appeared to be great columns of smoke billowing up and disappearing below the horizon in a cyclical manner, driven by a strong wind from the southwest.

Within a few minutes, the roar was overwhelming. I raced down a bluff, 200 feet in height to finally regard the Great Falls of the Missouri. Quickly scanning the area for the best vantage point, I leaped from rock to rock to take position on a pile of stones opposite the center of the falls. I stared in awe for several minutes, transfixed by the most magnificent vision I ever beheld.[15]

On the far larboard side, a tremendous volume of water flowed smoothly along the horizontal plane until it tumbled over a cliff of at least 80 feet where it acquired a frothy, white appearance before smashing onto the rocks below. After being beaten with great fury, a tremendous spray rose many feet from the basin where colors of the rainbow could be seen, while the sun's light passed through the foggy mist at the bottom of this splendid sight.

The remaining portion of the falls was comprised of two ledges separated by perhaps 30 or 40 yards. Spilling over the first and lesser of the ledges, the water temporarily collected in a roiling pool before being dumped over the greater ledge where irregular and projecting rocks received the beaten water, and further broke it into a perfect, white foam, which assumed a thousand forms in an instant — sometimes flying up in jets to a height of 15 or 20 feet that disappeared as quickly as they were created.

After writing this imperfect description in my field notes, I again gazed upon the falls and was disgusted with my attempt to capture its grandeur in words. I briefly considered penning another effort, but thought better. If gifted with the abilities, my wish would be to give you an enlightened idea of just how truly striking this object is in authenticity, which had been so long concealed from the view of civilized man. Even my drawing the scene would not have offered justice to its majesty. Conceding to my juvenile wordsmith and artistic limitations, I retired to the shade of a tree on the north bank where I determined we would make camp.

I lay there and waited for the others — having walked 51 miles in nearly as many hours. I was confident these were the falls the Indians had described, since it was much greater in height than an eagle's nest. The Hidatsa also said that underneath this falls, several people could walk abreast and safely pass from one side of the river to the other without getting their feet wet, which also proved to be true.

Limping from the ache of small puncture wounds in his feet, Goodrich arrived — followed by the others two hours later. They arrived with nothing, after finding the area devoid of game. But despite disappointment and the absence of game, they were as equally impressed with the falls, and relieved we had taken the correct route.

Searching for a suitable landing for the canoes to begin our portage around the falls, I walked alone downstream three miles. I found rapids and perpendicular cliffs up to 200 feet in height that rendered this section impossible as a staging area for the effort. Disappointed with my findings, I hiked back to camp where I ordered Private Joseph to deliver a note in the morning to Captain Clark, informing him of our great success, and to stay near the river for the purpose of finding a proper area to stage the canoes for the portage.

A few hours after Field broke camp the next day, I left Goodrich, Drouillard, and Gibson behind with instructions to hunt and await my return. My mission for this day was to investigate where the rapids above terminated. For several miles, the river was a continuous rapid interspersed with three small cascades, each about five feet in height. To my great surprise, four miles upstream, I happened upon another waterfall, crooked in nature, which was about 20 feet in height. From that fall, about a half-mile in the distance, I viewed another fall to which I anxiously hurried for closer examination. This was as equally handsome as the first, and from there, I could see yet another no greater than 400 yards from where I stood.

After finding four waterfalls, and more rapids than anticipated, I was determined to follow the river to the head of these protracted challenges, even if it should have detained me all night.

Three miles beyond the fourth fall, I discovered a fifth cataract. By then, the only solace with regards to discovering an easy portage was that the bluffs along the river were finally decreasing in severity. Hiking another two miles past the last fall I saw the river took a sharp bend to the south where at no great distance I observed herds of buffalo, and another river flowing in from the west. I feasted my eyes on this magnificent sight, and was convinced this was the river the Indians called the Medisun, and subsequently made my descent to the confluence of these two great waterways.

According to the Hidatsa, the north side of the falls was the area through which canoes and baggage could be easily transported to the Medisun. They also said the Medisun originated in the mountains west of the confluence. Opposite the headwaters of the Medisun River was another waterway, on the west side of the mountains that flowed into a large river, which they said was not navigable because of its violent rapids and shoals. The King and Arrowsmith maps suggested this was the Great Lake River, which Indians claimed was only eight nights from the sea. I believed this trail led to the conjectural north fork of the Columbia River. However, our orders from President Jefferson were to explore the region to the headwaters of the Missouri, and the maps indicated there was likely a south fork of the Columbia at approximately 45 degrees north latitude, and 114 west longitude. This was the route we were to follow; where the legendary, but speculative Northwest Passage was supposed to exist.

After studying the confluence area, and viewing suitable driftwood for fire and trees for shelter, I decided to camp at that spot, rather than rejoin the others at the first fall. Under this auspice, I hiked a short distance onto the plain and selected a fat buffalo to shoot for supper.

After unslinging my rifle, I placed the barrel of the weapon on the metal crossbar of my spontoon to steady my aim and fired. The ball found its mark in a lung, and I attentively watched as the poor animal began to discharge large quantities of blood from its mouth and nostrils. The great beast did not immediately fall, as I expected. It staggered and moaned in great agony. Its nose and tongue oozed huge quantities of crimson liquid. I could scarcely look on, as complex and conflicting emotions suddenly overwhelmed my being. I wished very much for the beast to die, rather than linger in its tortured condition.

I gazed a few additional seconds, and was about to reload my weapon when suddenly my attention was redirected. I sensed a disturbance from behind. Much alarmed, I quickly spun to find a large white bear had advanced to within 20 paces of me. Instinctively, I raised my gun to eliminate the impending danger, but instantly realized the folly of not immediately reloading after discharge. The bear was closing in, and I recalled the observations I had shared with the men less than two months prior about my being an equal match with the bear near the water or woods, but much less certain on the plain. Quickly weighing my options, I chose to retreat at a pace equal to the bear's advance. I slowly turned and took three steps at a brisk pace. Glancing back, I saw the bear charging toward me with its sharp, white teeth clearly visible, just as the natives said.

I sprinted for the safety of the river with the rifle in one hand and spontoon in the other. After covering about 80 yards, I could sense the beast gaining, and the thought overcame me that I should defend myself in the water at such a depth that I could stand and the beast would be obliged to swim. Dust puffed up from under my feet as I ran another few yards down an embankment. My feet and ankles splashed into the water, and soon I was waist deep in the river. At this instant, I turned to face the bear while slinging the rifle onto my shoulder. Within another second, I confronted the threat with the sharp edge of my spontoon directly pointing at the beast.

The bear was at the edge of the water and about to follow me into the river when my sudden change in defense and glistening metal of the spontoon in the late afternoon sun confused the animal. The bear locked its legs, skidded to a stop, and swiftly retreated back up the bank and onto the plain. Amazed and delighted with this twist of fortune, I waded out of the river and watched the frightened creature run at top speed for three miles until it disappeared into the woods along the Medisun River. During the whole of its unexpected withdrawal, the bear sometimes glanced back, as if expecting hostile pursuit. Analyzing what transpired, I was at a loss to explain the cause for the bear's alarm, but felt most gratified it declined combat. I reloaded my rifle, and retraced my path where I could see the ground torn up by the bear's great claws, which were directly imprinted on my own footsteps in the thin soil.

In nearly the same direction as the bear's flight, I walked the plain a short way to explore the Medisun River, and on my return happened upon an animal I initially thought a wolf. As I drew nearer, I could see this was not that creature, but something I had never seen. The strange beast crouched down like a cat about to pounce on prey. It was large, brown and yellow. The monster was aggressively stooped near a burrow, and appeared somewhat like a giant polecat. In no mood for additional threats, I once again teamed my rifle and spontoon for a steady shot. After firing the weapon, I watched the animal disappear into its hole, which signaled my aim was off, but the threat was still neutralized.

I reloaded, and had not moved on more than a few hundred yards when I saw three bull buffalo observe my movements. They subsequently became upset with my very presence. The bulls separated from the herd, which was within a half-mile of my position. After casting investigative stares in my direction and intently smelling the air, the trio suddenly charged toward me, running abreast at a velocity equal to that of the bear's retreat, as if possessed by a demon. I watched and listened, as their pounding hooves became louder. To entertain them, and retest my newfound defense, I defiantly walked out at a very swift pace to confront the group, in abundant frustration with the day's events.

As I angrily paced toward them, it seemed my predicament was that all the beasts of this neighborhood had formed a legion resolute on destroying me. I also thought it possible the pirogue's evil genie had abandoned the boat, and was then disposed to amuse herself at my expense. Regardless of the circumstance, I continued my brazen march, and could distinctly feel the ground shake and rumble. At a distance of about 50 yards, the three bulls suddenly slowed and stopped. They turned and darted back to rejoin the herd as quickly as they had separated from it.

Shaking my head in disbelief, I quickly concluded to leave this place; for prudence dictated such action. I started back to camp — passed the buffalo I killed — and decided to leave it as a sacrificial offering to the wicked legion.

The sun was beginning to set, and I should have believed these circumstances a terrible dream had it not been for the prickly pear needles puncturing the soles of my feet to remind me that I was still very much awake. Near eleven that night, I finally arrived at camp. The men were extremely uneasy about my fate. They had even planned search routes had I not arrived by sunrise. I shared my story with them, and enjoyed a well-deserved meal before retiring for the night.

While I was experiencing curious encounters with the unlikely legion of wildlife, at Clark's camp, three men, and Sacajawea were ill with symptoms not unlike the ones I had recently suffered. In addition, at about four in the afternoon, Private Joseph arrived with my note informing Clark of my finding the falls. After reading the note, Clark slept comfortably knowing we were on the correct route. The night passed, and after hunting and fishing all the next day, I watched a dark figure emerge from the dusk near our campfire.

"Private Field. Welcome back," I said to the soldier, as he placed his rifle butt on the ground.

"Thank you, Captain. I am happy to report I gave Captain Clark your note."

"Good," I replied. "And?" I asked, staring up at him from my seat on small log.

"They stopped near a creek," Private Joseph factually reported. "They can't go no further 'cause of the rapids, so they made camp on the south side. They're having a time with all the rattlesnakes."

I nodded my head, and thought for a moment before responding — thinking about the legion. I silently laughed to myself at the comical adhesion.

"In the morning, I want you to go back and tell the Captain two things: Bring up some men to take back this meat," I said, pointing toward 600 hundred pounds of dried beef, and dozens of trout hanging from branches in several trees.

"The other is he should start looking for a portage route on the south side. … The north side has deep ravines. It will be too difficult there. From what I can see, the south side appears flat. It should also be shorter, since the river turns south for as far as I could see.

"Understood?" I asked, glancing at his face for assurance that he was listening.

"Understood, Captain," the Private quickly replied.

While I issued the new orders to Field, Charbonneau was six miles downstream appealing to Clark for his family to return to the Mandan village, in light of Sacajawea's inability to recover from her illness. Clark explained the folly of such a move, and urged Charbonneau to allow us to properly treat her. After a bitter debate, Charbonneau reluctantly agreed to allow external treatments, but refused any other medicine without his prior approval. Clark disappointedly forwent any oral medication, and subsequently applied a Peruvian-bark compress to her lower abdominal region to which she responded favorably.

On the 16th of June, the men arrived for the meat and fish. My squad and I returned with them to camp about a mile below the mouth of the belted creek. Upon entering camp, I looked down to find an extremely ill Sacajawea lying on a buffalo robe. After briefly conversing with Charbonneau, Clark and I persuaded him to allow us to continue the bark compress treatment, along with administering to her a drink mixed with opium and water — the water of which was obtained from the sulfur spring I previously encountered during my search for the falls.

Had the Indian woman died, Captain Clark and I were of the opinion that the sole responsibility would rest upon her husband's failure to heed our medical counsels, and his callous disregard to earlier recognize her condition and accordingly act. If she did not soon recover, I feared her remains would soon be atop a scaffold facing west, and we would be without an interpreter to assist in our negotiations for horses with the Snake Indians. Having then seen the ranges we would likely cross, these horses were very likely needed for us to travel up and over those daunting mountains still to the west — the alternative being to pass on foot, hiking over unknown terrain for an equally unknown distance.

With these thoughts burdening my mind, I peered up at Clark. I changed the topic to the more immediate task as I knelt on one knee beside her.

"I figure the portage on the south side is about 16 miles," I said, as Clark watched me hold the compress on Sacajawea's abdomen.

She moaned and writhed in pain.

"That's too far to carry all the baggage and canoes," he replied, standing over both of us, simultaneously listening and watching me by her side.

"The south side is it. It's the best option," I emphasized.

"I agree. I already sent Shields and McNeal up this morning to assess conditions," Clark said.

"What did they find?"

"They haven't returned."

Thinking for a moment, I looked down, and glanced back toward Clark.

"We should leave the pirogue here. I can build the iron boat to substitute for it," I suggested, with a definitive aim to persuade.

"Alright then, we need to cache some more items to lighten the load ..." Clark added, and suddenly cut off his own remarks upon seeing the pair return from their scouting mission.

"Welcome back," he cheerfully greeted McNeal and Shields.

"Thank you, Captain," McNeal wearily said, exhausted from their day of hiking.

"Well, how was it?" I anxiously inquired.

"Not good, Sir," reported McNeal. "There are two steep hills on this side."

I shook my head in disappointment.

"The south side is the best option. For better or worse, this is it," I reemphasized.

"Right ... In the morning, I'll take five men out to stake the best route," Clark said.

"Fine ... This is gonna take a lot more than a half-day," I responded.

"It's gonna take more than a week to move all six canoes, maybe two," Clark speculated. "What if we build new ones upstream?"

"No. It took us nearly a month to make six last winter, and we already cached some axes," I reminded him.

"I suppose," Clark acknowledged, looking down and rubbing his hand over his chin, which was covered with a week's growth of stubby whiskers.

Turning my head away from Clark, I shouted, "Sergeant Pryor!"

"Sir!" Pryor replied, standing up, and jogging to me.

"I want you to take five men to the mouth of the creek, and find some cottonwood trees for eight wheels and two carriages."

"Yes, Captain," Pryor responded.

He quickly turned, selected a crew, and they immediately departed. By evening, they returned, after locating trees for the purpose.

Night passed, and in the morning, Captain Clark led his men to survey the portage route, while I had six men begin constructing truck wheels. The four sets of axels and wheels were to be built complete with couplings and tongues to carry our canoes and belongings. We were fortunate to find one tree that was nearly two feet in diameter, which was perfect for cross-cutting into all the wheels. Meanwhile, the remainder of the party was employed in pulling the dugouts nearly two miles up the belted stream, which we then called "Portage Creek." The voyage up the creek was quite arduous because of rapids and rocks that constituted its bed. This made pulling the vessels up the waterway a colossal effort. Nearly every man was required for the difficult task.

While these two groups were working separately, I discovered many of the elk skins that were previously procured to cover the iron-framed boat were in a state of decomposition that rendered them useless for the task; more would have to be harvested to complete the vessel. I subsequently gave an order to do just that in hopes that the *Experiment* would prove positive.

While our groups labored up the creek and on the plain, just above the falls, a large bull buffalo had trodden into the water.

A short distance away, the entire herd was scattered along the riverbank, watching the bull's lead.

He slowly moved into the swift current, and it rippled and flowed around his spindly legs. The bull took a few more steps. His hooves were suddenly swept off the riverbed, and the bull was soon immersed up to his neck in water. Then helplessly drifting into the main channel of the river, the huge beast frantically kicked its legs and made some progress in reaching the opposite shore. But the current was much greater than the bull's ability to fight the increasing force of the river, as it drew nearer a roaring precipice.

Carrying the doomed beast to the edge, it quickly disappeared under the horizon. Turning and tumbling in its long descent, the bull met fate when his head smashed onto a craggy rock at the bottom of the falls — shattering into many large chunks and small pieces. Floating downstream, the bull's headless carcass bobbed in the rough waters, leaving behind a crimson stream. It finally came to rest on the opposite shore, alongside the remains of many others that met a similar destiny. A few minutes later, a dozen more freshly mangled corpses from the herd joined the bull, where five white bears feasted on the abundance.

A short distance from this fall, on the opposite bank near a fine spring, Captain Clark unsheathed his knife to carve his name, date, and height of the Great Falls on a large cottonwood tree. Meanwhile, about five miles downstream, Sacajawea rested under a similar tree. She was feeling much better — free of fever and pain. Clark and I were quite relieved.

As she recovered, the following morning all hands were employed in the Herculean task of dragging the white pirogue into a dense thicket of willows, which was about 100 yards northeast of the area named "Lower Portage Camp." The men removed the plugs from the bottom of the boat, and covered her with driftwood and bushes in a manner similar to how we protected the red pirogue. One of my hopes was that this would appease the evil genie, and it would not haunt another vessel. By evening, the pirogue was secured, the carriages for the portage were complete, and Captain Clark discovered a giant spring between the fourth and fifth falls that greatly dwarfed the sulfur spring I had discovered.

The volume of water flowing up from this spring was simply enormous. Clark had little doubt this was the largest such fountain in America. This colossal source of pure water surged up from a bed of rocks into a large pool that lazily bubbled and flowed into the Missouri, but retained its crystal transparency with a beautiful blue tint for nearly a half-mile before it slowly diffused into the river's opaque waters. Like the falls themselves, to attempt describing to you its magnificent appearance in words is simply not possible.

By the 19th, a new cache by our camp was ready for storing goods. Also, Sacajawea had recovered enough that she was able to walk and search for white apples, at the badgering behest of her husband. She gathered and ate a considerable quantity of this fruit, along with dried fish. Consequently, she then quickly relapsed with a high fever. Through the interpretation skills of Labiche, I severely rebuked Charbonneau for allowing her to consume such food so soon after her ailment. Without his consent, and contrary to Charbonneau's wishes, I then gave his ailing wife saltpeter and a tincture of opium laudanum through the day and evening to combat her further decline.

As I tried to save Sacajawea, most of the party was preparing for the portage by making moccasins from elk and buffalo hides. I also dispatched Drouillard, Private Reubin, and Shannon to the north side of the Medisun River to hunt elk. After doing what I could for our ill interpreter, I toured the camp watching the men sew, well aware of how necessary the footwear would be to protect the men from the impending onslaught of prickly pear needles.

The elk-hunting party departed and made their way upriver. Focused on the order to proceed to the Medisun, Private Shannon quickly marched ahead of the others, and was soon out of range to hear the shouts of Private Reubin and Drouillard who stopped to pluck the troublesome needles from their feet.[A] Shannon continued to walk, unaware that he was then well ahead of his companions. Despite hurrying to catch him, the straggling pair not only lost contact, but they could not find Shannon on arriving at the mouth of the Medisun. They searched for several hours. Seeing no sign of him or elk, Private Reubin and Drouillard eventually returned to the falls for better hunting opportunities. They hoped Shannon was well.

As I sat at my field desk writing in my journal the following day, I patiently awaited Clark's return. Hearing a rustling noise, I glanced up to see Clark and five men returning from their survey.

"Well, how's she look?" I asked.

"It's gonna be tough. The best route is the lower part to the islands with all the white bears. We marked it with stakes," Clark replied with trepidation.

"No, it won't be easy," I agreed.

"We're gonna need nearly every person for this effort. In all, it's a little more than 18 miles. Lots of rocks, gullies, prickly pear, and two steep hills … sure would be great if we had horses," Clark summarized.

"Indeed. We best not send anyone back to St. Louis then," I said.

Clark thought for a moment: "If we did, the others might resent it."

"Right … I don't see a good reason to send back another party. Warfington is probably already in St. Louis, assuming the Teton didn't get 'em. … Besides, the party seems to have made up their minds to succeed or perish in the attempt," I concluded.

Clark silently nodded in agreement, and paused to evaluate how best to present the next topic of discussion.

"I must inform you of a strange noise. … When the men and I were on the plains, we heard a noise about five or six miles to the northwest. … I'm not sure what it was, but it sounded like a cannon with six-pound balls.[10] I didn't hear it, at first. Private Joseph brought it to my attention. … I thought it might be thunder, but then I heard it, too. I looked up, but there wasn't a cloud in the sky. I heard it twice more, and figured it was west. … I don't know what it was," Clark explained with a perplexed look about him.

I listened and thought, but was at a loss to account for such a bizarre occurrence.

"Strange — certainly. I haven't heard it, and no one else said anything to me. Hopefully, no one here has access to artillery. If they do, that would not be good for anyone," I replied.

I can't imagine the Indians having such an arsenal," Clark said. "The Brits or French wouldn't barter for that."

"No, I don't think so either," I responded. "Perhaps the Spanish?"

"Whatever the source, I'm sure we'll find it," Clark assessed.

"Perhaps," I said, paused and changed the topic. "I think while you supervise the portage, I will take three men to assemble the iron boat. … I'll have Joseph, Gass, and Shields help me with the boat."

"That sounds fine. We'll start the day after tomorrow. We need a day to get the baggage on the plain, and time to dry out the canoes," Clark said.

"And I need more elk skins for the boat. Most are not in good condition," I replied in frustration.

Clark shook his head and responded: "Buffalo skins, sure. But I haven't seen many elk, lately."

"We'll do what we need then. … Still can't figure on that noise," I responded in bewilderment, unsure about how to appropriately react.

"Hopefully, we'll find out," Clark concluded.

With the plan for the portage complete, and unable to satisfactorily explain the curiosity, we finished our duties and retired for the night, which was windy and cool, but still quite comfortable.

Being very close to the mountains, I could see ranges to the west and northwest still covered in snow, and just as the Indians described. More accurately, this was to say they glistened and shone when illuminated by the sun. But the mountains were at their most striking near sunrise and sunset when their immense contours were displayed under obtusely angled light that contrasted the numerous shades of whites, grays, oranges, reds, and yellows. As formidable as these peaks were likely to be in crossing, they were equally, if not more impressive to behold. I would have indulged another attempt to detail their grand beauty, but feared such an effort would be as fruitful as my vain and inadequate descriptions of the magnificent spring, plains, cliffs, and falls.

On the 22nd of June, to maintain the integrity of the lower camp during our absence, we assigned a small party consisting of Sergeant Ordway, Private Goodrich, York, Sacajawea, and Charbonneau to guard the remaining goods and canoes. Most of the baggage we planned to take had already been carried out from the creek bottom to await us on the plain, including the iron frame of my collapsible boat. Transporting the boat added another 100 pounds to the weight of the cargo. The rest of our goods we loaded into one of the 3,000-pound dugout canoes, which was situated atop the carriage near the creek.

To move the bulky vessel, four men wrapped separate ropes around each carriage axle near the wheel.[14] Ready to then ascend a steep gully, the other 21 men either pulled on a rope or pushed the canoe out of the creek bottom, up the hill, and onto the plain. After pulling and pushing with much effort, they briefly stopped to load additional baggage into the canoe, and soon resumed the mission. The wooden carriage wheels turned and rolled over many rocks that bounced the cart up, down, and sideways, which tested the durability of the carriage, and the men's strength and endurance. No greater than a mile from the gully, the men were already tiring. They were also having a difficult time with the prickly pear needles poking their feet. The exertion required to haul nearly two tons of weight over uneven ground, combined with enduring sharp needles puncturing our soles proved to be the biggest challenges of this day. Men fainted from thirst and fatigue. Frequent breaks were needed for recovery, during which some men were asleep in an instant. Despite this, no man complained, and was, to the contrary, content —and more than met the grueling task. However, the same could not be said about our equipment.

The question regarding the vigor of the carriage was soon answered only eight miles into the first trip when Captain Clark had the party replace a broken axle and tongue. The job of cutting new parts to get back on the trail took less than two hours, which involved replacing weak cottonwood with more sturdy willow timber. However, even the new tongue broke shortly after dark when we were within one half-mile of upper camp. Dejectedly, we unloaded what supplies we could carry, and trudged the remainder of the way to camp. All were exhausted when we arrived, and quite disappointed to discover that much of the meat Captain Clark hung at this place was taken by goddamn wolves. Regardless of the loss, everyone slept well in preparation for another tiresome day.

For about an hour the next morning, my group cut and hacked a clearing for our new upper camp, while Captain Clark and his men brought in the first canoe. Afterward, we ate a quick breakfast, and Clark then led his party over the plain and gullies to lower camp, arriving shortly before dark. Although tired, Clark delighted in the fact that Sacajawea had recovered from her illness. He also ordered the limping, weary soldiers to haul a pair of canoes to the foot of a gulley near Portage Creek. Before retiring that night, the men also repaired the soles of their moccasins from the shredding they succumbed to during the previous two days; shredding from the sharp needles of the prickly pears, jagged rocks, and rough ground torn up by the buffalo. Rather than simply replace the tattered and pierced moccasin soles, the men added a second layer for increased comfort and greater protection. This worked well enough.

While Clark made his way to lower camp that day, we assembled the iron-boat frame using metal fasteners. In the afternoon, I sent Gass and Shields out to obtain willow branches for attaching to the boat frame. My plan was to use willow rope to secure branches onto the interior of the frame, and affix them from bow to stern. After completing the boat skeleton, elk skins were to be sewn onto the frame. The seams between the sections of hide would be sealed with pine pitch. However, there being an obvious shortage of elk and pine in the area, this was a challenge. Regardless, I was determined to complete the *Experiment*, even if it required substituting materials.

Thoughts about the boat led me to concern about the elk-hunting party, since we had not heard from them for three days. I determined to have Private Joseph accompany me in the dugout, with the intent to descend the Missouri a few miles to the confluence with the Medisun River.

With great effort, we pushed the heavy vessel off the bank, further into the water, and leisurely floated with the current. After a brief ride, we turned into the gently flowing Medisun where we paddled about a half-mile upstream.

“There, on the starboard. Let’s land near that tree,” I said to Private Joseph, as he stroked from the bow and I steered from the stern.

The front of the canoe slid onto the bank, and we jumped into the water.

“Tie her up,” I said.

“Yes, Captain,” Joseph replied, as he grabbed the rope, sloshed through the shallows, and stepped onto the riverbank.

“Let’s head up a ways,” I shouted, while unloading our gear.

Joseph nodded, and finished tying a knot around the tree.

“If we both holler, sooner or later we should find ‘em.”

“Yes, Captain. Let’s go,” he anxiously replied.

For more than an hour, we walked and yelled, and approximately five miles upriver, we heard Shannon shout and wave to us from his camp on the opposite side of the river. Seven deer and four buffalo were suspended from nearby trees, which hung as great testimonials to his vastly improved skills as a hunter, and knowledge of the wilderness. This was a much welcomed divergence from his wayward days the previous fall.

“Where’s Drouillard and Field!” I hollered.

“I don’t know!” he yelled back. “I haven’t seen them in three days! The last I saw, they were at the first falls!”

I processed this news, and was puzzled why Drouillard and Private Reubin had not accompanied Shannon, but knew there must have been a sound reason, given Drouillard’s sensible use of initiative. I quickly recalled his brave encounter with the Missouria Indians the previous summer, which resulted in our first, important meeting with the natives of our new territory.

“We’ll build a raft and come over! We’ll stay at your camp!” I shouted.

“Yes, Sir!” he yelled back.

Private Joseph and I hastily built a crude, willow raft, and poled our way to the opposite shore.

"Good to see you," Shannon warmly greeted. "I got buffalo and deer, but no elk," he sadly reported.

"No, that's good, Private. I'm more happy to see you're safe. ... But it is unfortunate there aren't any elk." I replied to boost his spirits.

"No. ... No elk, Sir. I haven't seen Reubin or Drouillard since noon a few days ago. We were walking together, and before I knew it, I was alone. I kept goin' thinking they would show up, but they never did," Shannon summarized.

I thought for a moment.

"They may have stayed below for some reason," I said, pausing to think of a plausible alternative. "On the other hand, they may be further up this river," I concluded, turning to Private Joseph who glanced back at me in assurance that he was listening intently.

"Tomorrow, I want you to go up about four miles, and see if you can find your brother and Drouillard. ... Regardless of whether you find 'em, I want you to turn back after that. Understood?"

"Yes, Sir," he responded in commitment.

The night was cool, and a light rain had fallen before I set out early on the 24th of June. I walked back to upper camp while Shannon took the canoe up to meet Private Joseph. On my arrival at upper camp, I found Gass and Shields had made little progress in procuring suitable wood for lashing to the boat frame. The pair attributed the delay to the time required to change from cottonwood to willow and box elder, since cottonwood proved too soft and brittle to form to the frame. As they worked, I searched the riverbank, and found a few pine logs among the driftwood. I desperately hoped these logs would be enough to provide an adequate quantity of tar to seal the seams between the animal hides. Only time would answer that important question.

While we valiantly labored to complete the *Experiment*, Captain Clark's team had much more success. They hauled the last of the six canoes from the creek to dry out, and were able to take advantage of a favorable wind from the southeast. The soldiers constructed a brace in the larger of the two canoes to support a mast on which they hoisted a sail. The steady breeze was captured by the sail, and propelled the heavy vessel across the wind-swept plain. Functionally, the sail served as the equivalent of four men pulling on cords. Great progress was made until just three miles from upper camp when the wind changed direction, and a violent storm blew in from the northwest.

A huge, dark cloud billowed up high and wide into an immense plume — blocking the late afternoon sun. Hearing rumblings of thunder not far in the distance, but seeing no lightning, the men paused from their work to stare in awe at the grand spectacle of a colossal curtain of hail and rain blowing toward them at great speed from deep within the swelling wall of blackness. Sergeant Ordway glanced upward to see a cloudless, blue sky, and looked back to contrast the observation with the imminent storm. The temperature suddenly dropped, a fierce wind blew, and with it came hail — pelting the men with small stones comprised of solid ice. With no shelter other than the canoes, the men lay on the ground, and crowded under the carriage to wait out the squall. The hail soon ceased, and for the next half hour, the area was deluged with hard rain. Men not under canoes were standing in several inches of water. Contrary to being unwelcomed, the storm relieved the hot and thirsty men who happily dropped to their hands and knees to drink from refreshing puddles on the plain.

As quickly as it developed, the gale disappeared into the evening, which is when I greeted Sergeant Ordway, and the men at upper camp. The two canoes they brought descended a moderate slope, and coasted to a stop near my tent.

"Welcome back, Sergeant," I said warmly to him, as I examined the sorry looking group of wet and tired soldiers, which included Reubin Field.

"Thank you, Sir," Ordway responded.

"Where's Captain Clark?" I asked.

"Sore feet. He went back to lower camp not long after we got goin'," he quickly answered in a loud voice.

"Indeed. I believe whiskey is in order. How 'bout it, Sergeant. How's the supply?" I inquired.

"Running short, Captain. We'll be out soon."

"Then add a dram to the usual," I commanded.

"Aye," Ordway replied, as he glanced at the meat Shannon harvested, which hung from tree branches near the river.

"Private Reubin!" I shouted at him.

"Sir!" he immediately snapped in response, knowing the reason for the summon. "Tell me about yourself and Drouillard." I sternly commanded.

"We lost contact with Private Shannon on the first day, and couldn't find him. We got to the Medisun, but saw the huntin' was better at our camp above the last falls. Drouillard is still there," Private Reubin explained.

"Where's the camp?" I asked, content with the explanation.

"The north side," he quickly replied.

"I'll dispatch Frazer tomorrow with the canoe to bring back the meat. You return with the others for the next load," I commanded to conclude the exchange.

In the morning, the men placed the canoes near the river, and started back to lower camp, which consumed the entire day. Before retiring for the night, the men again repaired their moccasins.

By noon on the 25th, Drouillard had returned, just as Private Joseph had who was also traumatized during his recent elk-hunting trip.

Instead of bagging elk, Private Joseph was reeling from his latest encounter with white bears. Spotting two by the river, he took aim, fired, and missed. While he was reloading, a third bear had crept up from behind to within a few steps. This was oddly reminiscent of my own experience. The startled soldier turned in time to see the bear, and fled in the opposite direction toward a steep bank. He leapt and fell about 20 feet onto a stony bank where he suffered a cut hand, bruised knees, and bent rifle barrel. Fortunately, the bear opted to not pursue.

This was yet another setback to a devolving situation with regards to the *Experiment*. If more elk hides could not be obtained, I would be forced to utilize the skin of the buffalo. However, I had yet to abandon the plan in covering the boat entirely with elk hides. Therefore, I sent Private Joseph and Drouillard out to hunt, and set Frazer to work preparing more than a dozen elk skins that were worthy of his efforts.

While my group continued constructing the boat, Captain Clark let his feet heal, and had a few men fill our third cache with articles. Deposited in the lower-camp cache were my field desk, books, two kegs of pork, half-keg of flour, two blunderbusses, half-keg of ammunition, and other items needed on our return.

By evening, the men arrived with two more canoes. After a brief period of recovery, some men accompanied me to an island down river to kill bears that had become troublesome. The beasts had been staking out our campsite and stealing meat during the night. We were quite fortunate to have Seaman patrolling the area to give us notice of their menacing presence.

On the 28th, Clark and the men set out with the last canoe, and progressed to a creek with boxelder and willow trees where they camped for the night. They named this spot "Willow Run Camp," which was approximately seven miles from lower camp.

During the night, rain soaked the ground making it impossible for travel in the morning. Assuming Clark could not travel that day, Drouillard and I walked down river about seven miles to obtain water from the giant spring. Meanwhile, Clark began his morning by staring at the weighty canoe and carriage wheels, which were partially sunk in mud. He quickly decided to cancel their trip until the plain was sufficiently dried, and dispatched the men with what baggage they could carry back to lower camp. He ordered one man to stay at Willow Run to guard the canoe and cargo, until the men returned to collect the belongings.

Rather than return by way of the prairie, Clark, York, Charbonneau, Sacajawea, and Jean Baptiste followed Willow Run Creek toward the river to also obtain water from the giant spring. Along the way, York asked permission to hunt buffalo, and separated from the group, after being granted the opportunity. Eventually, Clark's group arrived near the first fall where he viewed more ominous clouds even larger and more alarming than the ones a few days prior. Clark looked for shelter, but saw none, without risk of being blown over a cliff adjacent to the river. Hurrying along the edge of the cliff, Clark observed a deep and narrow ravine. It was about one-quarter mile above the falls, and had a few projecting rocks under which the group could be protected from hail and rain.

At the same time, the men on plain returning to Willow Run saw the same approaching storm, and scrambled back to camp. Bolts of lightning streaked across the sky, as flashing shades of whites, reds, and oranges accompanied tremendous rumblings of thunder. Rain and hail up to seven inches in circumference began to fall, which knocked some men to the ground who lay there momentarily unconscious, and bleeding from their heads.

The heavy rain continued to collect and pool on the plain. Soon it started flowing toward the gulley in which Clark, Charbonneau, Sacajawea, and Jean Baptiste were dry and sheltered. However, the safety rapidly deteriorated when the flow changed into a torrent that cascaded through the ravine, driving uprooted plants, sticks, rocks, and mud before it. Over the noise of the downpour, Clark could hear the turbulent waters rushing down the gully, and recognized the peril. He motioned with one hand for the group to climb to higher ground, while reaching for his gun and possible bag with the other. Without hesitation, a terrified Charbonneau was first to scurry up the ledge, leaving his wife, infant son, shot pouch, powder horn, and tomahawk at the bottom of the ravine. The Frenchman turned to look down, and offered his hand to Sacajawea who was cradling Jean Baptiste in her right arm. She grabbed his hand, and he helped pull her up a few feet, as Clark pushed from below. The initial wave from the flash flood reached Clark, and soon he was knee-deep in the raging surge. Sacajawea took a few steps with the assistance of Charbonneau and Clark, and reached the safety of the ledge, but the water was still rising.

Clark was then immersed to his waist, and searched for a handhold to prevent being swept off his feet. Finding a rock to clutch, Clark attempted to climb out, but his foot slipped a few times off the side of the gully before he was able to gain a secure surface on which to step from the churning water. Within a few seconds, the group was making their way out of the steep ravine, but the flood was still threatening to sweep them into the current. Charbonneau frequently stopped to look behind him, and was paralyzed by fear of a possible future, until Clark pushed him back into reality and up the hill. By the time the group stepped onto the plain, water in the gully was 15-feet deep, roiling its way to the river, taking with it Charbonneau's goods, a surveying compass, umbrella, moccasins, and Jean Baptiste's cradleboard, clothes and bedding.

Greatly concerned for the welfare of the group, York had been searching and was much relieved at seeing them emerge from the battered ravine. As York walked towards the group, the rain eased, and Clark decided to return to Willow Run Camp for dry clothes. There, many of the men were bleeding from being hit by the large hailstones. To relieve their suffering and reward their efforts, Clark revived the party with our dwindling supply of grog.

While the men at Willow Run cursed the storm and hail, I delighted in its wonderful offerings. Being amply protected by trees and tents, we were afforded the great opportunity to collect hailstones in a bowl. In the bowl, I mixed the ice with spring water and whiskey to create a refreshing and intoxicating punch. But the enjoyment of our cold treat was tempered by our worry for the others, and anxiety of what was ahead.

On the final day of June, I became extremely impatient with our lack of progress in reaching our goal. The days were already decreasing in duration, and the travel season through the mountains would certainly be quite short. Nearly three months had passed since we left Fort Mandan, yet we had not entered the mountains or arrived at the three forks, and were nowhere near the ocean. I was of the opinion that we would not see Fort Mandan again this season, or even return to winter with the Snake Indians, as I previously hoped.

Regardless, I endeavored to use our time wisely by having my group finish preparing the animal hides for sewing, which then consisted of 28 elk and four buffalo skins. As Private Joseph, Gass, Whitehouse, Shields and I worked; Captain Clark assigned his party to various tasks, including retrieval of the lost goods at the ravine. By sunset, two soldiers returned from the ravine with only the surveying compass to show for the effort. They found the compass half-buried in mud and stone. The ravine itself was filled with many new rocks and boulders, which had tumbled from above during the violent storm.

On that same day, Clark and his party set out at dawn from Willow Run Camp with the last canoe, and arrived at upper camp by mid-afternoon. However, they were obliged to leave a few articles at the camp to lighten the load for travel over the soft ground. By evening, the skins for my boat were stitched together and ready for attachment to the iron frame. In addition, Drouillard and I were able to produce a sealant ingredient that consisted of 100 pounds of tallow, rendered from bear oil. My hope was to mix the tallow with pine tar to seal the seams between the hides. The tar would be collected from a catch basin that was at the bottom of a sloping trench, attached to a crude kiln made in an excavated pit. In the pit, I planned to burn enough pine logs, roots, and leaves that the viscous liquid could be equally mixed with the tallow.

On the 2nd of July, the remainder of our belongings was delivered to upper camp by Clark and his party. This happily marked the end of the difficult portage, which lasted eleven grueling days, covering 130 miles in seven trips over extremely difficult terrain.

For the next two days, almost everyone in the party collected timber, tended the kiln, or sewed skins to the boat. A few soldiers who had yet to view the falls were granted leave to observe these fine spectacles before we left the area. Despite all the cutting, collecting, hauling, and burning, we had yet to generate any usable tar. Putting this disappointment behind me, in the late afternoon, I recalled this was our second consecutive Independence holiday together, and ordered Sergeant Ordway to distribute the last of our allotted spirits for a celebration. The men danced to Cruzatte and Gibson's fiddle playing, until a shower ended the merriment at about nine that evening. Some of the men were obviously drunk, which was appropriate, given the occasion.

During our time in this region, many of our party, including me, occasionally heard on calm, clear days the strange noise that Captain Clark discussed with me a few weeks prior. We still had yet to account for this sound, but I thought it probable this bizarre acoustic could have originated from water flowing into mountainous caverns. I recollected the Hidatsa mentioning this noise, but paid little regard to the assertion at the time, supposing it false, phantom, or superstitious. I also recalled the boatmen saying the Pawnee and Arikara gave the same account about the Black Hills west of them. In any case, I was still at a loss to explain the phenomenon.

By late morning on the 9th, we had coated and dried the animal skins covering the iron boat, abandoned the effort of making tar, and opted to use a mixture of tallow, beeswax, and charcoal to seal the seams. The *Experiment* was then worthy of duty, alongside our six dugouts, which were loaded with baggage. They all lay like perfect corks in the water, and we were ready to depart when a sudden storm blew in that mandated our delay until the violent wind ceased.

By evening, the wind relented by which time I walked down to the river to check the status of my grand *Experiment.* I looked down in shock and dismay at discovering the sealant mixture had dissolved, and water had leaked through seams between the hides. I hung my head in dejection and watched the water sadly jostle in the bottom of my cherished boat. I trudged back to camp in defeat to sadly report my findings. Clark watched my approach, and observed the look on my face, as I turned to sit on a log next to him in front of the campfire.

I sighed heavily and dropped my head for a moment before announcing the result.

"It leaks," I stated, looking back up into the fire.

Clark did not say anything for a moment.

"Sorry about the boat," Clark finally remarked, as he placed his hand on my shoulder. "I know how much it meant to you, and how much work we all put into it. ... Better to find out now than paddling down river."

"Definitely," I said, thinking about what may have been had pitch been available.

“Tomorrow, I’ll take 10 men upriver to make two dugouts. Drouillard said there are some large trees up that way,” Clark stated.

“How far up?” I asked.

“About eight miles … by land. … We buried the truck wheels in the kiln pit, and made a small cache today. Tomorrow, we can put the boat frame in the cache with the other articles.” [B]

“That sounds fine,” I replied, thinking of how the season was wearing on, and reluctantly accepted the fact that we would not return home this year.

During the next five days, Clark established Canoe Camp — some 23 miles downriver where he found two suitable trees for cutting and chopping into dugouts — one 25 feet, the other 33 feet in length. On the 13th, I joined them early, having walked with Sacajawea, her son, and Private Lepage who was feeling ill. By the end of the next day, the canoes were in order. We were then prepared to leave the plains, and enter the mountains where the Indians said the land of plenty terminated and a terrain of uncertainty ruled.

CHAPTER FIFTEEN
INTO THE MOUNTAINS

July 15, 1805
Missouri River Canoe Camp: 2,609 miles above the Missouri confluence

Despite the assurance of soon losing our primary source of meat since late August of the previous year, we happily proceeded on with a considerable supply of grease and dried meat. As I walked on shore to relieve the party of my added weight, we quickly passed a watercourse that was about 80 yards in width. We named the river in honor of Mr. Robert Smith, Secretary of the Navy. Further on, I was afforded an impressive view of Fort Mountain to the northwest. This magnificent spectacle was no greater than 10 miles from my position — jutting up 1,000 feet above the surrounding landscape in spectacular fashion.

With Drouillard on my right, he shot and wounded a deer, which Seaman anxiously pursued into the river. The dog splashed into the water, drowned the beast, and dragged it to shore — exactly like the antelope in April of that same year. The men butchered the deer, loaded it into a canoe near the dried beef, and transported the cargo to camp. We stopped for the night nearly 20 miles from where we began that day, and the deer was the main course for supper.

The following morning, I could scarcely contain my joyous anticipation, knowing we would soon pass through the first mountain range. I decided to leave the party, and take three men ahead on a scouting mission. Not far up, Potts, Lepage, Drouillard, and I passed an abandoned Indian camp, which was comprised of 40 willow branch shelters. From its appearance, they seemed to be Shoshone shelters, vacated less than two weeks earlier. This was quite an encouraging sign that we should soon meet these yellow gentlemen. Numerous hoof prints in the soil indicated they had a great number of horses, which was also heartening for great prospects.

We walked the tangents for several miles along the twisting, turning bends of the river whose current was swift. Ahead and to the larboard, were several, low mountains. To the starboard, I observed the last of the plains, which were then interspersed with high, rolling hills. Hiking another 20 miles beyond, we finally arrived about a quarter-mile south of the entrance to the Rockies, where the river channel narrowed, and was confined by dark peaks. Also at this place was a towering rock — 400 feet in height. Immediately adjacent to the rock was an ancient Indian road, which was 300 yards west of the river.

With memories of the near tragic incident at Tavern Bluffs still in mind, only with great caution and some difficulty was I able to scale the towering rock. However, my efforts were rewarded with a spectacular view at the protracted summit. After reaching the top, I was breathing heavily, and turned for the view.

I fixed my eyes north to our past, and saw huge numbers of buffalo grazing on the plains, which stretched far into the distance. In the opposite direction, I gazed at our future, which pledged numerous imposing peaks, and a river that somehow carved its way through an intimidating landscape. After studying what was possible from this impressive point, I descended the rock, and we unloaded our belongings onto a nearby island that had a single large, pine tree.

While we made camp, Clark and his party were at a slough about six miles downstream. By eight the next morning, he and the remainder of the expedition arrived at our camp. I comfortably watched the group approach, and shouted out happily to greet them.

"Good to see you, on this tremendous day!" I yelled.

"Indeed. … This is tremendous, as are the goddamn mosquitoes!" Clark quickly retorted, striding toward me.

I smiled and laughed.

"You're in time for breakfast, Captain." I shouted.

They joined us, and found logs on which to sit. Privates Howard and Thompson then distributed a pound of dried buffalo meat to each member of the party. We ate leisurely and drank water from the river.

"After you left, I saw the poles of a huge lodge — about 60 feet in diameter," Clark said between chews. "Rocks from about eighty others were nearby. Looks like it was made last fall."

"Last fall?" I asked for reassurance.

"Yes, I'm sure we will meet the Shoshone, soon. Those are probably their lodges," he asserted confidently.

"They're likely on the other side of this range," I responded, after standing to retrieve the sextant from one of the canoes. "I'm going to take our latitude. Have the instruments taken around the rapids — There's an Indian road over there," I said pointing in the direction of the towering rock.

We finished our meal, and after an hour of observations, I determined our latitude to be 46 degrees, 42 minutes, and 14.7 seconds, which confirmed my prediction we would enter the mountains much further north of 45 degrees than the map suggested. Although this was an important landmark, I did not think it as significant as the three forks, and elected not to delay to collect longitudinal data, which would have required recording lunar observations.

Getting a later start than usual, we loaded the canoes, and had to double our efforts to haul the canoes against the strong current. As we proceeded into the mountains, the river had somehow eroded a route through very hard, black rock, which produced canyons and high, perpendicular cliffs that projected to the water's edge in many places. On some of these cliffs, we observed bighorn sheep nimbly traversing the rugged terrain with great ease. One false step by these creatures would have resulted in certain death, after a fall of at least 500 feet onto sharp rocks or into the water. Regardless, they moved about without concern for such hazards, and appeared secure from any predators including bears, wolves, and even armed men. I could not imagine an animal better-suited for living in such an environment.

Having traveled only about eight miles, we encamped on the starboard side in an area with abundant pine trees for fires. Near our tent, Clark and I discussed a strategy for our anticipated meeting with the Shoshone:

"We should be through this first range soon. ... Tomorrow we should send an advance party to meet the Indians. I don't want the hunters' gunfire scaring them further into the mountains," I suggested to Clark.

"I agree. It should be a small party. ... I'll march ahead on the road," he volunteered. "I'll take Private Joseph, Potts, and York."

"Alright, but don't get too far ahead. A few days, at most," I advised.

"Agreed — a few days," he responded. "If we come across extra game, we'll hang it from a tree."

Early the next morning, we passed a clear, bold river on the starboard side, and named it after Secretary of War, Mr. Henry Dearborn who was a veteran of the Revolutionary War. Shortly afterward, Clark and his team took to the Indian road, which was rocky, led over a low mountain, and crossed two creeks — the last of which he named after Sergeant Ordway. The creek had an abundant number of little prickly pears along its banks, and its naming after our First Sergeant was appropriate since he was a stickler for telling and receiving the whole truth, and was most diligent and dependable.

After advancing 21 miles, my group encamped on the larboard side amid a small grove of cottonwood trees. We proceeded on the next day against an increasingly strong current. The velocity became more powerful as the river constricted from several hundred yards in width to about 100 yards in many places. In the narrow valleys between the mountains, we were offered no relief from the heat in the form of shade or wind, yet I could see at varying turns in the river the lofty summits still covered with snow. With each new bend in the river, we stared in awe at morose and brooding cliffs. Towards evening, we passed the most spectacular ones in the series — some of which soared to a height of 1,200 feet above the river. As water gushed from interstices between the rocks, the haunting sound of splashing water echoed off the canyon walls, which gave this landscape a most glum and dramatic attribute.

For more than three miles, this section of the Missouri is of such a depth that use of the setting poles to propel us upstream was not an option. The same may be said about use of the tow ropes, since there did not exist a stretch of rock that was much less than vertical for a foothold. From the singular appearance of this place, I attempted to capture its grand character in one name by calling it the

“Gates of the Rocky Mountains.” It was well past dark before we emerged from its shadowy confines to find a spot large enough on which to camp. This we did in a small field near a handsome gulch.

While we struggled through the gates, Clark continued on the winding Indian road, which led over two mountains, into an enormous valley filled with prickly pears, and past willow-brush camp remains. He peered ahead a short distance, and saw the trail was embedded with unavoidable projecting stones and sharp rocks. With each step, the double-soled moccasins provided little protection from blisters, bruises, cuts, and needle puncture wounds to the soles of the men’s feet. Clark glanced to the sides of the road in search for relief, but saw the alternative was worse — offering an equal number of stones, and an even greater concentration of prickly pears. They limped along the continuously changing terrain of the rocky road, until Clark decided to halt for the night, some 16 miles upriver from us. As the campfire flickered late that evening, Clark painfully extracted 17 needles from his feet. The others in his party did the same, as equally, if not more uncomfortable than Clark. After removing the last needle, Clark felt a strange sensation on his head. He brushed his fingers through his hair several times, and three ticks fell to the ground.

“Goddamn ticks!” Clark grumbled to himself. “Even out here.”

Regardless of the challenges, the group was determined to not allow the injuries or pests hinder their search for the Shoshone the next morning.

Shortly after sunrise, we were beyond the first range of mountains, and Drouillard took advantage of the retreating peaks to hunt. He found a herd of elk not distant from the river. As we quietly towed the canoes with a light mist hovering immediately above the river surface, he silently placed the rifle butt against his shoulder in the still, morning air. He peered down the rifle sights on the barrel, found his mark, and squeezed the trigger. Instantly, a thunderous boom propagated outward towards the mountains, and down the immense valley. Nearby, startled magpies quickly dispersed in differing directions from tree branches, while the intensity of the sound slowly attenuated from its origin.

The sound wave continued to radiate, and soon reached the ears of a vigilant Shoshone warrior named “Jumping Deer” who was peeling bark from a pine tree for food and sap.[A] He was part of a small, hunting party from mountains several days’ travel to the southwest. Their mission was to harvest buffalo and bring dried meat to the tribe. However, they did this at much peril, and only when they were in great need of food. For in so doing, they risked being killed by better armed enemy Indians such as the competing Gros Ventre of the Prairie, Crow, Blackfeet, or Hidatsa nations.

Following the source of the sound, Jumping Deer mounted his horse, rode to a ridge, and viewed the flotilla of eight canoes being pulled upriver by the men. He turned, raced down the mountain, and searched for a suitable location to set a warning fire to alert his group. After carefully planning an escape route far west of the river, and waiting several hours to correctly time his signal, Jumping Deer set fire to the parched valley grass near a small creek. The fire quickly consumed huge amounts of dry vegetation. Immense clouds of gray smoke billowed up from the valley floor, and could be observed at a great distance.

Shortly before two in the afternoon, as we passed a stream that had signs of beaver activity, Sergeant Ordway glanced to his right and saw smoke about seven miles to the southwest over a ridgeline.

"Captain Lewis!" Ordway shouted, as he anxiously pointed and gestured toward the swirling smoke plumes.

I watched the puffs swell and spin, and could only wonder about their cause. But I immediately suspected the Indians had heard or seen us, and they were then in the process of fleeing farther into the mountains.

At that same moment, but nearly 20 miles away, Clark and his men took notice of the same smoke, and drew a similar conclusion with regards to its origin. Clark did this while they continued on the Indian road, which ran parallel and five miles west of the river. They slowly marched another eight miles with their feet in constant pain, before halting for the evening. They stopped just above a creek, which also showed signs that beavers were abundant in this area.

Meanwhile, at a point in a bend of the river between two creeks, we found elk remains, and a note Captain Clark left for us. The note indicated that he planned to search for the Snake Indians one more day, and wait for our arrival at some convenient spot upriver. At our location, we were surrounded by jagged, low mountains, and could not find ground suitable for camping. We decided to move a short way upstream, and eventually found an area on the larboard side, not completely covered in prickly pear.

Late the following afternoon, we entered the same immense valley Clark's party struggled to crisscross with injured feet a day earlier. The region was at least 12 miles in length and width, bounded by high mountains, with summits partially covered with snow. In the valley, the river widened to almost a mile from a mere 100 yards in sections of the first range. The river was interspersed with dozens of islands, side channels, and a shallow bed primarily covered with smooth stones. This made traveling easier, since it allowed use of the setting poles to push the canoes forward, but was still quite taxing. In one of these side channels, Seaman jumped into the water and caught several juvenile swans that had yet to learn how to fly. The men threw the birds on top of a deer in one of the canoes, and we advanced another few miles before stopping for the night. While we prepared the animals for supper, Sacajawea walked along shore gathering ripened yellow, red, and black currant to supplement our meal. This area contained an abundance of these delicious fruits, which was some relief from battling the increasing current, rapids, and riffles in the river.

By this time, the men were much fatigued, and wanted to rest. However, I could not permit this being in such close proximity to the Shoshone. But Clark and his group did exactly that to heal their badly battered feet. They backtracked four miles downriver to a better location for rest, and wait for us. We were then separated by less than 10 miles.

Late the following day, we finally caught them:

"Good to see you're still on this side of the prickly pears," I joked to Clark, walking towards him.

"Just barely," he replied with a smile, as he donned his moccasins. "My feet are in sad shape. ... The same for the rest of 'em," he commented, gesturing with his head toward York, Potts, and Private Joseph. "There's an island a few miles upstream where we can camp."

"Right, let's go," I acknowledged, and changed the topic to elevate the men's spirits. "I have great news."

"How's that?" Clark asked, as he rose to his feet.

"At breakfast this morning, Sacajawea said she recognized white earth along shore ... similar to the cliffs below Maria's River"

"That is great news," he joyfully reacted.

I stepped in closer, placing my left hand on Clark's right shoulder to emphasize my next remark, said with a broad grin: "She also said the three forks, and her people are of no great distance from there."

Clark smiled, looked down and nodded in restrained enthusiasm.

He glanced back up at me: "We'll start again in the morning."

All the party was much rejoiced upon hearing this jubilant news. At camp that evening, a reinvigorated Clark ordered the Field brothers and Frazer to prepare to accompany him. Curiosity or more likely suspicion about how the Shoshone might react to the reappearance of Sacajawea captured the better part of Charbonneau who asked to go with Clark. Although we were unsure of his exact motives, he was granted permission, if for no other reason than his apparent enthusiasm for the project, and possibly the use of his limited interpretive skills.

After a cool and pleasant night, the sun was about to break the horizon, as Private Frazer was preparing to shave more than a week's worth of whiskers from his face. He repeatedly splashed water onto his whiskers to soften the growth, applied a small quantity of soap to lubricate the process, and angled a dulling metal blade to his neck. Pulling upward, the razor sliced through the course hair, but not without difficulty. [B]

"Goddamn it!" Frazer cursed, after a small cut in his skin drew an insignificant amount of blood.

Nearby, Private Joseph snickered at Frazer: "You need to sharpen that tired blade real soon," he remarked.

“I need to make this one last until the trip back,” Frazer quickly responded, turning his head toward Private Joseph.

“Sure … and you’ll be lucky not to bleed to death by then,” Private Joseph quipped, as he heartily laughed.

They soon turned their attention back to more immediate tasks.

With the preparations completed for our next separation, we proceeded on: Clark with his men by land, and the remainder of us pulling the canoes. I ordered that small flags be hoisted in each vessel to signal the Shoshone that we were not Indians, nor their enemy. However, the message was not received. As we got closer to the three forks, two high ranges of mountains to the east and west obscured more distant and lofty ones beyond.

As I marveled at the scenery, I could not help but fear that we should soon meet an obstruction, which would impede our advancement. But Sacajawea assured me that no such obstruction existed between there and the three forks. I scarcely could believe a river flowing through such rugged country would not have dangerous falls or rapids, but again, she said the waters continued as we viewed it for as far as we cared to follow.

/With all this water and stagnant pools, came three evils in the form of mosquitoes, gnats, and prickly pears. So abundant and troublesome were these evils that we suffered, I thought they must be equal to the curses experienced by the poor inhabitants of ancient Egypt. Clouds of mosquitoes and gnats descended on us, causing indescribable misery. The only hope of immediate relief was the cool temperatures in the high mountains.

While we endured our pestilence of insects, during the next few days, Clark and his crew continued their march another 55 miles south and a sizable distance west of the river, but still had not sighted the forks or Shoshone. By early on the 25th of July, they advanced an additional four miles when Clark observed a western fork in the river, which was about 100 yards in width, and another that was approximately 30 yards narrower turning east.

“I’m not sure, but this might be it,” Clark said to the group, turning his head to assess the character of the waters. “Let’s go up this way to see if there is another fork,” he said pointing west.

The men hiked less than one quarter-mile, and spotted a middle fork flowing south, which was nearly as wide as the west fork. Momentarily forgetting the pain and swelling in his feet, a wide smile grew on his face.

“This is it! This is the place! Gentlemen, welcome to the Three Forks!” Clark exclaimed in triumph.

Like the extensive valley north, this area too was striking, expansive, and surrounded by high mountains to the west, south and east. After finishing breakfast, Clark left another note for us. He wrapped it around a tree branch, and secured the note with red ribbon, at the confluence of the middle and west forks. He then headed up the latter. On the north side of the west fork, blackened remains of recently burned grass covered a large meadow, but still they saw no Indians. Hiking another 20 miles upriver, the men passed steep, rocky cliffs, tall grass, and many islands, before stopping for the night. They stopped after Charbonneau complained his ankle was injured, and could go no farther.

Earlier that same day, my group traveled through a second chain of mountains, not as grand as the first mountain gate, however still impressive. The gravelly bluffs rose from 400 to 600 feet above the river. At the foot of one of these sheer cliffs, we pitched our tents for the night.

During the night, the temperature dropped to a comfortable 60 degrees Fahrenheit, before Clark broke camp with Frazer and Reubin Field. He left Private Joseph and Charbonneau at camp to allow them time to recover, while the trio hiked farther west.

For more than four hours, the men walked along the river, up rolling hills, and climbed a sharp ridge to reach the summit of a mountain covered with short grass and scrubby pine. From the top, the exhausted men had an unobstructed view of the valley, and meandering west fork that faded into distant peaks. After observing the landscape, the weary three men made their way down by way of an old Indian trail, which led through a treeless, deep hollow facing south. The trail offered no relief from the burning rays of the sun or heat radiating from the naked ground. Dehydration, extreme exertion, blisters, and prickly pear needles were taking a toll. Spotting a spring flowing into the hollow, they paused to allay their great thirst. They knelt down, filled their canteens, and quickly gulped the icy waters. The hot, parched group immediately felt the water's chill spread, and were suddenly overwhelmed with brief headaches, nausea, and cramps. Clark felt especially ill, but was resolute on returning to camp, and exploring the middle river, before heading back to the three forks. After a short respite, Clark summoned enough strength to lead once more. He struggled for hours to arrive at camp, which is where Private Joseph and Charbonneau were spotted still recovering.

"We're headin' back. … Come on, let's go," Clark said to his reunited squad. "We're goin' by the middle fork."

The men wearily gathered their belongings, and walked the short distance to shore. At this spot, the west fork was split by a large island. Between the two forks lay several miles of flood land. Stepping into the gently flowing water, the going was easy. At the point of crossing, the deepest part of the river only reached the men's knees. They emerged onto the opposite shore where their saturated moccasins dripped and dribbled, and they walked across the island towards the next bank. Upon reaching the bank, the group momentarily paused to survey the threatening water, which was much more rapid and deep in appearance than during the previous crossing.

"I'll lead," Clark stated. "Single-file goin' 'cross."

Clark motioned for Charbonneau to follow him, and give his rifle to Frazer, since he knew the Frenchman could not swim. The men slowly waded into the swift current, and carefully stepped toward the distant shore. Charbonneau's expression deteriorated from a look of concern to abject terror, as he felt the water rising from his knees to thighs. Smooth stones comprising the bed of the stream made for uneasy footing, as the water endeavored to topple them. Clark could feel large and small rocks rolling from side to side beneath his moccasins, which occasionally sent sharp pains through his legs.

"Face into the current," Clark shouted above the noise of the roiling water.

The soldiers began turning to their right. Charbonneau followed Clark's lead. By this time, the men were immersed to their waists when Charbonneau lost his balance during the turn, and the current began carrying him downstream. Charbonneau screamed for help. Clark immediately reacted to the cry. His eyes widely opened upon seeing the Frenchman being claimed by the cold waters. He quickly handed his rifle to Private Joseph, before diving into the river for the unexpected swim in the chilly waters.

Charbonneau continued to scream and flailed his arms, as his hands repeatedly slapped the surface of the churning river. Waves washed over his head several times, while he bobbed up and down, struggling to keep his mouth above the surface. Clark's strokes and kicks were quick and powerful. Within 30 seconds, he reached the wallowing Frenchman from behind, and wrapped his left arm around Charbonneau's torso. Clark swam on his side a few yards, towing Charbonneau, before his feet found the river bed. This permitted for a much easier rescue. He aided the weeping Charbonneau to his feet, and the two clasped hands, as they cautiously waded back to the bank where they had started. Being late afternoon, and deciding this was enough exploration for a day, the group returned to camp another night at the same spot, with plans to resume in the morning, after what they hoped would be a restful period.

Early on the 27th, my party awoke, and grudgingly took again to the tow ropes — slowly moving past high, limestone bluffs.

As we drew nearer the most distant fountain of this immense waterway, our advancement was not impeded by obstacles as I feared, but by the increasing speed of rushing mountain waters. But to focus on this truth is to neglect the immense labors of the men who greatly exerted themselves each day hauling the canoes. Each man was in a continual state of extreme exertion, which quickly weakened them. They rested, recovered, and reluctantly headed back into the river. This description of the growing physical demands of the journey was becoming but a repetitious narrative of the previous day, and was equal to, if not greater than the efforts put forth during the great portage.

However, some relief was at hand. About nine that morning, we emerged from a small canyon, and into an immense valley, which Clark had visited two days prior. The landscape suddenly opened to plains and meadows, surrounded by distant mountains capped with snow. On the larboard was a split in the river.

With almost certainty, I believed this was the three forks. I shouted for the men to take breakfast, while I ascended a high point to verify my observation.

The men happily obliged, pulled the canoes ashore, and joyfully dropped the cords onto the ground.

I hiked up the east fork about one half-mile to the top of a large rock, which was several hundred feet in height. There, I had a commanding view of the neighboring country, and confirmed this was indeed the spot. Between the east and middle forks spanned an immense range that possessed broken, irregular, and snowy peaks similar to the ranges that flanked both the east and west forks. In the river bottoms, sizable cottonwood and lush grasses covered moist soil, which was nourished by the waters of those three fleet and shallow tributaries. After quickly sketching the region in my field journal, I quickly descended the rock, and ate breakfast with the party. Sitting on a log next to Sergeant Ordway, I enjoyed roasted beaver tail and serviceberries, before indulging him in my grand plan:

"Sergeant, we will go up the west fork a short way, and find a place to camp. … I want the party to rest, while I scout the middle fork."

"Aye. The men will be pleased. Thank you, Sir," he replied.

"Certainly, Sergeant. … I'm guessing the west fork will lead to the Columbia, but I want to explore the middle fork to be certain," I stated.

We proceeded upriver immediately after finishing our meal. Walking on shore near the confluence of the west and middle forks, I observed a small, paper cylinder at the end of a stick. The message was secured to the pole with ribbon whose ends were easy to see fluttering in the breeze. I hurried forward and anxiously unrolled the paper. The note described Clark's planned route, and indicated that he would soon meet us at this place, provided he did not make contact with the Shoshone, or see signs of recent activity, which is certainly what I had hoped.

Having found a smooth plain at a point in the river less than two miles up, we stopped at an abandoned Indian camp to rest and wait for Clark to return. Given that we then had time for lunar observations, and believing this to be a critical point in the geography of the continent, I planned to collect its latitudinal and longitudinal data, if weather permitted.

While the party rested, I worked my way up the middle fork, and fretfully awaited Clark's arrival. In the late afternoon, dark images emerged over the southern horizon, as I walked toward the shimmering silhouettes. Ever slowly, I could see there was not one, but five figures, and was confident they were that of Clark and his party. However, experience and caution mandated that I prepare for an alternative outcome. I inspected my rifle to ensure it was ready and double-checked my possible bag for ammunition supplies. The images became clear, and I was quite relieved when I recognized Clark, Frazer, Charbonneau, and the Field brothers. After the Captain was close enough that I could examine his face, I could see he was in great distress. My grin changed to concern, but decided levity was the prudent greeting for this occasion.

"What took so long, you son of a bitch," I yelled jokingly in their direction.

"That would be funny, if I wasn't so goddamn sick," Clark responded.

"What's the matter?" I asked in a troubled tone, as I turned to hike with them.

"Fever, chills, muscle aches ... I'm exhausted," he responded, shaking his head and looking at his feet. "I haven't passed in several days."

"I have some thunderbolts at camp," I assuredly replied.

Clark nodded. The other men appeared almost equally drained. I determined that rest for everyone, and a few of Dr. Rush's cure-all for Clark would prove sovereign for all their ailments.

"What about this fork?" I asked.

"It's the west one," Clark confirmed. "This one goes who knows where?"

With my hypothesis supported, around the fires that evening, many expressed their increasing anxiety regarding our inability to meet the Indians and secure horses. I assured them that we would be successful, just as we had been to that time. I reminded them of our defusing of the Teton incidents, befriending the Indians at Fort Mandan, and our correct decision at Maria's River. While I voiced this to the men, writing in my journal that night, I reiterated a concern that had been haunting my thoughts since before the falls.

I feared that if we did not procure horses, the success of our expedition was quite doubtful, or at least made that much more difficult should we have been forced to march. I expected game to be scarce in the higher mountains, the trail unknown, and location of trees suitable for constructing canoes a mystery. Regardless of these ambiguities, I took comfort in Clark's words that the west fork could only be the waterway leading to the Columbia. And if an entire nation of Indians could live in these frugal mountains, this would bode well for our own subsistence. Therefore, I determined we must resume our search for these yellow gentlemen in a few days.

During our repose, the men hunted, mended holes in clothing, and prepared animal skins for new moccasins and clothes. Meanwhile, I ascertained our latitude to be 45 degrees, 24 minutes, and 54 seconds north. According to our maps, and Clark's mileage estimations, I guessed we were somewhere between 110 and 117 degrees west of the prime meridian. This meant we were about 300 to 600 miles from the mouth of the Columbia River, in a direct line. Unfortunately, I knew a direct line would not be the actual trail, and the actual trail would be much more in time, distance, and difficulty.

But such limitations in ascertaining our actual location were not a factor in naming the three forks. After little discussion, it was clear that to honor the creator of our enterprise, we should name the west fork after President Jefferson. The east fork was designated the "Gallatin," after the Treasury Secretary Albert Gallatin, and the middle waterway for Secretary of State James Madison.

Similar to the possible settlement near the confluence of the Yellowstone and Missouri rivers, I felt the three forks region would also support a fine community. This was due to its abundance of wild game, stone, timber, and rich earth for bricks. The game in this region included deer, elk, pronghorn, and many beaver. Considering the wealth of natural resources at this campsite, it was understandable why the Indians visited this fertile location. This was also the region where Sacajawea was captured by the Hidatsa four years prior. Near the campfire that night, Sacajawea recalled this harrowing event through the interpretation skills of Charbonneau and Labich:

The war party set out on horses from their villages near the Knife River in late spring with an ample supply of axes, muskets, and ammunition. After a month of travel along the Yellowstone River watershed, and crossing over a low, mountain pass, the Hidatsa closed in on their target. Before they reached the three forks, the war party was noticed by a Shoshone scout. He rushed back to camp to warn others that another hostile nation was near, and equipped with deadly thunder and lightning. The poorly armed Shoshone quickly fled up the west fork to conceal themselves in a grove of cottonwood and brush. But the raiders quickly discovered the deception and a skirmish ensued. As the battle raged, more than 10 Shoshone men, women, and boys were killed. The end of the brief combat was marked when outgunned Shoshone warriors mounted their horses and fled toward the southwest mountains.

Surviving members of the band were left to fend for themselves, including Sacajawea who was running for the safety of the woods, which lay on the other side of the river. She glanced back to see a Hidatsa fighter pursuing her on horseback. Sacajawea doubled her efforts to escape, as she splashed through the shallows. Not long after entering the river, the pursuing horse slowed, and the warrior reached down with one arm to easily sweep Sacajawea onto the back of his galloping stallion. ...

This was the last time Sacajawea had been with her family and her people, yet she was devoid of emotion when recollecting these events. She also showed no signs of joy at returning to her homeland. I was left to conclude that if she was provided with only the very basics for living, she would be perfectly content anywhere in the world.

But contrary to her satisfied demeanor, I would not be content if we failed to meet her people, or some other nation with horses, and discover facts about the Northwest Passage. It was imperative that we find the truth, and the morning of the 30th of July, Clark and I determined it was time to continue the important quest.

CHAPTER SIXTEEN
PASSAGE

July 30, 1805
Three Forks Camp: 2,848 miles miles above the Missouri confluence

The thick brush and luxuriant grass comprising the riverbank covering collapsed and crunched under the weight of our steps as I led Charbonneau, Sacajawea, and two injured soldiers downstream. After about five miles of cumbersome and unwieldy travel, we halted to await the rest of the party for dinner.

By that time, the group accompanying me had enough of difficult hiking. They elected to proceed on by boat.

Alone, I resumed my march on the starboard side, and was soon slowly slogging through thick muck and murky water up to three feet in depth. Great numbers of beaver dams and huts diverted my intended course, which only added to the challenge. My objective in this taxing endeavor was to avoid the many riverside obstacles by way of a high plain. However, after an hour of very difficult travel, I would have gladly rejoined the canoes had it not been for the fact that the path to the plain was then nearly the same distance as the path to the river. Soaked, sweaty, and exhausted, I finally gained the advantage of the plain, and moved on several miles, until the plain intercepted the river, which is where I arrived near sunset. All the effort yielded only six miles of displacement in a direct line from where I left the slow-moving canoes.

Observing no signs that the party was ahead of me, I fired my gun and hollered, but heard nothing other than the warm, evening breeze blowing past my ears. I silently stood for a moment, breathed deeply, and enjoyed the fleeting solitude and majestic landscape of this exceptional portion of Earth. Turning to face west, I squinted and gazed into the sun, as it began to disappear below the darkened peaks. I thoroughly enjoyed this tranquil moment, but soon reluctantly resigned myself to attend more urgent concerns.

I concluded my best alternative for a safe night was to first procure supper, and then a suitable site for camp, away from the clouds of mosquitoes that swarmed in this marshy portion of the Missouri. A roasted duck, willow brush, and large fire answered the call. I would have been afforded a most comfortable night of slumber had it not been for the troublesome mosquitoes, and a sudden, disconcerting noise in the very early morning.

On the stony bar on which I lay, the sound of weighty steps suggested an elk or black bear was nearby — the latter having been very abundant in this region. Throwing off my blanket, I strained my eyes expecting to view a shadowy form moving along the river, but saw nothing but the darkened figures of willow brush. I was quite alone, but quite comfortable with that circumstance.

Fortunately, no further incidents developed during the night, and by eight the following morning, I saw the hazy silhouette of person walking up shore. The form soon developed into that of Charbonneau.

"Good morning, Mr. Charbonneau," I greeted our contemptible interpreter.

"Merci, Captain Lewis."

"Where are the pirogues?" I asked.

"Below … water … rapid … twisting," he said, emphasizing his words with gestures to demonstrate the circuitous nature of the river.

A short time later, the party arrived.

We dined, proceeded southwest, and later passed a clear, flowing stream about 30 yards in width. It possessed a bed of smooth gravel and fine pebbles — much like the Jefferson at this juncture. We named this tributary, "Philosophy," from its calm resignation and nourishing flowage into the river whose namesake was the author of this grand mission. The banks of the Philosophy had abundant numbers of willows, and origins in the nearby snowy mountains situated between the Madison and Jefferson rivers.

Towards evening, Drouillard observed a black bear feeding on berries along the distant shore. Knowing we had yet to procure any fresh meat before settling into camp, he cautiously approached and positioned himself for a shot when suddenly the bear caught his scent and fled for the protection of the bushes. Drouillard quickly summoned others to aid in the hunt, and the area was then thronging with armed soldiers, including myself. For several minutes, we vainly searched for the beast that somehow managed to elude our capture.

Failure to kill the bear meant we were going to, once again, be without fresh meat for a meal. Despite my attempts to convey to the men the urgent need to be frugal with such commodities because we were in the mountains, they consumed whatever we harvested with complete disregard for thrift. Yet, I refrained from issuing an order for such thrift in hopes that voluntary action would prevail.

To that need, I remarked to Clark, while we ate a meager supper of salted pork, flour, and berries: "The Big Bellies were correct about game here."

"Sure," he responded, and thought for a moment. "The men should ration, but forcing them isn't the answer."

"I'm hoping they will realize it's in their best interest to be frugal. It's difficult to order men who work all day hauling canoes to not eat so much," I interjected between energetic chews.

Clark nodded agreement, but remained focused on eating his food.

I gazed up at the stars, which decorated the darkness, and my mind moved on to a topic of much greater concern than being frugal with our food supply.

"How do you feel about another scouting party?" I inquired.

Clark offered his usual pensive silence for a time.

"You should go ahead. You're in much better condition. My feet are still bad. I'm not feelin' strong," he replied.

"I haven't been 100 percent, either. I've had a bit of dysentery for several days."

Pausing to consider my options, I announced to Clark: "I'll take Sergeant Gass and Drouillard. Gass is probably better walking with me than hauling the boats, considering his condition."

Gass had injured his back earlier in the day, during a fall onto a gunwale.

"Charbonneau said he wanted to accompany us, if we sent another scouting party. He believes his ankle is healed," Clark reported.

Although I had serious doubts about Charbonneau's ability to endure the rigors of the march, he was again most anxious to meet the Shoshone, and I reluctantly indulged the man.

"Fine, but I'm confident he is overestimating his ability," I replied. ... "In case I forget in the morning, I want to wish you a happy birthday. Let's hope this is the last one in the wilderness."

"Agreed. Maybe next year at this time, we can celebrate in St. Louis or Virginia!" Clark hoped.

The new month brought more and differing impediments, as we drew nearer the most remote source of the Missouri.

In the violence of the rapids, the canoe rope snapped that was secured to the vessel hauling the captains' provisions. The current quickly swept the vessel downstream, and it crashed into a pile of large rocks. Shifting cargo tipped the gunwale toward the swiftly flowing water, but the dugout was stopped short of filling when the men righted it in a most timely manner.

Meanwhile, several miles upstream, my group was traveling on the north side of the river in an area Captain Clark suggested exploring, since he believed the Jefferson entered the mountains in this region. Clark's suggested route required us to scale a high, rough range, and we did this only after great effort.

The sun relentlessly drained us as we struggled over the mountain and into the valley. Without shade or even a light breeze, heat radiated from the hills through which we passed, and offered no relief. We baked in stifling temperatures, while the nearby tops of the mountains were still capped with snow: A contrast I thought hardly possible before the beginning this arduous voyage.

We turned to follow the watercourse into the mountains, and after leading the men up it for several miles, I was convinced this boulder-strewn creek was not the Jefferson. It wasn't until two in the afternoon before we regained the river — exhausted and fatigued. But our spirits were revived after we sighted an elk herd. Not long afterward, Drouillard and I successfully killed two elk for a large feast at camp. Indulging ourselves on the precious bounty, we consumed our fill, and hung the balance from a tree near the river for the remainder of the party.

At sunrise, we resumed our march hiking away from the river, and covered 24 miles of similar territory with similar trials, while Captain Clark and the rest of the expedition slowly advanced upriver. The pace of moving against the current was ever decreasing, the shallower and narrower the river became each day. Adding to this burden was the probability that Clark had been bitten by a vicious insect or spider, which caused the inner portion of his ankle much pain and swelling. However, even this did not hinder him from leading the determined party 15 miles before they decided to encamp on a level plain along the larboard shore. The party was exhausted.

"Sergeant Ordway," Clark yelled, as the sun dipped below the distant mountains.

"Sir," Ordway responded.

"Only three campfires this evening ... We don't have enough meat."

"Yes, Sir," Ordway saluted, and went on to instruct the privates of their duties.

The burning logs flickered in the cool breeze of the night at Captain Clark's site. Less than a half-mile away, Jumping Deer had returned. This time he was on a scouting mission, watching Clark's group from a distance. He was on horseback, and noticed strange lights near the river from the top of a small hill, upstream from Clark's camp. Leaving his horse on the small knob, the Indian cautiously made his way close enough to ascertain that the strangers were not members of enemy nations, but much different and unknown. Jumping Deer scampered back up the hill, remounted his horse and rode through the night far to the west to advise members of his nation of our progress.

By the next day, Clark was well enough to walk along shore where he observed a muddy footprint he surmised was that of an Indian who had seen their campfires the previous evening. Clark surveyed the area in the direction of the footprint, and guessed the Indian had probably viewed the party from a little hill on the larboard side.

Meanwhile, my group continued on the high plain, well ahead of the main party, but saw no sign of the Shoshone on the 3rd or 4th of August, which is when we discovered three new forks in the river.

The first fork was bold, rapid, clear, and cold. It veered more west than the other streams. I took these characteristics to signify it originated in the mountains immediately to our right, and found it utterly impossible to navigate with any semblance of safety, after a brief reconnaissance mission.

The middle fork was drastically different than the first fork in that its flowage was gentle, less in volume, more turbid, and much warmer. Given this information, I deduced this fork must have passed through a considerable amount of open country, before terminating in the mountains to the southwest.

The last tributary I immediately dismissed as the correct route, since it flowed from the area to the southeast, and had similar traits as the sharp western fork.

Between the junction of the west and southwest branches, I penned a note to Captain Clark that recommended he follow the middle fork, if I did not meet him before he found the message. Similar to the procedure at the first three forks, I secured a note to a sapling with ribbon, and then further explored the rapid fork to conclusively eliminate it as a possibility.

During our march those three days, Charbonneau repeatedly complained about pain in his ankle, just as he had in the region below the first three forks. His apparent ailment unduly detained us in our exploration, and was a great source of irritation to not only myself, but to the others. Out of respect for his ostensible limitations, we reluctantly returned downstream, and encamped on the riverbank near the confluence of the west and southwest forks, after hiking a grueling 23 miles that long day.

My thoughts during the night led me to the conclude that I must instruct the gimpy Charbonneau to accompany Sergeant Gass, with orders to proceed at their leisure about seven miles down the middle fork, and wait for Drouillard and me to return from our investigation of the west fork. When morning arrived, we handed them the burden of our packs, and bid them adieu.

Approximately six miles up the rapid fork, the snow-capped mountains closed in on both sides to lofty heights. Drouillard and I proceeded on where we spotted a high spur in the range and ascended the rocky hills for a commanding view of the country. After a half-hour of challenging climbing, we took advantage of the summit. From this eminence, we marveled at the valley below, and had a clear view of the middle fork for many miles to the southwest, before it disappeared into the distant mountains.

The southwest range was much lower and less rugged than those from which the adjacent forks originated. The rapid branch flowed from among a series of peaks — each one towering above the other, until terminating on the northwest skyline. Given these conditions, I did not hesitate in believing the middle fork was the one that would lead us to the most isolated spring of the Missouri, headwaters of the Columbia, and Northwest Passage between those two great waterways. A brief excitement overcame me at the realization.

Satisfied the view and consequential information was worthy of our toil, we resolved to descend the steep rocks, and cross the plain to where Gass and Charbonneau awaited. As we made our way down, Drouillard stepped on a craggy stone that rolled from beneath his foot. Instinctively extending an arm to arrest his fall, the index finger on his hand caught the edge of another rock that hyper-extended the digit, as his thigh simultaneously slammed into a projection from a large boulder. For nearly 20 minutes he sat writhing in pain, before he recovered enough to resume our rendezvous.

Upon regaining the middle fork, we happened upon an old Indian road that was large and prominent, imprinted along the river. Much to my disappointment, I saw no signs of recent activity. The only indications that it was used were horse tracks, which appeared to have been made in early spring.

We proceeded on, and it was well past sunset before we rejoined Gass and Charbonneau — after having hiked another 25 miles.

Unknown to us at the time we were making observations on the spur, Clark arrived at the mouth of the rapid fork, and decided to pursue the same, since it flowed from the west.

Unfortunately he had not received the note I had secured to the sapling, and he left a message of his own to me at the same confluence. After about a mile of very rough travel, his party encamped on a muddy island, which obliged them to make beds of pine brush to keep them dry. The men were so much fatigued from pulling the canoes against the swift current that they very much wished navigation by water was at an end, and we could finally go by land. Their feet were severely bruised from walking on the stony riverbeds and rocky shores all day, which made for a most agonizing process.

On the 6th of August, my group broke camp at sunrise in search of Clark, food, and Indians. With nothing for breakfast, I sent Drouillard west to hunt in the woods, while I gave Sergeant Gass orders to proceed with Charbonneau down the southwest branch, and watch for Captain Clark. Meanwhile, I directed my course between Drouillard and Gass to search for the Shoshone. My plan was for all of us, including Clark, to meet at the confluence of the west and southwest branches.

Clark's party proceeded up the rapid fork about the same time we left camp, but they stopped for breakfast about two hours later near a timber grove. There, Private Bratton was finishing his meal.

"Private!" Clark shouted, as Bratton gulped the last of his food.

"Sir!" Bratton responded, looking up from his plate.

"I want you and Shannon to hunt after you're done. Shannon go upstream, you go down."[A]

Yes, Captain!" the soldier promptly replied.

Moments later the pair departed, Shannon upriver, Bratton down.

Before he ate, Clark noticed a faint path leading west from the river, and pursued it a short way. After examining the trail a few minutes, Clark concluded this was another Indian road that led farther into the mountains, not a game trail to nowhere. He concluded that further investigation could be later warranted.

Less than a half-hour later, Drouillard was making his way through the forest when he heard voices to his right. Pushing pine branches aside and stepping over fallen timber, he soon emerged from the trees, and could see Clark and the party preparing to continue in the direction of Shannon.

"Captain! Captain!" Drouillard shouted.

Clark slung his rifle over his right shoulder, and briskly strode to meet him.

"Captain, you're going up the wrong fork," Drouillard advised. "Captain Lewis left a note to go southwest."

After processing the initial shock, Clark responded, shaking his head in disbelief: "I didn't see any note. It wasn't there."

Quickly turning on his heel, Clark shouted new orders: "Sergeant Pryor! Sergeant Ordway!"

"Sir!" both soldiers responded, nearly in unison.

"Turn the boats around! Head back to the forks!" Clark commanded.

The Captain turned back to Drouillard.

"George, I would like you to wait here for Shannon. He's out huntin' that way," Clark said pointing upriver.

"Of course. I'll wait here awhile, and if he doesn't come back, I'll look for him," Drouillard immediately responded.

Within a few minutes, the party finished breakfast and started downstream — toward Bratton, and away from Shannon and Drouillard.

The heavy canoes rode atop the cold waters as the river roiled, churned, and surged down the mountain toward the serenity of the forks. High, white-crested peaks swelled up from the depths of the river, while low troughs surrounded the crests, and the waters swirled over and around incalculable numbers of beaten rocks and boulders of all shapes and sizes. Near the banks, large numbers of driftwood floated on the incessant waves where fallen timber often protruded well past the shore to obstruct travel. Maneuvering with the churning current in the lumbering dugouts was proving to be a much greater challenge than anticipated. Keeping cargo dry was a futile endeavor with foreboding.

Peering forward from the bow of one of the canoes, Private McNeal dug hard with his paddle to avoid another downed tree. At the stern, Private Whitehouse was trying to steer away from the numerous sharp branches aimed at their heads. The vessel was almost clear of a tree when a deep thump sound was quite discernible over the roaring waters. The port side of the canoe had crashed against a large boulder, and the vessel lurched starboard. Fearing the dugout would capsize, Whitehouse unconsciously leapt into the chilly waters, and McNeal's knapsack, clothes, and moccasins were thrown into the river. The agitated tributary quickly swept the goods under the surface and downstream — lost forever to the dreadful torrent.

Pivoting around the boulder, the swift current easily pushed the heavy canoe toward the hapless Whitehouse, with McNeal still futilely paddling to escape the developing disaster. The bow swung away from shore toward the main channel where Whitehouse reached out to momentarily grasp the gunwale. Unable to jump into the vessel, the dugout continued on its powerful path, trapping the Private's leg in the process. Whitehouse was forced to release his grip when the great inertia of the bulky craft forced him under the boat. Pinned on his back between the rocky riverbed and 3,000-pound canoe, Whitehouse could only watch from the bottom of the icy waters as the boat passed over him inches from his nose, nearly crushing his lower leg in the process.

Seconds later, Whitehouse emerged from the river, and tossed his head aside to throw the water from his face. He was breathing heavily, as he stood and glanced down to check himself for injuries, quickly taking inventory of his possessions. Seconds later, the Private realized his shot pouch, powder horn, sewing thread, and spare moccasins were lost, but he was relatively unharmed.

The men behind witnessing the incident yelled and hollered when the dugout forced Whitehouse under the water and below the craft.

From far in the distance, down in the valley, I heard the men's loud shouts to my left, and redirected my route toward the disturbance, which I estimated to be much less than five miles above the forks.

Soon after Whitehouse recovered, another boat crashed into a rock, tipped, and partially filled with water — soaking its cargo. Fortunately, no one was injured during that mishap, but one powder keg and a rifle were claimed by the river — the mountain's toll for our misguided passage.[B]

Upon my arrival at the forks, I discovered the reason for Clark's diversion from my plan: The sapling to which I secured my note was gnawed down and hauled away by a goddamn beaver. Tracks in the area suggested it was a rather large creature, which was no doubt successful in not only constructing lodges and dams, but in delaying our expedition. I was not amused.

Finding a boulder on a large, gravely bar, I patiently sat and waited for Clark and the others. At midday, the dugouts rounded the bend, and headed toward the bar where I was resting. Most of the party were wet, including Bratton, Sacajawea, and York.

"Welcome, Captain! … I know what happened," I commented, as he began unloading his saturated baggage.

"How's that?" he asked.

"A beaver … it took the note I left over there," I said, pointing to the area where the sapling once grew.

Clark shook his head in disappointment. "Yeah, that figures, don't it. … Whitehouse was damn near killed in the rapids."

"What?" I asked in astonishment.

"The dugout was foundering. He jumped out, and the current swung her over him," Clark bluntly reported.

"Was he hurt?"

"His leg, but he's fine. … We lost a few items, and alotta shit got wet."

"Well, this is a good place to dry them. We'll camp here, and start fresh in the morning," I stated.

"Fine. That'll give Drouillard a chance to bring back Shannon," Clark replied.

"Are you joking?" I asked, disbelieving this could happen a third time.

"No, it's not like that. … I had him go hunt to the west about the time when George walked into camp and told us about your note. George said he'd look for him, if he had to. … I'm guessing you had no luck with the Indians."

"Nothing, but some old roads. They look like they passed last spring," I said. Glancing at Clark's inflamed ankle, I gave an upward nod: "How's that?"

"Worse than the last time I saw you. Hurts like hell," Clark said, as he bent over to rub the red, swollen joint.

The discussion concluded.

The remainder of the afternoon was spent washing clothes, mending garments, unloading the soaked baggage, and spreading items out to dry under a cloudless sky. Wood was plentiful in the area, and five campfires aided in speeding the drying process for our soaked articles.

By evening, many of the goods were repacked into the dugouts, and Drouillard joined us, but without Shannon. He reported his disappointment to us:

"I waited two hours, and then went up shouting, but got no answer," Drouillard stated. "I followed his trail, but he had too big a jump for me to catch."

Turning in haste I shouted: "Sergeant Ordway! Sound the horn! Shannon's lost!

Ordway ran to search for his bundle containing the horn, as I hurried to find Sergeant Pryor. Seeing him sitting on a log among a small group, I hollered:

"Sergeant Pryor!"

He spun around to focus his attention.

"Sergeant, after the horn, have three men fire their guns in succession!"

With the commands executed, the deafening signals reverberated off the mountains, and the night wore on, but Shannon did not return. We decided to not send anyone out in the dark to search for him, and hoped he would do well enough on his own for the time being.

Much concerned for his welfare, but unable to do anything more until morning, I warmed my hands by the fire, watching Clark work at his desk.

"What should we call the rapid fork," I asked Clark.

He thought for a moment.

"Seein' that we named the last one, Philosophy, we should continue with the grandest of life's virtues."

"Agreed," I responded without hesitation. "Name it 'Wisdom,'" I announced.

"What about the southeast fork?"

"Hmmm," Clark paused, rubbing his chin. "'Philanthropy'... we'll call it 'Philanthropy,'" he stated, then dipped his quill into a bottle of ink, and scratched the name on his map.

The night passed, and a brilliant sunrise greeted us on the 7th of August. Under the morning sun, we waited for the remaining goods that had yet to dry. Because Shannon was still somewhere in the wilderness, I dispatched the other Field brother — Reubin — to search for Shannon, since Private Joseph did the same the previous fall. He promptly packed, departed, and we took stock of our remaining goods, before heading upriver.

Our gifts and supplies were diminished to the point that we determined to proceed on with just seven canoes, instead of the eight we had brought. Pulling and dragging the heavy canoe through the brush, the men secured her to several trees in a dense thicket to prevent it from being carried off by spring floodwaters. We could only hope it was there on our return, if we returned.

Waiting for the baggage to dry allowed me time to repair my air gun, which was damaged during the ruckus on the rapids. By one in the afternoon, our baggage was sufficiently dry to enable the men to pack and reload the canoes. While Captain Clark and the party moved upstream, Sergeant Gass and I remained at the forks to wait for Shannon and Drouillard. While waiting, I completed my morning and afternoon latitudinal observations.

Based on these observations, I ascertained the forks to be at 45 degrees, 2 minutes, and 43.8 seconds north. Unfortunately, cloud cover during the night prohibited me from taking lunar observations for longitudinal calculations, but I knew we were many miles southeast of the Boars Tooth, and deep within the Rocky Mountains — somewhere in the vicinity of meridian 115, west.

Seeing no sign of Private Reubin or Shannon, Gass and I rejoined the remainder of the party at camp, just north of the river Philanthropy.

As the light from the campfire flickered in the twilight, I turned in the direction of cracking wood and crunching vegetation to view rustling branches from which Drouillard emerged with a small deer draped on his shoulders.

“Good to see you brought your own supper,” I joked to him, as he dropped the carcass on the ground with a low thump.

“Yes, but sadly it will not be shared with Shannon,” he replied. “I did not see him or Private Reubin.”

I thought for a moment about the possibilities for Shannon’s delay.

“He probably shot a big elk, and is waiting for us,” I speculated. “Eventually, he’ll figure out what happened. … Hopefully, Private Reubin has already found him, and they are both well.”

But this was not the case.

At noon the following day, Private Reubin caught up with us, as we traveled farther up the Jefferson River. Like Drouillard, he too had been far up the Wisdom River, but could not locate Shannon.

This was a source of great concern for all. Despite our distress, we could not wait for his arrival. My hope was that he would soon find us en route or in camp. To send more men back or to wait would result in an unnecessary delay that would likely prove very costly for everyone. To risk being trapped in the mountains by deep snow, with little or no food, and inadequate shelter was simply not an option. Hours, even minutes could be the difference between our success and failure in not only crossing the mountains, but living to tell the tale.

I had to do what was best for the entire expedition, not just one man, including myself. This dilemma consumed my conscience, but I knew we must proceed without him, and could only wish for his safe return.

Starving or freezing to death crossing the ranges was certainly a possibility, if we halted. But food supplies and the cold were not a concern for us on this portion of the Jefferson River. Although game was limited, the river abounded in beaver numbers thus far unsurpassed on our journey.

This fact played a curious and hopeful role in an observation made by the Indian woman toward evening.

From a distance of about 20 miles, Sacajawea recognized the point of a high plain she said was not very distant from the summer retreat of her nation. She added that the retreat was on a river beyond the southwestern mountains, and the plain we were observing was called the "Beaver's Head," from its resemblance to the creature when it swims on the surface of the water. More importantly, she assured me that we would find her nation on this river or on the one immediately west of the Continental Divide.

Upon hearing this, the men and I were overjoyed. I then carefully examined the character of the waters to gauge how much farther we would have to travel before reaching the ultimate source of the river. The Jefferson was then narrow and shallow, and continually diminished in stature each mile we advanced. I deduced the Divide could not be far off, and decided another search party was needed to hunt for the Shoshone. We traveled another mile before camping near a thicket on the larboard side, after proceeding 14 miles that day.

At camp, I watched Clark mend his shirt when he abruptly reached down to grasp his throbbing ankle.

"How's it feel?" I asked.

"Sore … very sore," he replied in great pain.

Shaking my head in sympathy, I responded: "I know you would rather lead the scouting party, but tomorrow I need to look for the Shoshone."

"I know. It's the right thing to do," he said dejectedly, nodding agreement.

I placed my hand on his shoulder to ease his disappointment. "I'll take George, Shields, and McNeal. Even if it takes us an entire month, we need to find them, and get horses."

"Yes. And not having horses means we'll have to leave a good deal of our provisions behind," Clark stated. "That can't happen. You should go … what about taking Charbonneau?"

"No. He'd be a burden," I quickly replied without further consideration.

I glanced to my right and saw Sacajawea nursing Jean Baptiste, while Charbonneau tended a small fire next to Private Labiche and a small group.

I removed my hand from Clark's shoulder, approached the group, and squatted down to speak with Labiche.

"Private, would you ask Mr. Charbonneau to ask Sacajawea what the name is for 'white-man' in Shoshone?" I inquired.

Labiche turned. He spoke in French to Charbonneau who relayed the message in Hidatsa to Sacajawea. She appeared puzzled, but responded a short time later.

"Tab-ba-bone," she said, studying my face.

She redirected her attention to Charbonneau, and continued to speak for a moment. The translation chain was reversed back to Labiche.

"Charbonneau said: 'Tab-ba-bone' is the word to use," Labiche repeated.

"Thank you, Private," I replied, standing up.

"Thank you," I said, directly to Sacajawea, and then gave a silent nod to her pathetic husband, before retiring for the evening.

The rising sun on the 9th of August projected distinct columns of red and orange lights of many shades toward the heavens, as it broke over the horizon. Minutes later, the column shades slowly disappeared, and gave way to a brilliant orange orb. This was the most auspicious start one could hope for during our quest for horses and I intended to capitalize on the provident signal.

With the morning sun illuminating our backs and knapsacks over our shoulders, Drouillard, Shields, McNeal, and I set out, and proceeded on very well across a gigantic plain nestled between distant mountain ranges.

During our march, the thought came to me that I failed to leave written instructions with Captain Clark, in the event some tragedy should befall us during our quest. We continued to a point where I expected the party to arrive by eight o' clock — our usual time for breakfast. At this spot, I penned brief instructions for Clark that included a short will in the event of my untimely demise. We waited for their arrival, but they did not appear.

We hiked a mile downstream where I saw Clark who was quite surprised to see our group. He grinned as we approached.

"You must have really missed us," he remarked sarcastically.

"Of course," I responded drolly. "I especially missed the fragrant, and appealing aroma exuding from your ankle."

He snickered. I handed him the note.

"If I don't return, I want you to have these instructions," I said in a serious, but low volume, as I stepped in close.

At that moment, looking downstream, I saw a lone figure materialize from the shimmering rays radiating above the horizon.

I tapped Clark's arm, and pointed north toward the wavy silhouette. He turned to face the figure. The crew noticed our gaze, and soon everyone was staring at the enlarging figure, not knowing whether it was an animal or human. Chatter among the party changed to whispers. Soon all were silent. Only gusts of wind and the babbling of the river current could be heard.

The figure continued to advance toward us, and became more lucid. I could see a slim protrusion jutting up from what appeared to be a person's right shoulder. Another quiet moment passed while anticipation mounted. A magpie crackled several times from a nearby tree branch.

Private Reubin squinted to be certain of what everyone hoped.

He focused, took a deep breath, and pierced the tense silence with a loud shout: "It's Shannon! Goddamn it! It's Shannon!" he happily exclaimed, grabbing the hat from his head and forcefully throwing it to the ground to emphasize his glee.

A loud cheer arose from the men nearly in unison. Everyone rushed out happily to greet him with broad smiles, slapping him on the back. His initial look of worry was quickly replaced with beams of joy at the enthusiastic reaction. He was disheveled and tired, but in much better shape than when he was lost the previous fall, or a month earlier. Shannon even brought back three deer skins for the party to cut into moccasins and other clothes.

I could scarcely contain my delight at his safe arrival for a third time.

"Well, Captain, now I can leave with a clear conscience!"

After the jubilant reception diminished to low chatter, I turned to Shannon with a big grin and asked the obvious: "Tell us, what happened?"

He momentarily hung his head, shook it a few times, and looked up to scan the crowd: "Well, I ended up huntin' in the mountains the whole day, and got back where we split the next mornin'. Everyone was gone, so I figured you was upriver, so that's where I went. I hiked until I knew you wasn't above me, and turned 'round. I got back to the forks, and could see you went up this branch."

With his explanation complete, my team re-grouped, and we made haste to move ahead. By day's end, we covered 16 miles, while the rest of the party was not far behind. By this time, the river was becoming so rapid and shallow I had sincere doubts about whether the men would be able to pull the canoes much farther upstream.

We set out early the following morning, anxious to meet the Indians.

After about five miles of travel through an immense valley, we crossed a large creek on larboard side. I named the creek after Private McNeal, since he did not yet have his name affixed to the landscape. Immediately on the other side of the creek, we happened upon an Indian road along the river, which led us 10 miles to another range of mountains and rocky cliffs, which were inhabited by numerous rattlesnakes. At this spot, McNeal, Shields, and I halted for several hours, built a fire, and waited for Drouillard to return from a short hunting trip. By noon, Drouillard brought three deer skins and the flesh of one, which made for a terrific meal that we quickly consumed, before proceeding.

I was determined to cover as much territory as possible before sundown, and we soon resumed our journey. Within several hundred yards of the cliffs, the mountains closed in on the road. We hiked fifteen additional miles before emerging into another large valley where the river forked once more into equally-sized tributaries. Nothing remarkable suggested the way forward.

One branch led southeast, the other southwest.

The only natural suggestion at this junction was the fact that this would be the point at which hauling canoes and cargo by water would finally come to a merciful end. The river was then but two small streams.

The Indian road also split at this confluence. Each road followed the streams into separate valleys from which they originated. I placed the butt of my gun on the ground, and surveyed the area. The men and I glanced from left to right, not knowing which road to follow.

“George, I want you to go west,” I said pointing in that direction. “Private Shields, go up the other way.”

“How far?” Shields asked.

“No more than a mile. ... I want to pursue the one that has the most recent tracks,” I stated.

The dispatched pair went their ways, while McNeal and I waited and watched for them and the Shoshone.

I took out my field journal and recorded McNeal’s name for the creek, and started writing a brief note to Captain Clark. I wrote that he should remain at this spot until my return. After completing the note, Shields and Drouillard returned at nearly the same time to report their findings.

“What’s it look like, Shields?” I inquired with excitement.

"It looks like it was traveled a bit this year," he promptly replied.

"George?" I asked, turning to him.

"Looks like much more than a bit, Captain."

Judging from their testimonials, it was apparent the southwest road was the one to the Shoshone. However, I thought it prudent to personally examine the southeast road to be sure it did not loop back to the west. I folded my note to Clark, advising him of the route we planned to take, secured it to a dry willow pole at the forks, and set out on the southeast road.

Less than two miles away, the path became so faint I determined it could not have been the one we had followed all the way from McNeal's Creek. We promptly made a retrograde march back to the forks, and traveled up the southwest road several miles to the point I was convinced it was the one and true route to further pursue.

We halted, and I penned a replacement message to Clark, and dispatched Drouillard back to the forks with the new note.

Since the sun was soon to set, we camped at this spot, which was below a rocky hill devoid of timber. Examining the topography while waiting for Drouillard to return, one could not help but notice that although the mountains very near us did not appear that high, most were still partially topped with snow. This fact convinced me that we had very slowly ascended to a very great height, although I had no means by which to calculate our elevation.[18] The ascending course we had taken since leaving St. Louis had been so gradual in height that it had been barely perceptible. What was equally amazing was the fact that the waters were still navigable through such mountainous terrain. I therefore did not believe there was a similar extent of country anywhere on Earth.

If the Columbia River proved similarly navigable, commerce and communication across the continent by water would one day be practicable and safe, assuming a suitable portage similar to the one around the falls existed.

However, I very much doubted such navigation was possible. I based this sobering conclusion on three geographical facts:

The first fact was I knew our position was approximately 115 degrees west longitude, and 45 degrees north latitude.

The second fact was the King and Arrowsmith maps indicated the mouth of the Columbia was at about 124 degrees west, and 46 degrees north.

The last fact meant that from where we camped, the mouth of the Columbia was almost directly west, some 400 to 500 miles, given there were about 50 miles between meridians at that latitude.

Piecing the puzzle together in my mind, the image was becoming clear that the waters west of the Passage must indeed be turbulent, having such a large height to fall over such a small distance. Conflicting prospects filled my thoughts.

Three thousand miles the waters flow from these rugged mountains, east to St. Louis, and still more to the Gulf of Mexico. Contrasting this flowage in the opposite direction with only a few hundred miles west to the Pacific Ocean from the same lofty altitude, one does not have to be gifted with a great imagination to recognize the probable dangers.

I did not want to think about what likely lay ahead, but concluded it very likely had to be chaotic and treacherous.

Drouillard returned, darkness fell, and I lay my head on a makeshift pillow, trying not to dwell on the trail beyond the Divide. Having walked 30 miles that day, I soon fell into a deep slumber to ready myself for another demanding outing in a few hours. The night was cool, but comfortable.

We set off at first light, continuing on the road we pursued the prior evening. Within two miles, the road faded to a trail that diminished into a faint path, and finally disappeared completely in the vastness of the valley in which we found ourselves. Small tufts of rough grass and short shrubs were everywhere, and nowhere were signs of the former road. Looking up at the western mountains, I resolved to proceed along the same creek we had followed, which led toward a narrow pass.[22] With hopes of regaining the Indian road, we hiked west for more than three hours, and still had not regained the road.

In need of a different plan, I signaled for the men to halt. I took the rifle off my shoulder, placed the rifle butt on the ground, and addressed the group.

"We need to find the road. ... If we separate by a few hundred yards, we have a better chance. ... George, I want you to go near the creek. ... Private Shields, I want you on the left. ... McNeal and I will take the center. If you find the road, place your hat on your gun muzzle and wave it. Pay attention, and try to stay abreast. Understood?"

The men nodded the affirmative, and we silently marched another five miles.

Under a warm afternoon sun, the only sound was that of our feet plowing through the dry, brittle grasses and vegetation, as they were pushed aside or crushed beneath the soles of our moccasins. I lifted my arm to wipe away the sweat from my brow when I paused in mid-motion at an astonishing sight that left me momentarily paralyzed.

"Stop," I commanded, and anxiously put out my arm to cease McNeal's advance. Drouillard and Shields continued on, having not seen us halt.

I quickly laid down my gun, and hurriedly rifled through my knapsack to fish out my spyglass. Peering through the device, the figure was quite clear and about two miles in the distance, riding an elegant horse through this grand valley — a spectacular valley situated between undulating mountain ranges.

"It's an Indian! An Indian!" I exclaimed to McNeal, as I continued to study the warrior through the lens. "This is unbelievable after all this time!"

It was Jumping Deer on another solo scouting mission.[C] His manner of dress indicated that he was a member of a nation we had yet to encounter. He bounced as he rode without a saddle, armed only with a bow and quiver filled with arrows. A small string answered as a bridle for the horse.

Now that I have done the business, I understand that North American horses were decedents of breeds brought to this continent by Spanish conquistadors in the 1500s. The great herds possessed by the Indians were acquired a relatively short time later, as horses rapidly populated the West.

I was delighted at the sighting of this yellow gentleman. There was no uncertainty in my mind that our introduction would be friendly and welcoming, provided we could get close enough to show him our group was white, and not in legion with their enemies. I therefore collected my belongings quickly, and resumed our march at our previous pace, slightly behind Drouillard and Shields.

At the distance of about one mile, the Indian stopped, having spotted the four of us walking toward him. Anxiously, I again laid down my gun, threw off my knapsack, and untied my blanket, which was secured to the rear of the knapsack. Quickly unrolling the blanket, I grasped one end at each corner, and began signaling the Indian by repeatedly waving it up and down, as if to spread it on the ground. The Indian stopped, but did not react.

I knew waving a blanket in this manner was a signal of friendship among tribes on the Missouri. The origin of this welcoming and simulated signal was the placement of an animal skin on the ground when hosting guests.

I proceeded this waving in groups of three. Regrettably, my frantic signals failed to have the desired outcome.

Jumping Deer remained steadfast.

I concluded he viewed with great suspicion the unwavering advancement of Drouillard and Shields, as they appeared to be executing hostile flanking maneuvers. Shouting for them to halt was tempting, but would prove futile, since they were too far distant to clearly hear any bellowed order.

Instead, I took from my pack strings of beads, a spyglass, and other trinkets.

"Wait here," I said to McNeal. "I'm going to try and catch up with them before they scare him off."

Holding the items up in front of me, I briskly walked toward the Indian — leaving behind my belongings and McNeal.

Hoping to overtake Drouillard and Shields before the warrior retreated, I arrived to within 200 paces of the Indian when he slowly turned his horse, and began moving in the direction from which he came. He looked back at us in frightened curiosity, but did not immediately run off.

"Tab-ba-bone! Tab-ba-bone!" I shouted to the Indian.

The warrior understandably seemed quite confused, as he struggled to make reason of the conflicting actions. By then, the rifles Drouillard and Shields possessed must have been visible, and a cause of great alarm — his being armed with only a bow and a few arrows. I recognized the devolving situation, and anxiously signaled the men by frantically waving my arms overhead.

Drouillard stopped, but Shields pressed on, seemingly unaware of my parley with the lone Indian.

The warrior slowed his retreat, as if to wait for me, but grew ever wary of Shields, and his deadly weapon that were then well within killing range. I was no greater than 150 paces from the yellow gentleman.

"Tab-ba-bone! Tab-ba-bone!" I again hollered.

I held the items in my hand high above my head, as the Indian stared back over his shoulder. His horse slowly moved away from us.

Seeing my intentions were not being received, I anxiously tossed the objects aside, and quickly rolled up my shirt sleeve in attempt to show him the portions of my skin that were not baked by the intense rays of the sun. I continued walking, holding back my shirt sleeve to demonstrate that I was white, and not from any native nation. I was desperate to show him who I was.

"Tab-ba-bone! Tab-ba-bone!"

Within 100 paces, Jumping Deer had seen and heard enough of Shields and me. He turned his head, whipped the hindquarters of the horse with a willow switch, and the elegant beast leapt a creek to disappear into the trees.

"Goddamn it!" I yelled to myself, thrusting my fists down into the air to emphasize my frustration. "Son of a bitch!"

For the time being, all hopes vanished in obtaining horses with the retreat of the Indian. I was sorely chagrined at the conduct of the men, particularly the aggressive folly by Shields. Seething with fury, I angrily gestured Shields towards me, and held my tongue until he was within reach. Suddenly, I grabbed his shirt and pulled him into me until he was close enough to feel my breath.

“What were you thinking?” I screamed in his face. “I signaled for you to halt! Did you not see that?”

I curtly pushed Shields back, and could see he was quite shaken at my unprecedented display of temperament.

“No, Sir. I did not see your signal,” he replied in a voice quaking with fright, panic and unease.

I shook my head in disgust, and rolled my eyes towards a solitary cloud in the sky, as if the answer were written on the vapors — a vain search for a single answer to my many questions.

“You may have cost us our only chance of getting horses!” I said in exasperation.

“I am sorry, Sir. I wasn’t sure how to approach,” he explained.

“You have a rifle. He had a bow and arrows. Did you not see that?” I asked.

“I am sorry, Sir,” he again apologized.

“Apologies aren’t enough, Private,” I said to him in fury. “A soldier also needs to use his initiative. ... And you need to use your goddamn head!”

I sighed heavily, and tried to calm myself at the prospect of another opportunity, but remained livid. Disgusted, I gestured for the others to join us. Upon Drouillard’s arrival, I reluctantly reprimanded him for his actions, but to a much lesser degree than Shields. Moments later, feeling some regret for the harshness of my rebukes, I placed a hand on each man’s shoulder.

“Gentlemen, we need to think to think like them,” I urged in a subdued tone, but feeling no need for an apology. “The lives of us all depend on it.”

Recalling I had left my spyglass and gifts on the plain, I sent Drouillard and Shields back to retrieve the goods, which afforded us time to separately compose ourselves. I paced about for a time contemplating my next action.

After concluding what needed to be done during their brief absence, I assembled a different assortment of gifts for the Shoshone, while McNeal collected wood for a campfire. This assembly I hoped would please the Shoshone, if we were fortunate to soon meet them again. Onto the end of a pole, I attached moccasin awls, strands of beads, a container of paint, one mirror, and our country’s flag. My intention was to have the gifts on the pole and readily available to show and give the Indians should we meet them, once more. McNeal had the fire started by the time I finished securing the items to the staff. After digging a small hole, I firmly planted the pole in the ground for easy access when the time arrived.

We camped near the narrow pass and confluence of two small creeks that originated in the mountains. I estimated our camp that night could not have been more than 15 miles west of our camp the prior evening.

After hiking many miles in various directions that day, falling asleep was again quite easy. However, staying asleep was not possible. Most of the night was spent tossing and turning during a series of historical remembrances and dreams I had about what could await us at the Northwest Passage.[D]

The Passage had been the goal of many explorers, since at least 1576 for reasons I earlier recounted, but now submit additional details for your mature deliberation and thought:

Finding this gap very likely meant prosperity for all inhabitants living along its entire route, which could only increase the wealth and security of the entire nation. For more than 200 years the intrepid — including Martin Frobisher and Henry Hudson — had been searching for it, and we then lay at its foothills.

I recalled that Hudson failed in his 1610 quest for the Passage after his crew mutinied, and sent him, his son, and loyal followers adrift on a raft amid the vast forest to the northeast.[15] They were never seen again. Hudson's crew organized the mutiny after becoming disgruntled with a winter similar to the one we had just endured on the plains. I dreamt of a similar scenario befalling Captain Clark and me, after we became trapped in these rugged mountains and faced another cruel winter in the wilderness.

Alarmed by the disturbing thought, my eyes shot open, and I was quickly relieved the tragedy was merely in my mind. I stared into the night sky for a moment before turning onto my side. Trying to forget the awful dream, my mind floated toward other musings.

When President Jefferson began his first term in 1801, four recent expeditions contributed a great deal to our understanding the West, but still huge gaps remained.[15,17,21] Those expeditions were led by British Sea Captain George Vancouver, Scottish trader Alexander Mackenzie, British merchants James Mackay with John Thomas Evans, and American sailing Captain Robert Gray.

Gray was a fur trader who on May 11, 1792, sailed his ship the *Columbia Rediviva* 36 miles into the mouth of an enormous river, which he named after his vessel. He and his men were hunting sea otters. Their plan was to obtain pelts for trade in China in exchange for tea, spices, and porcelain. Approximately five months later in October of the same year, Gray traveled north approximately 150 miles, and met Vancouver on the west coast of an island of the same name, and informed Vancouver of his finding.

With hopes of expanding British interests, and convinced Gray could not be credited with the river's discovery, Vancouver sent a crew south in a smaller boat. They sailed 100 miles inland to the southeast where they named two high peaks that were visible from near the river: Mount Hood and Mount St. Helens.

Vancouver was able to calculate the latitude and longitude coordinates of the region, which were eventually mapped by British cartographer Aaron Arrowsmith in 1802, and American map-maker Nicholas King in 1803.

The fact this river existed was a primary reason why Jefferson and I believed this watercourse may have been part of the yet-discovered Northwest Passage, and following the Missouri to its most distant fountain was the most logical route to discover this valued road.

According to Arrowsmith and King, this area was conjectured to be the south fork of the Columbia River. This meant if the maps were correct, the north and south forks were only eight sleeps from the ocean, if one believed Hudson's Bay Company Surveyor Peter Fidler and his source, the Blackfeet Indian Chief called "The Feathers."

Eight nights: I could scarcely contain my jubilation at the thought.

If we could obtain horses, in a little more than a week, we might be on the shores of the Pacific Ocean receiving news and much-needed supplies from a passing merchant ship. But that romantic speculation was soon married to a more harsh and realistic vision of the rapids and torrents we were sure to encounter, as the pure waters of the Continental Divide swiftly flowed toward the salty waters of the sea — waters that likely traveled 800 or 1,000 miles west, instead of more than 3,500 miles to the east.

I dozed a few hours, only to awaken once more with thoughts that eventually turned to the travels of Alexander Mackenzie in 1789 and 1793 when he vainly sought the Northwest Passage during two expeditions.

Beginning in May 1793 at Fort Chipewyan in Canada, about 800 miles north of our campsite, 10 men headed southwest in a 25-foot birchbark canoe toward the Pacific Ocean. Less than three months later, Mackenzie painted his name on a large rock on the Pacific coast, not far from Vancouver's island.

The rock bared the following message: "Alexander Mackenzie from Canada by land 22nd July 1793."

Mackenzie published a book about his travels in 1801 and called it: *Voyages From Montreal Through the Continent of North America to the Frozen and Pacific Oceans in 1789 and 1793.*

The book was delivered to Philadelphia in 1802, shortly before I arrived there in May 1803, as part of my training for leading the Corps. I read it, and was intrigued with the leadership skills Mr. Mackenzie demonstrated that resulted in his crew's unwavering loyalty.[11] His portage over the great Rocky Mountains — mere 817 paces — an easy passage by any standard.

My dream faded into slumber, and I was able to rest another hour before the sun started to illuminate the landscape. I suddenly stirred, and with great excitement threw off my blanket. Drouillard was already awake, and packing his belongings for an early start to proceed on.

"George," I called, striding toward him.

He glanced in my direction.

"Yes, Captain," he responded in a calm voice.

"I want you to go on a short scouting mission for the Indian's path," I said, spinning him to the west, and pointing toward the mountains. "No more than an hour out, and use your initiative."

"It shouldn't be difficult," he quickly and confidently replied.

Less than two hours later he returned to report his findings, as I ceased writing notes in my field journal.

"It goes just to the left of that gulch," he stated, looking west.

From our position a few miles east of the narrow pass, Drouillard said this as he used his right arm to gesture. He slowly moved it parallel to the ground from right to left, stopping to point at the shadowy gulch.

"I did not see the road, but that's where the horse tracks lead," Drouillard reported to me.

"Let's move out then." I concluded, folding the cover of my journal.

We collected ourselves, and were soon ready for departure.

"Same formation as yesterday. Shields left, George right. Keep your eyes open for the road and Indians. Let's not repeat yesterday. Keep within shouting distance. … Let's move out!"

McNeal grabbed the flagged staff with gifts, and we headed through the pass toward the base of the mountains where we crossed four small creeks. Near this spot were recently constructed willow-brush shelters, which were conical in shape. I called to the others, and we examined the area. Much of the soil had been upturned for what seemed to be a search for edible roots.

"We're close, very, very close," I said to the men. "Let's find the road."

Shortly after continuing our pursuit along the creek, Shields rediscovered the lost road. The trail followed a stout stream, which flowed from the mountains. We stopped briefly for breakfast, and quickly proceeded on. Still traveling to the southwest for several miles, the road and stream then took an abrupt turn to the west. Peering ahead, the stream left the valley, and was squeezed between high, rolling hills and ridges, but remained a gradual rise through the gap.[23]

Staring into the future while we marched, I could no longer silence my great anticipation: "Gentlemen, we shall soon be at the Passage. We'll be drinking from the waters of the Columbia by evening!"

A cheer rose up from the group, and we remained in high spirits, anticipating the great Divide. The stout stream had then diminished to a modest brook, only a few yards in width, and a few feet in depth. A few miles up, and six miles from the valley, the brook further shrank to a rivulet, only three feet in width.

McNeal looked forward, saw the waterway further narrow, and was overwhelmed with excitement and emotion. Without uttering a sound, he bolted in front us for 50 yards, and suddenly halted when he arrived at the correct location. We watched from behind as he placed the bottom of the staff down on the opposite side of the rivulet, and threw his right foot on the ground behind the staff. The soldier was then astride the mighty and heretofore seemingly endless, Missouri River — more than 3,000 miles from St. Louis. He gleefully thrust both fists in the air — rifle in one, staff in the other.

"Thank you, God! Thank you that I lived to see this day!" he loudly yelled to the heavens and his deity.

The three of us behind chuckled at the action, but shared his juvenile exultation, without the overt mannerisms.

To deem credit for our burdensome labors these many toilsome days and uneasy nights to a divine being seemed inappropriate, at best, and pathetically capitulatory, at worst. But it would have been equally pathetic for me to question, or show the folly of such a belief system in the presence of the others, at this joyous time, and especially as his commanding officer.

Instead, I ignored the reference, and focused on sharing in his delight by stopping to fill our canteens, and refresh ourselves by drinking from the waters that gushed so pure and cold. Judge then the pleasure I felt as the cool liquid allayed my great thirst, and the others.

For more than a mile, we resumed our climb, and the only obvious indication the brook was still on the surface of the mountain were the abundant numbers of lush grasses and leafy plants that mostly hid its presence from view.[E] Glancing up as we marched, I could then see an abrupt end to the lush undergrowth — beyond which lay a small grove of pine trees, and stubby, dry vegetation that terminated at a ridge.

The epic trek to the most distant fountain of the great river, which we had sought for so many grueling months, was about to conclude. There — bubbling up from the ground on the east side of the gentle mountain — was a tiny spring that continuously gave birth and helped nourish the mighty Missouri River in all its brilliance and splendor.[24]

"There it is, men. The start of the Missouri," I said as we hiked around the spring. "And on that is the Northwest Passage!" I exclaimed, pointing at the ridge.

Well aware of the immense possibilities, I could scarcely contain my thrill of anticipation as we trudged up the incline. With each step, the top of the mountain became more visible, beyond which lay the answer to the long-sought question. I glanced down to check my path for placement of my next steps, and then looked back up, as we drew nearer the summit. Drouillard, Shields, and McNeal walked on each side of me, while all four of us gulped air to endure the increasing ascent. The parched vegetation crunched and snapped under the weight of our feet, approaching the Divide. Only short grasses and shrubs were then between us and the top. I briefly turned my head back to examine the eastern view and saw low, rounded mountains surrounding the gap through which we had just traveled. Far off in the distance were the snow-capped peaks we observed from the basins feeding the Missouri.

Given this affable terrain to the east, I stopped in astonishment upon reaching the summit, peering west. The others followed my lead.

Knowing we were only a few hundred miles from the ocean and at a very high elevation, imagine my alarm when I discovered numerous and immense ranges of high mountains still to the west with their tops partially covered with snow, not rounded, gently sloping mountains similar to the ones we just passed, but rugged, sharp peaks that promised confrontation and challenge — the likes we had yet to experience.

Simple trigonometry would confirm my fears, but an exact enumeration was certainly not needed to prove what we were seeing. My previous belief about the navigability of the rivers appeared true. Our hope of a Northwest Passage seemed dashed by the imminent rush of the waters from these lofty points. Regardless, I had no time to contemplate these disturbing developments, and knew the procurement of horses, and journey over and through these mountains had taken on new and extremely dire significance.

We stared west in stunned silence, as a cool wind blew in our faces. I hung my head, and slightly shook it in dejection, as McNeal closely studied my reaction.

"Goddamn, Captain. ... They look as bad as the ones north. ... What we gonna do?" McNeal asked, while Shields and Drouillard listened intently.

Without hesitation, I boldly asserted: "We're going to find horses. ... There's still a chance a river cuts through these mountains. Think of the Gates," I stated, emphasizing the positive, but knew even if one did exist, it was likely not negotiable by any canoe.

"There's no time to waste then. Let's move out," McNeal energetically urged.

Disillusioned and worried, I led the men down a very steep and treacherous descent through grasses of all sizes, and groves of trees that grew from the rocky slopes. Although this was still part of the Indian road, the trail was faint, and would have been difficult to follow had it not led to a bold, handsome creek. At the spring that fed this creek, we again stopped to ceremoniously drink from the first waters of the great Columbia River.

We resumed our march into a deep hollow, and emerged into a clearing near which we found huge quantities of willow brush for fuel, and decided to encamp, after hiking 20 miles. Having not killed any game, we reluctantly dined on boiled pork, flour, and parched corn meal.

After lying down for the evening, I processed the emotional tumult of the day, and wondered how Clark and the remainder of the party were progressing. I could do no more than speculate, but imagined they were having a very difficult time lugging the dugouts through the demanding shoals. However, the definitive answer to that question would have to wait until we met again — where and when, only McNeal's God knew.

MESOLOGUE

Whatever we inherit from the fortunate
We have taken from the defeated
What they had to leave us - a symbol:
A symbol perfected in death.
And all shall be well, and
All manner of thing shall be well
By the purification of the motive
In the ground of our beseeching.

T. S. Eliot, 1942, "Little Gidding"

CHARACTER LIST

NAME	ROLE
Arcawechar	Yankton-Sioux Indian chief.
Arrowsmith, Aaron	British mapmaker whose 1802 map was used to make the Nicholas King 1803 map carried by the expedition.
Bates, Frederick	Secretary of the Louisiana Territory under President Jefferson.
Big Hawk	Fictional name of the son of a then deceased Mandan Indian chief.
Big Horse	Missouria Indian tribe chief.
Big Stealer	Hidatsa Indian chief at Mahawha village.
Big White	Mandan Indian chief of the lower or first village called Matootonha.
Black Buffalo	Teton-Sioux Indian chief.
Black Cat	Mandan chief of the upper or second village called Rooptahee.
Black Moccasin	Hidatsa Indian chief of the Metaharta village.
Blackbird	Omaha Indian chief; died before the expedition arrived in their region.
Boley, John	Private; return party member; discipline problem at Dubois Camp.
Bratton, William	Private; permanent party member; hunter, blacksmith.
Brave One	Fictitious name for an Otoe Indian warrior.
Budge, George	Hudson's Bay Company clerk.
Buffalo Medicine	Teton-Sioux Indian chief.
Calumet Bird Tail	Hidatsa Indian chief at Mahawha village.
Cann, E.	Engagé; probably return party member at Mandan villages.
Caugee, Charles	Engagé; probably return party member at Mandan villages.
Chaboillez, Charles	Trader and senior executive of the North West Company.
Charbonneau, Jean B.	Very young son of Sacajawea and Toussaint Charbonneau.
Charbonneau, Toussaint	Interpreter; husband of Sacajawea; good cook, bad spouse.
Clark, William	Second lieutenant/captain; co-leader of western expedition.
Collin, Joseph	Engagé; may have left at Arikara or Mandan village after service.
Collins, John	Private; permanent party member; best known for misbehavior.
Colter, John	Private; permanent party member; expert hunter; best known for his 1809 run from Blackfeet Indians after being stripped naked, and his 1807 wandering into what is now known as Yellowstone National Park, which was originally called "Colter's Hell."
Cruzatte, Pierre	Private; permanent party; best known for playing violin, limited vision.
Dame, John	Private; return party member; best known for killing a pelican.
Dearborn, Henry	Secretary of War under President Thomas Jefferson.
Deschamps, Jean B.	Engagé; foreman for the French boatmen.
Dorion, Pierre	Interpreter; Frenchman fluent in the language of Yankton-Sioux Indians.
Drouillard, George	Interpreter; civilian; valued hunter, and member of expedition.
Eagle Feather	Arikara Indian chief; died visiting Washington in early January 1806.
Fairfong	Frenchman who traded goods, and lived with Otoe Indians.
Fidler, Peter	Trader; collected information transferred to 1802 Arrowsmith map.
Field, Joseph	Private; permanent party member; selected for special missions.
Field, Reubin	Private; permanent party member; selected for special missions.
Floyd, Charles	Sergeant; victim of unknown ailment; died and buried Aug. 20, 1804; cousin of Sgt. Pryor. The only expedition member death during the trip.
Frazer, Robert	Private; permanent party member; best known for trading his razor with an Indian during the return voyage on June 2, 1806.
Gallatin, Albert	Secretary of the Treasury under President Jefferson.
Gass, Patrick	Sergeant/Private; carpenter; replaced Sgt. Floyd.
Gibson, George	Private; permanent party member; good hunter and violin player.
Goodrich, Silas	Private; permanent party member; best known for fishing skills.
Gravelines, Joseph	Interpreter and trader who lived among Arikara Indians for many years.
Grinder, Priscilla	Matriarch of inn for travelers on road known as Natchez Trace.
Hall, Hugh	Private; permanent party member; subject of court-martial.
Hebert, Charles	Engagé return party member, probably at Mandan villages for the 1804-1805 winter.

Henderson, George	Hudson's Bay Company trader.
Heney, Hugh	Trader for the North West Company.
Horned Weasel	Hidatsa Indian chief at Menetarra village.
Howard, Thomas	Private; permanent party member; tried for misbehavior.
Jefferson, Thomas	President of the United States; chief advocate and inspiration of the expedition; envisioned westward expansion of the nation.
Jumping Deer	Fictional Shoshone Indian warrior name for an actual person.
Jusseaume, Rene	Interpreter; trader from British Territory, hired by Lewis and Clark for trip to Mandan villages.
King, Nicholas	Mapmaker based in the United States; created map for expedition.
La Jeunesse, Jean B.	Engagé; went downriver in dugout canoe in fall 1804.
La Liberté	Engagé who spoke the Otoe Indian language, and deserted the expedition on or about July 29, 1804.
Labiche, Francois	Private; permanent party member; skilled Indian interpreter.
Lafrance, Jean Baptiste	North West Company trader.
Larocque, Francois-Antoine	Trader; executive for North West Company. Responsible for overseeing trade with Indians in the Mandan/Hidatsa area.
Lepage, Jean Baptiste	Private; Frenchman living among Mandan Indians who joined the expedition as replacement for Private John Newman who was discharged after a court-martial.
Lewis, Meriwether	Captain; leader of expedition called on by President Thomas Jefferson to explore what is today the western United States.
Lightning Crow	Arikara Indian chief.
Little Bear	Fictional name for very young Yankton-Sioux boy.
Little Buffalo	Fictional name for an Indian boy with frostbitten feet.
Little Crow	Mandan Indian secondary chief of Matootonha village.
Little Fox	Hidatsa Indian chief at the Metaharta village.
Little Thief	Otoe Indian chief who died near St. Louis in late 1805.
Loisel, Régis	Trader; businessman in village of La Charrette in today's Missouri.
Madison, James	Secretary of State under President Jefferson.
Makoshika	Fictional name of Teton-Sioux warrior. The name actually means "bad earth" in Sioux language, and is the author's salute to Glendive, Mont.
Malboeuf, Etienne	Engagé; return party member, stayed at Mandan villages for the winter.
McCracken, Hugh	Trader for the North West Company.
McKenzie, Charles	Trader and clerk for the North West Company.
McNeal, Hugh	Private; permanent party member; chosen for special missions.
Newman, John	Private; tried, expelled from the party for unknown mutinous expressions.
Ordway, John	Sergeant; permanent party member; known for his reliability.
Otter Woman	Other young Indian wife of Toussaint Charbonneau.
Pinaut, Peter	Engagé; probably return party member at Mandan villages for the winter.
Pocasse	Arikara Indian Chief.
Potts, John	Private; permanent party member; joined John Colter in 1809; killed during conflict with Blackfeet Indians near Three Forks, Mont., in what would later be known as "Colter's Run." His association and likely friendship with Colter was documented in the Lewis and Clark journals on April 22, 1806.
Primeau, Paul	Engagé; went downriver in canoe in fall 1804 from Mandan villages.
Pryor, Nathaniel	Sergeant; permanent party member; known for integrity, skills; cousin of Sgt. Floyd who died early in the expedition.
Radiant Day	Fictional Mandan Indian woman name.
Raven Man	Secondary Indian chief of the upper Mandan village, Rooptahee.
Reed, Moses	Private; tried, expelled from the expedition for desertion.
Rivet, Francois	Engagé; return party member at Mandan villages; known for dancing on hands, and spinning on his head during celebrations.
Robertson, John	Private; likely never left Dubois Camp, or was soon sent back to Dubois.
Roi, Peter	Engagé; return party member at Mandan villages who probably stayed among the Arikara until September 1806.
Red Shield	Hidatsa Indian chief.

Running Deer	Fictional name for Teton-Sioux Indian warrior.
Running Horse	Fictional name for a Missouria Indian man.
Sacajawea	Interpreter; Shoshone Indian; wife of Charbonneau, mother; saved valuable articles from destruction, recognized landmarks, pilot, facilitated horse trade with her people from her homeland, performed actions to help expedition, living peace symbol to other Indians. Also known in the journals by her nickname: Janey.
Seaman	Newfoundland dog owned by Captain Lewis.
Seeing Snake	Hidatsa Indian chief.
Serpent	Hidatsa Indian chief of the Menetarra village.
Shaking Hand	Yankton-Sioux Indian chief.
Shannon, George	Private; permanent party member; best known for being separated from the expedition three times during the journey.
Shields, John	Private; permanent party member; blacksmith, carpenter.
Smith, Robert	Secretary of the Navy under President Jefferson.
Standing Elk	Fictional Mandan Indian woman name.
Soaring Raven	Fictional name for a Mandan Indian warrior.
Struck by the Pana	Yankton-Sioux Indian chief.
Struck by the Ree	Yankton-Sioux Indian infant.
Tabeau, Pierre-Antoine	Trader who lived among the Arikara Indians; cousin of Jean Vallé.
Talking Crow	Fictional Mandan Indian woman name.
Tar-ro-mo-nee	Yankton-Sioux warrior.
Thompson, John	Private; permanent party member; experienced surveyor
Tortohongar (Partisan)	Name for Teton-Sioux Indian chief. He was also known by the name Partisan.
Tuttle, Ebenezer	Private; may have returned in June 1804 or April 1805
Two Bears	Fictional Mandan Indian warrior name.
Two Eagles	Fictional Hidatsa Indian warrior from the Mahawha village.
Vallé, Jean	Trader living among Arikara; cousin of Pierre-Antoine Tabeau.
Very Big Eyes	Missouria Indian warrior.
Warfington, Richard	Corporal; return party member; in charge of keelboat, April 1805.
Weiser, Peter	Private; permanent party member.
Werner, William	Private; permanent party member.
White Crane	Yankton-Sioux Indian chief.
White, Isaac	Private; may have returned to St. Louis in June 1804 or April 1805.
Whitehouse, Joseph	Private; permanent party member; tailor; kept journal.
Willard, Alexander	Private; permanent party member; largely known for mishaps and misbehavior, but still kept for the entire expedition.
Windsor, Richard	Private; permanent party member; skilled hunter.
Yellow Wolf	Fictional Indian name for the father of Little Buffalo at a Mandan village, which was located near present-day Fort Clark, North Dakota.
York	Participant; servant, black slave of William Clark; assisted in search for Shoshone Indians, demonstrated empathy, and conducted many actions in ensuring success of the mission, such as hunting and procuring food.

TIMELINE

YEAR	MONTH	DAY	EVENT
1500s			Horses brought to North America by Spanish conquistadors.
1576			Martin Frobisher fails to find Northwest Passage — water route to Pacific Ocean.
1610			Henry Hudson fails to find Northwest Passage; set adrift in Canada, never seen or heard from again.
1700s			Russians, Spanish, British explore northwest coastline of North America.
1743	March	30	Brothers Francois and Louis-Joseph La Verendrye fail to find Northwest Passage. Present-day Pierre, South Dakota area claimed for France by burying lead tablet on a mound now known as Verendrye Hill, which is a historic landmark.
1770	August	1	William Clark born in Virginia.
1770			York likely born, probably in Virginia.
1771			Sergeant Patrick Gass born in Pennsylvania.
1772			Sergeant Nathaniel Pryor born in Virginia.
1774	August	18	Meriwether Lewis born in Virginia.
1775			Sergeant John Ordway born in New Hampshire.
1775			Private John Colter born in Virginia.
1782			Sergeant Charles Floyd born in Kentucky.
1789			Sacajawea likely born, probably in present-day Lemhi Valley of Idaho.
1792	May	11	Robert Gray's men sail 20 miles up the Columbia River.
1792	October		George Vancouver charts mouth of Columbia River region.
1792			Clark joins United States Army.
1793	May	9	Alexander Mackenzie begins his second Northwest Passage search from central Canada.
1793	July	22	Mackenzie paints name on rock at the Pacific coast near Vancouver Island.
1794			Lewis joins the United States Army.
1795			Lewis meets Clark in Chosen Rifle Company, which is commanded by Clark.
1796			Explorer John Thomas Evans visits the Mandan villages on the upper Missouri River.
1800			Sacajawea claimed as war prize by Hidatsa warriors.
1801	February	17	Jefferson writes Lewis appointing Lewis to be Jefferson's private secretary.
1801	March	4	Thomas Jefferson begins his first presidency of the United States.
1802			British cartographer Aaron Arrowsmith creates newest map of western North America that includes secondhand information from surveyor Peter Fidler.
1803	January	18	Jefferson writes Congress proposing a western expedition.
1803	March	14	Albert Gallatin writes Jefferson about commissioning cartographer Nicholas King to create an updated map for the western expedition, which is later led by Lewis and Clark.
1803	Spring		Lewis visits Philadelphia for training, and to purchase supplies for the expedition.
1803	April	30	Louisiana Purchase treaty signed; greatly expands United States territory by 820,000 square miles.
1803	June	19	Lewis writes Clark inviting him on the expedition.
1803	June	20	Jefferson writes Lewis on how to conduct the expedition.
1803	July	18	Clark writes acceptance letter to Lewis about expedition.
1803	August	31	Lewis leaves Pittsburgh, Pennsylvania in a new keelboat for travel to Illinois territory.

1803	October	15	Clark joins Lewis at present-day Clarksville, Indiana on the Ohio River. Technically, Clark is a lieutenant, not a captain, but is known as "Captain."
1803	December	13	Construction begins on Camp Dubois in Illinois Territory on the Dubois River.
1804	May	14	Expedition leaves Camp Dubois; regarded by most as expedition's official start.
1804	May	16	Clark establishes St. Charles Camp in present-day St. Charles, Mo. Expedition begins in earnest from this location.
1804	May	17	Court-martial of Privates John Collins, Hugh Hall, and William Warner for infractions relating to their behavior associated with a celebration.
1804	May	20	Lewis returns from St. Louis to rejoin Clark at St. Charles Camp. He brings with him a special group from St. Louis.
1804	May	21	Final hiring and preparations complete; party leaves St. Charles to begin, in earnest, the journey up the Missouri River to its source and beyond, with the objective of finding the Northwest Passage, reaching the Pacific Ocean, meeting Indians, and documenting findings.
1804	May	21	Lewis ceases making journal entries until September 16, 1804. No one knows the exact reason for the cessation.
1804	May	23	Lewis nearly dies from fall at Tavern Cave bluff.
1804	June	12	Lewis buys 300 pounds of voyager's grease as a crude insect repellant. With the purchase, they hire Pierre Dorion.
1804	June	12	Captains hire Pierre Dorion as a Yankton-Sioux Indian interpreter. He proves to be an asset for Indian relations.
1804	June	29	Court-martial of Privates Collins and Hall for alcohol-related offenses. They steal whiskey and get drunk in the process.
1804	July	4	Independence Day ushered in with shot from keelboat cannon. The celebration is near today's Kansas City, Mo.
1804	July	12	Court-martial of Private Willard for sleeping on duty.
1804	July	28	George Drouillard meets the first Indians who are of the Missouria nation near today's Council Bluffs, Iowa.
1804	July	29	Private Alexander Willard forgets his tomahawk at previous camp; drops gun into Boyer Creek.
1804	July	29	Engagé La Liberté dispatched by captains to arrange meeting with Otoe Indians for a council.
1804	July	30	Sergeant Charles Floyd reported very ill by Clark in his journal. Floyd is dying from an unknown ailment.
1804	August	1	Private George Gibson sent to search for La Liberté and Otoe Indians, after La Liberté fails to return to the expedition.
1804	August	3	First council with Indians who were of the Otoe and Missouria nations near present-day Fort Calhoun, Neb.
1804	August	4	Private Moses Reed, likely friend of La Liberté, also deserts the expedition, based on deception of a lost knife.
1804	August	7	Search team sent to hunt for Reed and La Liberté.
1804	August	11	Expedition visits Chief Blackbird's burial site in present-day Nebraska on the Omaha Indian Reservation on U.S. Hwy. 75.
1804	August	16	Search team captures Moses Reed.
1804	August	18	Court-martial of Private Reed for desertion.
1804	August	19	Second council with the Otoe and Missouria nations.
1804	August	20	Sergeant Floyd dies likely from burst appendix; buried at today's Sioux City, Iowa on bluff overlooking the Missouri River and Interstate 29.
1804	August	22	Private Gass elected by fellow soldiers to replace Floyd.
1804	August	23	First buffalo killed by the Corps.
1804	August	26	Private Shannon becomes lost in present-day Nebraska.
1804	August	27	Expedition meets the Yankton-Sioux Indians.
1804	August	29	Expedition members feast on their first dog as food.

1804	September	11	Shannon rejoins the party in present-day South Dakota in the vicinity of the Snake Creek Recreation Area.
1804	September	16	Lewis resumes making journal entries.
1804	September	18	Lewis ceases making journal entries until April 7, 1805.
1804	September	24	Expedition meets the Teton-Sioux Indians.
1804	September	25	First altercation with Teton-Sioux regarding paying proper tribute for passage.
1804	September	28	Second altercation with Teton-Sioux on the same topic.
1804	October		Trader Régis Loisel from La Charrette dies in New Orleans.
1804	October	8	Expedition meets the Arikara Indians.
1804	October	13	Court-martial of Private John Newman for mutinous remarks.
1804	October	20	First grizzly bear encounter, which was experienced by Private Cruzatte, likely in present-day Morton County, N.D.
1804	October	24	Expedition meets Mandan Indians.
1804	November	2	Construction of Fort Mandan begins.
1804	November	4	Toussaint Charbonneau hired as interpreter to communicate with Shoshone/Snake Indians.
1804	December	17	Coldest day experienced by the expedition; 45 degrees below zero Fahrenheit.
1804	December	24	Construction of Fort Mandan completed.
1805	February	11	Sacajawea gives birth to Jean Baptiste Charbonneau.
1805	February	15	Expedition pursues Teton-Sioux in retaliation for taking their goods. This is the third negative encounter with the tribe.
1805	April	7	Expedition leaves Fort Mandan traveling west in six dugout canoes and two pirogues; return party heads southeast for St. Louis in keelboat with samples and specimens for Jefferson.
1805	April	7	Lewis resumes making journal entries.
1805	May	14	Sacajawea saves important items from being lost in the river.
1805	May	22	Corporal Warfington and return party safely arrive in St. Louis with the keelboat and goods for President Jefferson.
1805	May	30	Expedition enters the White Cliffs section of the Missouri River in today's Chouteau County, Montana.
1805	June	2	Expedition arrives at the confluence of Marias and Missouri rivers in present-day Chouteau County, Montana.
1805	June	9	Expedition members express opinions about which of the two waterways is the true and genuine Missouri River — the north river (Marias) or south river (Missouri).
1805	June	10	Red pirogue stored on island near Marias River.
1805	June	13	Lewis is first expedition member to view the Great Falls of the Missouri River, after choosing to further explore the "south" fork of the river.
1805	June	18	White pirogue stored along riverbank about 100 yards below Lower Portage Camp, which was approximately one mile below present-day Belt Creek.
1805	June	19	Private Shannon separated from the party for a second time.
1805	June	21	Portage begins by creating staging area for transporting six canoes around five waterfalls — a diversion of about 18 miles from northeast to southwest.
1805	June	23	Lewis has men begin constructing his iron-framed boat.
1805	June	23	Private Shannon rejoins the party.
1805	July	2	Portage completed in present-day southwest Great Falls, Mont., along Lower River Road.
1805	July	4	Last of the liquor is consumed during Independence Day celebration, after the waterfall portage is completed.
1805	July	9	Iron boat *Experiment* proves a failure when it leaks water.
1805	July	10	Iron boat frame is cached underground with other goods, and has still not been recovered as of 2015, despite numerous searches for its location, which is somewhere along the Missouri River near Great Falls, Montana.

1805	July	10	Two Cottonwood trees cut down above the five waterfalls to make two additional canoes to substitute for the pirogues.
1805	July	15	Party leaves camp with eight dugout canoes, south of present-day Great Falls, Montana.
1805	July	16	Lewis leaves the Great Plains and arrives at the foot of the Rocky Mountains at today's Tower Rock State Park.
1805	July	18	Clark starts search for Shoshone Indians with three other men, with a goal to trade for horses to help them portage through the Northwest Passage.
1805	July	19	Lewis names a geologic formation known as the "Gates of the Rocky Mountains" in present-day Montana.
1805	July	25	Clark arrives at the Three Forks of the Missouri River.
1805	July	27	Lewis and Clark reunite at the Three Forks, after Clark does not find the Shoshone.
1805	August	6	Private Shannon separated from the party a third time.
1805	August	7	One canoe not needed; stored on shore opposite today's Big Hole River mouth in Montana.
1805	August	8	Lewis starts search for the Shoshone with three other soldiers.
1805	August	9	Shannon rejoins the party for a third time.
1805	August	10	Lewis records doubts about the existence of a viable Northwest Passage.
1805	August	11	Lewis sights Shoshone warrior, but the warrior flees in fear after the party fails to persuade him of their friendly intent.
1805	August	12	Lewis and advance party arrive at most distant fountain of the Missouri River, and cross the Continental Divide at today's Lemhi Pass; The team finds many more mountains to the west, casting serious doubts on a viable Northwest Passage.

STORY NOTES

No book will ever be able to capture the all the adventure and facts of the Lewis and Clark expedition. However, I have attempted to capture the spirit through many years of research and site visits along the historic trail.

Early drafts of this book took far too many liberties with facts. But the weight of history, and respect for the Corp's achievements compelled me to change trajectory toward history and facts. However, sheer history and facts can be as sterile as the sums, products, and quotients of mathematics, and my aim was vibrancy, truth, and interest. These elements became the building blocks upon which the book evolved.

During the creation of this story, I lived in proximity to many Lewis and Clark sites, including South Sioux City, Nebraska; Glendive, Montana; and Helena, Montana. I learned a great deal by living in these areas and visiting many locations, which I hope is reflected in the book. Several visits to my brother's home in Washington state afforded me opportunities to visit Cape Disappointment, Fort Clatsop, the salt works in Seaside, Oregon, and other places near the Pacific Ocean and Columbia, Snake and Clearwater rivers.

Consistent with the rest of the book, imagining exact words for narration and dialogue was based on the best information I could obtain from numerous and notable sources — the most distinguished being the Gary Moulton version of the Lewis and Clark journals, James P. Ronda's book *Lewis and Clark Among the Indians*, David Lavender's *The Way to the Western Sea: Lewis and Clark Across the Continent*, and the voluminous tome by Edward S. Curtis on the Indians of North America.

Where gaps in information existed, I referred to published and unpublished sources listed in this book, maps, and my own personal experiences, which included visiting and revisiting many Lewis and Clark sites along the entire route from southwest Illinois to the mouth of the Columbia River in an effort to recreate what likely happened. Significant events were reconstructed, such as the capture of Moses Reed and George Shannon's wanderings when he became lost in what is now northeast Nebraska and southeastern South Dakota. Those events are disclosed for the reader in this section of the book.

Camp names were either taken directly from the journals or were in reference to an event, spirit, or landmark at that time. Throughout the book, I tried to enrich the reader's experience by interjecting history of which Lewis may or may not have actually been aware, such as the banishment of Henry Hudson and his followers in 1610.

The journals frequently use the term "squaw" in reference to female Native Americans. I opted to not include the term in this book because it is regarded by Native Americans as derogatory, and its use was not needed to tell an already compelling story. Early drafts of this book used the term out of respect for history, but I omitted the term after concluding the term was not advancing the story, and out of respect for native women. Conversely, I do not think its exclusion detracts or distorts the narrative.

Prologue

A. I chose the well-known poem by T.S. Eliot "Little Gidding" to start the book on the day I started writing this story, which was August 10, 2010. I did not print the poem from the cited Web site until March 21, 2012. And it was not until June 25, 2015 that I discovered Clay S. Jenkinson cited a similar section of the same poem in his book *The Character of Meriwether Lewis*, after I purchased it on June 20, 2015 at the gift shop at Camp Dubois in Hartford, Illinois. However, unlike Jenkinson, I included two additional parts of the poem for the mesologue and epilogue because of its relevance to this book.

One: INTO THE NIGHT

A. Rain has always been a point of frustration and discomfort for me whether camping, hiking, running or engaged in any other planned outdoor activity. Therefore, I thought the same likely applied to how Lewis must have felt on the journey. I used this as a minor issue throughout the book, but it took on special meaning after I read his morose thoughts he recorded about his birthday on August 18, 1805, and the shower that preceded his journal entry. The idea of the depressing effect of rain came to me when I started the book in 2010, but I did not become aware of the storm that came before his journal entry until 2014 when I wrote Chapter Eighteen.

Two: DEPARTURE

A. Much of this chapter was based on photos taken in 2010 of various exhibits at interpretive centers in Great Falls, Montana and Sioux City, Iowa — the latter which was about one mile from where I lived in South Sioux City, Nebraska in late 2010 and early 2011, and the former being less than 90 miles from my residence in Helena, Montana.

B. The exact number of people who departed as part of the expedition is not certain because Lewis and Clark viewed the hired boatmen differently, in terms of keeping records. Therefore, I left this number vague to be consistent with history, but feel 45 members may have been with the expedition after they departed from St. Charles. Journal Editor Gary Moulton addresses this topic in Appendix A of Volume Two of the definitive journals.

Three: AGAINST THE CURRENT

A. From this chapter forward into the book, I used the names of Privates McNeal and Shields to build them as characters for story purposes because of their importance in the roles they played crossing the Continental Divide at today's Lemhi Pass. When used, the journals may or may not have described their activity, but the event actually occurred, unless otherwise disclosed in these notes. I also found these individuals interesting characters.

B. The journals do not detail how Lewis saved himself with his knife on the bluff far above Tavern Cave. However, after reading how Lewis instructed Private Windsor to save himself from falling in a similar situation more than a year later on June 7, 1805, along Marias River, a few miles northwest of today's Loma, Montana, it seemed very likely to me this is also what happened at Tavern Bluffs.

Four: DISCIPLINE

A. After studying the desertions by Private Moses Reed and Engagé La Liberté, I thought it logical the two became friends and planned to escape, but had yet to plan exactly how and when it would be executed.

B. I thought it proper to set up Private Alexander Willard's own whipping, for later in the chapter after he witnessed the punishment of Privates John Collins and Hugh Hall.

C. How Private Willard lost his rifle is not detailed in the journals, but I tried to imagine the most realistic scenario, based on my own experiences as a child, and hiking in the mountains of Montana and Idaho. Specifically, I recall balancing and walking on railroad tracks bridging a creek near my home when I was young, and doing the same as an adult on logs over mountain creeks.

Five: FIRST MEETING

A. Wording for Lewis's speech to the Otoe Indians was taken from a handout obtained on March 18, 2011 at Gavins Point Dam Visitor Center near Yankton, South Dakota. According to the handout from the U. S. National Park Service, the decedents of Otoe Chief Big Ax donated an 11-page manuscript in March 2003, which was penned in Clark's hand, and detailed the speech Lewis gave to the Yankton-Sioux on August 30, 1804. My conclusion is this speech was probably originally written by Lewis at an earlier date, and similar to the one he gave to the Otoes at Council Bluff. How I believe Clark came to write a copy of the speech is detailed in Chapter Nine.

B. The journals do not specifically name many Indians they met. Running Horse is a fictitious name. I thought this Missouria Indian man played an important role in the expedition's first encounter with Indians, and thought he should be given a name for readers' enjoyment.

C. Anyone who has camped in the summer humidity of the Midwest can appreciate water accumulating on the interior of a tent during the night. This was the inspiration for the scene when I thought Private Shields could have been awakened the morning of August 3, 1804.

Six: CONSEQUENCES

A. Reconstructing Moses Reed's desertion and capture was difficult because it is not detailed in the journals. After considering the facts, it only seemed logical that Reed and La Liberté would form a team and meet at an Otoe village, since La Liberté was familiar with that nation and could speak the language.

B. I do not know whether Captain Lewis was, or was not aware of who Machiavelli or Vlad the Impaler were, and their relation to history. However, I thought the references were within reason, given Lewis' level of education, and flair for prose.

According to the *Encyclopedia Britannica* online, Vlad the Impaler was a member of nobility in 1400s Transylvania (Romania) who gained notoriety by the cruel methods he employed to punish his enemies. The same source indicates that Machiavelli's book *The Prince* was published after his death in 1532. The book basically states that for a prince to attain glory and survive, immoral means can be justified in achieving that goal.

After I learned about Chief Blackbird's methods of dealing with rivals, I believe Lewis may have recorded such a thought had he been writing in his journal either on the trip up the Missouri in 1804, or on the way back to St. Louis in 1806. However, we will likely never know, since no known record has been found, as of this writing on June 30, 2015.

Seven: CHANGES

A. The journals do not explain why Lewis and Clark chose the bluff where Sergeant Floyd was buried. However, after living about a mile from Floyd's final resting place, which is on a bluff overlooking the Missouri River along present-day Interstate 29, and not too far from Chief Blackbird's hill, it seemed logical after I visited both areas that Lewis and Clark would have been inspired by the Chief Blackbird site, and wanted to have something similar for Floyd. I believe they did well.

B. The flag scenes in this chapter and Chapter 13 on page 154 are not in the journals. The origin of the 13-fold burial flag is not known, according to The American Legion. However, the custom of flags on caskets began during the Napoleonic Wars (1796-1815), according to the U.S. Army Military District of Washington.

Eight: ADVENTURE AND MISADVENTURE

A. The procedure to elect Private Gass to his new status after the death of Sergeant Floyd described in this chapter was modeled after my own experiences teaching high school. The journals do not describe the election process, nor was I aware of any military protocol to select such a candidate.

B. How Private Shannon became lost is not known. I attempted to re-create the likely scenario based on what is known, and a hiking pace average of two to three miles per hour in mostly daylight hours, with time for rest, water, sleep, and eating. The terrain in this part of present-day northeast Nebraska and southeast South Dakota is mostly rolling plains on which huge herds of buffalo once grazed on short grasses. Having lived and worked in this region helped me imagine what may have happened and where.

Nine: WARNINGS

A. How Otoe Indians came to be in the possession of Lewis's speech at Calumet Bluff is not known, according to the U.S. National Park Service. However, I created the likely scenario in this chapter, which is based in Chapter Five. Putting pieces of history together, it seems only logical that the document was given to the Otoes by the Yankton-Sioux as part of a peace deal brokered by Dorion, and/or perhaps Joseph Gravelines, since the Otoe and Yankton-Sioux members eventually met Jefferson in January 1806.

B. Yankton-Sioux Chief Struck by the Ree helped negotiate a treaty in 1858 that secured Indian access to the red rock formation in today's Pipestone National Monument in Minnesota.

Ten: CONFLICT

A. The history of the mooring rope legend was attributed to Régis Loisel by me for story purposes to aid the reader. I could not find any definitive record that Lewis or Clark was aware of the rope-seizure legend, but I believe they were, and Loisel would have probably been the person to give them this information. The legend is detailed on page 132 of David Lavender's book *The Way to the Western Sea: Lewis and Clark Across the Continent*.

B. The fictional name "Makoshika" for the Teton-Sioux warrior is one I used to enhance the story, and honor a great state park in eastern Montana. The park of the same name is where I used to run nearly every day after work when I lived in Glendive, Montana. The name means "bad earth," and the park is a remarkable example of the beauty of the badlands, which is amid the vastness of the Great Plains. Readers are strongly urged to visit the park.

C. I believe the vow of celibacy for the reasons described in Chapters 10 and 11 by Lewis and Clark to be not only realistic, but sensible and probable, although the journals do not record such a vow during this period. However, the vow seems even more probable given the fact that such a promise was asked of the men by the captains on March 15, 1806. The vow was asked to avoid illness after symptoms of sexually transmitted disease were present among the party from encounters with Chinook Indians on November 21 and 22, 1805. This vow is only broken once on page 98, but reaffirmed on page 111.

D. There is no known documentation that the expedition's lost anchor was ever recovered from the Missouri River, according to a personal communication I had in 2014 with Gary Moulton via e-mail.

Eleven: TRANSITION

A. The journals do not detail the motive for Private John Newman's actions that resulted in his court-martial. Therefore, I created what I considered the most likely scenario, based on Gary Moulton's speculation in the journals (vol. 2, p. 519).

B. This part of the story is a summary of what is recorded in the journals about York. The humiliating ordeals York had to endure during the expedition, but more importantly how he positively reacted to the various situations, I believe is a testimony to his strong character, and ability to appropriately adapt to any circumstance. This is evident throughout the expedition.

Twelve: MANDAN

A. Controversy exists about the correct spelling and pronunciation of Sacajawea's name. After years of travel and research, I opted for the Lemhi-Shoshone spelling, rather than the Hidatsa pronunciation, which is "Sacagawea." I did this to honor her heritage and ancestry as a member of the Lemhi-Shoshone nation. The reasoning for the naming was apparent after visiting Lewis and Clark sites along the trail from Lemhi Pass to Lolo, Montana, a discussion on the topic I had with Shoshone leaders during a job interview on July 9, 2010, and reading various documents about these areas, which are listed in the source notes section of this book, which includes, but is not limited to sources for this chapter. The Gary

Moulton version of the journals uses the Hidatsa version, which I used for much of the draft of this book, until I wrote the initial draft of Chapter Eighteen.

B. Two Bears, Radiant Day, and Talking Crow are fictional Mandan Indian names created for the story about the real conflict between a man and his wife.

C. Two Eagles is a fictional Hidatsa Indian name created for the story.

D. The confrontation between North West Company representatives, and Lewis and Clark was based on an actual occurrence.

E. Almost any male skier, runner or participant in outdoor winter activities in cold climates can relate to the agony of a frost-nipped penis. The experience of it slowly thawing out is one of great pain. After I read that York experienced something similar, I knew how he must have felt, and could accurately describe the ordeal from personal experience. Fortunately, I suffered no long-term effects, and suspect York was also as lucky.

F. Standing Elk is a fictional name for a Mandan woman, based on an actual unnamed woman.

G. Little Buffalo is a fictional name for the Indian boy with frostbite whose toes were actually amputated.

H. Yellow Wolf is the fictional name for Little Buffalo's father. The inspiration for the name was a sign at the national Lewis and Clark museum in Great Falls, Montana, on which Gerard Baker is identified as Yellow Wolf.

I. The term "battered and blistered" was inspired by a terrific Pete Townshend song titled "I Am Secure" from the *White City* album. I credit my oldest brother, James, for introducing me to this album, and am ever grateful for his lifetime of positive influences.

Thirteen: RESUMPTION

A. Soaring Raven is a fictional name for a Mandan Indian warrior.

B. Lewis' recognizing a change in the climate near a beaver's hill is a salute to the communities of Glendive and Wibaux in eastern Montana where I lived and worked. There is a large mound in that region along Interstate 94 near mile-marker 241, which is known by locals as "Beaver Hill." Based on my own observations, this area seems to be a transition area to a drier, less humid region. The Koppen Climate Zone map from the U.S. National Weather Service confirms the presence of this transition zone in the same vicinity.

C. The description of the wet soil where Private Windsor slips in the area near today's Marias River is based on my own experiences hiking and running in the badlands of Makoshika State Park in Glendive, Montana. I visited this park almost every day during the years I lived in Glendive. This soil is known as gumbo, and is very slippery and heavy when wet. Credit to my friend Dennis Snow for informing me of this term. The area near where this event happened is laden with gumbo. Consequently, the section of the story detailing how Private Windsor saved himself from falling on the wet gumbo is based on journal entries, and mirrors how I believe Lewis saved himself at Tavern Bluff on May 23, 1804.

Fourteen: PORTAGE

A. How Private Shannon became missing for the second time is not detailed in the journals. I reconstructed the most likely scenario for how he became lost, based on an earlier fictional event in this chapter regarding Lewis' arrival at the Great Falls.

B. To the best of my knowledge, the iron boat that was cached after the first portage around the falls of the Missouri River has never been found, and may perhaps still be buried near Great Falls, Montana.

Fifteen: INTO THE MOUNTAINS

A. Jumping Deer is the fictional name for a Shoshone Indian. The name is based on an actual person, or event attributed to a person. The name was given to set up the first Shoshone Indian encounter described in Chapter Sixteen.

B. The section of this chapter describing Frazer's razor is to set up an event that occurs in Chapter Twenty-one. The event in this chapter may or may not have occurred. It is not described in the journals.

Sixteen: PASSAGE

A. How Private Shannon became missing for the third time is not exactly detailed in the journals. I reconstructed the most likely scenario for the story.

B. There is no record that the rifle lost on August 6, 1805 in the today's Big Hole River in Montana has ever been found. This river was named Wisdom by Lewis and Clark, and a tiny town by the same name is upriver, near the present-day Big Hole National Battlefield.

C. The actual name for the Shoshone warrior Lewis encountered on August 11, 1805 is not known. I created a probable scenario, based on the journals, with the fictional name Jumping Deer given to the Indian, as disclosed in the story notes for Chapter Fifteen.

D. The entire historical dream sequence in this chapter is background information for readers, based on facts. There is no record that Lewis had such a dream, but records do exist that Lewis was educated about the West before the expedition. I am not aware to what extent Lewis was aware of other explorers' writings and findings, but imagine it was sufficent, given his preparation for the expedition in 1803.

E. Words cannot describe the thrill I experienced the first time I hiked to ascend and descend the Continental Divide crossing at Lemhi Pass on July 16, 2010. I wrote this section of the book based on that experience, and that experience was largely afforded to me by my good friend Elizabeth Temple, who helped make this possible through her generous financial support during my devastating period of unemployment and wrongful home foreclosure by a large bank in the wake of the Great Recession.

Mesologue

A. Mesologue is a word I created for the book, since I am not aware of any word to address the circumstance of a middle discourse between prologue and epilogue. The prefix "meso" is from the Greek word "mesos," or middle, and the suffix "logue" for discourse.

SOURCE NOTES

Prologue

1. T.S. Eliot, "Little Gidding" Web page; New York: Columbia University; http://www.columbia.edu/itc/history/winter/w3206/edit/tseliotlittlegidding.html ; accessed August 10, 2010 and March 12, 2012.

One: INTO THE NIGHT

1. Gary Moulton, ed., *The Definitive Journals of Lewis and Clark* vol. 2 (Lincoln and London: University of Nebraska Press, 1986, 2002), p. 512.
2. David Lavender, *The Way to the Western Sea: Lewis and Clark Across the Continent* (Lincoln and London: University of Nebraska Press, Bison Books, 1988, 1998, 2001) p. 382-383.
3. Dayton Duncan, and Ken Burns, *The Journey of the Corps of Discovery: Lewis and Clark: An Illustrated History* (New York: Alfred A. Knopf, Inc., 1997, 2004), p. 8-15, 222-224.
4. Thomas C. Dansi, *Uncovering the Truth About Meriwether Lewis* (Amherst, NY: Prometheus Books, 2012), p. 104, 122, 142, 147, 223-227, 230, 232-235, 289.
5. John D.W. Guice, ed., *By His Own Hand? The Mysterious Death of Meriwether Lewis* (Norman: University of Oklahoma Press, 2006), p. xvi.
6. Ibid. Clay S. Jenkinson, "Introduction," p. 5.
7. John C. Jackson, "Reuben Lewis: Fur Trader, Subagent, and Meriwether's Younger Brother," article; *We Proceeded On* online magazine, November 2012, vol. 38, no. 4, p. 9 (fur company members); Great Falls, Mont.: Lewis and Clark Trail Heritage Foundation; http://www.lewisandclark.org/wpo/pdf/vol38no4.pdf#page=9; accessed June 11, 2015.
8. "Meriwether Lewis Park (Natchez Trace Parkway) Tennessee" Web page; Survey of Historic Sites and Buildings; U.S. National Park Service; http://www.nps.gov/natr/learn/historyculture/meriwether-lewis.htm; accessed February 22, 2012.
9. "William Clark to Meriwether Lewis, July 18, 1803" Web page; "The Thomas Jefferson Papers Series 1," U.S. Library of Congress; http://memory.loc.gov/cgi-bin/ampage?collId=mtj1&fileName=mtj1page028.db&recNum=905 ; accessed March 12, 2012.
10. "Transcript: Jefferson's Instructions for Meriwether Lewis" Web page; U.S. Library of Congress; www.loc.gov/exhibits/lewisandclark/transcript57.html; accessed March 12, 2012.
11. "ENVSIONING THE WEST: Thomas Jefferson and the Roots of Lewis and Clark; Letter from Albert Gallatin to Thomas Jefferson" Web page; Lincoln: University of Nebraska; http://jeffersonswest.unl.edu/archive/view_doc.php?id=jef.00114; accessed May 3, 2014.
12. "Presidential Oaths of Office" Web page; U.S. Library of Congress; http://memory.loc.gov/ammem/pihtml/pioaths.html; accessed January 10, 2012.
13. "Biography of Meriwether Lewis" Web page; Virginia Center for Digital History, Charlottesville: University of Virginia; http://www.vcdh.virginia.edu/lewisandclark/biddle/biographies_html/lewis.html; accessed April 27, 2014.

Two: DEPARTURE

1. Gary Moulton, ed., *The Definitive Journals of Lewis and Clark* vol. 2 (Lincoln and London: University of Nebraska Press, 1986, 2002), p. 1-42, 59, 188-189 (squads), 213-214 (rifles), 217-246, 254 (horses), 486-487 (distances), 511-529 (members).
2. Ibid. vol. 9 (1995, 2003), Ordway, p. 6-7, Floyd, p. 373.
3. Ibid. vol. 10 (1996, 2003), Gass, p. 8-9.
4. Ibid. vol. 11 (1997, 2003), Whitehouse, p. 1-11.

5. David Lavender, *The Way to the Western Sea: Lewis and Clark Across the Continent* (Lincoln and London: University of Nebraska Press, Bison Books, 1988, 1998, 2001) p. 41 (*Experiment*), 76-77, 89-90 (Chouteaus).
6. "Corps of Discovery: Preparing for the Trip West" Web page, "Medical Supplies of the Lewis and Clark Expedition"; U.S. National Park Service; www.nps.gov/archive/jeff/lewisclark2/corpsofdiscovery/preparing/Medicine; accessed January 17, 2011.
7. "Lewis and Clark Expedition Supplies" Web page; Washington, DC: National Geographic Society; www.nationalgeographic.com/lewisandclark/resources.html; accessed October 11, 2010.
8. "Seaman" Web page; Public Broadcasting System; www.pbs.org/lewisandclark/inside/seman.html; accessed December 19, 2010.
9. "Corps of Discovery: Preparing for the Trip West" Web page, "What did the men who went west with Lewis and Clark wear?" U.S. National Park Service; www.nps.gov/archive/jeff/lewisclark2/corpsofdiscovery/preparing/Clothing; accessed October 17, 2010.
10. Personal photographs 1-25, Lewis and Clark signs and exhibits; Sioux City Lewis and Clark Interpretive Center Association; Sioux City, Iowa: The Sioux City Lewis and Clark Interpretive Center; October 9, 2010.
11. Personal photographs 1-5, keelboat replica and signs; State of Iowa Department of Natural Resources, National Park Service, State Historical Society of Iowa, Lighthouse Marina; Onawa, Iowa: Lewis and Clark State Park; November 28, 2010.
12. Personal photograph, "Against the Current — The Omaha" sign; Big Muddy Workshop, Inc.; Decatur, Neb.: Chief Blackbird Hill Interpretative Pavilion; U.S. Highway 75; January 26, 2011.
13. Personal photographs 1-5, model boats exhibits and signs; U.S. Department of Agriculture Forest Service; Great Falls, Mont.: Lewis and Clark National Historic Trail Interpretive Center; July 18, 2010.
14. Personal photographs 1-11, Lewis and Clark exhibits and signs; Chamberlain, S.D.: Lewis and Clark Interpretive Center, Interstate 90 near mile-marker 264; July 13, 2010.
15. Personal photographs 1-5, full-scale replica boats and exhibit signs; St. Charles, Mo.: Lewis and Clark Boat House and Nature Center; Discovery Expedition of St. Charles, Missouri; October 7, 2012.

Three: AGAINST THE CURRENT

1. Gary Moulton, ed., *The Journals of the Lewis and Clark Expedition; Atlas of the Lewis and Clark Expedition* vol. 1 (Lincoln and London: University of Nebraska Press, 1983), p. 8 (Régis Loisel).
2. Gary Moulton, ed., *The Definitive Journals of Lewis and Clark* vol. 2 (Lincoln and London: University of Nebraska Press, 1986, 2002), p. 64 (campsites), 59,188-189 (squads), 246-329, 486-487(distances), 512-529 (members).
3. Ibid. vol. 9 (1995, 2003), Ordway, p. 7-18; Floyd, p. 375-384.
4. Ibid. vol. 10 (1996, 2003), Gass, p. 9-17.
5. Ibid. vol. 11 (1997, 2003), Whitehouse, p. 12-32.
6. James P. Ronda, *Lewis and Clark Among the Indians* (Lincoln and London: University of Nebraska Press, Bison Books, 1984, 2002), p. 9.
7. David Lavender, *The Way to the Western Sea: Lewis and Clark Across the Continent* (Lincoln and London: University of Nebraska Press, Bison Books, 1988, 1998, 2001) p. 76, 105.
8. Hugh Rawson, *Wicked Words* (New York: Crown Publishers, Inc., 1989) 174-175 (goddamn).

9. Dayton Duncan, and Ken Burns, *The Journey of the Corps of Discovery: Lewis and Clark: An Illustrated History* (New York: Alfred A. Knopf, Inc., 1997, 2004), p. 21-29.
10. Francis Grose, *1811 Dictionary in the Vulgar Tongue* Web page (vulgarities: bastard, bitch, shit); Salt Lake City: Project Gutenberg; http://www.gutenberg .org/cache/epub/5402/pg5402.html; accessed January 1, 2015.
11. Joseph Mussulman, "Hair-raising Hazards" Web page (Lewis' March 31, 1805 letter to his mother), Discovering Lewis and Clark; Washburn, N.D.: Lewis and Clark Fort Mandan Foundation; http://www.lewis-clark.org/article/1422; accessed March 10, 2012.
12. Ibid, "Osage River" Web page, Discovering Lewis and Clark; Washburn, N.D.: Lewis and Clark Fort Mandan Foundation; http://www.lewis-clark.org/ article/2957; accessed May 20, 2013.
13. "Sergeant Patrick Gass" Web page; Virginia Center for Digital History, Charlottesville: University of Virginia http://www2.vcdh.virginia.edu/ lewisandclark/biddle/biographies_html/gass.html; accessed November 5, 2010.
14. "Lewis and Clark Across Missouri" Web page: May 22, 1804 campsite map; Columbia: University of Missouri; http://lewisclark.geog.missouri.edu; accessed September 24, 2012.
15. Ibid. "Virtual Landmarks" Web page: May 23, 1804 camp and Tavern Bluffs.
16. "Transcript: Jefferson's Instructions for Meriwether Lewis" Web page; U.S. Library of Congress; www.loc.gov/exhibits/lewisandclarktranscript57.html; accessed March 12, 2012.
17. Personal photograph, "Up the Missouri" sign; Missouri National Recreational River, U.S. National Park Service; U.S. Army Corps of Engineers: Yankton, S.D.: Gavins Point Dam Visitor Center; March 18, 2011.
18. Personal photograph, camp layout exhibit; Sioux City Lewis and Clark Interpretive Center Association; Sioux City, Iowa: The Sioux City Lewis and Clark Interpretive Center; October 9, 2010.
19. Personal photographs 1-5, full-scale replica boats and exhibit signs; St. Charles, Mo.: Lewis and Clark Boat House and Nature Center; Discovery Expedition of Saint Charles, Missouri; October 7, 2012.
20. Personal photographs 1-15, Tavern Cave sign and site; Saint Albans, Mo.; October 7, 2012.

Four: DISCIPLINE

1. Gary Moulton, ed., *The Definitive Journals of Lewis and Clark* vol. 2 (Lincoln and London: University of Nebraska Press, 1986, 2002), p. 8-35 (journals), 64 (campsites), 188-189 (squads), 329-435, 486-487(distances), 512-529 (members).
2. Ibid. vol. 9 (1995, 2003), Ordway, p. 18-33.
3. Ibid. vol. 10 (1996, 2003), Gass, p. 17-24.
4. Ibid. vol. 11 (1997, 2003), Whitehouse, p. 32-49.
5. Clay S. Jenkinson, "Forward," David L. Nicandri, *River of Promise: Lewis and Clark on the Columbia*, (Washburn, N.D.: The Dakota Institute Press of Lewis and Clark Fort Mandan Foundation, 2009), p. xi-xii (journal writing, celestial observations).
6. Thomas C. Dansi, *Uncovering the Truth About Meriwether Lewis* (Amherst, NY: Prometheus Books, 2012), p. 71-77 (journal writing).
7. Hugh Rawson, *Wicked Words* (New York: Crown Publishers, Inc., 1989) 157-167 (fuck), 174-175 (goddamn), 366-369 (son of a bitch).
8. Francis Grose, *1811 Dictionary in the Vulgar Tongue* Web page (vulgarities: bitch, shit); Salt Lake City: Project Gutenberg; http://www.gutenberg.org/ cache/epub/5402/pg5402.html; accessed January 1, 2015.
9. Joseph Mussulman, "Rulo, Nebraska" Web page, "High Ground," Discovering Lewis and Clark; Washburn, N.D.: Lewis and Clark Fort Mandan Foundation; http://www.lewis-clark.org/article/2942; accessed May 20, 2013.

10. Ibid, "Tornado Damage near Logan, Iowa," Web page, "Another one for Alex," Discovering Lewis and Clark; Washburn, N.D.: Lewis and Clark Fort Mandan Foundation; http://www.lewis-clark.org/article/2939; accessed May 20, 2013.
11. Silvio A. Bedini, "The Scientific Instruments of the Lewis and Clark Expedition" Web page; *Great Plains Quarterly* 4.1 (1984): 54-69; Lincoln: London: University of Nebraska; http://lewisandclarkjournals.unl.edu /php/xslt.php?&_xmlsrc=http://lewisandclarkjournals.unl.edu/files/xml/lc.bedin i.01.xml&_xslsrc=http://lewisandclarkjournals.unl.edu/LCstyles.xsl; accessed March 10, 2013.
12. "Lewis and Clark in Montana—a geologic perspective: Navigation—Finding the latitude" Web page; Montana Bureau of Mines and Geology, Butte: Montana Tech of the University of Montana; http://www.mbmg.mtech.edu /gmr/lewis_clark/lewis_clark-nav.asp; accessed March 10, 2013.

Five: FIRST MEETING

1. Gary Moulton, ed., *The Definitive Journals of Lewis and Clark* vol. 2 (Lincoln and London: University of Nebraska Press, 1986, 2002), p. 64 (campsites), 65 (1803 air gun incident), 188-189 (squads), 435-438, 486-487(distances), 512-529 (members).
2. Ibid. vol. 9 (1995, 2003), Ordway, p. 33.
3. Ibid. vol. 10 (1996, 2003), Gass, p. 25.
4. Ibid. vol. 11 (1997, 2003), Whitehouse, p.50.
5. James P. Ronda, *Lewis and Clark Among the Indians* (Lincoln and London: University of Nebraska Press, Bison Books, 1984, 2002), p. 1-26.
6. David Lavender, *The Way to the Western Sea: Lewis and Clark Across the Continent* (Lincoln and London: University of Nebraska Press, Bison Books, 1988, 1998, 2001) p. 116-133.
7. "Captain Meriwether Lewis'speech to the Yankton Sioux, August 30, 1804" hard-copy document; Missouri National Recreational River, U.S. National Park Service; U.S. Army Corps of Engineers; Yankton, S.D.: Gavins Point Dam Visitor Center; acquired March 18, 2011.
8. "Telescope of Meriwether Lewis" Web page; St. Louis: Missouri Historical Society Collections; http://www.lewisandclarkexhibit.org/shared /specimen_window_fs.html?0; accessed October 10, 2011.
9. Joseph Mussulman, and David E. Nelson, "Animations" Web page, "An Air Gun of the Girandoni Type"; Washburn, N.D.: Lewis and Clark Fort Mandan Foundation; http://www.lewis-clark.org/article/1829; accessed December 11, 2010.
10. Ibid, "Incomprehensible" Web page, air gun details; Washburn, N.D.: Lewis and Clark Fort Mandan Foundation; http://www.lewis-clark.org/article/1828; accessed December 11, 2010.
11. "The first Indian council" Web page, "Lewis and Clark Historical Background," U.S. National Park Service; www.nps.gov/history/history /online_books/lewisandclark/intro22.htm; accessed November 15, 2010.
12. John E. Koontz, "Etymology, What is the origin of the word Dakota?" Web page; Department of Linguistics, Boulder: University of Colorado; http://spot.colorado.edu/~koontz/faq/etymology.htm; accessed November 15, 2010.
13. Personal photograph, trial of Moses Reed painting; Lewis and Clark signs and exhibits; Sioux City Lewis and Clark Interpretive Center Association; Sioux City, Iowa: The Sioux City Lewis and Clark Interpretive Center; October 9, 2010.
14. Personal photographs 1-11, Lewis and Clark interior exhibits and signs; Chamberlain, S.D.: Lewis and Clark Interpretive Center, Interstate 90 near mile-marker 264; July 13, 2010.
15. Personal photographs 1-31 of Council Bluff and interior exhibits; Fort Calhoun, Neb.; Fort Atkinson State Historical Park; June 21, 2015.

Six: CONSEQUENCES

1. Gary Moulton, ed., *The Definitive Journals of Lewis and Clark* vol. 2 (Lincoln and London: University of Nebraska Press, 1986, 2002), p. 64 (campsites), 188-189 (squads), 438-490, 486-487(distances), 512-529 (members).
2. Ibid. vol. 9 (1995, 2003), Ordway, p. 33-41.
3. Ibid. vol. 10 (1996, 2003), Gass, p. 25-29.
4. Ibid. vol. 11 (1997, 2003), Whitehouse, p. 50-57.
5. James P. Ronda, *Lewis and Clark Among the Indians* (Lincoln and London: University of Nebraska Press, Bison Books, 1984, 2002), p. 1-26.
6. David Lavender, *The Way to the Western Sea: Lewis and Clark Across the Continent* (Lincoln and London: University of Nebraska Press, Bison Books, 1988, 1998, 2001) p. 116-133.
7. Hugh Rawson, *Wicked Words* (New York: Crown Publishers, Inc., 1989) 157-167 (fuck).
8. "Moses Reed: Jefferson National Expansion Memorial" Web page; U.S. National Park Service; http://www.nps.gov/jeff/learn/historyculture/private-moses-reed.htm; accessed December 11, 2010.
9. Personal photographs 1-5, signs of Nebraska and Iowa Lewis and Clark sites; Lewis and Clark National Historic Trail; South Sioux City, Neb.: Scenic Park; October 22, 2010.
10. Personal photographs 1-25, Lewis and Clark signs and exhibits; Sioux City Lewis and Clark Interpretive Center Association; Sioux City, Iowa: The Sioux City Lewis and Clark Interpretive Center; October 9, 2010.
11. Personal photographs 1-8, various pavilion signs Big Muddy Workshop, Inc.; Decatur, Neb.: Chief Blackbird Hill Interpretative Pavilion; U.S. Highway 75; January 26, 2011.
12. Personal photograph, "Tonwantonga" roadside sign, Nebraska Historical Marker; Historical Land Mark Council; U.S. Highway 75; Homer, Neb.; January 26, 2011.

Seven: CHANGES

1. Gary Moulton, ed., *The Definitive Journals of Lewis and Clark* vol. 2 (Lincoln and London: University of Nebraska Press, 1986, 2002), p. 64 (campsites), 188-189 (squads), 490-499, 512-529 (members).
2. Ibid. vol. 7 (1991, 2002), p. 326, 328 (06/02/06: Floyd's tomahawk stolen).
3. Ibid. vol. 9 (1995, 2003), Ordway, p. 41-42.
4. Ibid. vol. 10 (1996, 2003), Gass, p. 29-30.
5. Ibid. vol. 11 (1997, 2003), Whitehouse, p. 57-59.
6. James P. Ronda, *Lewis and Clark Among the Indians* (Lincoln and London: University of Nebraska Press, Bison Books, 1984, 2002), p. 1-26.
7. David Lavender, *The Way to the Western Sea: Lewis and Clark Across the Continent* (Lincoln and London: University of Nebraska Press, Bison Books, 1988, 1998, 2001) p. 116-133.
8. "What is the origin of the 21-gun salute?" Web page; U.S. Army Center of Military History; http://www.history.army.mil/html/faq/salute.html; accessed January 12, 2011.
9. Joseph Mussulman, "Burial of Sergeant Floyd" Web page; Washburn, N.D.: Washburn, N.D.: Lewis and Clark Fort Mandan Foundation; http://www.lewis-clark.org/article/960; accessed March 10, 2012.
10. Personal photographs 1-21, Sergeant Floyd Monument; U.S. National Park Service; Sioux City, Iowa: U.S. National Historic Landmark at Interstate 29 near mile-marker 137; June 11, 2010; and June 21, 2015.
11. Personal photographs 1-25, Lewis and Clark signs and exhibits; Sioux City Lewis and Clark Interpretive Center Association; Sioux City, Iowa: The Sioux City Lewis and Clark Interpretive Center; October 9, 2010.

Eight: ADVENTURE AND MISADVENTURE

1. Gary Moulton, ed., *The Definitive Journals of Lewis and Clark* vol. 2 (Lincoln and London: University of Nebraska Press, 1986, 2002), p. 64 (campsites), 188-189 (squads), 499-508, 512-529 (members).
2. Ibid. vol. 3 (1987, 2002), p. 7-21.
3. Ibid. vol. 9 (1995, 2003), Ordway, p. 42-46.
4. Ibid. vol. 10 (1996, 2003), Gass, p. 30-32.
5. Ibid. vol. 11 (1997, 2003), Whitehouse, p. 59-64.
6. David Lavender, *The Way to the Western Sea: Lewis and Clark Across the Continent* (Lincoln and London: University of Nebraska Press, Bison Books, 1988, 1998, 2001) p. 116-133.
7. Hugh Rawson, *Wicked Words* (New York: Crown Publishers, Inc., 1989) p. 114-115 (damn), 174-175 (goddamn).
8. "Private John Colter" Web page; Public Broadcasting System; http://www.pbs.org/lewisandclark/inside/jcolt.html; accessed February 5, 2011.
9. "Private George Shannon" Web page; Public Broadcasting System; http://www.pbs.org/lewisandclark/inside/gshan.html; accessed February 27, 2011.
10. Personal photograph, "Walking All Night" roadside sign: Lewis and Clark National Historic Trail; St. James, Neb.: George Shannon Trail; December 16, 2010.
11. Personal photograph, "Lewis and Clark Campsite" August 21, 1804 roadside sign; Nebraska Historical Marker, Historical Land Mark Council; State Highway 12; Willis, Neb.; December 30, 2010.
12. Personal photograph, "Ionia Volcano" roadside sign: Nebraska Historical Marker, Historical Land Mark Council; State Highway 12; Newcastle, Neb.; February 3, 2011.
13. Personal photographs 1-7, wayside signs; Elk Point, S.D.: Union County, South Dakota Historical Society along Interstate 29 near mile-marker 18; February 19, 2011.
14. Personal photographs 1-14, various signs and landscape; Spirit Mound Trust; South Dakota Department of Game, Fish and Park; U.S. National Park Service; Clay County, S.D.: Spirit Mound Historic Prairie; February 19, 2011.

Nine: WARNINGS

1. Gary Moulton, ed., *The Definitive Journals of Lewis and Clark* vol. 2 (Lincoln and London: University of Nebraska Press, 1986, 2002), 188-189 (squads), 512-529 (members).
2. Ibid. vol. 3 (1987, 2002), p. 6 (campsites), 21-44.
3. Ibid. vol. 9 (1995, 2003), Ordway, p. 46-53.
4. Ibid. vol. 10 (1996, 2003), Gass, p. 32-34.
5. Ibid. vol. 11 (1997, 2003), Whitehouse, p. 64-68.
6. James P. Ronda, *Lewis and Clark Among the Indians* (Lincoln and London: University of Nebraska Press, Bison Books, 1984, 2002), p. 1-26.
7. David Lavender, *The Way to the Western Sea: Lewis and Clark Across the Continent* (Lincoln and London: University of Nebraska Press, Bison Books, 1988, 1998, 2001) p. 116-133.
8. Hugh Rawson, *Wicked Words* (New York: Crown Publishers, Inc., 1989) p. 114-115 (damn).
9. "Captain Meriwether Lewis's speech to the Yankton Sioux, August 30, 1804" hard-copy document; Missouri National Recreational River, U.S. National Park Service; U.S. Army Corps of Engineers: Yankton, S.D.: Gavins Point Dam Visitor Center; acquired March 18, 2011.
10. Dayton Duncan, and Ken Burns, *The Journey of the Corps of Discovery: Lewis and Clark: An Illustrated History* (New York: Alfred A. Knopf, Inc., 1997, 2004), p. 54-55.

11. "Grizzlies Tracks *and* Sign" Web page; State of Montana Fish, Wildlife *and* Parks http://fwp.mt.gov/fishAndWildlife/livingWithWildlife/grizzlyBears/trackSign.html; accessed October 30, 2011.
12. Personal photograph, "Captain Meriwether Lewis's speech to the Yankton Sioux, August 30, 1804" interior exhibit sign; Missouri National Recreational River, U.S. Army Corps of Engineers: Yankton, S.D.: Gavins Point Dam Visitor Center; March 18, 2011.
13. Personal photograph, "Council at Calumet" exterior sign; Missouri National Recreational River, U.S. Army Corps of Engineers: Yankton, S.D.: Gavins Point Dam Visitor Center; March 18, 2011.
14. "Pipestone" pamphlet (red stone story), Pipestone National Monument: Pipestone, Minn.; U.S. National Park Service; 2006, 2014; and personal photos 1-23 of site; September 1, 2015.
15. Personal notes on tipi sign on interpretive trail (eastern tipi openings); Salmon, Idaho: Sacajawea Interpretive, Cultural and Educational Center; recorded August 31, 2012.

Ten: CONFLICT

1. Gary Moulton, ed., *The Definitive Journals of Lewis and Clark* vol. 2 (Lincoln and London: University of Nebraska Press, 1986, 2002), 5-6, 23, 188-189 (squads), 512-529 (members).
2. Ibid. vol. 3 (1987, 2002), p. 6 (campsites), 44-125.
3. Ibid. vol. 6 (1990, 2002), p. 416 (celibacy).
4. Ibid. vol. 9 (1995, 2003), Ordway, p. 53-72.
5. Ibid. vol. 10 (1996, 2003), Gass, p. 34-48.
6. Ibid. vol. 11 (1997, 2003), Whitehouse, p. 68-91.
7. James P. Ronda, *Lewis and Clark Among the Indians* (Lincoln and London: University of Nebraska Press, Bison Books, 1984, 2002) p. 27-41.
8. David Lavender, *The Way to the Western Sea: Lewis and Clark Across the Continent* (Lincoln and London: University of Nebraska Press, Bison Books, 1988, 1998, 2001) p. 116-133 (rope seizure legend, 132).
9. Hugh Rawson, *Wicked Words* (New York: Crown Publishers, Inc., 1989) p. 174-175 (goddamn), 366-369 (son of a bitch).
10. Jean Clary et al., The Discovery Writers, *Lewis and Clark In The Bitterroot* (Stevensville, Mont.: Stoneydale Press Publishing, 1998) p. 57 (marriage traditions of Salish Indians).
11. Francis Grose, *1811 Dictionary in the Vulgar Tongue* Web page (vulgarities: bitch); Salt Lake City: Project Gutenberg; http://www.gutenberg.org/cache/epub/5402/pg5402.html; accessed January 1, 2015.
12. "Makoshika State Park" Web page (meaning of the word "Makoshika"); State of Montana Fish, Wildlife and Parks; http://stateparks.mt.gov/makoshika/; accessed May 15, 2011.
13. Edward S. Curtis, *The North American Indian* Web page, 1907, "The Teton Sioux," vol. 3, p. 3 (history), 31 (homeland), 77-78 (prayer); The University Press; Evanston, Ill.: Northwestern University Library; http://curtis.library.northwestern.edu; accessed October 2, 2011; and May 24, 2015.
14. "Arikara Indians" Web page; Public Broadcasting System; http://www.pbs.org/lewisandclark/native/ari.html; accessed October 19, 2011.
15. "Arikara Indians" Web page; Washington, DC: National Geographic Society; www.nationalgeographic.com/lewisandclark/record_tribes_202_5_1.html; accessed October 19, 2011.
16. "Equine encephalitis viruses" Web page (horse death); Madison School of Veterinary Medicine, Madison: University of Wisconsin; http://www.Vetmed.wisc.edu/pbs/zoonoses/eee-wee-vee/ewveeindex.html; accessed April 4, 2012.
17. Personal photographs 1-10: Pierre, S.D.: Teton council site; August 27, 2014.

18. Personal photographs 1-5: Pierre, S.D.: Farm Island State Recreation Area; August 27, 2014.
19. Personal photographs 1-3; live prairie dog photos; Williams County, N.D.: Missouri-Yellowstone Confluence Interpretive Center; State Road 1804; July 11, 2010.

Eleven: TRANSITION

1. Gary Moulton, ed., *The Journals of the Lewis and Clark Expedition; Atlas of the Lewis and Clark Expedition* vol. 1 (Lincoln and London: University of Nebraska Press, 1983), p. 8.
2. Gary Moulton, ed., *The Definitive Journals of Lewis and Clark* vol. 2 (Lincoln and London: University of Nebraska Press, (1986, 2002), 188-189 (squads), 512-529 (members), 519 (Newman's motive).
3. Ibid. vol. 3 (1987, 2002), p. 6 (campsites), 125-225.
4. Ibid. vol. 9 (1995, 2003), Ordway, p. 72-93.
5. Ibid. vol. 10 (1996, 2003), Gass, p. 48-76.
6. Ibid. vol. 11 (1997, 2003), Whitehouse, p. 91-107.
7. James P. Ronda, *Lewis and Clark Among the Indians* (Lincoln and London: University of Nebraska Press, Bison Books, 1984, 2002), p. 27-66.
8. David Lavender, *The Way to the Western Sea: Lewis and Clark Across the Continent* (Lincoln and London: University of Nebraska Press, Bison Books, 1988, 1998, 2001) p. 116-133.
9. John L. Allen, "Geographical Knowledge and American Images of the Louisiana Territory," James P. Ronda, ed., *Voyages of Discovery: Essays on the Lewis and Clark Expedition*, (Montana Historical Society Press, 1998), p.50 (Alexander Mackenzie).
10. Hugh Rawson, *Wicked Words* (New York: Crown Publishers, Inc., 1989) p. 114-115 (damn).
11. Jean Clary et al., The Discovery Writers, *Lewis and Clark In The Bitterroot* (Stevensville, Mont.: Stoneydale Press Publishing, 1998) p. 76 (body paint).
12. "Knife River Indian Villages" pamphlet (warrior culture); U.S. National Park Service; 2009.
13. Francis Grose, *1811 Dictionary in the Vulgar Tongue* Web page (vulgarities: bitch); Salt Lake City: Project Gutenberg; http://www.gutenberg.org /cache/epub/5402/pg5402.html; accessed January 1, 2015.
14. "Private John Newman: Jefferson National Expansion Memorial" Web page; U.S. National Park Service; www.nps.gov; accessed September 25, 2011.
15. "Grizzlies Tracks and Sign" Web page; State of Montana Fish, Wildlife and Parks; http://fwp.mt.gov/fishAndWildlife/livingWithWildlife/grizzly Bears/trackSign.html; accessed October 30, 2011
16. "King George III" Web page; The British Monarchy; http://www.royal.gov.uk/ historyofthemonarchy/kingsandqueensoftheunitedkingdom/thehanoverians/geor geiii.aspx; November 11, 2011.
17. "The War" Web page; Joe Medicine Crow, Montana: four feats of a Crow war chief; Public Broadcasting System, 2007; http://www.pbs.org/thewar/detail _5177.htm; accessed December 6, 2012.
18. Personal photograph, "Neuidia" (Mandan and Hidatsa Indians) display by Gerard Baker (Yellow Wolf), Fort Mandan exhibit, U.S. Department of Agriculture Forest Service; Great Falls, Mont.: Lewis and Clark National Historic Trail Interpretive Center; July 18, 2010.
19. Personal photograph, "A Communication Across The Continent By Water" sign, U.S. Department of Agriculture Forest Service, University of Montana Western; Lemhi Pass, Idaho-Montana border; July 16, 2010.

20. Personal photograph, bullboat exhibit; U.S. Bureau of Land Management; Pompeys Pillar National Monument; Yellowstone County, Mont.: Pompeys Pillar Interpretive Center; July 10, 2010.
21. Personal notes on Teton Indian and Arikara Indian signs along exterior walking path; Chamberlain, S.D.: Lewis and Clark Interpretive Center; Interstate 90 near mile-marker 264; October 3, 2011.

Twelve: MANDAN

1. Gary Moulton, ed., *The Journals of the Lewis and Clark Expedition; Atlas of the Lewis and Clark Expedition* vol. 1 (Lincoln and London: University of Nebraska Press, 1983), p. 8.
2. Gary Moulton, ed., *The Definitive Journals of Lewis and Clark* vol. 2 (Lincoln and London: University of Nebraska Press, 1986, 2002), p. 9, 188-189 (squads), 512-529 (members).
3. Ibid. vol. 3 (1987, 2002), p.202 (Knife River Indian villages map), 225-491
4. Ibid. vol. 4, (1987, 2002) p. 9, 84-85 (white bears).
5. Ibid. vol. 6 (1990, 2002), p. 86 (Yellowstone River exploration plan)
6. Ibid. vol. 9 (1995, 2003), Ordway, p. 93-125.
7. Ibid. vol. 10 (1996, 2003), Gass, p. 62-76.
8. Ibid. vol. 11 (1997, 2003), Whitehouse, p. 2-3 (campsites maps),107-131.
9. James P. Ronda, *Lewis and Clark Among the Indians* (Lincoln and London: University of Nebraska Press, Bison Books, 1984, 2002), p. 67-132.
10. David Lavender, *The Way to the Western Sea: Lewis and Clark Across the Continent* (Lincoln and London: University of Nebraska Press, Bison Books, 1988, 1998, 2001) p. 149-167.
11. Hugh Rawson, *Wicked Words* (New York: Crown Publishers, Inc., 1989) p. 114-115 (damn), 174-175 (goddamn).
12. Dayton Duncan, and Ken Burns, *The Journey of the Corps of Discovery: Lewis and Clark: An Illustrated History* (New York: Alfred A. Knopf, Inc., 1997, 2004), p. 79-82.
13. John W. W. Mann, *Sacajawea's People* (Lincoln and London: University of Nebraska Press, 2004) p. xvi (Shoshone Indian and Hidatsa Indian spelling/pronunciation of the name "Sacagawea" and "Sacajawea").
14. "Knife River Indian Villages" pamphlet (warrior culture); U.S. National Park Service; 2009.
15. John A. Alwin, "Pelts, Provisions and Perceptions: The Hudson's Bay Company Mandan Indian Trade" Web page; pelts, 1979, p. 16-27, *Montana: The Magazine of Western History* 29:3; Lincoln: University of Nebraska; http://lewisandclarkjournals.unl.edu/php/xslt.php?&_xmlsrc=http://lewisandclarkjournals.unl.edu/files/xml/lc.alwin.01.xml&_xslsrc=http://lewisandclarkjournals.unl.edu/LCstyles.xsl; accessed February 18, 2012.
16. "Our History: People" Explorers Web page; Toronto: Hudson's Bay Company; http://www.hbcheritage.ca/content/timeline; accessed January 22, 2012.
17. Joseph Mussulman, "Route to the Assiniboine River" Web page, Discovering Lewis and Clark; Washburn, N.D.: Lewis and Clark Fort Mandan Foundation; http://www.lewis-clark.org/article/1130; accessed January 16, 2012.
18. "Private Jean Baptiste Lepage" Web page; Public Broadcasting System; http://www.pbs.org/lewisandclark/inside/jlepa.html; accessed January 14, 2012.
19. Stewart Culin, *Games of the North American Indians* Web page; 1907, p. 512-513, Mountain View, Calif.: Google books; https://books.google.com/books?id=zYI6_uJ66jIC&printsec=frontcover&source=gbs_ge_summary_r&cad=0#v=onepage&q&f=false; accessed January 14, 2012.
20. I.A. Lapham , *The Antiquities of Wisconsin as Surveyed and Described* Web page; Mandan game tchung-kee, 1855, p. 87-88, The Smithsonian Institution; Board of

Regents of the University of Wisconsin System; Madison: University of Wisconsin; http://digicoll.library.wisc.edu/Antiquities/; accessed January 14, 2012.

21. "Gonorrhea" Web page; Atlanta: U.S. Centers for Disease Control; http://www.cdc.gov/std/Gonorrhea/STDFact-gonorrhea.htm; accessed January 14, 2012.
22. "Chlamydia" Web page; Atlanta: U.S. Centers for Disease Control;http://www.cdc.gov/std/Chlamydia/STDFact-Chlamydia.htm; accessed January 14, 2012.
23. "Syphilis" Web page; Atlanta: U.S. Centers for Disease Control; http://www.cdc.gov/std/syphilis/STDFact-Syphilis.htm; accessed January 14, 2012.
24. "Frostbite" symptoms Web page; U.S. National Institutes of Health; http://www.nlm.nih.gov/medlineplus/frostbite.html; accessed February 18, 2012.
25. "Mandan Indians" Web page; Public Broadcasting System; www.pbs.org; October 22, 2011.
26. "Corps of Discovery: Preparing for the Trip West" Web page, "Medical Supplies of the Lewis and Clark Expedition"; U.S. National Park Service; www.nps.gov/archive/jeff/lewisclark2/corpsofdiscovery/preparing/Medicine; accessed January 17, 2011.
27. "Toussaint Charbonneau: Jefferson National Expansion Memorial" Web page; U.S. National Park Service; www.nps.gov/jeff/historyculture/toussaint-charbonneau.htm; accessed January 23, 2012.
28. "Denning and Hibernation Behavior" Web page; Grizzly and Black bear behavior; U.S. National Park Service; http://www.nps.gov/yell/ learn/nature/denning.html; accessed March 24, 2012.
29. "Assiniboin Indians" Web page: Public Broadcasting System; http://www.pbs.org/lewisandclark/native/ass.html; October 19, 2011.
30. Karl Bodmer, "Indians Hunting the Bison" CD-ROM of illustrations; Omaha, Neb.: Joslyn Art Museum; 2000.
31. Ibid. "Winter Village of the Minatarees."
32. Personal photographs 1-18, U.S. National Park Service; Stanton, ND: Knife River Indian Villages National Historic Site; February 28, 2015.
33. Personal photograph, "Neuidia," Mandan and Hidatsa Indians display by Gerard Baker (Yellow Wolf), Fort Mandan exhibit; U.S. Department of Agriculture Forest Service; Great Falls, Mont.: Lewis and Clark National Historic Trail Interpretive Center; July 18, 2010.
34. Personal photographs 1-9 replica and signs; North Dakota Lewis and Clark Bicentennial Foundation; McLean County, N.D.: Fort Mandan replica, State Road 17; August 1, 2009 and February 28, 2015.
35. Personal photographs 1-7, signs and sites; State Historical Society of North Dakota; Stanton, N.D.: Fort Clark State Historic Site, North Dakota State Road 200A; August 1, 2009 and February 28, 2015.
36. Personal photograph, "Old Toby" display sign (Shoshone Indians); Lewis and Clark National Historic Trail backcountry at Trail Gulch, Salmon-Challis National Forest; Lemhi County, Idaho; August 4, 2013.
37. Personal notes on interpretive trail (Shoshone Indian life); Salmon, Idaho: Sacajawea Interpretive, Cultural and Educational Center; August 31, 2012.
38. Personal photographs 1-15, State Historical Society of North Dakota; Grant County, N.D.: Medicine Rock; February 28, 2015.
39. Personal photographs 1-2, windlass sign and replica; State of Iowa Department of Natural Resources, National Park Service, State Historical Society of Iowa, Lighthouse Marina; Onawa, Iowa: Lewis and Clark State Park; November 28, 2010.
40. Personal photographs 1-3, "The Portage at Great Falls: Pushing the Limits of Endurance" exhibit, dugout canoes; U.S. Department of Agriculture Forest Service; Lewis and Clark National Historic Trail Interpretive Center; Great Falls, Montana; July 18, 2010.

41. Personal on-site visit, Ma-ak-oti village; Oliver County, N.D.: Cross Ranch State Park; 25 Avenue SW; May 26, 2012.

Thirteen: RESUMPTION

1. Gary Moulton, ed., *The Journals of the Lewis and Clark Expedition; Atlas of the Lewis and Clark Expedition* vol. 1 (Lincoln and London: University of Nebraska Press, 1983), map 2.
2. Gary Moulton, ed., *The Definitive Journals of Lewis and Clark* vol. 4 (Lincoln and London: University of Nebraska Press, 1987, 2002), p. 96-277.
3. Ibid. vol.8 (1993, 2002), p. 219 (Private Hall's inability to swim).
4. Ibid. vol. 9 (1995, 2003), Ordway, p. 126-165.
5. Ibid. vol. 10 (1996, 2003), Gass, p. 77-101.
6. Ibid. vol. 11 (1997, 2003), Whitehouse, p. 132-193.
7. James P. Ronda, *Lewis and Clark Among the Indians* (Lincoln and London: University of Nebraska Press, Bison Books, 1984, 2002) p. 133-135.
8. David Lavender, *The Way to the Western Sea: Lewis and Clark Across the Continent* (Lincoln and London: University of Nebraska Press, Bison Books, 1988, 1998, 2001) p. 33-34, 189-210, 378, 381.
9. John L. Allen, "Lewis and Clark on the Upper Missouri: Decision at the Marias," James P. Ronda, ed., *Voyages of Discovery: Essays on the Lewis and Clark Expedition*, (Montana Historical Society Press, 1998), p.125, 135-136.
10. Hugh Rawson, *Wicked Words* (New York: Crown Publishers, Inc., 1989) p. 114-115 (damn), 174-175 (goddamn).
11. Edward S. Curtis, *The North American Indian: Volume 5*, "Mandan disposal of the dead" Web page; 1907, p.18, The University Press; Evanston, Ill.: Northwestern University Library; http://curtis.library.northwestern.edu; accessed December 25, 2011.
12. Joseph Mussulman, "Judith River" Web page; Washburn, N.D.: Lewis and Clark Fort Mandan Foundation; http://www.lewis-clark.org/article/3041; accessed October 22, 2012.
13. Ibid, "Who was Albert Gallatin" Web page; Washburn, N.D.: Lewis and Clark Fort Mandan Foundation; http://www.lewis-clark.org/article/299; accessed November 21, 2012.
14. Ibid, "Nicholas King Map (1803), Detail" Web page; Washburn, N.D.: Lewis and Clark Fort Mandan Foundation; http://www.lewis-clark.org/article/1132; accessed November 21, 2012.
15. Ibid, "Landmark – The Bear's Tooth" Web page; Washburn, N.D.: Lewis and Clark Fort Mandan Foundation; http://www.lewis-clark.org/article/2815; accessed November 21, 2012.
16. Ibid, "A Map for the Explorers" Web page; Washburn, N.D.: Lewis and Clark Fort Mandan Foundation; http://www.lewis-clark.org/article/1133; accessed November 21, 2012.
17. Trent Strickland, "The Corps of Discovery's Forgotten 'Sergeant'" Web page, *We Proceeded On*, vol. 31, no. 1 (February 2005) p. 13 (Corporal Warfington). Great Falls, Mont.: Lewis and Clark Trail Heritage Foundation; accessed June 18, 2015.
18. Stewart Culin, *Games of the North American Indians* Web page; 1907, p. 704-708 (football), Mountain View, Calif.: Google books; https://books.google.com /books?id=val_gaufljwC&pg=PA715&source=gbs_toc_r&cad=3#v=onepage& q&f=false; accessed January 14, 2012.
19. Howard Marshall, and Vivian Williams, New Columbia Fiddlers, *Fiddle Tunes of the Lewis and Clark Era*, compact audio disc liner notes: Malbrough s'en va-t-en guerre; Seattle, Wash.: Voyager Recordings; 2002.
20. "Toussaint Charbonneau: Jefferson National Expansion Memorial" Web page; U.S. National Park Service; www.nps.gov/ns/jeff/historyculture/toussaint-charbonneau.; accessed January 23, 2012.

21. "Map Collections" Web page; Aaron Arrowsmith 1802 map of North America; U.S. Library of Congress; http://hdl.loc.gov/loc.gmd/g3300.ct000584; accessed November 21, 2012.
22. Mark Chalkley, "Eagle Feather Goes To Washington," article; *We Proceeded On* online magazine, May 2003, vol. 29, no.2, p. 6-10; Great Falls, Mont.: Lewis and Clark Trail Heritage Foundation; http://www.lewisandclark.org /wpo/pdf/vol29no2.pdf#page=7; accessed February 7, 2015.
23. Personal photograph, "The Possible Bag" exhibit; St. Charles, Mo.: Lewis and Clark Boat House and Nature Center; Discovery Expedition of Saint Charles, Missouri; October 7, 2012.
24. Personal photograph, Glass Bluffs and confluence display sign; Williams County, N.D.: Missouri-Yellowstone Confluence Interpretive Center; State Road 1804; June 2, 2012.
25. Personal photograph, unnamed bluffs and hills along northern bank of Missouri River; Culbertson, Mont.; State Road 16; June 2, 2012.
26. Personal photograph, "Summits of High Hills Were Covered with Pine" display sign; Fort Peck Dam, Mont.; State Road 24; June 2, 2012.
27. Personal photographs 1-14, Chouteau County, Mont.: White Cliffs of the Missouri River; June 29, 2012 - July 2, 2012.
28. Personal photographs 1-2, cache exhibit signs; U.S. Department of Agriculture Forest Service; Great Falls, Mont.: Lewis and Clark National Historic Trail Interpretive Center; July 18, 2010.
29. Personal notes, William Clark descendants and family tree exhibit (naming Judith River); St. Charles, Mo.: Lewis and Clark Boat House and Nature Center; Discovery Expedition of Saint Charles, Missouri; October 7, 2012.

Fourteen: PORTAGE

1. Gary Moulton, ed., *The Journals of the Lewis and Clark Expedition; Atlas of the Lewis and Clark Expedition* vol. 1 (Lincoln and London: University of Nebraska Press, 1983), p. 5.
2. Gary Moulton, ed., *The Definitive Journals of Lewis and Clark* vol. 2 (Lincoln and London: University of Nebraska Press, 1986, 2002), Lewis and Clark, p. 5 (pre-expedition preparation).
3. Ibid. vol. 3 (1987, 2002), p. 367-368.
4. Ibid. vol. 4 (1987, 2002), p. 277-381.
5. Ibid. vol. 9 (1995, 2003), Ordway, p. 165-183.
6. Ibid. vol. 10 (1996, 2003), Gass, p. 101-111.
7. Ibid. vol. 11 (1997, 2003), Whitehouse, p. 193-226.
8. David Lavender, *The Way to the Western Sea: Lewis and Clark Across the Continent* (Lincoln and London: University of Nebraska Press, Bison Books, 1988, 1998, 2001) p. 41, 211-228.
9. "Map Collections" Web page, Aaron Arrowsmith 1802 map of North America; U.S. Library of Congress; http://hdl.loc.gov/loc.gmd/g3300.ct000584; accessed November 21, 2012.
10. Joseph Mussulman, David E. Nelson, Michael Stickney, "Thunderstorms and Cannons" Web page; Washburn, N.D.: Lewis and Clark Fort Mandan Foundation; http://www.lewis-clark.org/content-article.asp?ArticleID=1467; accessed November 21, 2012.
11. Ronald V. Loge, M.D., "Miracle of Sulfur Spring" Web page; Washburn, N.D.: Lewis and Clark Fort Mandan Foundation; http://lewis-clark.org/content-article.asp?ArticleID=850; accessed December 31, 2012.
12. Personal photograph, "Dugout Canoe" exhibit sign; St. Charles, Mo.: Lewis and Clark Boat House and Nature Center; Discovery Expedition of Saint Charles, Missouri; October 7, 2012.

13. Personal photographs 1-3, sulfur spring hiking trail signs; Cascade County, Montana; Morony Dam Road; July 23, 2011.
14. Personal photographs 1-8, various portage signs and exhibits; U.S. Department of Agriculture Forest Service; Great Falls, Mont.: Lewis and Clark National Historic Trail Interpretive Center; June 9, 2012.
15. Personal photographs 1-5, Great Falls of the Missouri; Ryan Dam Park; PPL Montana; Ryan Dam Road; Cascade County, Mont.; August 20, 2011.
16. Personal photograph, upper portage camp sign and landscape; Great Falls, Mont.; 4700 block, Lower River Road; December 1, 2011.

Fifteen: INTO THE MOUNTAINS

1. Gary Moulton, ed., *The Journals of the Lewis and Clark Expedition; Atlas of the Lewis and Clark Expedition* vol. 1 (Lincoln and London: University of Nebraska Press, 1983), map 2.
2. Gary Moulton, ed., *The Definitive Journals of Lewis and Clark* vol. 2 (Lincoln and London: University of Nebraska Press, 1986, 2002), p. 87 (longitudinal calculation), p. 200-201 (soap).
3. Ibid. vol. 4 (1987, 2002), p. 382-439
4. Ibid. vol. 5 (1988, 2002), p. 123 (Shoshone Indian life).
5. Ibid. vol. 9 (1995, 2003), Ordway, p. 184-191, p. 316 (Frazer's razor).
6. Ibid. vol. 10 (1996, 2003), Gass, p. 112-119.
7. Ibid. vol. 11 (1997, 2003), Whitehouse, p. 227-246.
8. James P. Ronda, *Lewis and Clark Among the Indians* (Lincoln and London: University of Nebraska Press, Bison Books, 1984, 2002) p. 135-138, 258.
9. David Lavender, *The Way to the Western Sea: Lewis and Clark Across the Continent* (Lincoln and London: University of Nebraska Press, Bison Books, 1988, 1998, 2001) p. 229-237.
10. Hugh Rawson, *Wicked Words* (New York: Crown Publishers, Inc., 1989) p. 174-175 (goddamn), 366-369 (son of a bitch).
11. "Helena National Forest" map (Lewis and Clark trail); U.S. Department of Agriculture Forest Service; ISBN: 159351026-8; Montana, 2006.
12. "Gates of the Mountains Wilderness and Recreation Area" map (Lewis and Clark trail); U.S. Department of Agriculture Forest Service; Helena National Forest Montana, 2001.
13. Francis Grose, *1811 Dictionary in the Vulgar Tongue* Web page (vulgarities: bitch); Salt Lake City: Project Gutenberg; http://www.gutenberg.org/cache/epub/5402/pg5402.html; January 1, 2015.
14. Personal photographs 1-5; State of Montana Fish, Wildlife and Parks; Cascade, Mont.: Tower Rock State Park; 2325 Old US Highway 91; April 27, 2013.
15. Personal photographs 1-4, Lewis and Clark County, Mont.: Gates of the Mountains Wilderness; July 25, 2011.
16. Personal photographs 1-10, Two Camps Vista; Lewis and Clark County, Mont.: Devil's Elbow Recreation Area; York Road; March 24, 2013.
17. Personal photograph, "Others Passed This Way" wayside sign; U.S. Department of Interior Bureau of Reclamation, U.S. Department of Interior Forest Service, U.S. National Park Service; Winston, Mont.; U.S. Route 287; March 18, 2012.
18. Personal photographs 1-13, White Earth Campground, U.S. Department of Interior, Bureau of Reclamation; Canyon Ferry Reservoir, Broadwater County, Mont.; April 27, 2013.
19. Personal photographs 1-25, Three Forks of the Missouri National Historic Landmark, Three Forks, Mont.: Missouri Headwaters State Park; 1585 Trident Road; July 14, 2010 and March 18, 2012.
20. Personal photographs 1-4, Missouri River east bank, north of York Road Bridge; Lewis and Clark County, Mont.; May 28, 2011.

21. Personal photograph, "BOZEMAN PASS" roadside sign; Interstate 90 near mile-marker 319; Gallatin County, Mont.; June 29, 2012.
22. Personal photographs 1-3, Apsaalooka (Crow/Rocky Mountain) Indian display sign; U.S. Department of Agriculture, Forest Service; Great Falls, Mont.: Lewis and Clark National Historic Trail Interpretive Center; June 9, 2012.

Sixteen: PASSAGE

1. Gary Moulton, ed., *The Journals of the Lewis and Clark Expedition; Atlas of the Lewis and Clark Expedition* vol. 1 (Lincoln and London: University of Nebraska Press, 1983), p. 5: maps 2, 65, 66.
2. Gary Moulton, ed., *The Definitive Journals of Lewis and Clark* vol. 2 (Lincoln and London: University of Nebraska Press, 1986, 2002), p. 2 (pre-expedition explorers).
3. Ibid. vol. 3 (1987, 2002), p. 368 (notes on geography and western Indians).
4. Ibid. vol. 5 (1988, 2002), p. 7-76, 85 (origin of Shoshone horses).
5. Ibid. vol. 6 (1990, 2002), p. 313-314 (origin of tribe horses).
6. Ibid. vol. 9 (1995, 2003), Ordway, p. 191-201.
7. Ibid. vol. 10 (1996, 2003), Gass, p. 119-125.
8. Ibid. vol. 11 (1997, 2003), Whitehouse, p. 246-266.
9. James P. Ronda, *Lewis and Clark Among the Indians* (Lincoln and London: University of Nebraska Press, Bison Books, 1984, 2002) p. 138-141.
10. David Lavender, *The Way to the Western Sea: Lewis and Clark Across the Continent* (Lincoln and London: University of Nebraska Press, Bison Books, 1988, 1998, 2001) p. 27-34, 42, 237-243.
11. David L. Nicandri, *River of Promise: Lewis and Clark on the Columbia*, (Washburn, N.D.: The Dakota Institute Press of Lewis and Clark Fort Mandan Foundation, 2009), p. 209 (use of Alexander Mackenzie's *Voyages* book).
12. Francis Grose, *1811 Dictionary in the Vulgar Tongue* Web page (vulgarities: bitch, shit); Salt Lake City: Project Gutenberg; http://www.gutenberg.org /cache/epub/5402/pg5402.html; accessed January 1, 2015.
13. Hugh Rawson, *Wicked Words* (New York: Crown Publishers, Inc., 1989) p. 114-115 (damn), 174-175 (goddamn), 366-369 (son of a bitch).
14. "The Appaloosa," Interactive Museum Tour Content Web page; Jefferson National Expansion Memorial; U.S. National Park Service; http://www.nps.gov /jeff/planyourvisit/interactive-museum-tour-content.htm; accessed February 23, 2012.
15. "Our History: People," Explorers Web page; Toronto: Hudson's Bay Company; http://www.hbcheritage.ca/content/timeline; accessed January 22, 2012.
16. "To the Western Ocean: Planning the Lewis and Clark Expedition, Part 4, Nicholas King. 'Map of the Western part of North America.' 1803" Web page; University of Virginia Library, Charlottesville: University of Virginia; http://explore.lib.virginia.edu/exhibits/show/lewisclark/westernocean/overview 4; accessed March 10, 2013.
17. "Alexander Mackenzie" Web page; Virtual Museum of Canada; Maritime Museum of British Columbia;http://www.beyondthemap.ca/english/explorer _mackenzie_expeditions.html; accessed October 29, 2013.
18. W.E. Knowles Middleton; "Aneroid Barometers and Barographs" section; *Catalog of Meteorological Instruments in the Museum of History and Technology*; Smithsonian Institution Press, 1969; p. 23 (history of elevation assessment tools); http://www.sil.si.edu/smithsoniancontributions /HistoryTechnology/pdf_lo/SSHT-0002.pdf; accessed March 10, 2013.
19. "A 125 Year History of Topographical Mapping and GIS in the U.S. Geological Survey 1884-2009, Part 1 1884-1980" Web page; U.S. Geological Survey, U.S. Department of the Interior; http://nationalmap.gov/ustopo /125history.html; accessed March 10, 2013.

20. Personal photographs 1-4, various landscape features, including Beaverhead Rock; Madison County, Mont.; State Highway 41; October 19, 2013.
21. Personal photograph, "THE RIVER OF THE WEST" display sign; Astoria, Ore.: Columbia River Maritime Museum; 1792 Marine Drive; May 25, 2013.
22. Personal photograph, narrow pass geologic feature; Beaverhead County, Mont.: County Route 324; October 18, 2013.
23. Personal photograph, western view of Shoshone Ridge; Beaverhead County, Mont.: County Route 324 at Lemhi Pass Road; October 18, 2013.
24. Personal photographs 1-30, Lemhi Pass; Montana-Idaho border; July 16, 2010; and July 4, 2011.

Mesologue

1. T.S. Eliot, "Little Gidding" Web page; New York: Columbia University; http://www.columbia.edu/itc/history/winter/w3206/edit/tseliotlittlegidding.html ; accessed August 10, 2010 and March 12, 2012.

Timeline

(sources not previously cited in chapters)

1. Personal photographs 1-10, lead tablet burial in 1743; Pierre, S.D.: Verendrye Site, National Historic Landmark; June 12, 2010 and August 27, 2014.
2. "Looking West: Lewis and Clark's Charlottesville *and* Albemarle County Virginia" Web page (pre-expedition history); Charlottesville: University of Virginia; http://www2.vcdh.virginia.edu/lewisandclark/video/section _4/1iv.html; accessed May 3, 2014.
3. "York Biography" Web page; The Oregon History Project; Portland: Oregon Historical Society; http://www.oregonhistoryproject.org/articles/biographies/ york-biography/; accessed May 3, 2014.
4. David Lavender, *The Way to the Western Sea: Lewis and Clark Across the Continent* (Lincoln and London: University of Nebraska Press, Bison Books, 1988, 1998, 2001) p. 9 (February 17, 1801).

BIBLIOGRAPHY

Published and unpublished sources

Allen, John L. "Geographical Knowledge and American Images of the Louisiana Territory," James P. Ronda, ed., *Voyages of Discovery: Essays on the Lewis and Clark Expedition*, Helena, Mont.: Montana Historical Society Press, 1998.

——. Ibid. "Lewis and Clark on the Upper Missouri: Decision at the Marias."

Alwin, John A. "Pelts, Provisions *and* Perceptions: The Hudson's Bay Company Mandan Indian Trade." *Montana: The Magazine of Western History*, vol. 29, no. 2 (1979). Lincoln: University of Nebraska Web site, accessed February 18, 2012.

Bedini, Silvio A. "The Scientific Instruments of the Lewis and Clark Expedition." *Great Plains Quarterly*, vol. 4 (1987, 2002), no. 1 (Winter 1984) London and Lincoln: University of Nebraska Web site, accessed March 10, 2013.

Chalkley, Mark. "Eagle Feather Goes To Washington." *We Proceeded On,* vol. 29, no. 2 (May 2003). Great Falls, Mont.: Lewis and Clark Trail Heritage Foundation Web site, accessed February 7, 2015.

Clary, Jean et al., The Discovery Writers. *Lewis and Clark in the Bitterroot.* Stevensville, Mont.: Stoneydale Press Publishing, 1998.

Culin, Stewart. *Games of the North American Indians,* 1907. Mountain View, Calif.: Google books Web site, accessed January 14, 2012.

Curtis, Edward S. *The North American Indian*, 1907. Evanston, Ill.: Northwestern University Library Web site, accessed October 2, 2011; May 24, 2015.

Dansi, Thomas C. *Uncovering the Truth About Meriwether Lewis*. Amherst, NY: Prometheus Books, 2012.

Duncan, Dayton, and Ken Burns. *The Journey of the Corps of Discovery: Lewis and Clark: An Illustrated History*. New York: Alfred A. Knopf, Inc., 1997, 2004.

Eliot, T.S. "Little Gidding" poem, 1941. New York: Columbia University Web site, accessed August 10, 2010; and March 12, 2012.

Grose, Francis. *1811 Dictionary in the Vulgar Tongue*, 1811. Salt Lake City: Project Gutenberg Web site, accessed January 1, 2015.

Guice, John D.W. ed. *By His Own Hand? The Mysterious Death of Meriwether Lewis*. Norman: University of Oklahoma Press, 2006.

Havens, Jeffrey P. Lewis and Clark sites (351 of 4,059 photographs in possession of author taken between August 1, 2009 and September 1, 2015).

——. Ibid. (unpublished notes on three Lewis and Clark sites in possession of author written between October 3, 2011 and October 7, 2012).

Jackson, John C. "Reuben Lewis: Fur Trader, Subagent, and Meriwether's Younger Brother." *We Proceeded On,* vol. 38, no. 4 (November 2012). Great Falls, Mont.: Lewis and Clark Trail Heritage Foundation Web site, accessed June 11, 2015.

Jenkinson, Clay S. "Introduction," John D.W. Guice, ed. *By His Own Hand? The Mysterious Death of Meriwether Lewis*. Norman: Univ. of Oklahoma Press, 2006.

——. "Forward," David L. Nicandri, *River of Promise: Lewis and Clark on the Columbia.* Washburn, N.D.: The Dakota Institute Press of Lewis and Clark Fort Mandan Foundation, 2009.

Koontz, John E. "What is the origin of the word Dakota?" Boulder: University of Colorado Web site, accessed November 15, 2010.

Lavender, David. *The Way to the Western Sea: Lewis and Clark Across the Continent*. Lincoln and London: University of Nebraska Press, Bison Books, 1988, 1998, 2001.

Lapham , I.A. *The Antiquities of Wisconsin as Surveyed and Described.* The Smithsonian Institution; Madison: University of Wisconsin Web page, accessed January 14, 2012.

Mann, John W. W. *Sacajawea's People*. Lincoln and London: University of Nebraska Press, 2004.

Marshall, Howard, and Williams, Vivian. *Fiddle Tunes of the Lewis and Clark Era.* Seattle, Wash.: Voyager Recordings, compact audio disc liner notes, 2002.
Middleton, W.E. Knowles. "Aneroid Barometers and Barographs," *Catalog of Meteorological Instruments in the Museum of History and Technology*, 1969. Washington, DC: Smithsonian Institution Press Web site, accessed March 10, 2013.
Moulton, Gary, ed. *The Journals of the Lewis and Clark Expedition; Atlas of the Lewis and Clark Expedition.* Lincoln and London: University of Nebraska Press, 1983.
——. Ibid. *The Definitive Journals of Lewis and Clark.* Volumes 2-11. Lincoln and London: University of Nebraska Press, 1986, 1987, 1988, 1990, 1995, 1996, 1997, 2002, 2003.
Mussulman, Joseph. "Hair-raising Hazards." Washburn, N.D.: Lewis and Clark Fort Mandan Foundation Web site, accessed March 10, 2012.
——. Ibid. "Osage River," accessed May 20, 2013.
——. Ibid. "Rulo, Nebraska," accessed May 20, 2013.
——. Ibid. "Tornado Damage near Logan, Iowa," accessed May 20, 2013.
——. Ibid. "Burial of Sergeant Floyd," accessed March 10, 2012.
——. Ibid. "Route to the Assiniboine River," January 16, 2012.
——. Ibid. "Judith River," accessed October 22, 2012.
——. Ibid. "Who was Albert Gallatin," accessed November 21, 2012.
——. Ibid. "Nicholas King Map (1803), Detail," accessed November 21, 2012.
——. Ibid. "Landmark – The Bear's Tooth," accessed November 21, 2012.
——. Ibid. "A Map for the Explorers," accessed November 21, 2012.
——. Ibid, and Nelson, David E., "An Air Gun of the Girandoni Type," accessed December 11, 2010.
——. Ibid, and Nelson, "Incomprehensible," accessed December 11, 2010.
——. Ibid, and Nelson, and Stickney, Michael, "Thunderstorms and Cannons," accessed November 21, 2012.
Nicandri, David L. *River of Promise: Lewis and Clark on the Columbia.* Washburn, N.D.: The Dakota Institute Press of Lewis and Clark Fort Mandan Foundation, 2009.
Rawson, Hugh. *Wicked Words.* New York: Crown Publishers, Inc., 1989.
Loge, Ronald V. M.D. "Miracle of Sulfur Spring." Washburn, N.D.: Lewis and Clark Fort Mandan Foundation Web site, accessed December 31, 2012
Ronda, James P. *Lewis and Clark Among the Indians.* Lincoln and London: University of Nebraska Press, Bison Books, 1984, 2002.
——, ed. *Voyages of Discovery: Essays on the Lewis and Clark Expedition.* Helena, Mont.: Montana Historical Society Press, 1998.
Strickland, Trent. "The Corps of Discovery's Forgotten 'Sergeant.'" *We Proceeded On*, vol. 31, no. 1 (February 2005). Great Falls, Mont.: Lewis and Clark Trail Heritage Foundation Web site, accessed June 18, 2015.
U.S. National Park Service. Knife River Indian Villages pamphlet, 2009.
——. Ibid. Pipestone National Monument pamphlet, 2006, 2014.

Websites

1811 Dictionary in the Vulgar Tongue, Salt Lake City: Project Gutenberg; http://www.gutenberg.org/cache/epub/5402/pg5402.html, accessed January 1, 2015
Alexander Mackenzie, Virtual Museum of Canada, Maritime Museum of British Columbia; http://www.beyondthemap.ca/english/explorer_mackenzie_expeditions .html, accessed October 29, 2013
The Antiquities of Wisconsin as Surveyed and Described, Mandan game tchung-kee, Madison: University of Wisconsin; http://digicoll.library.wisc.edu/Antiquities/, accessed January 14, 2012
Columbia Center for New Media Teaching and Learning, Academic Information Systems Columbia University; http://www.columbia.edu/itc/, accessed August 10, 2010; and March 12, 2012

Corps of Discovery: Preparing for the Trip West, U.S. National Park Service; www.nps.gov/archive/jeff/lewisclark2/corpsofdiscovery/preparing/, accessed October 17, 2010; and January 17, 2011

Denning and Hibernation Behavior, Grizzly and Black bear behavior, U.S. National Park Service; http://www.nps.gov/yell/learn/nature/denning.htm, accessed March 24, 2012

Discovery History, U.S. National Park Service, http://www.nps.gov/history/, accessed November 15, 2010.

Discovering Lewis and Clark; Lewis and Clark Fort Mandan Foundation; http://www.lewis-clark.org/, accessed December 11, 2010; January 16, 2012; March 10, 2012; October 22, 2012; November 21, 2012; and May 20, 2013

Equine encephalitis viruses, Madison School of Veterinary Medicine, Madison: University of Wisconsin; http://www.vetmed.wisc.edu/pbs/zoonoses/eee-wee-vee/ewveeindex.html, accessed April 4, 2012

Envisioning the West: Thomas Jefferson and the Roots of Lewis and Clark; Lincoln: University of Nebraska; http://jeffersonswest.unl.edu, accessed May 3, 2014.

Etymology, Department of Linguistics, Boulder: University of Colorado; http://spot.colorado.edu/~koontz/faq/etymology.htm, accessed November 15, 2010

Exhibitions: Rivers, Edens, Empires: Lewis *and* Clark and the Revealing of America, U.S. Library of Congress; www.loc.gov/exhibits/lewisandclark/, accessed March 12, 2012

Games of the North American Indians, Mountain View, Calif.: Google books; https://books.google.com/books, accessed January 14, 2012

Hudson's Bay Company, Our History: People, Explorers; http://www.hbcheritage.ca /content/timeline, accessed January 22, 2012

Jefferson National Expansion Memorial, U.S. National Park Service; http://www.nps.gov /jeff/, accessed December 11, 2010; September 25, 2011; January 23, 2012; and February 23, 2012

King George III, The British Monarchy; http://www.royal.gov.uk/historyofthemonarchy /kingsandqueensoftheunitedkingdom/thehanoverians/georgeiii.aspx, accessed November 11, 2011

Journals of the Lewis and Clark Expedition, University of Nebraska Press/University of Nebraska-Lincoln Libraries, Electronic Text Center; http://lewisandclarkjournals .unl.edu/, accessed August 10, 2010; October 11, 2010; December 23, 2010; October 22, 2011; February 18, 2012; March 10, 2013

Lewis and Clark, Public Broadcasting System; www.pbs.org/lewisandclark/, accessed December 19, 2010; February 5, 2011; February 27, 2011; October 19, 2011; October 22, 2011; and January 14, 2012

Lewis and Clark, Washington, DC: National Geographic Society;www.nationalgeographic .com/lewisandclark/, accessed October 11, 2010; October 19, 2011

Lewis and Clark Across Missouri, Columbia: University of Missouri; http://lewisclark. geog.missouri.edu, accessed September 24, 2012

Lewis and Clark in Missouri, Missouri Historical Society; http://www.lewisandclark exhibit.org/2_0_0/page_2_3.html, accessed October 10, 2011

Lewis and Clark: The Maps of Exploration 1507-1814, University of Virginia Library, Charlottesville: University of Virginia; http://explore.lib.virginia.edu/exhibits/ show/lewisclark, accessed March 10, 2013

Lewis and Clark in Montana—a geologic perspective: Navigation—Finding the latitude, Montana Bureau of Mines and Geology, Montana Tech of the University of Montana; http://www.mbmg.mtech.edu/gmr/lewis_clark/lewis_clark-nav.asp, accessed March 10, 2013

Montana Fish, Wildlife and Parks; http://fwp.mt.gov/fishAndWildlife/, accessed October 30, 2011

Natchez Trace, History and Culture, U.S. National Park Service; http://www.nps.gov/natr/learn/historyculture/index.htm, accessed February 22, 2012

The North American Indian, Northwestern University Library; http://curtis.library.northwestern.edu, accessed October 2, 2011; and May 24, 2015

Presidential Oaths of Office, Presidential Inaugurations, U.S. Library of Congress; http://memory.loc.gov/ammem/pihtml/pioaths.html, accessed January 10, 2012

The Roots of Lewis and Clark, Virginia Center for Digital History, Charlottesville: University of Virginia; http://www.vcdh.virginia.edu/lewisandclark/, accessed April 27, 2014

Smithsonian Institution, Aneroid Barometers and Barographs, *Catalog of Meteorological Instruments in the Museum of History and Technology*; http://www.sil.si.edu/smithsoniancontributions/HistoryTechnology/pdf_lo/SSHT-0002.pdf, accessed March 10, 2013

Thomas Jefferson Papers, U.S. Library of Congress; http://memory.loc.gov/ammem/collections/jefferson_papers/, accessed March 12, 2012

U.S. Army Center of Military History, origin of the 21-gun salute; http://www.history.army.mil/html/faq/salute.html, accessed January 12, 2011

U.S. Centers for Disease Control, sexually transmitted diseases; http://www.cdc.gov/std/, accessed January 14, 2012

U.S. Geological Survey, U.S. Department of the Interior; http://nationalmap.gov/ustopo/125history.html, accessed March 10, 2013

U.S. Library of Congress, Map Collections; http://memory.loc.gov/ammem/gmdhtml/gmdhome.html, accessed November 21, 2012; April 4, 2015

The War, Joe Medicine Crow, Public Broadcasting System; http://www.pbs.org/thewar/, accessed December 6, 2012

We Proceeded On online magazine; Lewis and Clark Trail Heritage Foundation; http://www.lewisandclark.org/wpo/, accessed February 7, 2015; June 11, 2015; and June 18, 2015

ILLUSTRATION CREDITS

Front Cover

1. Front cover design by Jeff Havens with valuable input from James R. Havens, Melissa Tuemmler, Jesse R. Havens and Robert J. Conboy.
2. Personal photograph, Two Medicine River at sunrise near the July 27, 1806 Fight Site; Pondera County, Mont.; May 1, 2015.
3. Map background, Nicholas King 1803 map of North America; U.S. Library of Congress; http://memory.loc.gov/cgi-bin/query/h?ammem/gmd:@field(NUMBER+@band(g4126s+ct000071)); accessed April 4, 2015.

Back Cover

1. Back cover design by Jeff Havens.
2. Personal photograph, Missouri River at North Dakota State Road 200A; Oliver County, N.D.: February 28, 2015.
3. Meriwether Lewis portrait by Charles Wilson Peale; courtesy of Independence National Historic Park Collection; Philadelphia, Pa.; 1807.
4. William Clark portrait by Charles Wilson Peale; courtesy of Independence National Historic Park Collection; Philadelphia, Pa.; 1807.
5. Personal photograph, dugout canoe replica; Clark Canyon Reservoir: Beaverhead County, Mont.; Route 324; July 16, 2010.
6. Personal photograph, White Cliffs, Hole-in-the-Wall section of the Missouri River; Chouteau County, Mont.; July 1, 2012.
7. Personal photograph, Continental Divide at Lemhi Pass in the Beverhead Mountains; Montana/Idaho border; July 4, 2011.
8. Map background, Nicholas King 1803 map of North America; U.S. Library of Congress; http://memory.loc.gov/cgi-bin/query/h?ammem/gmd:@field(NUMBER+@band(g4126s+ct000071)); accessed April 4, 2015.
9. Book logo by Jeff Havens with inspiration from James R. Havens and many Native American pictographs on rocks throughout Montana.

Book logo

Design by Jeff Havens with inspiration from James R. Havens and many Native American pictographs on rocks throughout Montana.

Map 1: Westward journey

Design by Jeff Havens with background from the National Park Service interactive Lewis and Clark map, and site locations from Volume One of the Moulton journals atlas (maps 1a and 1b).

Map 2: Fort Mandan region

Design by Jeff Havens with background from the National Park Service Lewis and Clark interactive map, and site locations from Volume Three of the Moulton journals (p. 202).

Map 3: Missouri River portage

Design by Jeff Havens with background from the National Park Service Lewis and Clark interactive map, and site locations from Volume Four of the Moulton journals (p. 322).

Book Interior

Design by Jeff Havens with inspiration for the Old West text from James R. Havens and Jesse R. Havens.

INDEX

ABOUT THE AUTHOR

Jeffrey P. Havens lived and worked in several places along Lewis and Clark trail, which afforded him many opportunities to visit and revisit sites to recreate the journey. At the time this book was first printed, he resided in Helena, Montana. He was raised in Loves Park, Illinois, which is a suburb of Rockford near Chicago. He also worked and lived in Minnesota, Nebraska and Wisconsin. Havens is a graduate of Western Illinois University with a degree in biology, and attended graduate school at Northern Illinois University. He authored a well-regarded essay about a strong arm of The Outfit (Chicago Mafia) for the 2014 book *Secret Rockford.*

Havens enjoys running, biking, hiking, backpacking, good lager beer, interesting people, and The Great Outdoors. His grizzly bear encounters in the Montana mountains have been few and fortunately uneventful, but always energetic. *Fraught With Difficulties* is his first novel, which was written at night and on weekends, due to day-job commitments. He works as a registered environmental health specialist.

Havens is also an award-winning, former investigative news reporter for a weekly newspaper in Rockford, Illinois. He was given the award in 2004 by the Illinois Press Association for writing a news series about widespread corruption and mismanagement at a community college in Rockford named Rock Valley College. In addition, Havens wrote extensively about the Rockford area's $160 million jail, the evolution of its pernicious "public safety" tax, and the region's long history with organized crime.

Photo: The author on the Continental Divide for the first time at Lemhi Pass on July 16, 2010 in the Beaverhead Mountains, along the Montana-Idaho border where Lewis and his men first crossed on August 12, 1805.